CAUGHT IN THE
DEVIL'S HAND

RUBY DUVALL

Chapter One

T he dawn was cold and damp. With the sunrise came an over-
cast sky, which drizzled upon a struggling village nestled in a
small valley. As the surrounding hilltops emerged from the
mists with the rise of the sun, smoke began to billow lazily from the
thatched roofs. Soon, those who were still of able body would leave
their homes, wearily hauling their tools to prepare the fields for
spring planting.

For the family in a scanty, weathered hut among a handful of
homes near the northern end of the village, today seemed like it
would be the same as the rest. They would rise, stiff from sleeping
on thin bedrolls with hardly enough warmth to let them sleep at all.
They would work in their isolated field, eke out a meager living selling herbal medicines, and return gratefully to their hard, narrow
mats for another night of rest.

However, these past few weeks had seen many villagers suc-
cumbing to a disease so deadly it was catastrophic. The entire village,
already at its knees, was now lying prone in the dirt. In her nineteen
years as the only daughter of a family of apothecaries, Shumei had
neither heard of nor seen so many people fall ill and die at once. She
could only pray to the Divine One that the worst was over and the
deaths would stop.

A muffled sound disturbed Shumei's sleep. She swallowed past
the itchy lump in her throat that bespoke of her overly salted meal
last night, and took in a shaky breath while denying the urge to

stretch, for she was already barely covered by a thin blanket. She opened one eye and realized with a mental groan that dawn had arrived.

She grudgingly lifted her head. Snuggled close within the curve of her body was her brother, only nine years old. He was sleeping peacefully enough despite his sickness. Beyond him at arm's length, their mother slept upon the larger of their two straw mats. Her mother's shoulders convulsed.

"Mama?" Shumei called, voice hoarse from sleep. She lifted herself onto her elbow.

"I'm sorry to wake you, baby," her mother murmured. "Did you sleep well?"

"Well enough. How are you feeling?"

When her mother rolled over, Shumei had to hold back a gasp. A blood vessel in her mother's right eye had burst, turning the white to red. Her skin was sallow and drawn. Mama was near the last stage of the disease.

"Well enough," her mother repeated with a resigned smile. "Where's your father? Already in the fields?" She shook her head. "That man works too hard."

Shumei lowered her face to hide her expression. Father had been dead for four years. Such confusion was another common symptom of the fifth day. Most people remembered a time in the recent past, but a few reverted several years. Breath hitching, Shumei suppressed the fearful sob that threatened to bubble up.

"I don't feel good today, baby. When your father gets back, ask him to rub my back." Her mother sighed and turned away. "I think I'll sleep a little longer."

"Yes, Mama," she said in a weak voice.

A month ago, an otherwise healthy boy suddenly fell ill. He didn't know how he had caught the disease. Several of his close friends became ill a couple days later. Then their parents, then their parents' friends...

Everyone began calling it the Burning, for the fourth day's fever was often lethal. It had spread like deadly fog through their tiny, poor village. Those who hadn't yet become sick, including Shumei, were counted as lucky, but they were a shrinking minority. Out of their tiny population of over a hundred fifty men, women, and children, over forty had died, and another fifty were still ill. The rest had either fought to recover from the disease or feared catching it.

The village leader and his wife had done nothing for the village except assure everyone they'd prayed to the Golden One—their preferred name for the Divine One. They didn't even leave their home, too frightened of the Burning to help those they were charged with protecting.

Instead, Shumei and her family's medicines had become essential to the village's survival. The *fuki* plant they cultivated had saved dozens from the fourth day's fever, although some had still gone on to the fifth day's symptoms: severe coughing and difficulty breathing. Two unfortunate souls had coughed so violently they'd broken their ribs and had ended up stabbing their lungs.

However, the Burning seemed to have nearly run its course. And just in time, too, for her family's supply of *fuki* was not only running dangerously low but also quickly growing stale. Her family still had the early-spring harvest of the herb to rely on, should the villagers have need of it, but picking it before it fully matured meant the medicinal properties of its large leaves would be less potent, and she would need to use more to produce an effective dosage. Doing so would also mean their supply for the rest of the year would be too small for comfort, and unfortunately, it was too late in the season to plant more.

Her lips trembled as she gazed at her brother's sleeping face. Today was his fourth day. So far, not many young children had survived the Burning's fever, and she could already see his cheeks warming to a deceptively healthy pink. He had cried throughout most of the first day, scared of dying and in a great amount of pain, making his initial symptoms much worse than they might have been otherwise.

He spent most of the second day silently weeping, body tense and occasionally convulsing as he endured a day-long headache. She managed to dull his suffering with a dose of *kavua*, but he still couldn't bring himself to speak through the haze of pain. He ate well on his third day but vomited the last of it a few hours ago. She had woken to find him emptying his stomach on the floor, and had spent an hour cleaning it up and giving him medicine before they could settle back to sleep again. Thankfully, he had yet to cough up any blood.

A splash of moisture landed on his rosy cheeks. She quickly wiped at her eyes and hardened her jaw, determined not to let her anxiety show. She was practiced at hiding her feelings, and this latest crisis would not be an exception. Pressing her lips together, she pushed the fear to the pit of her stomach and sat up, then scrubbed her face with her hands as if wiping away the last layer of sleep still clinging to her.

A movement in the corner of her eye caught her attention. A long-legged spider skittered across the dirt floor, headed toward the nearly dead fire in the center of their single room. Squeezing into herself, she felt the usual rush of fear and adrenalin as she silently panicked over what to do. A small mewling began in the back of her throat. Then her brother turned in his sleep, flinging out one arm and smacking the spider with the back of his hand, squashing it before it could even try to dodge.

Her jaw dropped. She sat there a moment, out of sorts, and her heartbeat slowed as she turned her mind to how she'd clean off Oka's hand. Her revulsion of spiders was so great that she even hesitated to use a rag. Perhaps a sage leaf, which she could then toss into the fire?

If only life had remained as sweet as when she'd been Oka's age. Her father had been alive, and his boisterous personality had overflowed their small house, leaving no room for despair. She had been his little garden imp, watching as he and her mother poured every bit of knowledge they had into caring for their field of medicinal plants.

Though the villagers and their thinly veiled animosity toward her and her mother for the color of their hair was always a deep wound, she was well shielded from their sneers and remarks by a loving father and well-spoken mother, both of whom could always make her feel better with a hug and a few words of wisdom.

Then Oka had been born. Even though neither of his parents was blond, he was, and the priests had proclaimed he'd been blessed by the Golden One.

Most of the villagers had brown hair, such as her late father. A small minority had black hair, like Shumei and her mother. Oka's blonde hair, however, was as rare as brown hair was common, and it had always fascinated her. She loved washing and combing it until it dried as golden as late-summer wheat.

As a young child, she hadn't yet understood the hierarchy of one's hair color. She remembered this time as being the happiest of her life, a time when nothing was shut away from her, when the world held no hatred and no danger. But an incident had changed all that, and she had quickly learned the dangers around her. The memories were fuzzy now, but she knew never to leave the village after sunset.

Daylight was safe. The Divine One sheltered and protected his people with the warmth of the sun's rays, so anyone with golden hair was more loved. Other than Oka, only two others in the village could claim to have been touched by the Divine One. One was the village leader, and the other was his wife.

The local priests taught that those with hair the color of the earth had been molded for the task of working with it, so most members of the village with brown hair tended the fields, save a few like the miller and huntsman.

However, those with hair the color of night were believed to have been tainted by the Damned One, also known as the Foul One. Her people's god had infinite forgiveness and patience, so those with black hair were forgiven for their nearness to evil. Forgiven, but not accepted. Not even when the brother and son to women with black hair had been blessed with blond locks.

Shumei had adored her brother from the day he'd been born, but the atmosphere around her had quickly grown hostile. The comments whispered near her had grown viler with each passing day.

Then one afternoon, her father's body had been found in the medicine field, and the cause of his death had been unknown. Sudden deaths weren't uncommon, but the villagers had gleefully shared various cruel theories with Shumei and her mother, the worst being that her father had ingested a poisonous plant on purpose. Never mind the fact that the only plant in the field that could kill if one ate too much of it would leave behind telltale signs.

Thus, the last four years since his death had seen a change in her. Once, she had been cheerful, talkative, and outgoing, but now she was quiet and reserved. Without her father to protect her from the villagers' contempt, their cruelty had grown exponentially. Their malice had forced her to close herself off and hide her emotions. Seeing any friendly expression on her face, let alone a smile, was now rare. Her eyes were always downcast, and she held herself closely, as if awaiting the blow of someone's fist.

With Oka, she spoke in a calm, gentle tone, though never with a smile. She could no longer bring herself to act the cheerful older sister, even for him. As a result, Oka had taken to being nearly as soft-spoken as she was, though much more physically active. He greatly enjoyed swordfights with imaginary enemies while she and their mother worked in the medicine field.

Their poor mother. Father's absence and the village's ostracism had aged her incredibly over those four years. Her youth had disappeared with her happiness, and though she was yet forty-one, she looked well past fifty, hair almost completely gray.

Shumei scratched an itch on her exposed lower shin, which poked out from the much-too-short dress she hadn't replaced since her father had died. Today was delivery day for the medicines they sold. Seeing as how both her mother and brother were sick, she knew the task of preparing and delivering the medicines to the households that had ordered them was up to her.

Selling herbal remedies was how her family made ends meet—the only way they were allowed to earn a living, scraping together enough money for food, clothes, and wood for the fire, but not much else. Even then, their food was always the cheapest and least nutritious, the bolts of cloth they purchased were of the lowest quality, and kindling was used sparingly.

The priests considered the medical arts to be "less holy" because only the Divine One could grant true salvation from injury and disease. But the benefit of properly prepared medicines could not be ignored, so they were declared a gift from the Divine One, who made his people from the same earth from which the medicinal plants sprang.

Shumei had never understood how something "less holy" was also a "divine gift." Then again, many things about how she and her mother were treated made no sense. But tradition demanded that crows and their families tend the fields. For generations, her ancestors had provided the village with medicines for a fee almost too meager to live upon.

Many times, she had wished for a different lot. Surely, she thought, life had more to offer somewhere else. She could make friends, find better work, and walk among other people without seeing disgust on their faces when they saw her hair. She wished to live in a place that didn't adhere to the caste system in which she found herself at the bottom, a place where she could find adventure, see new sights, and perhaps even experience love.

Even if she were attracted to any men in the village, which she wasn't, none of them would have her, save one—and she'd rather go unmarried than tie herself to him. Lately, she'd taken to nighttime fantasies of a handsome stranger, such as a traveling merchant or perhaps even a mercenary, who would pluck her and her family out of this miserable village. He'd look past her faded, worn-out dress and her tangled mop of black hair, and he'd see a kindred soul, one ready for life and passion.

More than once, such musings late at night had resulted in heady dreams, but in the morning, she'd always wake to find nothing had changed.

Sighing in resignation, she tucked the blanket more securely around her brother's feet and stood. She wiped his hand of spider guts, then prepared a variety of medicines in the corner of their hut, grinding together different mixtures of herbs and carefully packaging the results into small cloth bags. Her mother coughed a few more times but was otherwise still. Oka slept fitfully.

Upon confirming her list of orders matched her array of medicine bags, she packed everything into her delivery pouch and slung it over her shoulder. Before leaving, she knelt by her mother.

"Mama? I'm going out to deliver the week's medicine," she softly called. Nodding, her mother groaned a farewell. Shumei planned to make her deliveries as quickly as possible, purchase some meat to strengthen her ailing mother and brother, and return home to care for them. They were both at critical stages, and she couldn't stay away from them for too long. Pushing aside the reed door, she ducked out of the hut and surveyed the morning scene.

The day seemed destined to be gray and chilly. No doubt her shabby clothing would do little to keep her warm. One of her neighbors, a married man by the name of Akito, was just now leaving his home to go to the fields, but no one else was about. She waited until he had gone some distance before heading to her first and most hated destination.

The village leader's wife had been suffering stiff, achy joints ever since the onset of winter, and her condition was especially bad on days like today. She was taking a daily dose of white willow powder. Though Shumei was begrudgingly grateful the leader and his wife always paid for the medicine on time and in full, it was the same paltry fee everyone else in the village paid. The same medicines, she had heard, fetched ten times as much in the plains cities.

Of course, some villages had no crows to tend their medicine fields, so the task went to brown-haired farmers. Paying a brownie more for the same task was somehow equal to paying a pittance to a crow. Had her family known of this inequality before her father had passed, they would've asked for more money for his sake.

She hated delivering medicine to the leader and his wife. While other villagers openly displayed their contempt of her with sneers and rude remarks, the two blondies preferred to be condescending, lobbing insults at her from behind fake smiles. They always tried to make her stay and have tea so they could poke at her with their sharp tongues, but she wouldn't let them today. She had an excuse to escape them, one even they couldn't brush aside.

Walking quickly, head down, she took a path to the other side of the village that gave her the best chance of avoiding running into anyone. For once, luck was with her, and except for an elderly woman who simply turned her face away at Shumei's passing, she made it to the other side of the village without incident.

Cautiously, she approached the leader's front gate, two wood-paneled doors made of intricately carved whispering ash, and pushed open the left one because its hinges didn't squeak. After slipping inside, she mounted the worn stone steps leading to the leader's home.

While her family's cramped, drafty hut had a reed door, a partial wooden floor made of the cheapest and poorest wood, and a leaky, thatched roof, the leader's home was constructed of crimson cedar, cut and bundled in the famed city of Houfu in the plains to the west. It also had three glass windows, a finished wooden floor, and a solid front door made of stone oak. They never wanted for anything while Shumei and her family barely survived.

She wasn't allowed to use the knocker, so she rapped on the door. The unforgiving hardness of the wood stung her knuckles, and she sucked on them while she waited. A moment passed before she heard the shuffle of feet. She took a calming breath, schooled her face to look as blank as possible, and let her head hang low enough to show the one answering the door that she was being respectful.

But beneath the folds of her delivery pouch, she made a vulgar sign with her right hand, curling the third and fourth fingers.

The door slid open, quietly and smoothly riding its track.

"Ah, Shumei. Come in, child." Leader Kimen beckoned. His wife was nowhere to be seen.

"Thank you, Leader Kimen," she answered in a clear voice, hoping to alert Akki. She hated the woman, but Akki was the only person Kimen feared, and Shumei loathed being alone with the man.

Nearing fifty, Kimen was lanky in his limbs and sported a heavy gut from his drinking. His mottled complexion looked especially sickly when the light hit his blond hair just right, hair that was thinning and streaked with gray. His deep-set eyes were spaced wide, and his equally wide mouth sat under a long nose that was too big for his face. Every time she saw him, she likened him to a frog and often imagined him eating flies.

8

"Wipe your dirty feet on the towel here. Goodness, Shumei, will you never improve your appearance with a simple pair of shoes?" he asked with a smile. She hoped the sting of his jibe didn't show on her face, and couldn't help curling her shoulders inward, as if that would make the insults bounce off her. She would gladly garb herself better if she were paid properly for her and her mother's hard work, but the village would never pay them any better than they did now. She would never be able to "improve her poor appearance."

As it was, her feet were covered with thick calluses and caked with mud that only temporarily came off when she scrubbed them with sand from the riverbed when bathing. Her wavy hair, without the luxury of anything but the harshest soap, was rough and impossible to comb when the only tool she had was missing half its teeth.

Kimen knew she was too underpaid to afford shoes, yet he still insulted her. With no way to talk back, however, she silently and obediently wiped her mud-encrusted feet on a damp towel pulled taunt over a block of wood to the right of the door.

"Where is the mistress?" she asked, fighting to keep calm. "I have her medicine."

"Ah, then you should know that today's weather is particularly harsh on my dear wife. She's still in bed but will join us soon, child. Let us have some tea while we wait on her." He gestured her forward.

The smooth wooden floor Kimen stood upon was a small step up into their home from the entryway, and she could smell the sweet fragrance of a previously prepared pot of tea. They had such a lovely house, with small but pretty paintings and modest but comfortable furnishings. She hated how much she wished for something similar.

"As you've surely heard, Leader Kimen, my family has the Burning. I beg you to take the medicine now and let me leave with the fee so I can buy meat for them and help them survive this critical stage."

"Oh, a few minutes won't hurt, dear child. And we've things to discuss. Come in, have some tea, and I may let you go unscathed." His choice of words was not lost on her. She shuddered, an irrepressible flush of anger rising to her face. He would try it again today. She prayed his wife was hurrying her morning routine to interfere. Unfortunately, though, she may not even know Shumei had arrived.

Reluctantly, Shumei stepped into the leader's home and followed him to the warm parlor by the entrance. A small ceramic pot, steaming with hot tea, already sat next to three small cups on a low table in the middle of the room. He had been waiting for her. The thick, woven rug felt blissful beneath her calloused feet. Kimen bade her to sit, and she gratefully knelt to sit upon her heels. Kimen sat diagonal from her on a cushion.

"How is your mother, Shumei?" he asked, a bit of hope lighting his eyes. She knew it was *not* hope for her mother's recovery.

"Unfortunately, the disease has progressed with her. I shall try my utmost to keep her alive today, once I have finished delivering medicine," she explained slowly, hoping her urgent need to return home would penetrate his thick skull.

He frowned insincerely and tsked. "Her chances are slim, my dear. I'm sorry for the loss you're about to experience, and I would implore you to consider your next step after she passes. Akki and I know of a small handful of—well, somewhat *reluctant* men who are willing to take you to wife. You should consider their offers."

Shumei made the vulgar gesture with her right hand again, clenching her jaw. When her mother had first become ill, Shumei had known Mama's chance of survival was about one in five. She was nothing if not realistic. While her mother battled the disease, she had been preparing herself for the worst, if only to be brave in front of her fellow villagers, who were undoubtedly cackling with delight to hear a crow might die. She believed herself ready to accept what the leader predicted, but never would she give up hope.

"My mother may still recover," she bit out despite herself. "And even if she passed, I still wouldn't be ready for marriage." Realizing the level of her anger, she ducked her head to hide her face, and briefly closed her eyes to chide herself. Even if Kimen had been rude, as he always was, she couldn't let herself take his bait. She surmised that worry over her family had made her flippant.

The leader didn't respond at first. She didn't want to look up at him, for that would make matters worse, and hoped he didn't start lecturing her on her lack of humility.

"I was hoping you'd say that," he purred, putting her on her guard. She lifted her head a degree and stiffened as Kimen sidled toward her. "You're aware of how greatly I desire you." He spoke in a greedy whisper, leaning close to place his lips near her ear. She darted a glance at his wrinkly hand on her thigh and clutched her medicine bag to her chest.

"I-If I am to remain fit for marriage, I cannot accept your...advances. Besides, you are married, sir," she reminded him.

He pressed closer, pushing his pelvis against her hip. She suppressed a gasp, fearing the hardness against her backside. His tongue flicked out to leave a glob of his disgusting saliva in her ear, and she jerked her head away from his touch. Her hopes for his wife to appear snowballed until all she desired to hear was Akki stomping down the hall.

"Akki wouldn't know. I'd even compensate you for your time. You would like to eat more meat, wouldn't you?" She tried to lean away from him, but he pulled her body closer between his spindly thighs. "And I'd be more than willing, for you, to spill my purifying seed into your evil little pussy. Shumei, I could save your soul if you let me fuck you," he said, horrifying her with his confusing declarations. She knew of a physical act between married people, but he was using words she'd never heard before.

"I don't understand what you're saying, nor do I care to find out."

"Oh, I don't believe that. You know exactly what I'm talking about, don't you, Shumei?" He began grinding against her. "Like this, right? I pump my cock, and you moan like the wanton little witch you are."

"Stop it," she whispered vehemently, doing her best to put space between them. She tried to pull away, keeping her pouch close to her chest.

Heavy footfalls sounded from the opposite side of the house. Shumei gave a loud sigh of relief, never so glad for Akki's impending presence. Kimen was quick to put himself on the other side of the table. In record time, he straightened his robes and reverted to looking as innocent as possible.

"This discussion isn't over yet," he softly promised, catching her gaze for a fleeting second before Akki walked into the room.

"Why didn't you tell me my medicine was here?" she shrieked at her husband.

"My dear, I wanted to let you rest a bit longer," he cajoled, coming to a stand with a hastiness that was damning. Shumei could sense Akki's deadly glare. She could feel little pricks of suspicion and hate upon her bowed head.

"I'll rest better when I've had my medicine," Akki scathingly replied, stomping forward. She reached down and jabbed two fingers into Shumei's shoulder, her cue to bring out the medicine. Shumei quickly dug through her pouch to retrieve a larger cloth bag with seven small packets inside. "Pour the tea, you lazy bag of lard."

Kimen was quick to comply, and Akki yelped in pain as she struggled to kneel upon the cushion he'd vacated.

"Shall I add the medicine, Madam Akki?" Shumei asked only as loud as the huffing woman needed to hear her.

"With my hands the way they are, you stupid child, of course I want you to put the medicine in," she spat.

Shumei opened a daily dose, took a clean stirring stick, and mixed in the white willow powder, which quickly dissolved. Akki grasped painfully at the cup and attempted to down the steaming tea in only a few gulps.

This moment was one of the rare times when Akki's contempt for Shumei was not shrouded in her usual, mean smile. Despite being the lowest-ranking member of the village, Shumei was oddly privileged to see this side of the leader's wife, who always acted serene and spiritual in front of everyone else.

Akki had been a beautiful woman when she was younger, or so Shumei had heard from her mother. But despite her comfortable home and the power she held over the village, Akki hated her life, and it showed on her face. Lines of stress bracketed her mouth, which was nearly always pursed around her overly large front teeth. Permanent wrinkles furrowed her forehead. Her complaints, given "kindly" of course, were well and widely known, from the food she ate to the clothes she wore to the enviable amount of free time she enjoyed, time which she said was spent in "utter boredom."

Kimen and Shumei were both silent as Akki returned the cup to the table, hands trembling. Her eyes were closed, so Shumei didn't worry about being caught staring as she studied the older woman's complexion, noticing how pale she'd become. All the blood was gone from her face. Akki rarely went outside anyway, preferring not to work, even if "work" was simply visiting and speaking with the other villagers, but even for a woman who hardly saw sunlight, her skin was much too thin and gray. Something else was wrong.

Shumei stared at her hands and searched her mind for what could make someone appear so deathly pale.

"Dearest?" Kimen leaned toward his wife, and Shumei put aside her thoughts for the moment.

"Pay her the fee," Akki said flatly. Kimen reached into the fold of his shirt, pulled out a heavy coin purse, and withdrew a ten-kol piece.

Ten kols was enough to buy about three days' worth of meager meals for one person. The small, rectangular currency came in several denominations, but she'd never held anything higher than a ten-kol piece. The one time she'd seen a hundred-kol piece, it had been in the hand of another villager gushing about finding it on the western road.

Eight or nine kols was enough to buy the cheapest pair of shoes, but over the last year, only four traveling merchants had come through their village. Two had come without any shoes to sell, and the other two had been required by custom to sell to crows only after the rest of the village had made their purchases, so they had sold out of any affordable shoes. A run of bad luck. But when had she ever been lucky?

Kimen tossed the ten-kol piece to her from across the table, and it landed on the medicine pouch in her lap with an unceremonious plop.

"Have you seen my symptoms, little Shumei?" Akki asked with a sneer.

"Yes, madam." She closed her fist over the money in her lap.

"As observant as ever."

Shumei didn't respond.

"Find a cure for it, then."

She nodded without looking up. Perhaps her mother would have some advice.

"Now then, I suppose you should be going, child," Kimen said, making to rise.

"Not yet, idiot. We've yet to discuss her future husband," Akki pointed out, swiping her hand through the air as if cutting off someone's head. Kimen settled, nodding uncertainly. Akki turned her attention back to Shumei. "It's pitiable someone like you cannot marry by virtue of her own qualities when you are so lacking, but the job of any village leader includes arranging a husband for you on your twentieth birthday. We've collected a few offers for your...hand in marriage," she finished with a gulp, as if disgusted.

"If you please, Madam Akki—" Shumei tried to say, hoping to leave soon.

"Don't interrupt when a Blessed One is speaking," she snapped. "As I was saying, this village may have lost many of its finest members thanks to that cursed disease—and we may be temporarily abandoned by our neighboring villages who are too cowardly even to trade with us—but of the men here, three have said they're willing to take you to wife. And because he asked to be mentioned first..." Akki paused, sighing and rolling her eyes. "Akiji has begged that you 'accept his undying love and unending passions' when choosing a husband."

Shumei wanted to laugh but managed to keep her face still.

"The miller's two sons also agreed to be candidates, though it was difficult to garner their acceptance. I actually had to praise you once to make them say yes," she said, shifting uncomfortably. Shumei nearly couldn't suppress a disbelieving scoff.

"Madam Akki, I know I'm not worthy of your efforts, but right now, my mother and brother are at critical stages of the dis—"

"By the dueling gods, child, calm down. We can talk of this next week. But be sure to save that darling brother of yours. If you fail, and a Blessed One is lost to the Burning, I doubt even my husband and I could find or approve of any match with you."

Shumei nodded while silently fuming at Akki's coldness toward her brother's health. Blondies cooed at each other constantly for being so wonderful, but even that level of self-absorption was an illusion. Shumei was one of the few who knew the truth: blondies despised other blondies. The fewer of them there were, the more they were loved, appreciated, and worshipped. A spoiled blondie hated competition.

"I will take my leave, Leader and Madam," she said as she stood.

"Yes, you should be off to deliver those medicines, I'm sure. Perhaps you'll be able to afford some meat this week," Akki said with a grimacing smile, one that didn't reach her eyes. Not giving the woman the satisfaction of a reaction, Shumei showed none of the anger she felt as she forced herself to bow in respect before leaving.

Upon shutting the door behind her, she breathed in the fresh morning air and was only a little saddened to see it had begun drizzling, but she would rather be chilled and wet than remain in that house another minute.

Huddling over her pouch of medicines, she took the path that ran along the edge of the village even though it was a less-direct route to her next stop. It had the most trees and would keep her drier. A moment later, she knocked on the door of a family whose oldest daughter was pregnant and needed medicine for her morning sickness. After exchanging the medicine and fee, only two kols, the door was all but slammed in her face, but she paid it no heed. Two more families earned her six kols, and then it was time to visit her biggest customer.

The witch. At least, everyone said Majo was a witch. But no one had yet revealed any solid evidence to support such an accusation, or even to suggest it at a volume louder than a whisper.

In an obvious attempt to discover such evidence, Kimen and Akki had asked once what kind of plants Majo ordered from Shumei's family—as if they would know which ones were suspect, which of course they didn't. Knowledge of magic was forbidden. Even if they had conjured up a flimsy reason or a dubious claim, Shumei doubted they'd have the courage to confront Majo.

What Shumei knew about magic could be summed up in one word: nothing. But after dozens of weekly visits to Majo's home, she had never seen anything she might think was any sort of magic, which was all she could say in response to Akki and Kimen's questions.

Not that Majo wasn't a strange person. She always asked for an odd assortment of herbs, fungi, and roots. When Shumei once asked why, the witch had merely smiled and said she liked to cook. For a woman of her years—Shumei assumed somewhere around forty—Majo was rather fresh-faced and beautiful compared to anyone else her age. Of course, no one knew her exact age, but no one was brave enough to ask, directly or indirectly, Shumei included.

Majo's home was on the west side of the village and, like Shumei's house, was set farther back because, also like Shumei, Majo had black hair—the only other person with black hair in the village besides Shumei and her mother.

Shumei didn't know where the witch earned her income, but she always paid for her delivery in full and purchased more per week than the rest of the entire village did. Shumei had never seen her working on anything, so what she did with all those plants and extracts could only be guessed at. Perhaps she made and sold secondary medicines, but evidently not to anyone in the village as far as Shumei could tell. No one had ever mentioned buying anything from her—not that anyone would necessarily admit it.

The witch's home was far sturdier than Shumei's, having been constructed of yellow birch, a strange and rather paranoid choice. It was a type of wood that didn't burn easily, but other people would have chosen a prettier, longer-lasting wood. Yellow birch was unfortunately vulnerable to rotting, and it was also an unattractive shade of yellowish-green, which made for a home that stuck out like mold on a piece of bread. Her front door, which swung rather than slid, was decorated with an odd arrangement of dried flowers.

Shumei raised her hand to knock, but before she could, the sickly green portal yelped and shuddered as it pulled free of a catch in the doorjamb. Slowly but steadily, it swung inward.

"On time, as always." Majo draped one hand over the top of the door.

Shumei didn't respond, though perhaps visibly swallowing could be considered a response. Strangest of all Majo's habits was her manner of dress, and it was doubly so today.

With the exception of the leader and his wife in their relatively lavish home, most people in their village were of very limited means, including fashion. Men wore bland-colored, traditional clothing, which consisted of loose, dark pants that cinched tightly around the ankle, and thigh-length, robe-like shirts and jackets held shut with ties. The only real difference between what any of the men wore was the quality of the fabric and how well it fit.

Women wrapped themselves in long-sleeved, ankle-length dresses that closed at the waist with wide belts of cloth. If one could afford an under-robe, it was worn to provide extra modesty at the neck. Wealthy women wore bright, fine materials laden with intricate embroidery, but even Akki hardly wore her finest dress and was usually seen in more modest garb, albeit something finer than Shumei had ever owned or even touched.

Majo, on the other hand, had somehow acquired enough wealth to clothe herself extremely well. She always forewent the under-robe and cinched her belt to show off her cleavage, but her fine silk dresses boasted bold, beautiful patterns, such as red butterflies, black birds, or white roses.

Shumei was unavoidably jealous, but she wasn't alone. All the other villagers sulked about how Majo had far finer clothing than they did, and this, however petty, was the real reason they believed her to be a witch. How else would a crow have nice things?

Today, Majo wore a red robe covered with a peculiar black pattern, and Shumei had to wonder why Majo would choose something as disturbing as spiderwebs. It was a beautifully made dress, but it made Shumei shudder all the same.

"Do you have time to visit with me this week?" Smiling, Majo took the hand Shumei had left hanging in the air and pulled her inside. "I have a surprise for you."

"I'm sorry, Madam Majo, but my mother and brother are still both quite sick. I'd be glad to visit with you another day," she offered, even though she disliked spending time with the witch. Majo had never been unkind toward Shumei, but something about her felt off. Even dangerous.

Majo closed the door, leaving Shumei fidgeting under the full effect of her home's interior. There were no windows, only a small hole in the roof to let out smoke, so Majo's solution for creating light was candles—but not just one or two. Half a dozen red candles, worth ten times what Shumei's family made in a week, were always burning. And she had never seen them burned lower than halfway.

The floor of the hut was a cheap but smooth wood, and one threadbare rug covered a large, open area near the entrance. Majo's cooking pot sat to the left beneath the roof's smoke hole, and her thick sleeping mat lay to the right. All around were large cabinets and shelves filled with books and baskets of plants. A small, locked case sat in a far corner of the room.

Shumei had often stared at the books at the back of the hut, wondering what was inside. She couldn't read well, but she still wanted to look. What people, ideas, or places did they describe? Did they all speak of real events, or were fables and epics mixed in with historical accounts?

"A few minutes is all I ask," Majo pleaded, sandwiching Shumei's hand between her own. Not wanting to upset her best customer, Shumei hesitated and wondered why she couldn't bring forth her meager supply of courage in such a simple social situation.

But she had been away from her home only about forty-five minutes at this point, and she had five more deliveries. If she stayed at the witch's house for a short visit, then made her deliveries, she estimated she'd be home within the hour. Surely her mother and brother could be by themselves until then.

"All right," she said, giving in to Majo's cajoling. The woman smiled in relief and led her farther inside.

"Have a seat here." Majo swept her hand toward her sleeping mat, which was made up with a soft, woolen blanket. "Mind your feet, please."

Shumei sat with her legs angled away from Majo's clean blanket and tried to relax while Majo retrieved a jug and a cup from one of her cabinets. The witch rested on her heels on a cushion nearby and set her burden next to the still-steaming tea she must have been drinking before Shumei had arrived.

As Majo rearranged the items around her, Shumei dared to look a little closer at the witch. She saw only a couple of laugh lines around her eyes, the irises of which were nearly black. They sometimes crinkled as if she delighted in knowing something others did not, but more often they were cold and calculating. No doubt the reason Majo's lips were usually painted blood-red was to distract from her piercing gaze. Shumei was tempted to wipe her finger across

Majo's lower lip and wondered how she might look with a painted mouth.

Such thoughts always led to wondering what it'd be like to actually be Majo. To be independent. Mysterious. Feared and yet desired. Shumei didn't have to know much about sexual intimacy to understand the undercurrent to some of the villagers' whispered comments about the witch.

"I've been trying my hand at distilling spirits and managed to make rice wine," Majo revealed. Her long, unbound hair swept over her shoulders as she leaned forward to touch the jug. "I want you to be the first to taste it."

Shumei nodded rather than return Majo's smile, but her heart secretly raced with the bit of mischief Majo often brought out in her. A sip of alcohol today, a juicy piece of gossip last week. Mama had always strictly forbidden rice wine, even at village festivals, only one of which crows could attend, so to have an opportunity like this made Shumei feel lucky, if also a little guilty. She always tried to deny temptation in order to refute the bad reputation automatically cast upon her, but she had so easily nodded. Although, why shouldn't she enjoy something nice once in a while?

Majo presented the small cup of rice wine to her, and Shumei bowed her head as she took it. The wine's pungent scent filled her nostrils as she glanced up at Majo, who raised her eyebrows in question.

"Do I sip it?" Shumei asked.

A smile melted onto Majo's face. "If you like."

She raised the cup to her lips and took a small sip. Its smooth taste was a surprise. Whenever other villagers drank rice wine, they always winced after swallowing. "It's wonderful," she said, thoroughly enjoying the small flare of heat spreading inside her. Preening, the witch said her thanks.

When Shumei had finished her serving, she set down the cup and reached into her pouch to retrieve the largest packet, which was filled with roots, small bags of medicinal powders, and bundles of herbs. She laid it in front of Majo, who picked it up with yet another smile and inspected its contents.

"Wonderfully prepared, as usual," she praised, setting it aside. Moving with enviable grace, she then went to the chest in the corner and unlocked it with a small key she kept inside the belt of her dress. The heavy bag she retrieved was no doubt filled with more money than Shumei could ever hope to have. Majo counted out the payment and locked the chest again before returning to sit on the cushion.

"Hold out your hand, dear," she said. Shumei did so, bowing her head without thought. Twenty-five kols spilled into her hand, eight kols more than the expected fee. Shumei stared at the three coins in her hand with disbelief.

"For trying my wine and always doing such a wonderful job with my order, I wanted to give you a tip this week. Save it for yourself, okay?"

Shumei's eyes stung, and though she was grateful, she couldn't help feeling suspicious, which only made her feel worse. Majo was a crow like her and had always been generous. But Shumei just couldn't shake the feeling the witch's generosity, if accepted, came with a price. But what else could she do but accept what little kindness was given her?

With a quiet thank-you, Shumei put the money away and set her satchel aside. Majo poured more wine. "Have another before you leave," she said, holding the cup out. Bowing her head yet again, Shumei accepted a second serving and brought it to her lips. She took larger sips this time and marveled at how light the wine made her head feel.

"It really is delicious. Thank you for sharing it with me."

The witch smiled again, a little too slowly. Shumei couldn't help noting the direction of Majo's gaze: Shumei's chest. Glancing down, she wondered if she had spilled the wine, but there were no wet spots on her clothes.

"I wonder why you haven't yet purchased yourself new shoes, Shumei. You have enough money to afford a pair, don't you? I hate to see your pretty feet in the mud all the time."

Shumei curled her toes self-consciously, lamenting how calloused and dirty her soles had become since outgrowing her old pair of shoes. She wordlessly set down her empty cup.

"Oh, don't worry too much about it, dear. Though I do hope you use my tip to buy some shoes, I'll be happy as long as you use the money on yourself."

"Yes, madam," she murmured. She felt strange—in more ways than one. She was certain she was a little drunk, but more than that, she had grown reluctant to leave. Yes, she was dressed far more poorly than her host, but here she was warm and receiving small but highly appreciated gifts. She thought of her sick family at home, and guilt pulled her shoulders into a slouch.

"Shumei?" Majo softly called. She had leaned forward, hands out. Looking up with a bit of a start, Shumei straightened. Then her jaw dropped, for Majo cupped Shumei's breasts as casually as if shaking her hand.

Shumei was so shocked she couldn't move. All she could do was sit there while Majo tested the weight and shape of her breasts with the same sort of thoughtful and determined expression one would see from a physician.

The witch lifted her gaze to Shumei's stunned reaction and gave her a sly smile. "Does this feel good?" she whispered, brushing her thumbs over Shumei's nipples. At last, Shumei was galvanized to push the woman's hands away. Face red, she wrapped her arms around her chest and turned away.

"Why did you do that?" Shumei asked, voice shaking. Majo hadn't hurt her. In fact, the revulsion she felt around Kimen and Akiji was absent, but the witch had never given her any indication of such...interest before, and it had completely blindsided her.

"You're going to be twenty soon, right?" Majo asked. Shumei nodded. "Then no doubt the leader and his wife have mentioned marriage."

"Yes, not even an hour ago."

Majo sighed. "They will probably force you to choose that bully, Akiji. He may declare his love for you, but he only wants one thing from you. You know that, right?"

Shumei did know and swallowed her unspoken anxieties. Like all young, unmarried people, she was quite curious about "the marital act." She had heard of a body part on men that moved on its own, and positions the couple assumed. She wondered how much of it was true. Her mother had never explained much, and she had never felt she could ask.

"Why do I have to marry?" She sank into herself as sadness settled over her, and stared at a candle in the corner, its flame steady in the still air.

"No doubt they hope you'll soon be with child. Another crow for them to exploit."

"Is that why you refused a husband?"

"I had...many reasons."

Shumei rubbed her arms, gaze falling away from the candle. She could now guess at least a couple of those reasons.

"You should be going now," Majo said, dress rustling as she stood. "Your family is waiting for you, right?" Shumei grabbed her medicine pouch and stood. Though she faced the witch, she couldn't look her in the eye and instead stared at the floor. "The same order for next week will be fine, dear." Majo folded her hands together as if she were as proper as any other matronly villager.

"Yes, madam," she said, backing up to the door.

"Oh, and Shumei?" the witch called. Shumei made the mistake of looking up. "If you ever want me to touch your pretty breasts again, come by anytime. I can do that and much more," she said with a wicked grin, stroking her hand over her hip. Taken aback, Shumei could only stutter. She flung the door open and made a hasty exit. The last thing she heard before shutting the witch's door was lilting laughter.

Shumei beat a fast pace to her next stop. Embarrassment heated her cheeks. Her nipples tingled. Majo had never done or said anything like that before. And to think Shumei had been trying to give Majo the benefit of the doubt.

The next four deliveries went by quickly and without a problem. However, her last stop of the day still loomed before her—a man who regularly bought medicine for his hangovers. Where he got his drink, or with what money, was a mystery, but her mother suspected he used part of his crop to distill whatever could get him drunk despite how little surplus their village could produce.

His son was the infamous Akiji, who had been pursuing her since she was thirteen. At first, Akiji's overtures had been sweet, even thoughtful. But as everything else in her life, his attention had become something wrong and uncomfortable. That she had thus far escaped any serious incident with him was a miracle, for she was never surprised to see a new bruise on his face. He was always getting into fights, though she had never seen this herself, and his tendency toward violence seriously worried her, especially if she were forced to marry him.

She frowned when Akiji's home came into view and looked around for any signs of him or his pockmarked father. All was quiet. She lightly rapped on the door, medicine packet in hand, and waited. Almost a minute passed before she heard noise inside, but she knew she had to be patient with this delivery. Knocking more than once earned far more ire than it was worth. When the rickety wooden door was abruptly whipped open, she was rather glad it was Akiji's father, and not Akiji himself.

The man clearly had yet another hangover and had been sleeping until a moment ago. Where his wife was at this hour, Shumei didn't know, but she could guess the woman was filling in for her husband in the fields until he could pull himself out of his drunken stupor long enough to go do his own work.

"What do you want?" he grumbled. He wasn't in a good mood, so she meekly held out the cloth bag.

"Your medicines, sir."

He thought for a brief moment, rubbing his bumpy face, and then told her to wait a minute. He disappeared inside his dark home and came stumbling back with her fee. After slapping the two rectangular pieces into her palm, he grabbed his medicine. She brought her hand back just as he slammed the door in her face.

Sighing, she placed the money into the only other bag in her medicine pouch, which now held the day's earnings of exactly fifty kols. About half would go toward meals for her family this week, and another fifteen kols would go toward firewood because they had neither an ax nor the time to chop their own. That left ten kols, eight of which were from Majo's tip, for Shumei's use. She decided to take the witch's advice and use them for a pair of shoes. That assumed, of course, that a traveling merchant would come through their village again anytime soon.

The week's deliveries done, Shumei turned in the direction of the village huntsman, and she jumped in surprise to find Akiji standing between her and the path, arms folded and shoulder propped against the wall of his house. His smile was possessive, and a fresh bruise colored his left eye.

"Lovely to see you this fine morning," he greeted despite how obviously poor the weather was.

"Did you get into another fight?" she asked without inflection, having recovered from her shock. She made to walk past him, but he caught her arm in a firm grip.

"You always misunderstand me," he said, low and far too intimate. Compared to his father and most of the men in the village, Akiji was quite handsome. Straight teeth, light brown eyes, a strong jaw, and a fine figure. His sandy-brown hair was cut short and curled a bit.

But what value was there in good looks when she held absolutely no feelings for him, except perhaps pity and no small amount of fear? According to others' opinions of his temper and her own experiences with his bullying nature, she had the strong feeling his future wife would have her own share of bruises.

"I misunderstand nothing. Please let go of me," she said, attempting to jerk her arm out of his grasp. His grip only tightened. "My family is sick, and I cannot waste time here with you."

"I merely wish to know if the leader and his wife told you of my marital intentions."

"They did. Now let me go." She tried to break free once more, but he only pulled her a step closer.

"But what of your answer? Will you be my wife?"

"I... I didn't finish talking with them this morning due to my urgent business at home, so I won't have an answer until that discussion is over," she stalled, not wanting to say outright that marriage to him had no chance of happening.

"That you know of my intentions is enough of a discussion. I love you and want to marry you," he declared, though his voice nearly broke on the word *marry*. He briefly touched his bruised eye and winced as if it still greatly pained him. "We'd both be better off, don't you see?"

"But I don't love you," Shumei said, having given him a similar answer countless times over the years. She hoped this time he would let it go.

But he hardened his jaw and then clamped her against his wide chest, crushing her against him. "You'll come to love me, Shumei. I know it," he whispered. She turned her face when his mouth came dangerously close. "When you feel our first child growing inside you, you'll realize how much we love each other." She wedged her arm between them and wrenched free of his grasp. Stumbling back, she clutched her medicine pouch to her chest like a shield.

"Why is everyone after me today?" she panted. When he didn't advance on her and only looked at her with confusion, she straightened from her defensive posture. "My family needs me." Without bidding him any sort of farewell, she turned and walked away. He let her go this time, though she did hear him quietly call her name.

As her feet carried her toward the huntsman, Shumei's mind whirred with dread and confusion. Why hadn't her mother warned her turning twenty would be such a rocky experience? Leader Kimen, who had already propositioned her before, was stepping up his efforts. Then there was Majo, who had been like an older sister to her, albeit an intimidating one. Now she was also taking liberties and offering "much more." Lastly, there was Akiji, who had always pursued her as he had today, but now he wanted her hand in marriage rather than a kiss, a few of which he had successfully stolen over the years, much to Shumei's dismay.

Though her twentieth birthday was still a couple months away, it now loomed in her future like a storm on the horizon. The only question remaining was how much damage that storm would do.

Chapter Two

O ka would not live through the night if his fever wasn't brought down. With her hand on his forehead, Shumei looked at her mother and shook her head. Mama lay on her side. She was awake, but her breathing had become labored. Next to her, their cooking pot simmered over a small fire, steeping the last of the *fuki* they had at the hut. Shumei only hoped the herbs were still fresh. When she had dumped them in, the normally pungent, earthy scent was far too musty for her liking.

"Hot," Oka moaned. She patted his shoulder and blinked back her tears.

"Hush now. Let your body fix itself," she quietly ordered, brushing the hair from his forehead.

"I think it's...ready, baby," her mother weakly called. Shumei padded over to the pot and lifted the lid. The fetid stench that greeted her nose said it all.

"Oh no!" She sank to her knees with dismay. "The herbs must have been too old, and we don't have any more of them here." She glanced at her brother, who had tossed to his side. She couldn't lose him, not like this.

"Can't you...fetch some from...the field?" her mother asked.

Shumei bit her lip to stifle her response. The Burning had been tricking her mother's senses all day. Thus, Mama hadn't noticed the sun would soon set, and their field wasn't a short walk away. Leaving now was risking a lot.

She berated herself for not going earlier while she still had plenty of sunshine to spend. The heavy gray clouds had blown away by midday, revealing a weak, spring sun that had dried the paths in only a couple hours. She had seen their supply of *fuki* was low while cleaning up after lunch, but villagers had been showing up nonstop to request medicine for the Burning.

Now, Oka would most certainly die without it. If she wanted to save him, she had to risk herself. She had to go to the medicine field...or die trying.

Nodding to her mother, she stood and reached for the empty basket on the rickety shelf against the wall. Her mother lay back, closing her eyes as though she hadn't a care in the world. Shumei silently prayed for Mama's life, for no amount of *fuki* would help her chances, and hoped the Divine One would spare her mother tonight. Then she knelt next to Oka long enough to kiss his forehead before pushing aside the reed door and leaving.

Besides one person in the distance, probably hurrying home, no one was about. Too many people were sick, and it was too close to sunset. Not needing to hike up her skirt because it was already too short, she ran down the familiar path toward the medicine field. She might make it there and back before dark if she cut her travel time in half.

Tall poles stood at even intervals around the village, and a single rope connected them at the top. From the rope hung small wooden blocks with prayers etched into them by the priests from the local temple. When strung in a complete circle, the prayers formed a barrier that evil couldn't cross. A similar circle of prayers was staked around the medicine field, but there were no prayers to protect her along the way. She tried to ignore the jolt to her heart as she left the safety they provided.

The path beyond the charms turned rough fast. She thought of Oka's life on the line as she ran, scrambling up the abrupt hills and then skidding down the other side. The impending sunset kept her legs moving, even as her lungs burned for air.

Eventually she came to a large clearing covered with fragrant, early-spring grass, a sea of green broken only by a thin dirt path. She and Oka often played tag here. On summer days when the grass was tall, they would play hide-and-seek. Though she was tempted to check the level of the sun, she knew she'd likely turn and run back home if she saw how little daylight remained, so she kept her eyes on the gap in the tree line where the path continued.

The deepening darkness was frightening enough on its own. Strange shapes and shadows began to emerge. As she weaved through the trees, following the rambling path, each suspicious outline seemed scarier than the last. Had any of them moved after she'd passed?

Her chest heaved with strain as she leapt over a thin, meandering stream, only a couple more minutes from her destination. Sunlight flashed through a break in the newly budding branches, then disappeared as she left the stream behind.

At last, she arrived at the field, uncertain how long it had taken her to get there, but certain she had less time than she wanted. She knelt by a patch of the correct plant, which her mother had sown at the beginning of the season in half-frozen earth, and began harvesting the leaves of the most matured plants, which she placed quickly but carefully into the basket. She would need enough for several families; many more would come to the door that night looking for medicine. She glanced at the sun only once, feeling safe as long as its light touched her.

But by the time the basket was half-full, the sun was below the tree line, only a few moments from disappearing entirely. The pale face of the waxing moon sat low over the eastern rise of trees, heralding the coming of night and warning her to hurry. Tears streamed down her face as she tied the basket shut.

Whenever the sun sank below the horizon, other things rose to greet the night—and they weren't stars. Elders would tell children stories of these monsters, warning them never to leave the safety of the village at night. Shumei had heard the most powerful monsters could come out into the daylight in defiance of the Divine One, but everyone dismissed such tales as mere rumor.

As surely as there was a Divine One and a Damned One, there were demons to prey upon humans. Sent from the Damned One's domain of Oblivion, these creatures killed to gain power, eating children and mauling the occasional desperate traveler in obscene ways. Their predation was a by-proxy war between the Golden One and the Foul One, though Shumei thought demons had an unfair advantage. No human could win a one-on-one fight with any of the Damned One's minions.

Glancing around the edge of the field, she sprinted back the way she'd come. Normally, the woods seemed peaceful during the day. She usually didn't even think of the horrid monstrosities that prowled the forest while she slept, but now she feared one of them was watching the path, hoping to snatch up an unlucky soul. Which one might it be? She'd heard many stories of different kinds of demons. Almost all of the tales agreed they were ugly creatures made of disparate parts. Some chose specific victims or killed in specific ways. Most simply ate humans.

But the sort of demon that had always held her morbid interest was the kind that ravished humans as their source of energy. Sex demons. They were said to be sinfully beautiful—not out of vanity, of course, but as a means of ensnaring new victims. They'd whisk away a young man or, more often, a young woman and feed off her energy for as long as her spirit lasted. Shumei didn't know of anyone who'd ever been taken by such a demon, but everyone she'd ever overheard talking about them said the body of a missing woman typically showed up a few weeks or even months after she'd been taken.

Running at top speed for over twenty minutes since leaving her home had left Shumei's throat parched. Every breath was both agonizing and loud. Thankfully, the stream had appeared up ahead, and though she had skipped it on her way to the field, she knew she would have to stop for a few precious seconds to catch her breath and relieve her thirst.

She skidded to a stop at the muddy bank and dropped to her knees. Panting, she scooped water into the bowl of her hands and drank greedily. The relief was so great her eyes went out of focus, and the tips of her sorely tangled hair became wet as she leaned over the stream for another drink. Counting down from ten, she took one last gulp and drew her sleeve across her wet, open lips. Just ten seconds and she'd have to keep going.

A twig snapped. She gasped, hand already on the handle of her basket. Her other hand she pressed to her heart, which was ready to burst. Peering intently in the direction of the sound, she tried to discern what had nearly given her a heart attack, but the trees were tucked tightly against the stream, and she found it difficult to see much in the low light. She carefully rose to her feet and waited another breath. Had it been an animal?

Then a large shadow emerged, much closer than she'd expected. It had a head, shoulders, arms...

She ran, whimpering as she kicked up dirt in her haste to leave that enormous shape behind. Over the sound of air sawing in and out of her lungs, she heard rapid, heavy footsteps in a familiar cadence, like a horse's gallop. From which direction, she couldn't tell, but she almost sobbed when she spotted the clearing ahead. At her current pace, she'd be home in a few minutes.

Breaking away from the tree line, she neither let up speed nor looked over her shoulder, too afraid she'd see something out of her nightmares charging to catch up to her.

But it was too late. A movement from out of the darkened forest path ahead drove fear into the base of her spine like a hammer on a nail. Her legs faltered, and the world slowed. Her heartbeat sounded slow in her ears, but she knew it had never pounded as fast or as hard as it did now. The basket slipped from her fingers to land in the grass as an enormous black horse, gleaming with sweat under the moonlight, entered the meadow.

And the most handsome man she had ever seen was its rider. His hair was as pale as hers was dark, cut just above his shoulders and fluttering in the breeze. Was he a blondie? Had to be, but she couldn't tell. Nor could she tell much about his build due to his dark clothing, but his sharp, well-defined jaw made her think he was fit and strong. Beneath his prominent brow, his eyes were shrouded in shadow, but below his hawkish nose, the expression on his wide mouth was unmistakable: a smile of delight.

Something inside her twisted, making her stomach clench. He could see her with more than his eyes, she could feel it.

"Good evening," he greeted in a smooth, deep voice, one that sounded human. "Aren't you old enough to know it's dangerous to be out past sunset?"

She hesitated to answer, wondering what response would get her home safely. If he were human—one bold enough to travel at night and harass young women—she could point out he was also out past sunset. If he weren't human...

"Please don't hurt me," she panted, still winded. She picked up her basket. "O-Or make me go anywhere with you. I need to get back to my village."

He dismounted, and only then did she notice the sword attached to his waist. Was he planning to use it on her? She clutched her basket to her chest.

"I can promise you both of those things," he said, stroking his horse's neck as he strolled toward her. She backed up. "But I need something from you first."

He's lying was her first thought. *He just wants to get close enough to kill me.* But then she realized he could have run her down on his horse already and been done with it.

"What do you want?" she asked warily. Indeed, he could be lying, but she had to try to negotiate.

He stopped several paces away and cocked his head, considering her. "Should I try honesty?" he murmured, as if to himself. "Hmm, yes." He straightened. "Lie with me."

She balked. "What?"

"Lie with me. I shall give you pleasure, and it shall feed me."

"I-I don't— What, here? Now? With me? You can't be serious," she scoffed despite knowing deep down he was entirely serious. She had wondered whether she'd meet a demon, whether the kind that ate lust even existed. Now she'd wonder no longer.

He smiled, and Divine One did it do things to her heart that were so very wrong. If she weren't already hot from running, she would've turned bright red. "It's a pleasant enough evening. And one as tender as you hasn't crossed my path in many years."

"But I, I must return home at once."

He gestured at the basket in her arms. "Precious cargo?" She hesitantly nodded, worried he would take it from her. "You see, I am also desperate. I must feed, and I can tell you will be...quite nourishing."

She really wished he'd stop referring to her as food. "And if I weren't interested?"

Still smiling, he took another step toward her and his voice went low. "Oh, but you are. The delectable details are vague, but I know you think about, what to call it... A clandestine encounter? Someone new, mysterious, and exciting. Not someone from whatever village you call home."

Her eyes went wide. "H-How—" She shook her head. He was a demon, of course he had powers she didn't understand. "No, I cannot delay. I'm needed now."

Another step. "For someone as young and inexperienced as you, I'll need only a few moments to have you crying out in ecstasy."

"Oh," she gasped, shocked by his confidence. She regarded him for the space of a breath. His handsome smile, broad shoulders, large hands. Wait, she couldn't really be considering...? "B-But you're not human."

"I look human, don't I? I also feel human, I can promise you that," he purred. Another step closer. "True, you may never find with a human man the pleasure I can deliver. All the more reason to accept my offer."

Shumei couldn't help thinking of Akiji and how she'd likely be forced to marry him, sooner rather than later. She could run away, she supposed, but what about her mother and brother? What would become of them? And what were her chances, really, of a happier life somewhere else? She was still a crow.

"Shall I give you a taste, sweet miss?" He edged nearer, as if she were a spooked mare. "Reassurance of my skill?"

She gulped. "I s-shouldn't..." Now that he was closer, she could see his eyes were a light color, though their exact shade would remain a mystery in the weak moonlight. She wanted to see kindness in those eyes, but behind his hunger for her she saw...nothing.

"I'm offering you your fantasy," he whispered, close enough to touch. He was so tall. "Should I start over? Should I claim to be a...wandering mercenary, is that right?" She gasped. How could he see her most secret desires? *How*? "Someone bold who can take care of you—who wants to—and who'd whisk you away from this life?"

"It's only a fantasy," she stammered in reply. "Please stay out of my head."

"So is that a no to a show of my talent? You're not curious at all?"

Divine One help her she was intensely curious. And she knew she'd likely never get an opportunity like this again. To have a taste of forbidden passion before she was tied inescapably to both Akiji and her village, despite all her protests.

"You're hesitating," he slyly observed.

"All right," she blurted. Her heart still hadn't slowed from when she'd been running, nor would it anytime soon. "S-Show me what you can do."

The hunger in his eyes grew while his smile sharpened, turning predatory. "Shall I be your mercenary?"

"No," she said. He was already more than intimidating. "As you are."

"Whatever you desire." He touched her hand with warm fingers, gently urging her to lower the basket. She held it at her side. Her cheeks were so warm she could tell exactly how red she'd become: very.

With nothing left between them, he slipped his arm around her and pulled her against him. She sharply inhaled. He did feel human. More specifically, he felt male. The hardness pressed against her stomach certainly wasn't his sword. And his scent—something spicy that smelled familiar and even safe, but she couldn't quite place it.

He tilted up her chin. "Close your eyes," he urged in a bare whisper. Heart pounding, she complied. "And just feel."

Oh, his lips... So warm and gentle. They touched the corner of her mouth and were gone in an instant only to reappear on the other corner. Then he laid a tender kiss on her bottom lip, one that made her heart skip. She gripped his arm, finding it firm and muscular.

He held her closer and deepened their kiss, a growl rumbling in his chest. She heard a strange, throaty sound. Had that come from her? He pulled back to change angles, giving her a scant second to gulp for air, and when his mouth returned, she heard that sound again. A soft moan, and she had made it. By the dueling gods...

Something warm and wet swiped between her lips. His tongue. He dipped it into her mouth again, shallow but sensual. Without thinking, she opened wider, and when the heat of his tongue slipped alongside hers, she curled her fingers into his sleeve. How was she light-headed already?

His free hand was not idle. He ran it over her hair, somehow managing not to get his fingers tangled, and swept her messy locks over her shoulder. Having exposed her neck, he stroked her from earlobe to collarbone, his touch so light she shivered. But she wasn't cold. Everywhere he touched was feverish.

He continued downward, slowly dragging his hand over her breast. When his thumb reached her nipple, he rubbed and teased her through her thin, worn dress. She made a sound of surprise, arching her back without meaning to. The tip of her breast stiffened, and he pinched it through her clothing. She dropped her basket.

"Oh!" She pulled her mouth away and blinked up at the demon holding her. He hadn't drastically changed in appearance, but something about his eyes was different. Wilder.

Still tugging on her nipple, he brushed another kiss across her cheek and spoke into her ear. "Let me pleasure you, sweet miss." Oh Divine One, he was wrenching so much sensation from her breast. He hadn't come near to touching her between her legs, and yet she'd grown so warm and heavy there. "Let me worship you." He touched his wet, smooth lips to her neck. "Let me feast upon you. Say yes."

"Yes," she groaned. "To all you've promised."

He swept her into his arms and easily carried her several paces off the path into the meadow. His horse had moved off to graze. He spoke without strain as he lowered her to the grass. "I'll keep you warm." Then he was tugging at the collar of her dress, and indeed, his hot breath on her skin kept the cool evening breeze at bay. He lay alongside her, his leg draped over hers, and mouthed the upper swell of her breast. His hair tickled her and only added to the wash of sensations sweeping up and down her body.

Having parted the collar of her dress as far as it could go, he yanked impatiently on her belt, which was almost as old as she was. Thus, rather than loosen at the back where she'd tucked and folded its length into a simple knot, it ripped partway.

But before she could think to worry over her clothing, he parted her dress and sealed his lips around her nipple. Wet heat, suction... She moaned as she speared her fingers into his hair, for each pull sent a sharp tingle through her core. Had she been so sensitive here, all this time? The pleasure heightened when he swirled his tongue around her aureole, then flicked the hardened tip.

She felt his hand on her bare stomach, slowly sweeping down and parting her dress as it went. "O-Oh my! I—" She tried to clamp her legs shut, instinctively shy, but his leg was in the way, and she could not stop him from cupping her mound.

She gasped once, softly, then again louder as he massaged her. It felt so good. She knew it would, but— How many times had she woken from a dream, sex tingling with desire, without the privacy to explore herself? How many times had she gone down to the river for a "bath" and stifled her cries while hiding among the shrubs that lined its banks? Too many to count, and yet the way he groped at her—pushing and sliding her moist lips together, teasing at more to come—was so deliciously lewd that her mind went blank.

He released her well-loved nipple, and she shivered as he trailed passionate kisses up her chest. When he reached her neck, he slipped his finger between the folds of her flesh and quickly found what he sought.

"Ah!" she keened, thighs twitching. She felt his lips on her cheek a second before he captured her mouth, and she let him swallow every moan she made. He knew just how to touch her, not too directly and not too hard. Well, of course he knew, but he so effortlessly followed the ebb and flow of her pleasure, pushing firmly when doing so would feel good and pulling back the instant before it became too much. She found herself grasping his shoulders, kissing him back, and squeezing her thighs around his leg and hand. In moments, her entire body from head to toe became sensitized to his touch. Hadn't he promised he could bring her to the brink in no time?

"The sweet cries you make, they're like music to my ears," he said against her lips. "And your response is...persuasive." His caressing voice turned rough on that single word. "You make it easy to enjoy you."

If Shumei weren't lying on the ground, she'd have thought she was flying. Her lover's touch had overwhelmed her. She rolled her hips involuntarily, seeking something. The peak of pleasure, yes, but also fulfillment.

Pulling his hand away, he lifted his head and spoke in a voice pitched low with desire. "I can wait no longer." He pushed her knees apart and crawled over her. She lay meekly beneath him, both hands by her head as he slid his arm between their bodies and hurriedly pulled at his belt. He set aside his sword, then he curled closer and slid his hand into his clothes.

For a split second, she was nervous about what would soon happen. They would come together, though she wasn't sure quite yet how, and when her peak came, he would somehow consume it. Would feeding him be painful? Would it be scary?

He settled against her, not too heavily, and a part of him butted against the swollen lips of her sex. "Lift your knees." She did as he said and found the cool grass with her soles. He nudged her entrance. Pressure. Then he bucked, ripping through her virginity like paper. Yelping in pain and shock, she grasped fistfuls of grass and slowly tore them out. Tears sprang to her eyes. She looked up at his tense face, dismayed the pleasure had ended so abruptly.

"Forgive me, sweet miss. I'll help you." He stroked her cheek and uttered a few whispered words that sounded foreign.

The pain receded as if it had never happened. She was able to relax and really feel how they'd become connected, how completely he filled her. The part of him inside her was so warm and hard, so...invasive. Should she like it as much as she did? And had that been magic just now? Had he called upon it using that strange language? Before she could ask, he began to move. And all thought flew out of her head.

She gave a choked groan and wrapped her arms around his back, holding fast to his trim sides. The motion was so compelling, so singularly fixating. She couldn't think of anything but the friction, and how he felt over her and inside her. Every thrust built upon the tension sizzling in her core. Wanton sounds escaped her throat. Her breath hitched with every jolt of pleasure.

"You're mine. By the dueling gods are you mine," he growled. A gentle breeze brushed against her bare legs, reminding her unexpectedly that they were outside and on the ground. The weight of their bodies was crushing the newly grown grass beneath her and releasing its herbal scent. The stars swaying overhead were partially obscured by her lover's shoulder.

"I-I'm losing my mind," she groaned, closing her eyes. He was quickly building her back up, changing angles often and going deeper every time to find new, pleasurable places to stimulate. What made her moan the loudest was holding her legs back and grinding, followed by short, deep thrusts. The tension inside her coiled tight.

She almost didn't want to come. Maybe feeding him would be painful. No, the real reason was she didn't want their interlude to end. The rubbing and plunging and grinding felt too good. She hadn't known how wet she could get, having only ever touched herself while bathing. Oh, but her climax was inevitable. And for the first time, she'd be clenching around something. That thought alone—

"O-Oh gods," she panted.

"That's it, sweet miss. Come hard. And feed me." He gave a long, strangled moan and pressed deep. "*Omae wo shibatteyaru...eien ni na.*" He lifted his head to the sky. The sizzle of an impending lightning strike charged the air. Thunder rumbled. But no lightning appeared.

She pulled him close. Her heart seemed to thud as loud as a drum. Then the tension in her core melted into bliss. It stole her voice and rolled up her body.

The pleasure had her reeling. She trembled, barely able to breathe. With every pulse, she thrust herself against the demon buried inside her. The sounds he made were so low they were inhuman. When the stranglehold on her throat eased, she gasped for air and opened her eyes to find a white mist floating up from her body, rising in immense waves that matched each tremor in her loins and each passionate cry torn from her throat. Her lover absorbed the mist like rain hitting thirsty soil. He rolled his hips, drawing out the ecstasy rippling through her, and all at once, it hit her.

She had done something terrible. She had lain with a demon. Willingly. She hadn't chosen someone she loved, or even liked, for her first experience. She had pursued pleasure only, and not even with a human.

Why hadn't she been stronger? Why had she let lust cloud her mind and make her forget her urgent task at home? Why him and why now? Had he cast magic on her to make her forget, to make her willing? Or had an incredibly stressful day pushed her to seize something for herself, no matter how wrong it was and in so many ways?

She dared not even think which one it'd been. She would break. Already she'd gone empty and expressionless. The heat was still there, but it was fading. The demon raggedly sighed and pulled free of her. Sword in hand, he stood to adjust his clothing, and she gingerly sat up, bringing her legs together.

Her belt was still partly intact, but she had to hold her dress shut as she stood and looked around for her basket. Spotting it, she took a few steps to retrieve it, and froze when something wet ran down her thigh. Divine One help her, how had she forgotten he'd likely spend himself inside her? Frightened and mortified, she snatched up her basket and turned to the path, desperate to leave his presence.

"And where do you think you're going?" he asked, voice stony. The charming lover was gone.

She stopped and turned, eyes downcast. "Home."

"I don't think so. I'm keeping you." His footsteps approached.

She hastily backed away. "You said I could go home after you fed. I hold you to that promise." She hugged her basket to her chest. "W-What happened should never—*will* never happen again."

He didn't answer at first, so she dared to lift her gaze and found him staring at her with naked longing. Her answering desire sent her to the deepest depths of guilt to which she had yet sunk. Would the Divine One ever forgive her for this transgression?

"The Divine One knew what he was doing when he made you," he snapped. "He put you here to torment me."

The demon was angry with himself, and at the god who despised him so much. In truth, he had grown to revile intercourse, but his continued existence demanded sexual energy, and he wasn't about to let his distaste be his killer. Almost a full moon had passed since he'd last eaten a woman's lust, and finding one lately was proving difficult. If he ventured too close to a village to slake his hunger, he risked rousing a large-scale demon hunt, which he did not need when all he had wanted was to visit his old estate on his way to Stillwood.

He had been close to death yet again and was in search of a new village from which he could tempt a female for her favors before the month's end. He hadn't had any luck, though. The sun had set and his horse had needed water, so he had stopped by an obliging creek. Then a young slip of a girl had appeared so suddenly he hadn't been sure at first if she was even human. He'd slowly revealed himself, and her instant flight had confirmed she was as human as they came.

Catching her had been easy. She'd stuck to the winding path, so he'd cut through the woods to intercept her. And she was so young. Not much older than twenty, he was sure. Her heart-shaped face held large, dark eyes, a pert nose, and full lips meant for all things carnal. Her wavy hair, misused and tangled, needed only gentle soap and gentle hands. She was a tad skinny, but her obvious poverty was likely to blame, and he would have no problem getting her the meals she needed.

Women her age, though not at their sexual peak, had the stamina he looked for when selecting women to steal, and a single mating with her had completely replenished him, confirming she did indeed have black hair—the moonlight wasn't tricking him. With the last woman, whose hair had been a light brown, he'd had to take her three times to feel full again.

He was angry at how strongly he still desired this young crow, even though he no longer needed her energy. He wanted to lie between her thighs once more, feel her rise beneath him to meet his thrusts, and hear those high, shy moans that had brought him so quickly to climax.

He normally had no inclination toward sex, yet the thought of slipping into the role she'd fantasized for him was greatly appealing. Out of impulse, he had even cast a binding spell upon her. She would have been the perfect choice to sustain him for years, but he had made a promise he hadn't intended to keep, and the binding enforced that promise. He cursed violently, taking a step back.

"I shall ensure you reach your village, but I would ask you something before you go." She simply stared at him, saying nothing. His jaw stiffened. "Tell me your name."

She seemed surprised at the question and backed up another step. "Shumei."

"I am called—"

"No, don't," she vehemently whispered. He balled up his hands. "I can't know that. I can't ever see you again."

With that, she turned and ran, leaving him there. He swore under his breath.

Shumei ran as if the Damned One himself were on her heels. Tears ran down her cheeks as she thought about the crime she had committed. Her first sexual experience had been with a creature of Oblivion. Worse, she had enjoyed it immensely. Worst of all, she was certain she'd not be able to put the encounter out of her mind. She'd remember it often, and with no small amount of guilty satisfaction.

The villagers had been right about her.

Chapter Three

Shumei crested the top of a hill, hoping to see a sign of where she was, but the moon was hiding, and she could see only a few trees in front of her. She waited with a petulant frown, mad at the moonlight for playing tricks on her.

Mama had been mean tonight, saying she couldn't go to the festival tomorrow, so she had run away and she was never going back. She would live off nuts and berries. She'd grow her own crops and kill deer, just like Mama and Papa.

She could only think of one place to go, but finding the medicine field was a lot harder than she'd thought. The sun had set an hour ago, so she couldn't really see anything. The moon was playing peek-a-boo with her, hiding behind big clouds and only coming out long enough for her to see she was still lost.

She heard the snap of a twig and gasped in surprise. Looking around, she searched the underbrush near her to see if it'd been a rabbit, but it was too dark to see anything but shapes. Horrible prickles skittered down her back. Something was wrong.

More noises. Snapping twigs, crunching leaves, and groaning trees when there was no wind. Mama had said not to come here at night, and now she wished she hadn't. Fisting her hands in the skirt of her new blue dress, she fought the urge to curl into a ball.

"Little one, little one," a husky voice called. She shrieked in fright and whipped about in all directions, searching for the source of the voice, but saw nothing but trees and deep shadows. The tears began. She ran down the hill. She hated the forest, hated the moon!

More snapping twigs and groaning trees. It was following her.

"Come play with me," the voice called again. She sobbed, still running. Branches and underbrush scraped and scratched at her with every step.

"Little one, little one," it sang. "You look so sweet."

"Go away," she screamed, flinging her arms at nothing as she turned to follow a deer path. "I don't want to play!"

The voice giggled, low and fast. "But I want to play with you. So sweet, so soft. I wonder how old you are." It was definitely behind her, but whenever she darted a scared glance over her shoulder, she saw nothing.

"Leave me alone," she cried, pumping her legs as fast as she could. She wanted Mama and Papa. She wanted to be home safe, tucked into a ball on her bedroll.

"All right," the voice said with disappointment. "Good night, little one."

She ran and ran and ran until she could barely lift her feet. Exhausted, she chanced another look over her shoulder and clumsily tripped over a tree root. Her hands went out, but the ground was steeply sloped downhill and she couldn't catch herself. Instead, she landed hard on her stomach, knocking the air out of her, and slid until another tree root caught her. She lay there a moment, panting, before shakily pulling herself to her feet.

Leaning on the rough bark of the tree trunk next to her, she gripped the collar of her dress and listened carefully over her thundering heartbeat. The tears were starting to dry on her cheeks, but more threatened to spill forth, and she wondered if she'd ever be able to find Mama again.

Nothing but silence. No snapping branches, no creaking trees. The voice had left her alone.

"Mama," she wailed, dropping to the ground. She hugged her knees to her chest, letting the tears fall freely, and muffled her hiccupping sobs in her skirt.

Her new dress. Dirty, torn, and wet with her tears. Mama was going to be so angry.

Something grabbed the back of her clothes and lifted her off the ground. Her first reaction was a gasp, her second an earsplitting scream. It had been above her the whole time.

"Little one," the voice sang. It was a scratchy, hollow sound. "Little, little, little." A long, hairy limb grabbed her right arm. Another grabbed her left arm. She began kicking, her shrieks piercing the night.

A third hand grabbed one of her ankles. A fourth grabbed the other. She widened her teary eyes in disgusted shock, realizing the monster that had her in its grip was definitely not human-shaped.

"So sweet, so soft," it rasped. "Scream for me, little one."

She did, over and over while struggling vainly against the monster's hold. Hot, disgusting breath washed over her neck.

The voice spoke inches from her face, deep and growly. "I'm. So. Hungry."

She let out another scream, her loudest and longest yet.

A shout rang out. The monster dropped her. She didn't fall far and balled herself up. More shouts and screams. Dead leaves crunched and branches snapped.

At last, all was quiet except for soft footsteps. She sniffled, convinced her nightmare wasn't over. But a smooth, deep, *human* voice shushed her cries. Gentle hands lifted her and held her against a warm, solid chest. With great relief, she put her chin on the man's shoulder, taking comfort in his scent—like Mama's spicy winter stew—and wrapped her arms around his neck.

"Let's take you home," he whispered.

Chapter Four

Shumei slowly opened her eyes to the sound of birds chirping. Her dream faded, and though she tried to hold on to its remnants, they eluded her grasp.

The sun had risen, heralding the start of a new day. But something wasn't right, and she wondered at the sense of foreboding in her chest. It was just morning as usual. Oka would be asleep next to her, her mother would be getting up any minute now, and they would spend the day on household chores.

Then she remembered Oka's fever and bolted upright even though he lay right in front of her. She touched his forehead, which now felt much cooler, and came away with perspiration on her hand. His fever had broken. Briefly closing her eyes, she sighed with relief before glancing at their cooking pot, which held a few more doses of steeped *fuki*. Next to it was her mother on her bedroll, still asleep.

Almost all of the leaves she had harvested had been used as families came to their door the previous night, requesting medicine. And her family hadn't earned a single kol. *Fuki* had become so important for saving lives from the Burning's fever that Kimen had decreed it would be free to whoever needed it. Despite the lost income, Shumei hadn't minded—saving lives was most important—but she also hadn't been able to afford any of the huntsman's cuts of meat yesterday. Instead, she'd been forced to haggle with a neighbor for part of a fish he'd caught. But at least her family had eaten something more than vegetable stew.

She smoothed her hand down her dress and felt something rough wrapped around her waist. A makeshift belt made of an old scrap of cloth was keeping her dress closed. Her skirt had fresh grass stains, and her entire body ached, especially...

Her mad dash to the field. The setting sun. Running from shadows. A demon with a smile that twisted her up inside. He'd made her an offer, and like the selfish fool she was, she had embraced him beneath the early evening sky.

The foreboding in her chest clarified into guilt, shame, and, worst of all, yearning. Her stomach cramped with remorse even as she blushed at the most vivid of her memories. She could still feel his lips and his hands. She swore she could even smell him on her.

Conflicted, she glanced helplessly around the one-room hut and wondered what she was supposed to do with this new and haunting memory. No one could know how much last night had changed her, but how was she supposed to look or act in order to keep it a secret?

The first thing she wanted to do was take a bath, but she forced herself to pour the last of the medicine from the pot into an empty jug. The pungent aroma of the *fuki* made her gag, and she realized she wasn't well. Perhaps she needed something in her stomach? If so, that had to wait because her next task was cleaning out the cooking pot so they could use it for breakfast.

The smell of the herbs hit her again. Her throat seized. She dove toward the area that would be easiest to clean and lost what little food remained inside her. She gasped for air, vision blurry with tears.

Taking a break outside, she walked around her home a couple of times. On her fourth circuit, her stomach rebelled again, and she leaned down to retch in the tall grass where no one could see her. Hoping she had a moment of reprieve before it happened again, she cleaned the spot in the hut where she had previously thrown up and decided to leave washing out the pot for when she returned from the river. She looked to her mother, whose chest slowly rose and fell as she slept. Then she grabbed a pat of soap and a handful of mint leaves.

The rest of the village was already awake. Smoke rose from several roofs, and a couple doors were open. The last of the villagers who hadn't succumbed to the illness were busy working the rice fields down the hill. A light rain overnight had been good for the newly sown crop but had also muddied the paths. Shumei was too filthy to care.

The river between the village and the local temple was the only place where anyone felt safe bathing. Not only was it protected by the barrier charms, but bushes lining the banks also afforded small spaces where people could bathe with some privacy.

As she walked toward the river, chewing on fresh mint, memories of last night haunted her mind's eye—and her mind's skin and nose and ears. Memories of a slow, wicked smile, of slick friction and passionate kisses, of spicy cologne and gravelly moans. As it had ten times already that morning, a cold wash of shame followed those memories. She told herself that hiding her crime from the rest of the village wouldn't be hard—no one cared about her enough to notice any change in her. But hiding it from her mother and brother?

She was only a moment away from the river when she passed the home of one of the wealthier families in their little community. Ikuro, the lady of the house, was outside, observing one of her sons as he scrubbed the porch.

"Once you're done with that, you can have breakfast. That is, if you apologize to your sister when you come in. No more pulling on her braids," she admonished, lightly whapping the boy on his head. He was the same age as Oka and already handsome, and he stuck out his tongue at his mother before returning to his chore. Ikuro turned to go back inside her house, which was when Shumei noticed Ikuro was pregnant with what would be her fifth child.

Shumei continued walking, lips tight, hating Ikuro's good fortune. Her children were wonderful, she was a wonderful mother, and even her husband was wonderful. Though they weren't rich, they had enough, and that was wonderful too.

She was jealous, yes, but not of how well off Ikuro's family was, although that was certainly enviable. Rather, she coveted Ikuro's family. She wished for a partner and for children of her own. Though Oka was still young, he was her brother, not her baby.

Tears slipped down her face as she thought of how her lost virginity, if anyone learned of her indiscretion, would severely and irrevocably narrow her options for an honorable husband. Not many families would accept a black-haired bride. Almost none would tolerate a "lustful" one. Of the few offers of marriage the village leaders had secured, all but Akiji's would be withdrawn if anyone were to find out what she'd done. And if they learned who she'd done it with? She'd be lucky to escape the village alive and in one piece.

At the riverbank, she slipped between her favorite grouping of bushes. Though the branches were thorny, they extended well over the water—enough to offer some concealment from the other side of the river, and if she was careful, she could hang her clothing to dry. The water by the bank was only hip-deep, but it was clear and clean, and sometimes had tadpoles in summer. When she was small, this private section of river was enough for her and her mother to bathe together, but it would hardly fit two adults.

The water would be quite cold, but she was too desperate to be clean to care, and quickly undressed. She left her makeshift belt hanging on a branch but brought her soiled dress and the soap into the river. Goosebumps rose on every inch of her skin.

Letting her lower half get used to the temperature first, she found a couple of large, smooth pebbles and leaned down to begin scrubbing at the stains on the back and skirt of her dress. A few spots of mud came out quickly, but she grew more and more dismayed as the grass stains resisted. Her mother's soap could usually get anything out. She flipped her clothing over to find another spot to work on, and then stopped and stared at a few red streaks inside her dress. With a swallow, she soaped up the area and began scrubbing. Thankfully, the bloodstains quickly vanished.

When satisfied, she wrung out her thin dress and hung it over the side of the bush where the morning sun would hit it—assuming the sun came out soon. Then she returned to the water and sank to her knees. Using the last of her soap, she methodically washed every part of her body and scrubbed especially hard over the places where he'd touched her, hoping she'd not be able to smell him on her skin afterward. Not that she'd need the reminder. His scent was imprinted on her.

Having soaped up her hair, she leaned to rinse it out, and gasped at a strange stirring in her core. Was she going to throw up again? All that was left in her stomach were the mint leaves she'd eaten specifically to cleanse her mouth, and she really didn't want to see them again.

She lifted her head out of the water and ran her hands through her hair for any soap she'd missed. Finding some over her left temple, she leaned down again, but a jolt of some indefinable sensation shot through her loins. She held her breath and slid her hand between her legs, wondering if he had left some sort of magic there. The feeling grew, and she softly moaned, eyes fluttering. Eager to be out of the water, she rinsed herself off and stood.

Her sex throbbed and her knees shook as she waded toward the grassy riverbank. Water dripped from her body, but she was wet in another place for an altogether different reason. She cursed the demon for leaving his magic on her and tried not to panic over how she'd remove his evil charm without anyone's help. She was about to step onto the bank when the sensation flared, lighting her up with desire. She stumbled back.

Then she heard a rustling as someone entered her sanctum. Her head snapped up. Her heart leapt. Before she even saw him, she knew it was the demon. When he appeared, though, her first reaction was neither anger nor fear. Rather, she was surprised to see his hair wasn't blond, but white. Stark white.

And his eyes, they were the purest blue she'd ever seen, save perhaps a clear, winter sky. The color betrayed the coldness of his soul—while the rest of him produced only heat. Though she knew last night's transgression was the result of her own weakness, she couldn't help blaming him as well. He had seduced her with his wickedly attractive looks and a voice that could soften stone.

"How are you standing in daylight? You're a demon," she said.

"Yet here I am," he replied, which didn't speak to her confusion in the slightest. The evasion frustrated her. His presence enraged her. Why was he even here?

She lowered herself into the water, anger keeping her warm, and hid her nudity from his possessive stare.

"You're angry," he observed.

"You used my desires against me, seduced me. I'll be angry for the rest of my life."

"At me or at yourself?" he asked, stepping forward.

"Don't come any closer, demon. Y-You...you spun your magic and confused me," she said. "You're cruel to return and taunt me."

"Cruel? I pleasured you greatly, and even cast a spell to suppress your virginal pain. As promised, I did not kidnap you. In fact, I made sure you returned home safely. I could have left you to fend for yourself. Other things in that forest would have done far worse than a brutal death, and you say I am cruel?"

"You are the lesser of many evils, nothing more. I'm grateful to be alive, but you have no claim over me. None," she insisted.

"Oh, but I do have a claim on you. And I shall demonstrate." He narrowed his eyes, and she swore they glowed. The arousal humming through her grew tenfold.

"Ah!" she moaned, slipping her hand between her legs and hoping that holding herself would somehow lessen the sensation. "W-What is this magic?"

"My kind call it sympathetic binding. We now feel what the other feels—physically, at least. And by simply thinking it, I can arouse you nearly to bursting." His smile wilted slightly. "However, the price we pay is to obey all contracts made between us, past, present, and future."

"You placed this curse upon me? And you still think you're not cruel?" But despite her anger, she began teasing the same spot he'd so expertly pleasured the night before.

His gaze slid down. "Can't help yourself, hmm?" She froze, horrified. "Don't stop, Shumei," he said with a sigh, sitting back on his heels. "Why deny something that feels so good? For both of us?" He tugged on the ties to his clothing. His jacket sagged open. She fearfully watched as he delved into his loosened pants, and gasped when he gripped himself. As he'd said, she felt the mirror sensation in her body.

He held eye contact, willing her not to look away from his pure blue stare as he rubbed himself. She groaned, feeling every stroke just as surely as if his hand were between her thighs instead of her own. Her fingers twitched involuntarily, nudging her most sensitive spot, and she heard a catch in his throat.

"W-Why do you haunt me?" she asked, panting as the pleasure climbed higher.

"I promised not to abduct you, but I didn't promise to leave you alone," he reminded her. She made a small noise of reluctant defeat, knowing she could not argue—not in that distracting moment. "You think I left a mark on you, and though that's true, you do not realize the mark you left on me. I want you, Shumei," he declared, pumping his hand faster. She gave a broken cry, vision blurring.

She had refused even to think it, but the thought now blared inside her mind: she still wanted him too. He, a demon, had made her feel more alive than she had at any other point in her twenty years of life. He hadn't done it selflessly, but then neither had she.

"I can take care of you—I want to. Tell me to whisk you away from this life," he said, reminding her of her fantasy. "Say yes and save yourself."

She didn't answer him. She was on that final climb and eyeing the way his hand moved inside his clothes. Somehow, watching the fabric shift and bulge only intensified the sensations echoing in her body. She moaned and sighed and bit her lip in anticipation. Her eyes watered, so she closed them, ready to catch the brunt of the pleasure about to rack her body.

Then it all stopped. She glared at him with a grunt of disappointment. "D..." she began, but the sound froze in her throat when she realized she was about to say, "Don't stop." He gave her a knowing smirk, and she tightened her lips in anger. She wasn't sure what enraged her more—his arrogance or that he had denied her. "Damn you. Damn you!" She huddled even deeper into the water.

His smile faded. "I am already damned," he said, voice flat. She felt the change in his mood as if it were a change in temperature and shivered.

How overbearing would he be with several strapping field workers running to the sound of screams, she wondered. She gathered a deep breath.

He darted forward faster than her eyes could follow him. His clothes were instantly soaked, water splashing everywhere. She flinched away from him. A tiny shriek was all she could get out as she scampered back, brushing up against the prickly riverside bushes. Then he clamped her against his chest, trapping her arms between them.

"Scream, and anyone who comes will die," he snarled. Unable to move, she couldn't cower from him, so she chose anger instead.

"Then how do I make you leave?" she bit out. He released her.

"I've already given my offer. You're the ideal source of energy for a demon like me, and though I cannot steal you away, thanks to some stupidly uttered words on my part, I can offer you a better life in exchange for agreeing to come with me."

"I refuse. What you ask risks my soul, and I will not abandon my mother and brother."

"Think of your fellow villagers, Shumei. If you agree to be mine, I won't have to seek out other females to ravish." His eyebrows took a teasing slant as he smiled at her. She suppressed the urge to splash him, but only barely. Then he grew serious. "Nor would I reveal myself or our relationship."

She paled at that, realizing her worst fears could easily come true. Despite his white hair and his outsider status, he could announce to the whole village what she'd done, and he'd be believed. She and her entire family would be run out, if not worse. Of course, the villagers could attack him as well, but she wasn't worried about his safety, and she doubted that a demon who carried a sword worried over it, either.

"As for your soul," he continued, "do you think any of your 'pious' neighbors have not risked theirs? I've spent some time observing your village. I'm sure you're aware your pockmarked neighbor beats his son, but did you know the married man next door to you sneaks off to the widow at the center of the village and make the obscenest noises I've ever heard out of a man's throat? Did you know the woman at the west end of the village practices dangerous magic?"

"S-She does? They've done those things?" she asked, taken aback.

He let her go and nodded. "I'm willing to accommodate your brother at my dwelling if his welfare is the only barrier to making you mine. I'll even teach him how to fight if you submit to me whenever I please, but mark my words, Shumei..." His expression turned grave. "You can either make a deal with me, or I'll ensure the village learns of what we've done together," he said with finality.

"You'd be forcing me, then," she pointed out. "It would be no different from—"

"Despite what you may think, forced pleasure produces poison for my kind. It would not kill me but it would not nourish me, either."

"Then what are you saying?"

"You seem to forget what I can do, Shumei. Whether you like hearing it or not, I fulfilled your fantasy last night, and I can continue doing so. Isn't it true you've dreamed of a secret lover?" he asked. She swallowed, wide-eyed. "Of trysts in the forest, and gifts you can't explain to others? Of passionate pursuit?"

She wanted to scream a denial, but she didn't have it in her to outright lie. Perhaps she could by omission, but never outright. To say she hadn't entertained a long, complex fantasy of forbidden courtship—based wholly on a tale she'd heard as a young girl of a disgraced brownie warrior who secretly romanced a blondie princess... That would be a big lie. The demon before her was no human warrior, but then, neither was she a blondie princess.

However, bringing a fantasy to reality? Could a demon, even one as handsome and adept at seduction as this one, really imitate how her private desires made her feel, how they kept her warm at night and often tinted her dreams? Or would their relationship be something darker, more dangerous, and more carnal?

And, Divine One help her, did she find that even more tempting?

"You want a deal, then," she said, not answering his earlier questions.

He slowly smiled. "I do."

"You need to eat once a month, correct?" she asked. He nodded. "Then, one day a month, I'll meet you and give you the energy you need, but you must promise never to accost me until that day."

"No, from now on, it must be at least every other day."

"E-Every other? But I— Fine, two days a month," she bargained, sitting up straight. His gaze drifted down to her breasts. He swallowed. She curled back into herself.

"Three days a week," he said, grinning.

"Three days a month." She jutted her chin. "Final offer."

His grin fell. "Once a week. *My* final offer." She frowned at how quickly and easily his mood seemed to shift.

"Then, I..."

She stared at her bare knees through the water and thought not of the specific terms she was about to agree to, but of whether what was said about crows really was true: that they were drawn to evil. Or at least that evil was drawn to them. She wondered if her soul really had been infected by the Damned One, and if that taint meant having more bad luck than good.

"What is your answer?" the demon asked, voice oozing with annoyance.

"I will agree to once a week if you include one last thing," she said, trying to look him in the eye and having trouble.

He sighed, impatient. "And that would be?"

"You won't leave your seed inside me ever again."

He hesitated for the space of a breath. "Done." She glanced up at him, but his face was as blank as snow. "Now, I have a couple of my own stipulations to add." His indifferent expression turned into a satisfied smile. His mood had swung yet again.

"*More* stipulations?"

"You will not allow another man to enjoy your favors. Not even a kiss."

"My brother is only nine. I give him kisses all of the time," she exclaimed.

"I will permit affection between you and your brother."

"And why should it matter to you if a man were to kiss me?"

"Because I would feel it through the binding, which sounds unpleasant." Then he frowned. "And because you are mine."

The first part made sense, she supposed. But the second? "You may have bound yourself to me physically, but you don't own my heart or soul. I am not yours." Lips pressed flat, he didn't respond. She sighed. "Is that all?"

"Just one more thing." His focus on her seemed to grow sharper and warmer at the same time. "During our interludes, you must be an active participant. I won't embrace a meek doll once a week."

"I don't understand your meaning," she said, hoping to feign ignorance.

He unfolded his arms and leaned toward her. "When we have sex, I want to hear you moan. I want your hands on my ass as I push myself into your body," he said, low and hard. Oh dueling gods, did he enjoy making her blush bright enough to glow at night? "I want you eagerly kissing me and begging me to bring you to the joyous, wet climax you surely remember from last night."

"Enough," she begged, covering her red ears. One corner of his mouth lifted in amusement, and she bit back her saucy retort, if only to avoid angering him.

"If you break your end of the deal, all contracts between us shall be void, including the one that prohibits me from plucking you out of this tiny village. Do you understand, Shumei?" he said, speaking slowly and clearly.

"I may be naïve, demon, but I'm not stupid. I understand you," she ground out. "If you break your end of the deal, all contracts between us shall be void, and you will never approach me or anyone I care about in any fashion for the rest of eternity. Is that understood?"

He lowered his head, but not in apology or submission. It was the way a dog hunched into itself when it growled at you. "It is. Do you agree to our deal, Shumei?"

"Yes," she said in the barest of whispers, and the air between them shuddered. Her heart seized, both at the subtle flex of magic and at the terms it would enforce.

She watched him like prey watches a predator, lips barely touching the surface of the water. Gods, she was freezing. Now that he had his deal, she hoped he would leave, but something told her he wasn't done with her yet.

"Then let us fulfill our bargain," he said, opening his arms to her. She looked at him as though he had broken her favorite possession.

"But you had me last night. You can't have me again until six days from now," she said, shaking her head.

"Our deal was 'from now on.' Once a week begins today, and today, I will have you."

Her mouth fell open in surprise, and she wanted to scream with frustration. Instead, tears pricked at the backs of her eyes.

"I meant from last night," she insisted, despite knowing she'd lose this argument.

Displeasure supplanted his smug expression. "It's too late to change your wording. I will have you now."

Fisting her hands, she sat there defeated and waited for him to ravish her once again. But he didn't move a muscle. He simply sat there, arms crossed, making her edgy as the silence between them stretched on. What was he waiting for? An invitation? He'd not get one, and besides, she didn't even know what to call—

"What is your name, demon?" she asked, realizing she should know the name of her lover.

He seemed mildly taken aback. "Vallen," he revealed. She nodded, trying his name out in her head. She wondered who had given it to him—his father, or the Damned One? Perhaps it'd been both?

Another moment passed, and she wondered again why he hadn't moved or said anything. Why didn't he take her in his arms and overwhelm her like he had last night?

"Well, what do you want me to do?" she asked, enormously frustrated.

"I thought you'd never ask," he teased, earning an angry glare. "Come straddle my lap."

The anger on her face fled before a wash of anxiety. The position was immediately clear in her mind's eye, and she knew how vulnerable she would be with her legs spread around him.

"Shumei. Now," he ordered. Though her normal reaction would be anger at his gall, the thought of what she was about to do, in broad daylight, made her heart rise in her throat.

"But the water's cold," she said. Indeed, her fingers were starting to ache.

His brow softened. "I'm not."

"Oh." Those two words sent a welcome flare of heat shooting through her.

She moved forward hesitantly, finding one of his thighs and then grasping his hips. If he felt any reaction to her hands on his body, he didn't show it and she wouldn't have noticed, anyway, so shy she could only look at his chest. She pulled herself onto his lap, and besides uncrossing his arms, he didn't budge.

He really was warm. Very warm. She hadn't planned on fitting her naked body so tightly to his clothed one—thighs squeezing his hips and chest pressed to his—but she'd gone stiff from sitting in the cold river and was desperate to thaw. Even so, she was too shy to take her arms out the water and wrap them around his neck, so she curled her fingers into the wet cloth of his dark blue jacket and absently noted the fabric was finer than anything she'd ever touched.

He lifted his arms, and she couldn't help flinching. He paused. "Why do you cower?"

She couldn't look at him. All she would find there would be his arrogance, his cruelty, and his lust. She couldn't see that last one, too afraid of how quickly she'd reciprocate. "You made me bargain with you while cold and naked, and tricked me into...feeding you again. How do I know you won't hurt me, sooner or later?"

Another pause. Then he touched his warm, firm lips to her forehead. "I'll make you another promise," he murmured. "I'll never hurt you, at least not without your permission. If I break this promise, all agreements between us shall be void, and I'll never come near you again."

She gasped in astonishment, greatly surprised he would make such a promise—and greatly comforted. However, why he had included "without your permission?" When would she ever want him to hurt her?

"I'm going to touch you, Shumei. And only pleasure shall follow," he whispered, pressing another kiss to her forehead.

She cast aside all thoughts of his promise and focused on the present. Water swirled behind her as he moved, laying his palms on her lower back. He moved them slowly, exploring the shape of her waist, the line of her spine, and the ridges of her shoulders. She melted a little more as his hands infused her cold skin with blessed heat.

"Look at me," he said, not so much an order as a request.

She met his eyes. They were full of lust, to be sure, a drugged expression that hinted of carnal knowledge and deep longing, but there was no arrogance, no cruelty. He palmed her hips and rubbed his heat into them before sliding his hands to her thighs. She swallowed, fingers curling tighter.

"I knew you'd be soft here," he whispered before glancing at her mouth. She edged closer to him, sliding her arms around his back. His voice went lower and hungrier. "You know what to do."

Indeed, she knew what he wanted—what they both wanted. She leaned forward and tilted her head, eyes falling shut. She rubbed her lips against his, gently brushing them while he did the same to hers. The kiss had barely begun when he lifted his mouth.

"Shumei," he sighed, wrapping his fingers around her wrists. He draped her arms around his neck and took her mouth in another kiss. This one was more intimate, closer to the wanton kiss they had shared last night. He slipped his tongue between her lips, sealed their mouths together, and enveloped her in his arms.

She sank into his heat and into herself. His kiss was intoxicating, filtering up to her head and making it tilt and spin. Even though they'd been conversing at a regular volume until now, she was afraid of moaning, worried someone would hear. She was also reluctant, despite herself, to enjoy the demon's attentions. If last night were any reliable measure, however, she knew she soon wouldn't have the capacity to care how loudly she made her pleasure known.

How soon turned into a surprise, for when he squeezed his hand between them to cup her breast, she gasped into his mouth and then groaned as he thumbed her puckered nipple.

"My, my, that does feel quite good, doesn't it?" he rumbled against her lips. "How about this?" He captured her nipple between his fingers and pinched. They both gave sharp moans, and it hit her that he could also feel how sensitive her breasts were. The thought thrilled her. "Now I have to know."

He lifted her as though she weighed nothing. Water dripped from her naked body, and though the air was almost as cold on her wet skin as the river had been, she wasn't chilled. His greedy lips and hot breaths kept her warm as he mouthed the peak of one breast and massaged her other with his free hand. She gripped his shoulders, not for support but for assurance that she wouldn't float away. Moaning, she let her head roll back and her eyes flutter shut. The position arched her back, pushing her flesh deeper into his mouth. Before she could even think to want it, he sucked hard. Her core pulsed, blooming into delicious, tingling heat. She gave a shaky cry and felt the puff of his pleasured grunt against her skin.

Vallen spent far longer on his lover's breasts than he'd meant to, going from one to the other until her nipples were flushed and swollen from the attention. She was so responsive he didn't need to do so much to ensure her readiness. But the binding had given him such a delicious insight into her pleasure, and he found himself craving more of what she felt.

What would it feel like to tease her clit? To lick it and suck it? He almost gave himself permission to find out, right then and there, but they weren't somewhere even close to ideal for such enticing exploration, nor was he a stranger to anticipation.

Next week, he promised himself.

Shumei was vaguely aware of him doing something beneath the water, bumping her with his arm while he nuzzled her breasts. She hadn't had the presence of mind to suppress even a single groan, but she refused to feel embarrassed by it. After all, he was quite talented—hands down the most practiced lover she would ever have—and he had demanded she not hold back her pleasure. At least she hadn't been too loud to draw unwanted attention.

"Your first time was just last night, so I will say some words to ensure you feel no pain," he said, breathing heavily. "I wouldn't wish to break my promise so soon."

It took her a second to realize he was about to enter her again. "Oh." Would it feel as good as it had last night? Better?

Wait. "You mean"—she gulped—"sitting up like this?"

He didn't answer, only lowered his head in concentration. Strange sounds flowed from his lips. They sounded hollow, echoing as if spoken inside a cave. Heat and weight flowed from her head to her toes, leaving her heavy but relaxed. She sank in his embrace and dug her fingers into his shoulders as his sex nudged between her legs before sweetly piercing her.

"Yes, take me," he brokenly sighed, pulling her snug against his body. She clamped her thighs around his hips, knuckles white against his shoulders and teeth biting hard into her lower lip. She could feel the effects of the binding, as he had called it. In a somewhat unsettling way, she felt as if she were penetrating and being penetrated at the same time.

The sweet joining of their bodies was doubly good, doubly wicked. He was warm and thick, but she could also feel how warm and snug she felt around him. As an experiment, she clenched the right muscles and gasped at the jab of pleasure that bounced back. Groaning, he gripped her hips and bucked, sliding even deeper. Her vision shimmered. Oh dueling gods, would they even last two seconds when they started to move?

She looked at him. A mistake. His brow was tight, his mouth ajar. She could make out a flush in his cheeks, but his eyes were still so cold. Cold and empty. With his strange abilities, he saw so much of her, and yet he didn't see all of her. That numb gaze, however intimate it seemed, made her feel vulnerable and alone.

As if aware of her withdrawal, he pulled her into a kiss. She closed her eyes and was quickly overwhelmed again by the succulence of his lips. He tasted faintly of rice wine, she realized. Wanting more of that flavor, she coiled her arms around him and slid her tongue into his mouth. Grunting, he dug his fingers into her waist as he ground her against him.

Her whole world shrank, becoming as small as that little space between the bushes and compressing to their soft, shared breaths. He clamped his strong arms around her torso, holding her flush against him as he moved her over his lap. He sucked at her mouth as if he needed her air in order to breathe. Her head felt so light she wasn't sure if she would be able to sit up on her own if he were to let her go.

"Mm, yes," she groaned into his mouth. She felt overwhelmed by the power surging between her thighs. The way his body sought hers, the way it moved against her... He didn't just need her. He wanted her.

"Call my name," he bade. She had no trouble participating fully as he'd asked. She moaned wantonly, face tight with pleasure. When his demand penetrated her brain, his name did come to her lips, but she held it back, not wanting to give him that. To use his name out loud, she was sure, would give him the last bit of her soul she still retained.

"My name. Say it, Shumei."

She felt a new pressure deep inside and groaned when she realized—

"It's getting...b-bigger." The last was wrenched from her throat. Forming words was becoming difficult.

"I'll soon burst. You can feel it, can't you?" he groaned. He kissed her once more, massaging her lips with expert skill. She ardently reciprocated while rolling her body against him. The push and pull of his hands on her hips made following his rhythm easy.

"Yes. *Yes,*" she moaned, dragging her mouth across his smooth cheek as she wrapped her arms around his shoulders. She was close. They both were.

"Call my name." He was begging. She could hear it in his voice.

"I-I cannot. I cannot call it," she cried out, doubling her efforts to reach that wonderful, dizzying climax from last night. He made a pained noise, fingers tightening upon her.

"You're welcome to...break your end of the deal, Shumei. Don't forget...you must participate fully," he gasped.

She pressed her face into his shoulder, more desperate than angry. Oh, what did it matter now? She had become a sex demon's lover, and she was gladly feeding him.

So she took a deep breath, and as the tingle of her orgasm gathered deep inside, she moaned his name. It fell easily from her lips, as if she had used it countless times before, so she said it again and again.

Pleasure broke open, hot and sweet and plentiful. An agonized groan shook through him, and he squeezed her hips almost to the point of pain. Small noises eked from her open mouth in unison with the twitching in her fingers and the convulsions between her thighs.

Experiencing her release while unable to immediately follow it with his own was the greatest pleasure and worst pain Vallen had yet experienced. To add kindling to the flame, the sound of her high, delicate voice reduced to an achy moan as she spoke his name only fueled his urgent desire to flood the gates of her body with everything he had within him to give.

But he had made a deal. So, in the two or three seconds it took to pull out of her clenching warmth, he nearly lost control.

Shumei winced as pleasure and restraint warred within her until her lover pulled free and climaxed, releasing them both from the tension choking them. She couldn't lie to herself and say she wasn't a little disappointed he'd remembered not to come inside her. After all, if he hadn't, she would've won and he would've never had hold of her again.

But in a small, shameful place in her heart, she was also disappointed because she had liked how it felt when they'd throbbed together, coating each other in their pleasure. If only doing so didn't risk leaving her with child.

She watched the white mist, now gray in the wan daylight, flow from her to him. She couldn't help another moan as the full effect of his reflected orgasm hit her, resulting in a riot of renewed pulsations. The mist billowed out of her with every surge of pleasure, a fascinating sight.

Then she noticed how tightly he held her. The side of his face rested against her neck, and puffs of warm air hit her shoulder as he panted.

"And so it is fulfilled," he said.

She pulled her arms from his shoulders and sat nearly limp in his arms, waiting for him to let her go. When he raised his head, she schooled her face to look as blank as possible. Despite her flushed cheeks, he seemed to understand her silent hint.

He wasn't rough, but neither was he gentle as he pushed her away from him. He was angry, but she didn't care. He had the energy he supposedly needed, so he had no reason to come near her again for seven days. She almost felt exultant now that he was cut off for a week. She could have even rubbed it in, if she had wanted. He certainly deserved a few snide comments, such as a cut against his skills as a lover, but that would be a lie.

"Finish your bath. I shall return in a moment," he said, stepping onto the riverbank. Water dripped from his soaked clothing. She pinched her eyebrows in confusion, and she wondered what he wanted now. Whatever it was, she would refuse.

But he was gone before she had a chance to say anything, and she sat there for a moment in indecision. She didn't want to stay in the river any longer, but she didn't want to be nude in front of him any more than she had to, and she knew without even touching it that her dress was still quite damp. Should she put it on, anyway?

No, the binding would ensure he behaved himself. Making her decision, she climbed out of the sandy riverbed to kneel on the cold, wet grass, and shivered in the breeze filtering through the bushes. Having forgotten the small, half-broken comb she usually brought to the river, she used her fingers to work on a few knots in her hair before a sound alerted her to Vallen's return.

And even though she had already told herself she shouldn't be nervous to be naked in front of him, she found herself grabbing her damp dress to shield herself. The cold, wet fabric clung to her skin. Shivering, she hunched to conserve warmth.

Vallen slipped into the bushes, taking up what little space was left on the bank. She couldn't help a small oh as she took him in. Before, he had been wearing fine but plain traditional clothing. The black jacket he now wore bore intricate red embroidery along the sleeves that depicted flames licking up his arms. His shirt ties were bright red, and the well-tailored fit showed off his toned physique. He had changed his pants and boots as well, both embroidered to match. And in his arms he held something large and soft under a white towel.

"You look like a drowned rat," Vallen wryly observed, lying through his teeth. True, her hair was impossibly tangled, but she still looked absolutely delectable despite the hideous garment she held against her flawless skin. To have the honor of bathing her in Kaisuian soap would be a pleasure. He made a mental note to do just that someday soon.

She hardened her jaw, but her voice was calm and steady. "What's worse? Being a drowned rat or trapping one for sex? One is much more disgusting than the other."

He tsked at her, grinning. "Now, now. Don't lie about that." He inwardly winced at his duplicity. After all, he had just lied to her about her appearance. "You came to me freely, and we both know you enjoyed it immensely." He gloated at her blush. She dropped her gaze, tucking the tattered garment tighter to her body.

"What do you want, demon?" she asked, emphasizing the last with an extra ounce of venom.

"Don't be so aloof," he said as he lowered himself on bent knees. He tilted her face up with one hand on her chin. "True to my word regarding your fantasy, I've brought you presents."

Shumei resisted the urge to jerk her chin away and instead watched as he folded back the thick towel. Gasping in surprise, she was taken aback by the finely made dress he'd revealed, one that would undoubtedly fit her much better than the stained, heavily maintained dress she had covered herself with. The new dress was black with a simple gray pattern on part of the skirt.

He also held a pair of leather boots that looked not only comfortable and durable but also never before worn. She spied a matching set of socks.

Her hands itched to touch the dress, but she loathed the idea of letting him see that she was at all tempted by his gifts. She turned her head to hide her desire.

"I cannot accept that. My family is too poor to afford such a rich garment, and everyone in the village would be suspicious of how I'd gotten it." None of her neighbors had ever realized or cared about the cruel hypocrisy of them owning decent clothes, usually more than one set, while ridiculing her for what little she had. They could afford to clothe themselves well only because they assigned no value to her skills. Skills which they could hardly live without.

"You will take this dress, and you will wear it," he snapped. Blinking in surprise, she looked up at his angry expression. "If anyone asks, tell them it's none of their business." He set the robe on a dry bit of grass.

"They won't accept that excuse," she scoffed. "They'll assume I'm whoring myself for the luxuries they believe only they are entitled to."

"Why do you care what these cruel people assume about you? Why do you languish here when I've given you a way out? You and your brother. My offer to bring him with us still stands. Both of you would want for nothing."

"I don't want my brother to be taken under your wing. He's as precious as the first blossom of spring, while you are as tainted as a salted garden," she spat. His nostrils flared in anger.

He reached forward and pulled her dress from her arms, upsetting her balance enough to half tumble her back into the river, though only her shins were wetted again. With one pull of his strong hands, he ripped her dress in half. Seeing her one and only piece of clothing for the past several years irreparably torn, she dropped her jaw in shock.

"Y-You h-horrible child!" She climbed out of the river to grab at the remains of her old dress, no longer caring if she was naked or not. Not even the anger he had shown her so far would frighten her now. She literally had nothing left of her own.

Vallen tossed the two halves into the river behind her, then grasped her wrists as she tried to catch the tattered dress. He hauled her to her feet, picked up the towel, and roughly began drying her.

"D-Don't you touch me." She tried to squirm away from him, but his hold on her wrists was too strong. "You are breaking your end of the bargain by groping me in such a manner."

He made a mocking snort. "When I am touching you sexually, you will know. I am merely drying and dressing you before you actually do catch some sort of disease. If you become ill from this stupidity, your next meeting with me might be more nauseating than the normal repugnance you feel for me."

"Stupidity? If you had never harassed me in the first place, I would have finished my bath long ago. You were the one who kept me in that cold river and tricked me into—"

"Crying out with pleasure?"

"Into making a deal with you," she supplied, forging onward, "and then you tore the only thing I had left to give me any semblance of decency in this ungrateful village."

"I believe you were rather warm and comfortable when we were locked in that last embrace," he said, pulling her closer. "And when I would give you a better garment to keep you warm, one that would give you more decency than that rag behind you, you were just as ungrateful as the rest of your fellow villagers by not accepting my generosity."

"Generosity? When have you been generous?" Anger clouded her vision. "You seduced me! You blackmailed me into bearing your lusts once a week. You belittle me needlessly. You destroyed my only dress, however poor a dress it was. And you expect me to be grateful?"

She frantically scrambled for the worst insult she could think of, something that would specifically hurt him.

"You are the King of Oblivion himself, and everything about you is evil."

"Enough," he growled in the same inhuman voice she'd heard last night. "If you insult me again, then the next time we meet, I shall draw out our coupling to last the entire length of the sun's trek across the sky. You'll be begging for release. So help me, Shumei, I can drive you insane if I want to." She hastily nodded. "Now hold still. You'll be dressed in only a moment."

Shivering in the cold, she didn't resist as he dried her. He spent no more time drying her intimate parts than he did the rest of her, but she felt small, teasing pulses of desire coming from him. However unwillingly, she ached for another round, but dared not show him any encouragement. She didn't want him to touch her any more than he had already threatened.

Satisfied she was dry, he laid the towel aside, unfolded the dress, and pulled it across her shoulders. She put her arms through the loose sleeves, silently pleased they reached her wrists, unlike her old dress's. Then she held the folds of the dress in place while he tied the plain, black belt around her waist, deftly forming a large, flat knot against her lower back. The hem touched the tops of her feet, the perfect length. He let her lean against his shoulder as he knelt and slid on the socks and boots, and she was hard-pressed not to notice the gentle way he held her ankles.

She relished the feel of socks and shoes on her freshly cleaned feet. The boots were just as comfortable as she'd guessed—they even fit rather well—and the dress was warm and fine. She bit back a thank-you rising up her throat and stared at him while he quietly studied her. A pulse of desire from him told her how much he liked seeing the dress on her.

"Where did you get this?" she asked, wondering how this garment had been so readily available.

"That is a long story, indeed. I may tell you next week."

"Why not now?" she asked, even more curious.

"If you don't leave me now, I will not be able to stop myself from taking you again," he uttered, rubbing his hand across his belly as if he were hungry.

"I shall take my leave, then," she mumbled, hoping he would move out of the way so she could push past him and escape their little pocket of privacy.

"Do I not get a goodbye kiss? Until we meet again next week?" he asked, touching her shoulder. He hadn't grabbed her, merely stopped her with the gentle pleading in his voice.

"That wasn't in our deal," she hedged, expecting to hear he'd slipped yet more tricky language into their agreement.

"No, it wasn't. I'm merely hoping for one last taste of you before you leave."

"Oh." For once he hadn't demanded something from her. She lifted her head and gasped at how close his face was. "Vallen," she stammered, looking at his parted lips.

"Please?" His mouth dipped closer, but he didn't close the distance.

With the thought that rewarding this kind of behavior was a good idea—she refused to think she also wanted one last kiss—she tilted her face up the last inch that separated them.

Eyes closing, she held back a moan as he took total possession of her mouth. Though he moved his lips slowly, sweetly, and stroked her cheek while sighing with pleasure, she was no less overwhelmed than when they'd both been in the throes of ecstasy. Arousal had turned her soft by the time their kiss ended, and she knew only some of the sensation was mirrored from Vallen. The rest was her.

"Go, then," he whispered as he brushed his thumb along her jawline. "The seventh dawn from today, meet me in the field where we first met. I shall take up your entire morning, so be prepared." He abruptly turned and left. She heard his retreating footsteps for only a few seconds, and then he was gone.

She waited a moment before emerging, and only when she had left the river behind her did she realize something that put a pause in her step.

Vallen, a demon, had been inside the barrier charms.

Chapter Five

As Shumei walked back home, she luxuriated in the feel of fine cloth against her skin—not to mention the easy warmth lingering in her limbs from her passionate interlude. The chances of running into someone at this time of the morning were small, so she was able to duck into her home without anyone seeing her or her new dress.

Kneeling next to her brother, she checked his forehead again and found his skin dry and cool. He was sleeping peacefully, and she intended to leave him like that until he woke on his own. After tucking the blanket more securely around him and sweeping a few stray golden locks of hair off his forehead, she stood and walked to her mother, who was in the same position as when she had left her.

Last night, Oka had been awake long enough to take a cup of water and a little broth, but Mama had refused both. Thinking her mother would be thirsty, Shumei sat next to her. Explaining the new dress would not be easy. She would have to tell the truth, or at least most of it, and the truth wasn't pretty.

She grasped her mother's thin shoulder and gave her a gentle shake. But her body rocked as if she were frozen with cold. As if she were dead.

Shumei stilled. Hoping Mama was merely holding her body tightly in her sleep as many do in a cold room, she shook her mother's shoulder again, harder.

Mama's white-streaked hair slipped across her face, revealing a pair of blue lips. Chest seizing, Shumei forcefully pulled her mother onto her back. Mama's arms slowly fell to her sides, half-stiff with rigor mortis. She had definitely died, though probably not more than two hours ago. Perhaps only minutes after Shumei had left to bathe.

Her mother had been breathing when she'd left, she was certain. Or was she? A sob escaped. She covered her mouth, eyes scrunching up as she looked upon her mother's slack face.

"Mama... Mama, I'm sorry," she whimpered as tears ran freely down her cheeks. She swallowed several times to keep the massive lump in her throat down, but it rose without stopping until it broke free, turning into a harsh cry. The first of many.

She couldn't suppress the sobs that racked her body and made her gasp for painful, shallow breaths. Her face grew hot. A headache throbbed in the back of her skull and slowly traveled through to her forehead. Her cheeks and fingers were wet with tears. Nothing had been easy for her mother, and now she was dead.

"Mama," she cried, heart breaking. A hand touched her shoulder and she started. Her brother stood beside her, face tight. His beautiful brown eyes were red with anguish.

"Is Mama gone?" he croaked, lip trembling. Another sob escaped her, but she wiped at her cheeks and sucked in a calming breath. She nodded.

Oka put his chin to his chest. Tears fell. She pulled her brother into her arms and held him close as he sat sprawled across her lap. They wept together and embraced the last person they had left to call family.

***

HAVING RETURNED TO his horse, Vallen checked the soggy clothing he had hastily thrown over a low tree limb and found it still soaked. He patted the muscular neck of his mount while mussing the back of his hair to speed the drying process. Then he turned to the saddlebags on the ground and dug through them for his collapsed bow.

He was pulling it out when a tight, cold pain seized his chest. Gasping in agony, he slapped his hand against the horrible ache and nearly fell to his knees as it spread.

Shumei was in immense emotional pain, and it took him only a second to realize she must not have known her mother was dead.

64

Before he'd followed her to the river, he had been watching her home from beyond the tree line. She had first emerged shortly after the sun had risen, and he had nearly run to help her when she'd retched in the tall grass only fifty feet from him. She was important to his survival, but he'd restrained himself from sprinting to her side, not wanting to reveal his presence just yet. After she'd recovered, she had returned to her home with more energy in her stride, which had greatly relieved him.

A few moments later, she'd left again. He'd seen the soap in her hand and the direction she'd been taking—the river. Seeing his chance, he had waited until she was well away before stealthily approaching her hut, trying not to alert any of her neighbors. Inside, he had seen how little she and her family had. Not much food, all of it low in nutrition. A small, sad stack of firewood. Two thin bedrolls. Most of the rest of their possessions were related to caring for their field of medicinal plants. A young boy, asleep and unaware of Vallen, had moaned softly and turned to his side.

He had assumed the child was her brother. As for the older woman lying only a few steps away, undoubtedly Shumei's mother, his demonic senses had told him she had recently died, judging by the vapors coming from her body. Wondering if perhaps Shumei had gone to the river to cry alone, he had followed her there, only to forget any intention to comfort her when he saw her.

After all, he was used to cruelty, and more than used to human mortality. More of his past lovers—in fact, the vast majority—had died of old age than still lived. And he had seen plenty of humans take death in stride. That was the world they all lived in, so he had somehow convinced himself Shumei had been prepared for her mother's death.

Thanks to the binding, he was now experiencing her pain. He could practically hear her screams of grief in his head. Though normally a human's tears were annoying, especially after all the lovers he'd met and discarded throughout his existence, Shumei's weeping affected him—more than just physically. Chalking it up to another effect of the binding, he knelt by his saddle until the acidic pressure in his throat eased a few moments later.

He sighed in relief when the pain faded. His tightly held muscles slowly relaxed. He swallowed, glad it was over, though he wasn't sure if it was because his pain had dulled, or because hers had.

⁎

THE NEXT MORNING, Shumei and Oka watched as two field workers took up the temporary duty of gravedigger and helped bury their mother. Luckily, today was the last day of the month because only then did priests visit the gravesites of crows to pray for their souls. Any other person would have a priest the day of their funeral.

Shumei had paid twenty kols for the cheapest coffin, the only one she could afford, which used up this week's money for her mother's food and the ten kols she had planned to use for new shoes. Those present at the funeral included the village leader and his wife, the local priest, and a couple of curious villagers with nothing else to do.

Oka stood pressed to her side, his eyes fixed on the rapidly filling hole in the ground. She held him close with an arm across his back while absentmindedly stroking his soft hair with her other hand.

"She's really gone," he whispered, hugging her tighter.

"I know," she said, having spent her tears. She didn't intend to shed any more in front of anyone here. "But we still have each other."

The priest, having finished his sermon earlier, waited until the last shovel of dirt was thrown on top of the grave before making his way back to the temple. As soon as he was out of earshot, the village leader and his wife descended upon her. Akki, of course, was the first to speak.

"My, oh my, where did you get that dress, Shumei?" she asked, acting as though she was being genial, but she'd spoken too quickly to sound anything but suspicious. "It's a fitting color on a day like this."

"My mother told me as she was dying that my father had given it to her when they married, but it was too fine for working in the fields, so she never wore it. She wanted me to have it because my other dress was in such disrepair," she explained, having worked out an excuse with Oka late last night.

Oka remained passive at her side, and his face gave away nothing when Akki's gaze shot to him to see if he was at all surprised by Shumei's answer.

Shumei had been forced to tell Oka about Vallen. She had left out the worst details, only saying she had agreed to "work" for the demon in exchange for sparing her life—technically not a lie. Fortunately, her brother had not pressed for a more specific answer.

"I see," Akki said slowly.

"I had wondered how Father had afforded such a dress, but it was not an appropriate time to question Mother about such things." She turned her gaze to her brother. "I'm simply grateful Oka is alive. He's very precious to me."

"As he is to us all," Akki agreed with a smile Shumei almost believed. Almost. Shumei had learned never to trust anyone's outward demeanor. Many villagers had told her she was going to Oblivion someday while wearing smiles that, at a distance, made them seem as though they were paying her a compliment.

"Thank you, Madam Akki," she said, wishing she could make the vulgar gesture without being seen.

Glancing over Akki's shoulder, she was briefly ensnared in Kimen's lustful expression. He looked like he was about to eat a mouse.

"Well, Kimen and I must be going. I'm sure you have a lot of work to do in the fields today now that your mother is gone," Akki prodded, smile growing as she relished the cut to Shumei's composure. But Shumei gave no outward reaction. Clearly disappointed, Akki abruptly turned away and walked past her husband, who stared a moment longer before turning away as well.

Shumei and Oka watched as the gravediggers patted the dirt down, spreading out the remainder to make the extra volume of soil less obvious.

The burial site was in a smaller cemetery behind the regular cemetery, which was now much fuller than it had been before winter. The smaller cemetery was meant for black-haired villagers, and it only had two more places left before it would be full. An extension would have to be made someday.

If one wanted to read the names of deceased black-haired villagers, one wouldn't find any. To give a crow's soul a clean slate and prevent any lurking evils from following their soul to the Garden of the Divine One, a black-haired villager was buried with no name on their tombstone—only a date of death. Each grave marker was a simple, stone column. Nearly forty crows had been buried here. The oldest tombstone was close to three hundred years old. In fact, several black-haired villagers seemed to have died at the same time.

"I wonder what a priest might say during my funeral," a sultry voice said. Turning in surprise and jostling Oka, Shumei found the somber face of the witch. "I heard what you said about your new dress, and I must say I'm ever so curious to know how your father obtained such a fine piece of work." She gestured at the embroidery along the bottom. "Water lilies suit you rather well, though I might've chosen a different color for the dye work."

"Did you need something, Madam Majo?" Shumei asked, a blush coloring her cheeks despite her best attempts to prevent it. Even after what she'd done with Vallen, twice, the memory of Majo's hands on her breasts still flustered her.

Majo smiled and folded her arms, which made her breasts swell upward. She glanced at Oka, who regarded her silently.

"I wanted to inquire after your health, my dear," she said. "It would be a shame if you were to come down with the Burning as well."

Though the nausea had returned earlier that morning, she felt fine now. When she had woken, sleeping on her mother's old mat with her brother tucked in front of her, her chest had felt constricted, as if her dress were tied too tightly. Then the nausea had begun. She had left Oka sleeping while she'd endured it, and it had lasted a couple of hours.

"I'm fine, Madam Majo. I haven't had any of the usual symptoms." Of course, vomiting was not a symptom of the Burning, so she wasn't lying—not really. Majo's gaze slid down to Shumei's chest, and she blushed brightly when Majo's smile widened.

"You certainly look healthy, my dear," she said with overt mischief. "Ah, but take care of yourself anyway. I look forward to your delivery next week." Of the three idling villagers still milling about, the two men ogled the witch and the old woman scowled at her, but she paid them no heed as she swept past, walking sedately back to her home.

Now that their entertainment for the day was over, the villagers meandered away, and Shumei wondered why they didn't help in the fields, seeing as how the village was already shorthanded. Many people were still sick.

"We're done," one of the gravediggers called. Oka moved away from her.

"Thank you for your hard work, sirs," he said as he tipped his head down. The gravediggers exchanged confused looks, no doubt because Oka outranked them despite his young age. They returned his bow.

"It was no problem, Master Oka," the bigger one said. "We have to get back to the fields now. S-Sorry for your loss." With that, the two of them left, carrying their tools with them.

Shumei watched their retreating backs for a few seconds before approaching her mother's grave, which had been dug into the southeastern corner of the cemetery. She'd easily be able to pick out this spot again, so she would have no trouble praying at the right grave in the future.

"Mother has happiness now. You know that, don't you?" Oka said quietly as he pressed close to her side again. She put her arm around his back. "She's in the Garden of the Divine One with our father. She knows no sadness now."

"I know that, Oka, but I mourn the life she had when she was here. I mourn that her passing wasn't easier and that we didn't have more time with her."

They fell silent for a moment, both gazing sadly at the fresh marker driven into the ground at the head of their mother's grave.

"Why is life so hard?" Oka eventually asked, sniffing.

Shumei brushed her fingers through his hair and gave him an honest answer. "I don't know."

**

THAT NIGHT, SHUMEI lay awake. Her brother was curled up in front of her, one arm thrown out toward the dying fire. Her head rested on her bent left arm, and she rubbed small circles on Oka's shoulder. He wasn't sleeping peacefully, and she wasn't sleeping at all.

Thinking maybe he was cold, she flipped her side of their blanket over him and tucked it tight around him. She didn't especially need another layer, for her new dress was much warmer than her old one and was pretty much a blanket on its own. Aching, she stood to stretch and raised her arms above her head. The dress slid along her skin as it moved with her, and thoughts of Vallen came rushing forth. His voice, his hands pulling her closer, the way he sometimes looked at her...

She smoothed her dress down and watched the small fire, wondering why she wasn't angrier when she thought of Vallen. Hadn't he made her life ten times more difficult than it already was? Hadn't he disrupted her already miserable existence? Hadn't he berated her, manipulated her, and lied to her?

But not much had changed, truth be told. She had a new appointment every week, but it was one that didn't involve getting paid a pittance for backbreaking labor. Instead, she would enjoy the pleasures of the flesh with someone who could make her thighs clench simply by licking his lips. The virginity she'd lost had never helped her before. She was as hated in her village as she had been before Vallen had entered her life.

She had berated him as much as he had berated her, and though he had used her own desires against her, he had never failed to give her exactly what he'd promised. The blackmail still sorely rankled her, but he hadn't lied to her or broken his word. She was just too inexperienced at dealing with people like Vallen to come out the victor.

She recalled their conversation at the river as she stretched her back, arms straight behind her. He had told her he was willing to do anything to have her and her favors at his disposal, even take her on as what she assumed would be his mistress, though she wasn't quite sure if that was the word. Was a mistress anything other than a "kept woman"?

She frowned as she relaxed, rolling her shoulders. She would not be his mistress, then. Although, looking at the dress she wore, she wondered if she hadn't already taken on that title.

Her mind moved on to when he had said he would take her and her brother to live with him. The idea was ludicrous, of course. Just pack up and leave her home to live with some man—or rather, some demon—and pretend to be genial as he attempted to help raise Oka while spending each night on top of her? Although, that sounded rather like what would happen if she married Akiji.

She shivered despite her warm clothing. Akiji made her nervous. Of course, so did Vallen, but she saw gentleness in Vallen that he hid—and that Akiji faked. The promise Vallen had made to never hurt her hadn't been part of their bargain but a gesture to show her he wouldn't use force—would never need it. He had asked honestly and sweetly for her kiss, had given her clothing because she needed it rather than wanted it, and...

Shumei shook her head, hair flying about her face. Why was she thinking this way? She should be thinking of ways to escape her entanglement with him. As secretly tempting as his offer to take care of her and her brother was—

Wait. Vallen had never included her mother in the deal. Now that her mother had passed, the deal made sense. Had he already known?

Her jaw tightened with anger as she realized he most likely had known that her mother was dead when he'd approached her at the river. After all, he had known all those other things about the other villagers. He had been spying on her, on them. He must have snuck into her home. He must have known, and he hadn't told her.

Why? Did he really think she had gone to the river to bathe while her brother slept in the same room as his dead mother? What if Oka had woken up first? She would never have left the two of them like that had she known.

Vallen couldn't strike her, but that didn't mean she couldn't strike him, and the next time she saw him, she was going to hit him hard enough to make blood flow, she was sure of it.

**

A FAINT RUSTLING woke Shumei with a jerk. Softly moaning because of a slight headache and a parched throat, she sat up, careful not to rouse her brother. The sun was an hour from rising, but she had slept enough. She needed to make breakfast before she and Oka went to the field today.

Oka, lying on his back, was deep asleep. His mouth was open, his face slack. She hated to start making noises that would wake him. Looking around the room to delay standing, her gaze fell on a small bundle sitting just inside their flimsy reed door. Confused, she walked over to the package and knelt to inspect it. Where had this come from?

Deciding to unwrap it, she pulled at the knot in the brown wrapping and swept aside the edges. Inside sat several small bundles, four in total. Each was tightly wrapped in the same rough, brown cloth. She unwrapped one and gasped. The bundle contained what she rarely had the privilege of eating: meat.

Deer meat, judging by the color, cut into thin strips and made into jerky. There was enough for several days, even if they ate it at every meal. Though delighted, she couldn't help worrying there'd been a mistake. What in the world—

"What is it?" a sleepy voice asked. She turned to her brother, who had sat up.

Lifting a strip of deer jerky for his groggy contemplation, she gave him a small smile. "Someone left us a present."

71

Chapter Six

S humei had perhaps three hours of daylight to spend before the sun would set, and the day's labors were almost over. After weeding, checking for pests, and sprinkling a compound to combat them, she had planted a large crop of *kavua*. In small quantities, it relieved general body aches, especially menstrual pain, and it was her most popular medicine lately. She would need all the income she could scrape together, so she'd decided to have more than enough on hand.

Her midday meal of rice, fresh, leafy vegetables, and a good helping of deer jerky sat warm in her stomach, even though she didn't need the extra warmth when the day was turning out rather humid. It didn't help matters that her dress was black and sucked in every ray of sunshine.

She looked up from the shallow hole she had dug in front of her, and found Oka at the edge of the field, shouting distance away. In his small hands, he held his version of a sword—a tree branch he'd found a few weeks ago. With a warrior's determination, he slashed at invisible enemies and tested different moves and stances.

She might have thought he was merely playing hero with that fallen branch, but his expression and intense concentration told her he was practicing for something real. Frowning, she realized how much of his childhood Oka had missed. He didn't laugh much. He didn't play with the other village children, mostly because they had often said mean things about Mama. A brazen young boy had once thrown a rock at Shumei and had giggled when Oka yelled at him.

Because of her and Mama, he'd been forced to see such hatred. Some boys would lash out with anger and violence—although, she supposed hours of sword practice counted as violent—but Oka had never been particularly disobedient or short-tempered, and he had never gotten into any fights. He was quickly becoming an adult at the tender age of nine.

A drop of sweat rolled down her temple, and she resisted the urge to wipe at it with her dirty fingers. Though the sun shone down from a perfectly clear sky, the ground was still sticky and wet from a heavy rain a couple of days ago. In an effort to keep her dress clean, she had brought along the cloth that had been wrapped around the jerky, and had laid it on the ground to protect her skirt while she knelt in the soil.

Looking down at her work again, she pulled two large seeds from the pouch slung around her torso and pressed them into the bottom of the hole, careful to make sure the fatter end of the tear-shaped seeds was facing up. This would be the last plant, and then she and Oka could go home, eat a hearty supper, and retire early.

Tossing her head to fling her hair out of her way, she carefully spilled dirt back into the hole and sprinkled in the occasional handful of plant feed, a mixture her mother had taught her how to make. Mama had also taught her how deep and how far apart to place different seeds. She and Papa had taught her how to pair plants to reduce pests, and problems to keep an eye out for as the plants matured. That she even had half a chance of sustaining Oka and herself was thanks to them. Holding back tears, Shumei swallowed the ache in her throat.

As she was about to stand, an unsettling dizziness upset her balance, and she threw out her hands to keep from falling into the row of flowering *yagikusa* next to her. Closing her eyes, she concentrated on breathing evenly.

She hadn't felt nauseated since yesterday, for which she was grateful, but after that and Vallen's binding spell, she wasn't sure what her body was doing anymore. All morning, it felt like something alive was moving inside her, undulating as if stretching after a long nap.

She'd never suffered heartburn before, something her mother had complained of on occasion, and wondered if she was experiencing it. But the sensation wasn't like burning—just warmth and movement. And though she felt a small swipe as high as her heart, the bulk of the strange sensation's weight sat solidly in her stomach.

"Ah, Shumei," a familiar voice called. She turned in the direction of the voice, but everything swung slower than it should have. Eventually, her eyes settled upon the tall, wide-shouldered frame of Akiji.

She heard small feet running and knew Oka was rushing to her side. Akiji approached. She managed to stand, albeit shakily, and wiped her fingers on a rag.

"Working hard, I see. I wanted to talk to you," he said, setting his hands on his hips.

"Then speak," she said. Akiji's mouth twitched.

"I have it on good authority that you obtained a generous amount of deer meat," he said mildly, as though speaking of the weather. "And yet Ryoushi says you didn't buy any from him."

Ryoushi was the village huntsman, and though he couldn't leave the village before dawn to be in position for bow hunting or to place traps, he still managed to kill enough wildlife for those who could afford the meat he sold every week. It had been a long time since Shumei had purchased any of his offerings.

She didn't know how to respond. She had known instantly that Vallen had killed the deer and prepared its meat for her. It had been left inside her door well before dawn, and no one else would dare leave their hut at night, even if the village grounds were considered safe from monsters.

That had been the most shocking part. Vallen had definitely passed the barrier charms, which made him uniquely powerful compared to other demons.

It hadn't escaped her notice that the only way Akiji could have found out about the deer jerky would be if he'd gone poking around her home without permission. But now was not the time to confront him about it.

So instead of trying to explain—or worse, lie—she asked him a question of her own. "What are you trying to say?"

"Who gave you that meat, Shumei? I know you didn't kill the deer yourself. You have no hunting experience, no weapons, and you don't have the strength to drag a deer anywhere suitable for field-dressing the body."

"Why should I tell you who gave it to me? Is it any of your business?"

He clenched his hands. "As the man who would be your husband, I have the right to ask. Though gifts aren't a bad thing, the way you might repay someone is what worries me. I don't believe for a second the dress you're wearing came from your mother."

"For the hundredth time, I will not marry you," she said, voice tight. She decided not to touch his insinuation that she'd instantly resort to offering sex when presented with a gift. "My refusal negates any right you think you have to know my personal affairs."

"You *will* be my wife," he spat, face twisting with rage. "Now tell me who is giving you these things."

She couldn't hold back her surprise at his temper. Normally, he acted like a petulant child when she rebuffed him, throwing a mild tantrum or pretending to suck it up and walk away. But ever since the village leaders had broached the topic of her marriage partner, his reactions had escalated.

"N-No." Though it was the wrong thing to say, she could give him no other answer. If she even hinted at Vallen's existence, she might lose her home, her brother, her life, or all three.

Akiji hardened his jaw. His wide stance radiated frustration. "You'll be no one's whore but mine."

His hands shot to her shoulders and clamped down, their grip painfully tight. She gasped in fear as he dragged her to him. He had never resorted to physical violence in front of Oka. Her heartbeat thundered in her head as a deep, pulsating hum. It rose inside her, drowning out Akiji's growling grunts as if someone had rung a large bell.

Time slowed. She heard Oka yelling, and saw him reaching for her in the corner of her eye. Though he was only a couple steps away, his voice was so distant. Akiji pulled her toward him in a bruising grip, clearly about to force a kiss, but it happened so slowly that it seemed she had as much time to react as she wanted. She braced her hands on his chest.

"Get away from me," she screamed. Something inside her surged, swelling outward from her stomach and stealing her breath. Energy and tension sizzled down her arms. Wind rushed overhead as time resumed its normal speed. The sounds of the forest pressed close against her eardrums. The chirping of birds, the rush of the breeze through the newly grown leaves...

Akiji flew back and landed on his rear with a pained yell. Oka had stopped dead in his tracks. Cursing wildly, Akiji stumbled to his feet.

"Shumei... How?" Oka asked. She looked at her hands, slowly turning them. They were still dirty, still small and weak. She shouldn't have been able to do that.

Akiji gaped at her as if she had sprouted warts all over her face. She wanted to say something but didn't know what—certainly not an apology. She was as confused as Akiji was. Without another word, Akiji ran back toward the village, sparing a single, fearful glance over his shoulder before disappearing among the thick trees lining the path.

"Is it because of him? Did he make that happen somehow?" Oka asked. Shumei didn't have to ask who "he" was. She put her hands down and turned to Oka, who regarded her with worry.

"I don't know. I don't think so." A lot of magic had been directed at her lately, and she didn't know enough about it to understand what kind of consequences it wrought. Though Majo had often vehemently denied it, she knew the woman practiced the forbidden art. Vallen had told her so.

It was time to pay the witch another visit.

SHUMEI HAD TWO days left until she saw Vallen again. Each day she'd been busy with spring planting, and now that she was the only one working the field, wanting to spare Oka the worst of the backbreaking labor, she had to use every second of sunlight she could spare to finish planting.

She hadn't had time to visit Majo and ask the questions that had been blaring inside her head after the incident with Akiji, whom she hadn't seen since, but no one had come to her door with accusations. Though she didn't know what to think, she knew what that shove had looked like. Magic. Which meant Akiji was keeping her secret for now.

Thankfully, she had caught up on planting and had kept the weeds to a minimum. Oka had repeatedly tried to help her, but he had neither the knowledge of what was a new seedling versus a weed nor the stamina to remain bent much of the day, and she wanted him to relax until at least the harvest next year.

Seeing a couple of hours were left to burn until sunset, she decided to give herself a break and leave early. She could wash at the river and meet with Majo before coming home and helping Oka with dinner. Wiping her hands as she stood, she looked across the field at Oka, who was trying his best to walk around on his hands.

"Oka?" she called before picking up the cloth she had been kneeling on. Her brother clumsily flopped to one side, his little legs flying, and his head popped up from behind a row of comfrey, used for wounds both big and small to speed up healing and leave less scarring. She carefully stepped over rows of plants toward the path home. "Let's go home a little early today."

Oka was instantly up and jogging around the edge of the field to catch up to her. She held his hand as they walked home, and he apprised her of all the tumbling he'd done as well as an interesting bug he'd found.

Having asked Oka to clean and prepare their only pot for dinner, she left him at their hut and made her way to the river for a much-needed bath. Then as she was dressing, having washed away the day's labors, she couldn't help but stroke the material of her dress, still incredibly grateful to have it, though she would never say that to the demon who had given it to her. After combing her hair, she walked back to the village and headed in the direction of the witch's home.

However, the closer she drew to Majo's hut, the more fretful she became, and as the hut came into view, she found her feet slowing to a stop until she stood a few feet from the door, fidgeting with the sleeve of her dress and wondering if this visit was a good idea. The last time she had entered the witch's hut, she had left tipsy and groped.

Gathering her courage, she strode forward and raised her hand to knock. But before she could make contact with the door, it swung inward, revealing a smiling Majo in yet another of her revealing dresses. This one was white and embroidered with a rosebush heavy with new buds. The witch's gaze darted to Shumei's chest for half a heartbeat, long enough to make her blush.

"Why, Shumei! It's a delight to see you here without your delivery bag. Come in, come in," she invited, oozing kindness, though now it didn't seem nearly as sincere as before. She asked Shumei to leave her shoes near the door, and ushered to her usual seat on the thick, comfortable sleeping mat.

"Would you care for some tea, dear?" she asked, elegantly gesturing at a kettle sitting by the fire.

"No, thank you, madam," she demurred.

"Suit yourself." Majo smiled before sitting on her cushion. "Now then, what brings you to my home today?" She leaned forward, supposedly out of curiosity, but Shumei suspected she did it because it made her chest swell dangerously close to falling out of her dress.

Shumei looked into the witch's dark, twinkling eyes. "Please, madam, answer me truthfully. Do you know anything about magic and its secrets?"

The witch sat straighter. Her smile now had an edge to it. "Because you're a crow I shall answer you truthfully. I do have knowledge about magic. Why do you ask?"

"Something strange happened the other day. I think I did it." Her story came out haltingly as she tried to express what she'd experienced in actual words. The witch's face revealed little the entire time, though her eyes did widen when she came to the part about shoving Akiji.

"How I envy you," Majo said, breathy. Shumei blinked in confusion. "What you and I have is intrinsic magic, my dear. Those with black hair have the potential to possess it. Not all crows are so blessed, though. Only some carry the warm weight of magic inside."

"W-Wait, are you saying I'm a magic-user?" Shumei asked, mind reeling. She braced her hand on the bedroll beneath her as she swayed in shock. She had thought perhaps what had happened was a side effect of Vallen's magic when he'd cast the binding upon her, but apparently not.

"One of the few, dear. Your power likely rivals my own."

"Why didn't you tell me all this before?"

Majo shrugged. "Your magic hadn't manifested. Only a few things awaken it in a crow. A demon or another magic-user casting a spell on you, for instance. Then there's a serious illness, a traumatic experience, and sometimes sex. I suspect the loss of your mother was the trigger in your case."

Shumei rather suspected the other triggers had helped. Not only had Vallen made love to her on a couple of recent occasions, but he had also placed the binding upon her, and though she hadn't experienced any symptoms of the Burning, she had been periodically nauseous earlier in the week.

Her mind tripped over itself stringing together dozens of questions, the most haunting of which was whether or not the village would execute her should they ever discover her ability.

"How do I keep it from coming out?" she asked, looking beseechingly at the witch. Choosing to be a magic-user and getting yourself executed was one thing, but being a magic-user by birth and not knowing how to hide it was another.

"For someone like you with no training, the best way to keep it calm is by controlling your emotions. You're actually rather good at that. With Akiji, however, you had no other recourse."

Though she had meant them to be comforting, Majo's words didn't make Shumei feel any better. She didn't have much confidence in her ability to mask her feelings anymore. The village leaders, Majo, Akiji, and Vallen had all proven quite capable of cracking her shell lately. Ever since the damned Burning...

"Why? Why do I have this?" she whispered, hands fisted on her thighs. "Does that mean crows truly are evil?"

"Only some black-haired people, especially women, have intrinsic magic, but brownies and blondies try and sometimes successfully acquire some level of magical talent. Their power can be just as strong or stronger than intrinsic magic, depending on the user's determination. And Shumei..." Majo said, leaning toward her, though this time it wasn't a ploy to show off her breasts. "Unlike what blondies would have you believe, magic is not evil, nor is it good. It is neutral. I don't know why crows have it intrinsically, but I know it's not a mark of evil."

"But demons use magic," she said, thinking of Vallen and binding.

The witch straightened, brows raised. Shumei resisted the urge to slap her hand over her mouth, or to even react at all. Apparently she had revealed too much.

"How did you know that?" Majo asked.

Stomach sinking, Shumei gathered every ounce of control she had to look as guileless as possible. "Is it not common knowledge? I heard it from my mother after my incident. And besides, I heard you say earlier that a demon's spell could trigger one's magic."

Indeed, she had known before meeting Vallen that demons could use magic. Though the memories were vague, she knew something bad had happened to her—had *almost* happened to her—when she was quite young. She remembered a long lecture from her mother on the dangers of demons. Everyone in the village had found out about her nearly fatal trip into the forest. Many had cruelly accused her of trying to join the demon hordes.

"Ah, yes. I suppose your mother would have known."

"What do you know of demons, madam? Are they all evil, mindless creatures?" she asked, for the witch's knowledge seemed to encompass more than magic.

Majo smiled like a cat after it had eaten a mouse. "For answers to those kinds of questions, you'll have to pay a price in return," she purred with one hand on the wooden floor. The fire beside them snapped, and a log fell into the base of the flames. Shumei jumped.

"What kind of price?" she asked, thirsty for knowledge about demons and yet not wanting to give up anything in return for that knowledge. She had little money as it was.

The witch eyed her as if she were a piece of meat. "First, a kiss. I shall then tell you the basics about demons."

Shumei's jaw dropped. "A kiss? But I'm a woman." Moreover, Vallen had said kisses were off-limits, making Majo's offer a fast method of breaking her end of the deal. Although, he had only stipulated men.

"Doesn't matter. In fact, I want a kiss even more because you are a woman."

"Then, do you not like men?"

"Not as much as women. However, I appreciate pleasure above all things. Your lips look very pleasurable," she murmured.

Shumei's face grew hot and she couldn't maintain eye contact with the witch. Something uncurled inside her, as if turning over in its sleep.

"Calm down, child. You are letting your emotions run too high, and your magic is leaking. It's only a kiss, dear," Majo sighed, sounding impatient as she straightened.

"Is that what I'm feeling? My magic is...leaking?"

"Yes. It sometimes moves on its own, and you'll have to learn to calm it, a basic skill you can master quickly."

"If I kiss you, will you tell me about demons *and* how to calm my magic?"

Majo smiled slowly, as if she had deciphered the winning move in a game of strategy. "I'll even let you ask one extra question about demons if it is specific enough," she said, stroking the rosebush pattern on her skirt.

"It's a deal, then," Shumei said with more bravado than she felt. She was making a lot of deals lately.

The witch rose to her knees, sliding her hands forward—a cat rising from a nap. She crawled toward Shumei, whose heart thudded so loudly it was a wonder the witch couldn't hear it.

"I won't hurt you, dear," Majo whispered, now close enough for Shumei to smell her perfume. Majo's long hair flowed quietly over Shumei's hands, which sat in her lap.

Shumei stiffened as the witch slid one arm behind her, pulling her closer. Majo's other hand held her weight, pressing into the sleeping mat next to her thigh.

"Close your eyes."

"You know what to do."

Shumei remembered Vallen's whispered words at the river. Though she couldn't force herself to meet the witch's kiss, she tilted her head and shut her eyes as Majo pressed her lips against Shumei's.

Unsurprisingly, she didn't get the same thrill as when Vallen kissed her. Her heart raced, to be sure, but only because the experience was novel. Majo tightened her hold, pulling Shumei against her chest as she slowly and gently slid her tongue in and out of Shumei's mouth.

She couldn't help but compare the witch's kiss with the demon's, and found that Vallen's rougher, more demanding ones were the kind she liked. Although, her preference could lie in the fact that Vallen was male.

She realized her hands still sat in her lap, curled with nervousness, but lying there all the same, and remembered how she had eagerly gripped Vallen's shoulders as they ground against each other in the river only a few days ago. The memory sparked a bit of longing within her, and she guiltily wished the one bargaining for her kiss wasn't the witch, but someone else entirely. She shouldn't be longing for the demon's attentions.

Eventually, Majo withdrew, sucking on Shumei's lower lip in parting before releasing it and leaning back with a satisfied look. Shumei wanted another kiss, but from the one whose spicy scent set her heart at ease and whose desire brought out her own in equal measure.

"If only you were interested in women, dear Shumei. What pleasure we could have in the privacy of my hut," she said. Shumei was tempted to wipe her mouth but resisted the urge.

"Please, Madam Majo. I willingly gave you the kiss. I am most eager to learn about demons and their properties," she said. "What I know of them is very little and most likely contains exaggeration."

Majo lightly chuckled. "You speak of them as if they're medicinal plants. Very well, let us not waste daylight."

The witch was clear and succinct as she outlined the origins and motives of demons. Most of the information Shumei had already known from eavesdropping near the elder members of the village, who loved to flap their mouths about the Damned One and his minions.

What she didn't know was interesting and frightening at the same time. She hadn't realized how much danger lurked outside the barrier charms, and knew she would have nightmares that night. According to the witch, demons only felt basic needs—none of them healthy. The Damned One released these creatures with only one purpose in mind: to kill any human they could find, making the death as painful and as violating as possible.

Majo wouldn't give her details on any specific types of demons, and she wondered with a great deal of trepidation what kind of price she would have to pay for that information.

Next came a brief but detailed explanation of controlling one's magic. Doing so took concentration, but reining in her magic was no different from using a muscle, like closing one's fist or swallowing. She didn't have an immediate chance to practice, but she was at least more confident about being able to stop her newfound power if she lost control of it again.

"It couldn't be simpler, dear. The only thing easier is breathing," Majo assured. She stretched elegantly, rolling her head in a circle. "Now, if you would like to ask your extra question, I can answer it and retire for the night. Sunset is coming."

Shumei pressed her lips thin as she considered which question to ask. She knew she wanted to know more about the kind of demon Vallen was and the magic he could do, and Majo had said the question had to be specific, but asking about the binding or about why sex demons could pass through barrier charms was far too specific to be anything but suspicious.

Hoping Majo would be lenient, she went with a more general inquiry. "Tell me about s-sex demons," she said, frustrated when her words didn't come out smoothly.

The older woman looked at her with mild surprise. "Sex demons? Why would you ask about them?"

"I once heard some other girls talking about them."

The witch stared at her for a moment, but Shumei's mask was in place, and Majo would find nothing in her face to give her away. "Well, that type is certainly interesting. If it weren't for the fact they kidnap their prey and exhaust them to the point of death, I wouldn't mind meeting one someday."

"Why are they interesting?"

"Most demons are the creations of the Damned One, but a precious few types are...shall we say, born from another source? The spell to create sex demons is quite complicated, which is all I really know about the ritual. Oh, I do know the main spell component is the seed of a male specimen, and that by using it you can curse that male to be reliant on sexual energy to live. Thus, a human becomes a demon. Quite cruel indeed," she clucked, crossing her arms and drumming her fingers.

Vallen used to be human. Shumei had to use all of her concentration not to gasp in shock or show much more of a reaction than a surprised jump of her eyebrows.

"Do they become immortal, then? Invulnerable?"

"The curse gives men the status of a demon but forces them to either fulfill their role or die. If a sex demon does not consume the energy of a woman by the end of a full moon's passing, the human soul is doomed to spend eternity in Oblivion. In exchange, he has certain unearthly abilities that lend themselves to his sensual task, though I do not know what they are or how long they last. I do know that sex demons weaken the longer they go without sexual energy."

Shumei nodded slowly, feeling a great swell of pity. No matter her lot in life, she was at least still human, but Vallen...

"Dear Shumei, you seem quite lost in thought. I fear I confused you more than enlightened you, but if you wish to ask more questions, I'll be glad to answer all of them should you decide to pay the right fee," the witch said, lips curving into a smile.

Shumei shook her head and stood. "Thank you for your wisdom this evening. I shall leave you to your rest, Madam Majo," she muttered, wishing to return home before Oka began to worry. Indeed, the sun would be setting soon.

Majo remained seated, arms crossed. "You're welcome, dear Shumei. Feel free to ask more questions in the future."

Shumei pulled on her boots at the door, feeling an awkward silence settling over her shoulders as Majo watched her from her cushion. She reached for the handle of the door, but a thought made her pause.

She looked over her shoulder. "Madam, why do you stay in this village?"

The woman smiled. "Unfinished business," she said, a reply surely as vague as she had intended it. Shumei nodded and left, not wanting to press any further. She shivered as she closed the door behind her.

Chapter Seven

Dawn pressed close, not yet over the horizon, but the incessant chirping of birds told Shumei she'd soon see Vallen again. All day yesterday, her mind had been consumed with thoughts of him, and it had left her tense and irritable. The night had crept along, and only her brother's sleeping presence kept her from screaming with impatience.

Her control certainly had been stripped from her in the past week. When dawn did arrive—and the fact it eventually would was her only comfort—she told herself she would sprint to the meeting place and demand two things of the damnable demon.

First, she wanted to know why he hadn't told her Mama had died, and that her brother was sleeping a short distance from the cooling corpse of their beloved mother. Had he thought she already knew? Had he thought she'd skip down to the river without seeing to her mother's body, or making sure her brother didn't discover her first?

Second, she wanted him on top of her, inside of her, rubbing and sweating against her as they kissed and moaned until they reached that vision-blurring, spine-bowing climax for which she'd been aching more and more.

She had already told Oka she would be gone most of the morning to "work" for the demon. He still didn't know what she did specifically, and she hoped he didn't find out for a long time, if ever. He had instructions to sleep in, clean up, and prepare the seeds of which he had knowledge for planting that afternoon.

Sitting awake at his side, she looked at the edge of the door and confirmed the sun had risen above the horizon. She kissed Oka's cheek, and he frowned in his sleep as though he would wipe it away. Then she stood, put on her boots, and slipped through the reed door.

No one was about, but they soon would be to start the day's labors. Carefully surveying for any spying eyes, she took the path that led to the medicine field and the meeting place. Anyone who did see her would likely assume she was heading out to work, but they might also notice she wasn't carrying any seed bags or tools. Once she was among the trees, she picked up the pace.

All she could think about was the demon she was about to meet. The timbre of his voice, his harsh breaths while he drove himself inside her, and the way he made her feel—heavy, soft, and warm. She also remembered the bite of his insults, the grip of his fingers around her wrists, and the demands he made of her.

Halfway up the first hill, she spotted a flicker inches in front of her face and stopped, a gasp trapped in her throat. The silky, tenuous threads of a spider's web, only just begun, were stretched across her path, anchored by a few branches hanging low and close together over the path.

Fear gripped her, and she took several hasty steps back. Pressing her hands against the flutter in her chest, she stood there in indecision while flicking her eyes about, looking for the web's architect. She soon found it wiggling with constructive haste on the branch to the right. The eight-legged menace was perhaps the size of a *kavua* seed, not very big at all, but size didn't matter. She was utterly terrified of it.

The web was high enough that simply ducking would clear her of the lowest threads, but there was no way she would walk under it. However unlikely, the chance that a spider would drop onto her neck and crawl beneath her collar kept her from moving forward. A pitiable, mewling noise welled up in her throat.

She couldn't be late meeting Vallen. She couldn't skip. She had to get past the web. Oka would be able to remove it later—it had become his job, seeing as how she was useless when it came to spiders—but for now she had to deal with this obstacle on her own.

Stepping carefully, she left the path and traipsed through the forest to avoid the spider and its partially finished web. The morning dew clinging to the underbrush dampened her skirt, and when she reemerged on the path, dead leaves were stuck to her dress. She impatiently brushed them off.

After taking a breath to calm herself, she continued walking, but she couldn't help scouring the path in front of her for any other "construction sites" as she came closer and closer to the meeting place. Thankfully, she saw none.

Up ahead was the clearing, and she clenched her hands as if holding tight to the courage it would take to scream at the demon waiting for her. She couldn't let him control the conversation, at least not until she'd said her piece.

Then arousal hit her full force, flushing her cheeks and making her stumble. The gasp from earlier that had never managed to escape her throat broke free. She hugged herself, hoping she could somehow contain the waves of heat washing up and down her body. Her magic stirred, and she worried she wouldn't be able to put another foot in front of her.

"Damn you," she hissed, livid he would use his magic on her already. After shaking her head and blinking a few times, she managed to walk, but only because she was now determined to kill him.

The morning sun greeted her when she emerged into the meadow—cranky and aroused. She found Vallen standing to the left in a spot where the grass was crushed. Hmph, as though she even needed a reminder of where they'd first embraced. Each time she had passed through this clearing on her way to the medicine field, she would remember the night he'd caught her, and the feel of his warm lips against hers.

Today he wore a dark blue jacket with gold ties. It framed his broad shoulders perfectly, and its decorative, gold seams complimented the lines of his chest and sides. His black pants wrapped snugly around his long legs, but the jacket fell too far for her to see the erection she knew was there.

Her sex flowered with excitement, but she held back the needy groan rising in her throat. Even at a distance, she saw his knowing smile. Forcing herself to walk to him, she waded through the ankle-high blades of grass until she came to a stop an arm's length away from the man whose touch had haunted her for the last week.

"Good morning, Shumei," he rumbled, voice rolling over her body. She shivered.

"Why didn't you tell me my mother had died that morning?" she bit out, ignoring the dizziness in her head and the clenching arousal in her sex. She needed answers now.

"I thought you already knew," he readily answered. "I followed you to the river, thinking you had gone there to mourn in private, but seeing you naked distracted me."

She balled up her hands. "Distracted you?" she scoffed. "And yet you managed to coax that deal out of me. Are you really so single-minded, you damned de—"

"Yes, I am," he said, eyes flashing. "This way of life is all I have known for a long time. I rarely think of anything other than my next meal."

She had no immediate response. She also rarely thought of much else besides how to keep her and her family fed and sheltered—at least until Vallen and her intrinsic magic had entered her life.

"I have a question of my own," he said, leaning forward. His cold eyes stared straight into hers and she almost looked away. "The evening before last, you received quite a kiss, but from whom I could only assume was another woman. Tell me what you were doing."

"Trading for information, that's all," she said, not wanting to admit what she now knew about his nature.

"Trading with whom?" he whispered, taking a step forward. She had to tilt her head up to maintain eye contact.

"With—with the witch." She saw no reason for holding back that detail, yet he inhaled swiftly, a raw emotion passing over his face.

"She is dangerous, Shumei. Do not trade anything else with her," he warned. "She already cast one spell on you, and thankfully its effect was rather pleasant." He said the last with a small smile and glanced at her chest.

Her breasts! Realizing he was right, she gasped and laid her hands protectively over her bosom. Her old dress had become tighter across her chest, but it had been so ill-fitting already that she hadn't thought much of it, and then Vallen had given her a new dress. With everything that had happened in the last week, the subtle growth of her breasts had been the last thing to capture her notice.

Majo must have put something into that rice wine, and Shumei's nausea had been a side effect. It all made sense now. She was doubly glad she hadn't taken any of the witch's tea the other day. Who knew what that might've done to her?

"She was probably experimenting on you, and let's be glad her experiment was successful. Improperly mixed potions can kill, and the ill effects often look like a disease to outsiders," he explained. Shumei blanched. "Fortunately, most crows have more than enough magic to fight off these ill effects, but everyone else...?"

The Burning. Had it been Majo's fault?

"Then the witch..." was all she could say. It was too horrible even to imagine. That Majo would be so reckless and kill so many people, including Shumei's mother...

"What information, Shumei? What was it you wanted to know so badly that you would kiss such a creature?"

"I kiss you, don't I?" she replied dryly. The way his jaw stiffened told her she had hit her mark. "I wanted to know more about demons."

"And what did you learn?"

"Very little, unfortunately. I already knew most of what she told me." She injected some bitterness into her voice in order to sell her half-truth. Yes, she hadn't learned much, but what she had learned had been important. He tilted his head, eyes narrowing slightly, and she realized he knew she had omitted something. However, he didn't say anything further and straightened to his full height.

"Let us not delay any longer. I have prepared a place for us, and my loins ache to be inside you," he uttered thickly. The abrupt change in subject and his blatant admission had her speechless and blushing. He held out his hand. Dazed, she took it. He turned to the woods behind him and led her to the tree line.

"How far are we going?" she asked.

"Far enough."

His hand was warm, his grip firm. They entered the trees, though this time there was no path, so the underbrush quickly turned into a hindrance. The ankle-length dress shortened her gait, and she had to stop to pry out every single branch or thorn that snagged her skirt. Vallen seemed patient at first, but the fourth time it happened, he turned and heaved a sigh of frustration.

She eased yet another thorn out of her skirt, face flushed with exertion. She was really trying to avoid damaging her new dress, but the material seemed to catch on every little thing, and its proper fit meant she couldn't lift the hem more than a few inches. He had said they weren't going far, but they'd stopped so many times that she could still see the clearing through the trees behind her.

Leaves crunched. Then he was right next to her, practically a hand's breadth from her side. She looked up at him in question.

"It'll be faster to carry you," he said, snaking his arm around her back.

"Wait," she stammered, not comfortable with being in his arms like that, even though she was about to be a lot more intimate with him. But it was too late for protests.

He swept her off the ground. "Think of it as part of foreplay. You're fulfilling your end of the deal by letting me carry you," he murmured, holding her tight against his chest. Then, voice tinged with effort, he said, "But it'd be easier if you put your arms around my neck."

She didn't believe for a second that Vallen needed her to do anything to make her easier to carry. Demons had superhuman strength. But before she realized it, she had laced her fingers together on his far shoulder.

"What's foreplay?" she asked. "Is it a kind of magic?" She heard him choke and wasn't sure if it was a laugh or a cough.

"Some would call it magic," he teased, eyes twinkling. Ah, it'd been a laugh, then. "But no, foreplay is not the kind of magic you're thinking of."

"I don't understand," she said, fighting not to squirm. Being in anyone's arms felt awkward, his arms especially.

"Don't worry, I'll show you," he promised, glancing down at her. For a split second, she saw something other than emptiness in his blue eyes—something gentle—and a small gasp popped out of her mouth. But as quickly as his gaze fell to her, it rose again, looking ahead.

In the silence that descended, she began to notice other things about Vallen. His white hair brushed her hand, tickling a bit. She fought an insane urge to play with it. A faint scent drifted to her nose, a mixture of a hot night's breeze and sun-warmed skin. It also strongly hinted of his spicy soap, and underlying it all was a light, manly musk. She shivered in longing even as she wished his smell was less alluring.

Vallen's thoughts were of a similar bent. She felt so light in his arms. Soft. He wanted to sink into that softness and wrap it around him. Her hair smelled of earthy plants, and her dewy skin glistened under the dawning sun's intermittent rays. He hadn't wanted a woman like this since the one who had been his downfall.

He wondered why it was Shumei he hungered for. Though she shared a few physical traits with Miharu, her personality and background were radically different. The whole world had been radically different back then.

He spied their destination up ahead. His steps quickened. She turned her head and stiffened in his arms.

"W-What is that?" Shumei squeaked, having expected a simple blanket on the ground, if anything. She wasn't sure what to call this structure. A cloth house?

"It's a tent, which I obtained long ago in Kurosa, the City of Dunes. Wait until you see inside."

She studied it as they neared, barely noticing his imposing horse standing behind it. The framed fabric was a rich green, and its seams were laden with heavy gold ropes that were furred on the end, a strange flourish she didn't even have a word for. The entire structure was at least the size of her paltry hut.

She expected to be set on her feet, but Vallen continued around the tent to the side with an opening. He easily steered them through the cloth door that was already drawn open, and she gasped at the sight within. Dozens of pillows were strewn across the cozily lit space. They were varying hues of purple, and the rug that stretched from wall to wall was a dizzying mix of red and gold. Several burning candles sat on metal plates far from where any…activity might occur.

"Where did all of this come from?" she asked, still in his arms.

"My original estate is not far from here. No one has disturbed it since I last visited it, so it must be as hard to find as ever."

"Estate? How can you own an es—" she said before remembering that Vallen had once been human. Who was to say he hadn't been a rich human, perhaps even a lord?

"Wealth is acquired over time, and demons have a lot of time."

Or that, she supposed. "How long are you going to hold me?" she asked, having gone cold now that the magic he had used on her had died away.

"All morning." He slowly smiled, teeth gleaming even in the dim interior. A wave of arousal rolled over her, and she knew he'd pulled the strings on his magic again, renewing her hunger. He lowered her to the lush carpet and set her back against several pillows. She wanted his arms around her, his body warming hers, and couldn't help clinging to him as he pulled away to close the tent flap.

He chuckled at her eagerness. "Don't worry, dear Shumei. I will return to your arms soon."

Still of enough sound mind to feel embarrassed, she was grateful when he secured the flap against even the smallest seam of light, for anything brighter than a candle would let him see the blush crawling up her neck. But even the heat of her shame was nothing compared to the sexual excitement budding within her, turning her heavy and sluggish. She squirmed among the pillows holding her up as if she were an offering to the Divine One. Or a sacrifice to a demon.

She tried to push the thought away and told herself he wanted a steady source of energy. He wasn't looking to gorge himself on her, yet the idea of being so literally consumed...

He returned to her side, the fine lines of his face betraying his hunger, tightly reined. His expression somehow thrilled rather than frightened her.

"Do you wish to see foreplay, then?" he asked, settling against her right side. He slid his arm beneath her shoulders, and his face drew near. Her heart leapt.

"Can't you just tell me?"

Laying his hand on her knee, he smiled as though he knew a secret. "That could be just as delicious, I suppose."

Another pulse of arousal made her back arch, forcing a sigh from her lips. She thought that maybe they should take off their shoes.

"I'd start by removing your belt and kissing your petal-soft lips," he said, though his actions didn't mirror his words. Rather, he drew up her skirt, slowly revealing her ankles and shins. "Then I'd part your dress and marvel over the sliver of porcelain skin I find."

Her skirt traveled higher, passing over her knees. Her heart pounded in her ears, and she found herself softly panting.

"I should touch you gently and savor the feel of your skin, but I'd be far too impatient." The last came out as a harsh whisper. "My lips would travel lower, tasting your neck, your breasts, and the dip in your stomach."

She shivered as phantom sensations manifested where and how he'd described them. Was this magic, or just the power of his sultry voice? She felt silly clutching her hands to her chest, but her nerves wouldn't let her relax.

"Then I'd lie between your legs and nuzzle the sweet treasure between your thighs," he said with a low moan. "What a delicious pussy it'll be."

She blinked in revelation. "That's what a pussy is? Down there?"

He smiled, clearly amused. "You did not know?"

"No," she mumbled. "I mean, I've heard that word, but I...didn't know its meaning at the time."

He made a pensive sound and slipped his hand into her dress. Taken by surprise, she grabbed his wrist.

"Gods, Shumei, don't stop me when I'm so close," he groaned, pulling her hand up to his shoulder. "Hold me here instead. Squeeze when I make you feel good." She looked at him with a mixture of arousal and uncertainty but kept her hand in place.

He found her knee again and delved under the skirt bunched up on her thighs. She wanted to pinch her legs shut, embarrassed by how wet she'd become, but he already knew just how ready she was for him, didn't he? What he didn't know—couldn't know—was how much she'd imagined his big, warm hands seeking out her most secret places over the last week. After all, the binding only worked over a short distance, right?

A small flicker of heat lit his cold, calculating eyes, which watched her closely as he stroked his hand up her thigh. He cupped her mound without hesitation, and she took in a shaky breath.

"This is your pussy," he said, massaging gently. She shut her eyes, too embarrassed to meet his gaze any longer. "And between your lips"—he split her open with two fingers—"is a sweet bit of flesh that makes you moan my name." She dug her fingers into his shoulder. "My favorite part of foreplay is sucking a woman's clit."

"Clit?" she hoarsely repeated. Another new word.

The rest of his sentence hardly registered, for he swiped his finger through her arousal and used it to tease and swirl that sensitive nub. Waves of heat. Tingles. She would've moaned but her voice was gone, so he groaned for her and pressed his erection against her leg. She could sense his ache for her. It was sharp, almost painful. Or was she feeling her own pleasure, pulling her deeper into the pillows and twitching through her writhing body, while at the same time lifting her up to float near the cloth ceiling? In either case, she wanted more.

She was easing her thighs farther apart when his hand left her without warning. She glanced at him in time to see his slick middle finger disappear between his lips. Her heart jolted. Was he...tasting her?

"Now then," he said roughly. He was breathing hard, and that flicker of heat in his eyes had grown warmer. "Any other words you wish to know the definitions of?"

"Other...?" Caught off guard, she had to think for a second. "I think it was...cock?" She wasn't sure if she had remembered the word right, but he was quick to grin in response.

"Gods, Shumei, you are a delight." He took her hand from his shoulder and pulled her close, turning her toward him. When he placed her fingers over the bulge in his pants, she stiffened in shock and pleasure. The latter came from Vallen. Well, most of it. "This is a cock," he said gruffly. "My cock."

His face was mere inches away, his eyes closed in bliss. He tightened his grip on her hand, making her squeeze him harder. It felt so good they both grunted in response.

"Say you want me," he groaned. "Say it."

"I—" She did want him, and he knew it, but pride and shyness choked her.

He stared hard at her, almost glowering. "You've craved me all week, especially late at night. Every night. Admit it."

"Y-Yes," she said, needier than she'd meant to sound. Oh dueling gods, the binding wasn't as limited as she'd thought.

"Then say it."

"I want you."

She'd hardly gotten the words out before his mouth was on hers, demanding, stroking, delving deep. She arched and pressed her breasts against his hard chest. It was the only way she could be closer to him, trapped as her arms were between them. He let go of her hand, but she kept it cupped over his groin while he worked on loosening the knot holding her belt together. He was so adept at it that he was able to tug blindly, still kissing her, and get the job done. Molding her fingers around the shaft trapped under his clothes, she rubbed cautiously and was rewarded with a flare of pleasure that made him sigh roughly against her lips.

Her belt went slack. Then, in a slick whip of sound, it disappeared. He rolled her onto her back again and rose above her. She licked her wet, swollen lips. Panting, he roughly pushed open her dress and paused to regard her naked form only about as long as it took to swallow with hunger. She hadn't imagined his earlier description of foreplay quite so eager and rushed, but she had no complaints about this version. She was as desperate for more as he was.

"Beautiful," he groaned, straddling her thighs. She eyed the lines of his chest and shoulders underneath his shirt and realized she had never seen more of him than his cock.

"I..." she began, hesitant to say anything. Accepting his touch, even eagerly, was one thing. Taking initiative was another. Was asking for more going too far?

He braced himself on his elbows and nuzzled her chin higher. "What is it?" he whispered, covering her neck in soft kisses. Shivering, she grasped his shoulders.

"I want to see you too," she breathed, barely loud enough for him to hear. A heady pulse of satisfaction swept through her. She'd evidently delighted him.

"Your wish is my command." He straightened, breaking her grasp on his shoulders, and snatched at his jacket ties with efficiency. Then, with deliberate care, he swept aside the folds of his clothes, revealing his smooth, sculpted chest. His pecs were high and tight, his abdomen ridged with toned muscle. She wanted to touch him, and though she was sure he wouldn't mind, she refrained. Feeling desire and acting on it, those were different things, right?

He tugged on his sleeves behind his back and rolled his massive shoulders as he pulled his jacket off. His arms were long and well shaped. She traced with her eyes the healthy veins that fed his strength. He could carry his own horse, she was certain, and yet he touched her so gently, held her so ardently. Soon, he'd be sliding that warrior's body against her. She clenched her thighs in impatience. He inhaled deeply, chest swelling. Her heart flipped as he slowly leaned over her again.

"You're pleased, I can tell. That gladdens me." He touched his lips to her collarbone and kissed his way down to her breasts. He didn't linger long, as impatient as he had described earlier, and quickly moved on, pausing only long enough to dip his warm, wet tongue into the hollow of her navel. She squirmed at the ticklish sensation and heard a soft laugh.

He settled between her legs, and she looked down at him from her elevated position. He pressed her thighs apart, opening her to his close inspection. Her face became so warm so fast that she was convinced she was as bright as a candle. Then he licked his lips. Wait, he was really going to put his mouth—

"Don't stare," she begged, cupping her hands over her red cheeks. He lowered his head and breathed her in. "Oh, gods!"

"You're like a flower here," he said, low and needy. "Beautiful pink-and-red folds. Your scent makes my mouth water." As if invoked by magic, her sex pulsed and tingled, ready to bloom.

"Vallen," she keened. His head snapped up, and he looked at her with such desire that she couldn't help a whispered oh. The flicker of heat she'd seen earlier was now a bright flame, one that almost overpowered the cold emptiness of his blue eyes. Another pulse of their heady magic filled her, and she restlessly rubbed her bare calves against his flanks.

"Say it again." He slid his warm hands over her hips, gaze fixed upon her face. She hadn't meant to call his name but it had slipped out. Why was hearing it so important to him? Because she avoided using it? "Shumei, please."

Or maybe he liked knowing just how little composure she had left. She curled her hand in front of her mouth and hid behind it as she gave him what he wanted. "Vallen," she groaned.

His eyes glazed. His lids drooped shut. Then he plunged his face between her legs and nuzzled into her flesh. Something hot and wet pulsed against her.

Crying out, she slammed her hands onto the thick rug and pressed her head into the pile of pillows beneath her. Instinctually, she drew her legs back, boots scraping the rug. With more room, he was able to slip his fingers between them and spread her lips like the petals of a flower. His hot breath felt amazing. Then he found her clit with his tongue—

She jerked in reaction. So did he, shoulders jumping under her thighs.

"V-Vallen," she gasped. She lifted her hips, seeking more.

Vallen panted openmouthed against her pussy, for he felt the pleasure just as she did. He dipped his tongue between the shivering walls of her sex and felt the wave of bliss in his loins. He flicked the smooth, slick knot of nerves above her entrance and his hips cupped the floor of the tent. He repeated this endlessly, shoving his tongue inside and then retreating to tease her clit. He still hadn't taken it with his lips as he had said he would earlier, convinced it would undo them both far too quickly for his liking.

Then again, he was close to falling apart just from tasting and smelling her arousal. He pulled back.

"No, don't stop," Shumei begged, even as she gratefully relaxed her shaking lower half. Her lover rose to his knees. His lips were glistening.

"You are glorious," he said, voice incredibly low—inhuman. Its resonance went straight through her. She shivered, not sure whether from fright or anticipation. What sensations would follow if he lost all control?

He stared at her as he loosened the ties at his waist. He could have undone the flap in front, but instead he shoved the last of his clothes down to his knees. His cock emerged, long, thick, and flushed. The tip glistened, and the shaft bobbed lightly in time with his heartbeat. She mewled at the sight and barely resisted pulling him in with her legs.

"Tell me what you want, Shumei," he said in that impossibly low voice. She shivered again, her desire deepening. "What do you want? And where?" He held his sex in his hand and looked pointedly at the crux of her legs. She knew exactly what he wanted to hear.

"I want your cock," she breathed, emboldened by her lust. "My pussy wants it." He shuddered at her plea, sending back a wave of satisfaction that made her melt. She twisted with impatience. "Please, Vallen. Hurry."

Taking her legs with him, he leaned over her and caught his weight on his palms. Her feet were in the air, her hips tilted at the perfect angle for her body to accept the cock waiting a kiss away from her core. She moaned at the open, erotic position he had put them in. Her knees were close to touching her shoulders, but her legs were spread wide around his torso, so she had room to breathe. Swiveling his hips, he dragged his sex over her mound and prodded for entrance.

"Vallen, there's one more word I don't know," she panted, heart hammering. His blazing blue eyes, so close to hers, were wild with want. But the emptiness in them now pulled at her, begging for something more than pleasure—even if he didn't say so, even if he didn't know so.

"What is it, then? Before I go mad," he said, guttural.

"What does *fuck* mean?"

A great wave of need washed over her, one so powerful it drew a broken cry from her throat.

"It's what I'm about to do to you," he said, nudging the head of his cock into place. "I'm going to fuck you until this insanity leaves me."

He was still speaking when he pushed into her, sliding smoothly all the way in. They both cried out, feeling the sensation twofold. She white-knuckled the pillows beneath her, toes curling inside her boots.

Vallen had to admit that though the binding had prevented him from stealing Shumei away, its physical effects more than compensated. To think he had regretted using it for the first time, or that he had even thought to abduct her when watching her resist her desires, and then submit to them, was so satisfying.

96

He hadn't discarded all his dastardly strategies—he did want her in a way he had trouble articulating, and not just as a reliable source of energy. But seeing her reach for him, hearing her moan his name and beg for his cock after sensing how hard she tried to deny the pleasure she wanted—pleasure from him... After the life he'd once lived, he shouldn't derive so much gratification from it. But that was it, though, wasn't it? Gratification, not triumph. He needed her energy, yes, but he somehow also needed to be the one to fulfill her.

He pulled out slowly, watching for her reaction. Though she had closed her eyes the way many women did, he loved the way she sank her teeth into her lip and turned her head aside when the sensations were too intense. He thrust, marveling at the warm suction of her body pulling him in. Her brow tightened and her lips parted around a sharp moan. He did it again, earning a new sound. He did it again and again.

Shumei was drowning in bliss, awash in heat that slowly covered her in a thin film of sweat. Her legs bobbed lightly in the air as he rocked over her, sighing harshly with every thrust. The sound of it and the motion and the thick, heavy air... But his rhythm was too slow, his strokes too shallow, and she was left at a plateau of sensation with nowhere higher to go.

"Tell me to fuck you hard," he growled in his demonic voice. "I won't hurt you, but by the dueling gods, I'll come close."

"That's what I want," she panted, looking up at him. There was a hint of worship in his blazing eyes.

"I want you to say it." He thrust a little deeper, eliciting a gasp. "You know how."

She did, and she couldn't hide behind her hands this time. "F-Fuck me, Vallen," she said, forcing past her shyness. "Fuck me as hard as you want."

He leaned into her, pushing her knees to her shoulders, and gave her what she'd asked for. The only thing louder than the deliciously vulgar slap of their skin was her long, lurching moan. His reflected pleasure bombarded her. Her legs bounced wildly. She had a death grip on the pillows. Her mind was going blank.

Her lover let out a roar of delight, one that made her heart jump. The sound thrilled her, for its inhuman quality reminded her that what she was doing—what she was letting him do, begging him to do—was forbidden. She had met him in secret and had disappeared into the forest with him. She had eagerly spread her thighs for a

97

demon. A devastatingly handsome one, but a demon nonetheless. And he'd more than fulfilled her fantasy—he'd surpassed it. Her abdomen seized, and with a final, scratchy gasp of air, she cried out his name.

Something uncurled inside her and flung out a tendril of sizzling power that made her body arch. Vallen had pulled out, letting her legs fall to either side of his hips. The power jumped from her to him, and he gave a shocked groan. His pleasure splashed onto her stomach. He gripped her knee hard and pumped his other hand up and down his cock.

Eyes half-open, she writhed with ecstasy and watched him do the same. She reveled in it, especially the way he stared at the mess he was leaving on her. His abdomen spasmed with every pulse of his seed. He threw his head back, which made his animalistic groans even deeper, and the tense column of his neck was muscular and beautiful.

Seeing his broad, strong body trembling before her made her feel incredibly powerful. And so did the waves of pleasure he emitted. His desire for her had left him in this state, choked and transported.

He gave a final jerk, then a tired sigh as he sank to his heels. Their bodies quieted. Still catching her breath, she savored the afterglow settling deep in her bones.

Her magic had come out again. She hadn't tried to stop it, forgetting she could try, but when it had hit Vallen, she could feel a bit of what Majo had described when telling her to simply pull it back, hold it still, and keep it quiet. Like stopping one's hand from hitting someone or shifting one's balance to avoid bumping into something.

"You are a rare treasure," he croaked, voice almost normal again. His eyes had dilated. "At the end, though, what did you do to me?"

"I don't entirely know," she admitted. "How do you feel?"

"Drugged," he answered. He rolled his head around his neck. "Demons cannot feel the effects of medicinal plants, but we can feel the effects of magic." He looked straight at her. "You have a lot of power. A lot."

Shumei gulped. "Oh." Her magic squirmed like a child trying to escape their mother's arms. She seized her chance and clamped down on it, willing it not to move. It quieted, as easily shushed as Majo had said it would be.

Her lover smiled and his shoulders shook with silent laughter. He brought his hand to his face, rubbing the euphoric expression off as if it were dirt. He was high, she realized, something she'd seen when administering too much *kavua*. Patients would smile for no reason and giggle at the strangest things.

She watched Vallen closely, and when he lowered his hand, he seemed to be in control again. He sat back to remove the rest of his clothes, and his shoes and pants ended up in the same pile as his jacket. Then he stood, rising gracefully, whereas she could barely coax her limbs in the direction she wanted. Was she still sluggish from sex, or was her lethargy a symptom of being fed upon? She supposed time would tell.

Vallen walked to a corner of the tent where a small case and a few other items sat. The way his muscles rippled was fascinating. His rear was especially good-looking in the candlelight.

Next to the case was a stack of cloths. He grabbed a couple and carried a bowl of water over. She laid her legs flat and helped him clean herself up, but she was more of a hindrance than anything.

This wasn't the first time he'd cared for her after sex, and they had already done carnal things together—several times—but she grew embarrassed anyway. She crossed her arms over her bare chest and pinched her thighs together. She hadn't thought ahead to what happened after she'd fed him. Should she get dressed and walk out? *See you in a week?* Did they need to discuss where to meet next time? And did she know the way back to the clearing? She hadn't really been paying attention. Should she ask him to take her back?

The only thing she could think of to lessen her embarrassment was talking. "Why didn't the mist come out? I thought that was how you fed."

"The energy came with that touch of power you gave me," he said. "Much faster than the slower absorption of the mist. I suspect my giddy state was because I took in too much too fast."

Yes, she supposed that made sense. Her magic had woken only recently, some time since she'd last seen him. Did that change how she'd feel afterward, physically? Did that mean she wasn't a normal human woman anymore, or at least not like most others?

He finished drying her and tossed the towels aside. She began to draw her dress shut, but he stopped her with a light touch on her wrist.

"Please, not yet. A few moments more," he whispered. The emptiness in his eyes had grown, and though she wanted to be free of his intoxicating presence, she couldn't deny the plea she saw in them. The loneliness. She pushed her dress open again.

He moved slowly but surely over her, and she couldn't help covering her breasts. They had been kissing and groping and so much more just moments ago, and yet now the intimacy seemed too much to bear. Why did she feel so self-conscious?

"I wish to hold you," he murmured. "Let me share in your warmth."

Why? she wanted to ask, but she couldn't speak. Her thoughts were a jumble. Was he doing this as part of his pledge to fulfill her fantasy? The forbidden lover, dangerous and passionate but also sweet and dedicated? Or was this his own desire? She couldn't know which, not when he was so quick to hide behind that emptiness and the cruelty it had bred.

He laid on the pillows beside her and pulled her into his arms. Her heart leapt, and she prayed he couldn't feel it through the binding. He kept one arm banded around her and drew her against him with his other hand on her bare hip. Though his cock had softened, that she could feel his loins brushing her stomach made her keenly aware of him. The warmth of his firm chest under her hands, the strength in the arm behind her back, and the scent of his skin, still complex but less subtle than before they'd so vigorously enjoyed each other.

"You smell good," he said. He was also noticing her, it seemed. A smile threatened to curl the corner of her mouth.

"You said this tent was from a place called Kurosa," she said, matching his low, intimate volume. "I've never heard of it. You said it's the City of Dunes?"

"Kurosa is the largest city in the Black Sands, far to the south. If you traveled nonstop on the fastest horse and had no trouble along the way, you could reach Kurosa in two weeks."

"Two weeks?" she gasped.

"Kurosa is not exactly in the Black Sands. It occupies a thin strip of land between the desert and the ocean, so it takes two weeks to reach it because you have to travel around the sands to reach Kurosa safely."

"You can't go through the desert, even with provisions?"

"You cannot walk through the Black Sands during the day. No matter what footwear you have, the heat of the desert will burn your feet and cook the rest of you. One could ride on a desert creature known as a *rakuda*, which can withstand the temperature, but the heat waves rising off the desert are still so great you would pass out in minutes."

"You've traveled a great deal, then."

"I've seen most of our continent, yes."

She tilted her head back to look at him. "Tell me more?"

Though she hadn't smiled when she'd asked, Vallen could hear the fascination in her voice, much like when she'd asked about all the adult words she'd heard. Hers was an adventurous soul, one yearning for more than what little bit of life her village allowed her. They'd even convinced part of her that such limitations were for her own good. She had been stiff earlier but was now relaxed in his arms. He resisted the urge to stroke her side.

"The continent is shaped like a great ox running north. There are many peoples living very different lives, and they all have different names for themselves and their piece of the world. The mountain range we're in is most commonly known as the Jagged Peaks. They are the ox's spine. Your valley is rather isolated, which is why not many merchants come here. The river where you bathe is actually the head of a large branch of rivers that feeds the plains to the west and southwest. Most of the population resides there in dozens of cities and villages. The largest is the capital, Houfu."

"All the goods that make it here come through Houfu."

"Before I discovered you, I was traveling to Stillwood, an immense forest southeast of here. Fewer people live in Stillwood, but its largest city is still something to behold."

Her lover continued his story, describing places she had never heard of nor thought even to imagine in such detail. Ensconced in their cozy, candlelit world, she dreamed of something wider, bigger. She lusted to travel as much as Vallen had with no worries about money or time.

"So the bulk of Kito doesn't touch the ground?" she asked, trying to picture trees large enough to hold up a city.

"Yes. The city's biggest threat is a forest fire, whether born from nature or arson, so they maintain a large unit of citizens dedicated to guarding against them."

"It sounds so unreal and far away," she sighed.

Vallen admired the dreamy look in her eyes. The lust for life he saw in them was infectious. Something softened inside of him, while another part stirred.

"Not so unreal. Not that far away," he said, voice unobtrusive to the naked wants playing across her face. He had suspected she'd been tempted the first time he'd offered to take her away from her village, to give her everything she wanted if only she'd let him have her. She had rejected the offer so unequivocally, but he had been right. Now the question was whether he could tempt her again, this time successfully, by presenting it right. He turned the matter over his mind.

"Vallen," she said quietly, rousing him from his thoughts. He focused on her sober expression, and for half a heartbeat, he wondered if she'd bring up his offer herself. "You were human once, weren't you?" she asked, matter-of-fact.

Shocked, he struggled to form words. "You... H-How did you know?"

"I asked the witch about sex demons."

"So your kiss did buy some information after all." Vallen let his arms go slack, and his erection vanished. Being confronted with one's past could do that.

"How did it happen? Who cursed you?" she asked.

He refused to look at her. "A magic-user, who else?"

"Why?"

A simple question with the most complicated answer to anything she could've asked him. To ask why was to dig up a past he hadn't even thought of, let alone shared with another, for longer than she had been alive.

And yet he found himself searching for a place to start. He wanted to tell her.

"My father was one of the empress's commanders, back when we had an empress. Thus, I was born to wealth and power, and surrounded by people like me. I lived my life as if I'd suffer no consequences—selfish and arrogant." He glanced at her, realizing he was still selfish, still arrogant. Her only reaction was to lift her eyebrows and encourage him to continue.

"My two best friends and I spent most of our time pursuing the ladies of the court—particularly the modest ones—as if they were prizes. We broke many hearts. And then the fresh-faced daughter of a widowed noblewoman came to the capital. I was the one who seduced Miharu and then rejected her. I boasted to my friends of my latest conquest, and my comments about her were...cruel." *And untrue*. But what did it matter now? Miharu and her sweet, trusting nature were both long gone.

"I never suspected the revenge her mother had planned. She had been secretly tapping into the power of the Damned One through his high general, a demon known as Bane."

No one alive at the time had ever seen Bane in the flesh, for the Dark Court's war with the demons had turned away from most face-to-face battles in favor of undermining from within. To Vallen, the demon general had seemed more like a scary tale for children.

"I'll never forget the night we were cursed. The pain was excruciating," he said, closing his eyes. He had been too drunk to move, or even be aware, but the agony of having his magic ripped out had instantly sobered him. "My hair had been black then, reflecting my magical talent, but after the ritual, it was white."

Shumei watched him intently, lips parted and heart pounding. A million questions buzzed in her mind, but she didn't dare interrupt him.

"When we woke the next morning, we were starved for sex. We fell upon our current lovers, and while I stopped before I killed Suzuku, my two friends didn't come to their senses until their lovers had perished. My father slew the noblewoman in a rage, effectively destroying any chance of learning about a cure."

Shumei couldn't help stiffening, but she managed to show little on her face at the mention of a potential cure. The thought had never occurred to her since she had learned the truth from Majo, but if magic worked the way she thought it should, then a cure was a sensible leap of logic. After all, if one magic-user could curse you, couldn't another break the curse? The magic inside her twitched.

"Though my father tried to protect me," he went on, "I was cast out of the court and for a while lived in the hidden estate my father had set aside. Yasuke, the youngest of us, died within a year. And after my father passed away of old age, I wandered the world with my third friend. We sometimes returned to the estate, but we spent more time walking in silence under the moon than anything else in life. It's been fifteen years since I last saw him, and I know not if he still lives or if he lay down somewhere and wasted away."

He sighed deeply, as if the words had cost him more energy than he had gained that day. He no longer held her at all, though she was still tucked close.

"Your third friend, what's his name?" she softly asked.

He stared at the cloth ceiling. "Rosuke. He's Yasuke's older brother."

"You said you had magic, and your black hair reflected that?"

"In my day, crows were the ruling class because we could wield magic, and no one had ever questioned whether magic-users should govern. The darker your hair, the stronger your magical potential. Women always have stronger powers, so the highest seat of authority was that of the empress."

"But that... Well, what happened? I-I've not heard any of this," she scoffed.

"Many in the Dark Court abused their power. Not most, but enough, and the lower classes rose up against us. Blondies are generally free of magic, so they 'humbly' accepted leadership, and slowly erased history so crows wouldn't know what they had once been. They burned the court library, and for time slaughtered anyone who spoke of magic with any sympathy. Some families passed down stories to their children, but they were lost as time went on. Those with black hair neglected their magic because using it had been outlawed, and breaking the law was punishable by death."

"You're saying my—our ancestors were once the rulers? Everything I've been told a-about my soul being tainted, that's all lies? A bunch of blondies made it up?" Bitter anger flooded her chest. He smoothed his hand along her side to soothe her, but it didn't help.

"Magic had been used to hurt them, or at least, those who could wield it had hurt them."

"Why didn't they just kill anyone with black hair?"

"They did. Then black-haired children were born to family lines that had never borne them before. When blondes realized magic would continue to reappear, they...adjusted their narrative."

"So everything people said about magic being evil—"

"Magic is not evil, nor is it good. It is neutral," he explained, and she recognized the same words Majo had used.

"Why do some crows have it intrinsically?"

He shook his head slightly. "All crows have magic."

"What? But Majo said only a few with black hair had it."

"Either she was mistaken or she lied. All black-haired people have magic, almost always stronger than those who acquire it through ritual and study."

"Then...my mother had magic?" she said with no small amount of surprise, wondering how Mama had hidden it her whole life.

"It's possible to smother one's magic," he said with hesitation, as if trying to be delicate. "If you restrict it long enough, you'll kill it. Your mother's magic may have died long ago."

And if Mama had lived, no doubt she would've taught Shumei how to kill her magic too. It wriggled as if sensing her thoughts, and she let it, no longer comfortable squeezing it until it stopped.

"The Divine One chooses to whom he grants magic and how much," Vallen continued. "But his will often seems mysterious. For example, black-haired families usually produce only black-haired children, but occasionally, a child is born blonde, like your brother. There were theories as to why, but no one knew for certain."

"But you said some people can acquire magic. Even blondies?" she asked.

He spoke as if hadn't talked of such things for a long time, his words coming to him slowly. "A blondie would have to pray and perform many complicated rituals over many years, perhaps decades, before they would even feel the slightest touch of magic. Those with dark brown hair can acquire a sizeable amount in only a couple years using simple rituals."

"So you were a warrior of the ruling class. You protected the people from the Damned One."

"Yes, although my friends and I didn't yet have formal ranks."

"Who protects people now? Who fights the demons?"

"They're not demon hunters, but the Divine One's priests do what they can with the barrier charms. Perhaps you haven't met many priests but all of them have dark brown hair."

"I hardly know the local priest," she muttered. "I have to give worship outside the temple."

He sighed with sympathy, pressing his lips into a thin line. "They are among the few who know what the world was like before. They're not substitutes for black-haired warriors, but their dark hair is a sign they have some magical ability. And they're all the people have now to keep them safe."

"How are you able to pass through the barrier charms? I mean, you..." She stopped, no longer comfortable calling him a demon to his face, not when his worst crime had been callously breaking a woman's heart, a crime many men were guilty of.

"Barrier charms work because of the prayers etched into the wooden slabs, written in the language of magic. Most priests can write the phrase but don't know its direct meaning, so there's a couple versions of the prayer out there. One keeps out 'demons,' and the other bars 'creatures of Oblivion.' I am not a creature of Oblivion, so while some barriers can keep me out, yours cannot."

Nodding, she thought of the gifts he had left inside her hut throughout the week, the start of which had been the deer jerky. The next morning, she found a beautiful, sturdy wooden comb, with all of its teeth, sitting in the middle of her palm. Knowing he had been that close to her had made her heart skip. Two mornings later, a bar of sweet-smelling soap was left sitting near her head. Its scent had entered her dreams, giving her visions of strong arms wrapped around her and large, soapy hands running over her naked body.

When Oka had asked her about the gifts, she hadn't been quite sure what to tell him. Even she didn't know why Vallen had been giving her such things.

"Is he trying to win your favor?" Oka had asked. "Does he want something else from you?" Shumei had stared at her brother, breath held. Vallen had said he wanted her to become his mistress, to bring along her brother... Perhaps the gifts were his way of wooing her?

"It's possible," she had confessed. "He wants me to leave the village with him and bring you as well."

Oka's expression had lit up. "Is he strong? Can he fight? Use a sword?"

"I don't know—"

"If he can, you should accept. We wouldn't have to live here anymore. He could protect us," Oka had urged her with more emotion than she'd seen from him in a long time. His plea had nearly left her speechless. She couldn't blame him for urging her to accept Vallen's offer, but he didn't know all the facts. She had told Oka that being friends with a demon wasn't a good idea, and he had seemed to drop it.

"What are you thinking of, dear Shumei?" Vallen asked, soft and close. Goose bumps rose on her skin. His voice still profoundly affected her. Was it one of his demonic powers? Or was it the way he'd said her name?

"Why have you been leaving gifts in my home? I mean, they're appreciated, but I don't know how to feel about them given the nature of our...relationship. And they've caused me some trouble."

With each gift, she had been pleasantly surprised, for all of them had been either sorely needed or greatly wanted. But such gifts weren't easy to hide, especially when the poorest person in the village received them. The soap and comb had done wonders for her hair, which hadn't gone unnoticed. And though she hardly spent much time with others, a couple of people had remarked on the sweet scent she exuded—usually by way of mentioning how she "used to smell." Then there was Akiji, who had gone snooping inside her home...

On top of it all, the gifts were from a sex demon. Harboring any soft feelings for him had to be a bad idea, right? Whether or not he had been human once, he was a demon now.

"What sort of trouble?" he asked, eyebrows coming together.

"Someone found out about the venison, and he confronted me. He suspects a story that's somewhat close to the truth, and..." She averted her eyes. "Well, I can't say anymore that I don't enjoy our arrangement—even if I still resent it on some level—nor can I say the opinions of the villagers would be any lower of me should they discover the truth, but Oka? I don't know what would happen to him if the village learned of us."

Oka might lose her, either to death by angry mob or banishment. He might be forced to live with Kimen and Akki, or struggle on his own to eat and stay warm. At best, he and Shumei would both be banished, but she had no way to guarantee their safety, even if Vallen's offer were still an option. She'd once heard an old farmer whisper to his wife that he wished Kimen would banish Majo...right at sunset.

"Worse, I accidentally used magic on the one who confronted me—when he grabbed at me, and...if that came out, I could be executed."

She took a deep breath, nauseous with worry, and laid her cheek on his shoulder. Vallen said nothing for a moment, just stroked her arm with his thumb, but she waited patiently as he collected his thoughts. He seemed to be the type who wished to say something once and say it right.

"Ever since I met you, I've been...consumed with thoughts of you. I've wanted to touch you," he uttered, sweeping his hand up her flank. She arched in response. "To please you, but I would never risk breaking our deal and losing any chance of seeing you ever again, so I spent my spare time retrieving those gifts. They were my way of showing my desire and, selfishly, a way to keep me in your thoughts. They were never meant as anything else."

"Vallen," she whispered.

"I'm glad to hear you no longer regret the relationship we established, despite its risks. I want you any way I can get you," he uttered, drawing her closer. "And I know I alone cannot change the deal we made. I cannot have you as I truly wish."

She raised her head to look at him. "Is that why you've been more patient? Trying to prove something to me?"

"I've never fixed my worst flaw. From my selfishness and arrogance comes cruelty, and... Well, I thought if I at least tried to be less demanding—"

"That I noticed is a good sign," she said. A genuine smile tugged at her cheeks, but it didn't quite make it to her face.

"I want the name of the man who grabbed you," he said with an edge to his voice.

"Why?" she asked with suspicion. She was certain she didn't want Vallen interfering in any way. If he did, the chance of their relationship becoming known would greatly increase. He must have seen the distrust furrowing her brow, for he was quick to reassure her.

"I promise not to hurt him or even contact him while our deal still stands, but give me his name."

She pressed her lips together, waffling on whether to tell him. But he had made a promise and he hadn't broken one yet. "It's Akiji."

He nodded in response and held her a little closer. She had so many more questions for him, such as the magic language he'd mentioned, but she had already tarried long after their agreed-upon exchange and her lethargy from earlier had thankfully vanished.

Any moment now, she'd pull away and get dressed. She'd ignore how soft his lips looked and stop thinking of all the sensations his mouth and hands had wrung from her. She'd not be tempted to linger in his warm embrace. Any moment now.

"The candles are low," she said, gazing into his heavy-lidded eyes.

He gently stroked her hip. "I have many more."

"But we've already..." she said even as warmth flowered between her thighs. Only some of it was from him.

"Only if you want me. It's your decision." He sounded calm, but everything about his expression pleaded with her to say yes. His furrowed brow, his hot stare. Watching him struggle to rein in his dominant streak was...affecting.

He had told her to clear her entire morning, yet she hadn't been gone more than two hours. Oka wouldn't expect her for several more.

She definitely wanted him again. She wanted him as much now as when she had first seen him that morning, and she didn't even feel all that guilty about it.

"Shumei?" He blinked as if pulling out of trance and tried too late to conceal his longing. He shook his head. "It's al—"

"Yes," she said quickly, quietly.

That look came into his eyes, one full of hunger but also elation in gaining control—so typically male. He was going to free his passions, overwhelm her, and usher them both to a wet, noisy climax.

She yelped as he pounced on her, rolling her beneath him once more, and this time she almost grinned with excitement.

Chapter Eight

S humei rapped her knuckles on the hard wood of the village
leader's door. It was delivery day again, and Akki would need
her medicine. Surprisingly, the door opened in a matter of seconds, and Akki's smiling face greeted her. Well, it was a sunny morning after all, so her joints wouldn't be bothering her as much as usual.
Akki's smile was as false as ever, though.

"I was wondering when you'd get here. You always make us wait,"
she clucked. Shumei regarded her blandly, for she was half an hour
earlier than usual. Kimen stood beyond the entry, sulking. She realized Akki was up early to make sure he couldn't try something again.
Akki was a mean woman but also a jealous wife, for which Shumei
was grateful.

"Good morning, Madam Akki, Leader Kimen," she said, bowing
her head. Akki made a pleased hmm at her deference.

"Well, come in, child. Leave your nice new shoes at the door and
have a cup of tea with us. We have much to discuss," she gushed,
waggling her fingers within Shumei's lowered line of sight.

Shumei had decided to arrive early, knowing that Akki and Kimen would keep her longer this morning. She still had things to do
at the field before dusk, and no doubt Akki would want to talk about
marriage.

Once they were all seated around the table with three cups of
steaming tea in front of them, Akki paid for and took her medicine.
Though she was still as pale as before, the good weather had made

whatever illness she had more bearable, and her improved mood meant she was all too happy to dish out her insults with a smile.

"Well, now. Your twentieth birthday is almost here. How inspiring that you made it so long, especially after losing your father," Akki needled. Shumei kept her eyes on the steam rising from her cup. "You'll need to marry soon to take some of the burden from your shoulders. You can't take care of your brother and the medicine field all by yourself. Your mother barely managed it and look what happened to her."

Shumei barely suppressed the snarl that threatened to curl her lip. "Your thoughtfulness truly humbles me," she replied, glad she could keep her tone even. Akki wasn't wrong about working the field alone and still providing for Oka, but Shumei was doing it. In fact, the field seemed to be flourishing lately. The plants were growing fast and full.

"Akiji tells me you rejected his offer of marriage. Why would you do that, Shumei?" she asked, smile hardening.

"I do not love him."

Akki waved her hand in front of her face as if shooing a fly. "Love is not a factor when it comes to marriage to a crow. You should count yourself lucky Akiji has deluded himself into thinking he loves you. How you feel is irrelevant." She pointed her thin finger at Shumei. "The miller's sons learned of your pickiness and withdrew their offers of marriage, so Akiji is the only one who wants you now, and you should be grateful he didn't withdraw his offer as well after your rejection." Akki sounded as though she was trying to be the well-intentioned auntie, but her words burned like acid.

"I don't want to marry him." Knowing Akki and Kimen only had power because Shumei's ancestors had been overthrown made her resent them even more. She glanced at Kimen's reaction to her denials and immediately regretted it. He looked at her as if he would eat her.

"You *will* marry him," Akki said harshly. "What other choice do you have?"

"I will marry no one."

"That is not a choice."

Anger boiled inside Shumei. She made a vulgar gesture under the table, but it didn't make her feel any better. Her magic trembled.

"This is one thing you cannot take from me. I will marry no one," she said forcefully, making eye contact with Akki for the first time since their conversation began.

Eyes wide with contempt, Akki jutted her chin. "You dare to take that tone with me a-and look me in the eye with such rancor."

Shumei didn't try anymore to hide her hate. Hiding it had done her no good. If she was to be treated like dirt no matter what, then she would no longer soften her words.

"Any discussion of my marriage to anyone is over and will never be brought up again. It's none of your business," she bit out, glancing from Akki's livid face to her husband's stunned one. "Leader Kimen, if you would please leave the room, I need to examine your wife. She said she wanted a cure for some illness plaguing her, did she not?" Having Akki sneering at her during an examination was bad enough, so she wanted his lecherous stare out of the room.

"But she's my wife. There's nothing I haven't already seen," he said, confused.

"I will not have you talk over me like a child," Akki railed, slapping her hand on the table. "And Shumei, you will apologize to me with your forehead on the floor, or else I won't buy your medicines anymore!"

"Then you can suffer from aching joints until the day you die, Madam Akki, and you can expect no further help from me for any other ailment."

"Y-You ungrateful little tramp," she screamed.

"I shall take my leave if that's what's required," Kimen announced as he stood, though Shumei suspected he was merely escaping his wife's rising ire.

"Where are you going, Kimen?" Akki yelled, rising to her knees. Kimen, for once, ignored his wife, sliding the door shut and walking away. Akki made a frustrated noise and sat on her heels once more.

"If you'll please face me, Madam Akki," she calmly but firmly ordered, using *please* out of habit.

"What do you think you could do, huh?" Akki said, confrontative even as she turned.

Shumei barely suppressed a gasp. Her magic had done the equivalent of a somersault in her stomach, and though it wasn't nauseating, it was certainly off-putting. And now that it was "at attention," she sensed something.

"Just relax and stay still. It won't take long," she whispered.

Her magic moved excitedly, extending itself into her arms as she raised her hands. There was something in the air around Akki. Or rather, something attached to her. Akki had frozen, possibly aware of the tension between them, but Shumei doubted the woman could feel the touch of magic.

That was it. There was a spell on Akki. Something had been cast on her, and it was clinging to her like a creeping vine. Shumei needed to find the source of it—the head of the plant, as it were.

Shumei reached out, pushing through the force around Akki's body. It gave some resistance, like thick mud. Draped over Akki's shoulders were strands of magic, thin and new. She traced them with her fingers, looking for the root.

"What's happening?" Akki said, voice small. Shumei ignored her and examined the invisible vines of power wrapped around the woman's waist.

There. On her stomach. She found a sort of mass, like the center of a weed, tough and bumpy. She curled her fingers around it, tightening her hold on the spell.

Akki gasped but didn't move. Shumei tried to pull it out like she would with any weed, and Akki gave a pained grunt. Shumei pulled harder, feeling the roots of the weed loosen. Akki croaked, cheeks growing paler as she clenched at her skirt, but she stayed still like she'd been told, though perhaps it was too painful for her to move.

The weed was stubborn, so Shumei let her magic out, and it sizzled along her arm, flicking at the spell in her hand while she pulled. The spell popped out with a jerk. Akki braced both hands to one side, nearly collapsing to the floor, and her breaths came in shuddering gulps.

Shumei could feel the spell sitting free in her hand, dripping down her arm, though the drips seemed to be harmless. Then it began to shake, and her hand trembled as she tried to hold on to it. A high-pitched whining grew inside the room, and she realized she needed to let go of the spell. Now. She twisted and tossed it into the air behind her. Half a second later, it burst with a loud pop and a red cloud rose to the ceiling out of nowhere.

"W-What was that?" Akki asked, breathless.

"Someone cast a spell on you. I removed it, and it exploded...I think."

Shumei couldn't help wincing. Her secret was no longer a secret now. Yet she wasn't as upset by this development as she had thought she'd be. Already, she was mulling the many ways she could escape the village if Akki decided to raise an alarm.

"A spell?" Akki asked, pressing her hand to her stomach. She took in a deep breath and her cheeks flushed with blood. She smiled, a genuine one this time. In fact, she looked ten years younger.

"Madam Akki, this started at the beginning of winter, right?" Shumei asked, wondering how much longer the woman could have withstood the curse.

"I...don't know," she said, confusion replacing her smile. "Why can't I remember that? And why didn't I know it was on me? What would've happened if you hadn't...?"

The most important question, the one Akki didn't ask, was who had cursed her. For a second, Shumei worried she would be Akki's first suspect, but then she realized Akki already had someone else in mind, undoubtedly the same person who had cast a spell on Shumei as an experiment. The one who had unleashed the Burning, and who had admitted to Shumei that she had "unfinished business" in the village.

She couldn't accuse Majo without direct evidence, though. And the witch could still prove useful. Shumei had no one else from whom she could learn about her magic. Although, Vallen had been a magic-user as well, and still was to a lesser extent...

Shumei mentally shook her head. Asking for tutelage from Vallen was perhaps even more dangerous than dealing with Majo. She could stand to let the woman have a few more kisses, but the only thing Vallen would ask for as payment would be meeting even more frequently. She didn't know if she could handle that. Her feelings about him had already grown past what was safe.

"I'm not sure, Madam Akki, but I can find out. However, my concern now is what you'll do with me," she said, giving her a pointed look.

"What...do you think I should do?" Akki asked in a careful tone.

Akki was offering her a way out of this. Yes, Akki could reveal Shumei as a magic-user, but if she'd been cursed once, she could be cursed again. And if Shumei were either banished or executed, Akki would have no one to protect her.

"In exchange for removing the spell, you won't tell anyone of the abilities I've discovered, and I'll find a way to keep this from happening again. We will continue as before," Shumei suggested.

Akki thought about it for a moment, and Shumei waited with bated breath to see if the woman would be spiteful or smart.

"I can agree to that," she replied. "I believe you even cured my stiff joints with that little show. I will no longer be needing your medicines, then."

Shumei quietly regretted the extra income but rejoiced in both the fact her secret was still safe and the fact she would never have to visit the leader and his wife again.

"Agreed." Shumei grabbed her medicine bag and made to leave, but Akki's hand on her sleeve stopped her.

"I won't need the medicine you just sold me. I want my money back for the unused portions." Her face held a hint of malicious joy, and Shumei wondered if Akki and Majo were more similar to each other than either of them would admit.

She tossed Akki's hand from her sleeve. "No refunds." Then she walked out of the house, hopefully for good.

*
**

NOT BOTHERING TO raise her hand this time, Shumei stood in front of the witch's door and waited for it to open. Majo had changed her order midweek, requesting almost twice as many ingredients. She was up to something, and Shumei wanted to know what.

She couldn't let Majo set loose another disaster like the Burning. The villagers were horrible and cruel, but testing spells on them was equally as cruel, and it went against the teachings of the Divine One. The mere thought of a second Burning, or worse, made her feel ill.

Majo's door opened slowly today, and her pale, elegant hand caressed its way around the edge. The outline of her face appeared but was mostly hidden in shadow, so Shumei couldn't tell if she was smiling.

Shumei was careful not to let any of the apprehension she felt show on her face. If her guess was correct, then Majo most definitely knew her curse had been uprooted. The only question was whether she knew who had done it.

"I have your order for this week, Madam Majo," she said, gesturing to the bag sitting on her hip.

"Come in, child," Majo bade, voice sounding deeper, older. "I'm...feeling a bit under the weather."

Shumei stepped inside and shucked her boots, keeping the witch in sight as the older woman closed the door. The candles looked to be newly lit, as though Majo had been resting in the dark before

115

Shumei's arrival. Majo walked slowly, feet sliding as she made her way to the chest in the corner.

"Have a seat. I'll be with you soon," she said.

Shumei's eyes adjusted to the candlelight, and she noticed Majo was wearing a plain black dress. It was the first time she had ever seen the witch in anything so normal. She sat in her usual spot and pulled large bundles of roots and bags of crushed, torn, or powdered herbs from her medicine bag. Majo made her way over, hand clenched around the kols in her fist.

"Thirty-four kols, dear. Thank you for your prompt delivery," she rasped.

"Do you have a sore throat? I can return with the proper medicine to clear it up," she offered.

Majo shook her head and lightly coughed. "That won't be necessary," she said in a stronger voice.

While the witch inspected her order, Shumei looked as closely at Majo as she dared, trying to decipher in the soft candlelight whether Majo had been sucking the life from Akki to stay younger. She didn't appear to be any older, though, not even by a few years.

"Everything's in order. I suppose you'll be leaving, then?" Majo asked with raised eyebrows.

"Actually, I had some questions, Madam Majo," she said uncertainly, wondering if she had the guts to withstand more payment for the information she sought.

"Questions about magic?"

"No, demons."

A smile curled Majo's lips. "Are you willing to pay for the answers?"

Resisting the urge to gulp, Shumei nodded. The thought of kissing the person responsible for the Burning turned her stomach, but the one question she couldn't ask Vallen was the one she wanted the answer to the most.

"What is the question, then?" Majo asked, leaning close.

"If someone can curse a man to be a sex demon, then can another person undo the curse? Is there a cure? How does one administer it?"

Asking for such specifics was risky. If Majo wasn't suspicious of her preoccupation with sex demons before, she certainly would be now. Indeed, the witch's smile wilted, and she narrowed her eyes.

But having removed the spell on Akki, Shumei was hopeful. If she could cure Akki, then maybe she could cure Vallen. Then she would not only free him but also herself. The binding and their deal would be dissolved.

And that was what they both wanted...right?

"Why the interest in sex demons?" Majo asked.

"I was shocked to learn some demons are human-born. You had said other demons were made through ritual, but only mentioned sex demons in particular, so that's why I mentioned them. You also seemed to know of the ritual to make a sex demon, so I thought you might know of a ritual to unmake one," she said, hoping she didn't sound rushed.

It seemed her acting skills hadn't failed her, for Majo's tight expression smoothed as Shumei explained her reasons. The witch's smile grew.

"Your payment shall be a kiss and a touch," she said, curling her fingers against the smooth wood floor as if imagining it already.

Shumei stiffened, ill at ease with the new level of intimacy Majo demanded, but if she was asking for payment, then she must have an answer for her. Shumei reluctantly nodded.

Licking her lips, Majo crawled toward her. She sat next to Shumei and leaned close, holding her weight on one hand. Shumei closed her eyes, telling herself it would be over soon, and it indeed was. The witch withdrew after a moment, pulling her hand from the fold of Shumei's dress and licking Shumei's lips one last time before sitting back.

Shumei could neither repress the shudder that swept over her nor could she stop herself from wiping her lips with the back of her hand. She wished she didn't have to trade something like this with such a monster. Hopefully, this would be the last question she would need answered. She didn't want to know what any future payments would be.

"Do not recoil so. You'll get what you asked for. Now listen carefully. I shall say this only once." The witch seated herself on her cushion again, hands folded in her lap. Shumei gave Majo her full attention.

"In my years of personal study," Majo began, "including a recent, enlightening trip to Houfu, I acquired a great deal of magical knowledge. However, I cannot decipher some of it. Having grown up in this backwoods village, I hadn't learned how to read or write well in my own language, let alone the other languages of the world, some of them old and rarely used—some of them forbidden. The process of learning a new language, or rather, an old one, is time-consuming.

"For this reason, I cannot give you a detailed answer, but according to what I can read, the Incubus Curse can be cured. The curse itself requires a special circle drawn upon the floor, and an altar must stand in the center. The focus, or magic-user, must obtain the curse's main component, semen, from the one to be cursed, who must also be in the circle, upon the altar.

"An invocation must then be spoken, but I cannot decipher it, nor can I read what exactly is done with the main ingredient. However, an outline of the ritual for a cure follows the curse. It is done in the same manner, but the invocation is different, obviously. The main component is used in a different manner as well."

Nodding, Shumei felt a spark of hope. She could cure Vallen, she knew it. New questions were popping up like daisies, but the one to ask was not sitting in front of her.

"I see. Thank you, madam."

Something about Majo's explanation was bugging her, though. The witch had mentioned a special "circle" as if she had seen something too complicated to describe. She had talked of not being able to read something—old languages and invocations.

The witch had a book. A spell book. Slowly, Shumei turned her gaze to the thick volumes sitting in a tall stack by Majo's sleeping mat. She had a feeling the witch wouldn't keep such a thing sitting out, though. It would be somewhere safe. Somewhere with a lock.

"Ah, sweet Shumei. How glad I would be to tell you all you ever wished to know, if you would only give me access for the night." Majo sounded as breathless as she looked, and Shumei gulped as the witch seductively drew her hand down her neck.

Shumei hastily stood, her nearly-empty medicine bag in one hand.

"Until next week, Madam Majo," she blurted, walking to the door and slipping on her boots. Majo bid her a good day, but Shumei didn't bother to acknowledge it as she whipped the door open and darted outside. She ran all the way to her next delivery.

Chapter Nine

Lying in Vallen's arms, Shumei sighed in contentment as the flutters in her belly continued to send little pulses of remembered pleasure throughout her loins. When she had come to the field at dawn today, the binding had combined his ache and hers, creating a pulsing fire in her sex and making it dripping wet as she emerged from the trees. Whereas he had been calm and composed last week, this morning had found him agitated, pacing back and forth impatiently.

He swept her up in his arms before a single word had been spoken. After swiftly carrying her to the tent, in a new location today, he had wasted no time shucking their clothing. The next fifteen minutes had been nothing but hard, sweaty, toe-curling sex. However, he had been in his right mind enough to have a small cloth on hand this time to catch his pleasure after he had pulled out, saving them from cleaning it up afterward.

Having caught her breath, she curled closer to the warmth of her demon lover and remembered the news she had wanted to tell him since yesterday morning. She had many questions to ask him, not all of them about his curse, but for now, she enjoyed the orgasm still sitting warm inside her.

Vallen held Shumei close, a little saner after a week without her. He had nearly screamed in his need to be kissing her, holding her, pleasuring her so well that her nails left indents in his skin. And the last few minutes of waiting before she'd arrived had been the most gut-wrenching moments he'd had in too many years to count. He had watched her walking toward him, impatience clawing at his insides. He knew every curve hidden under her dress, but he'd wanted to see her naked flesh. He knew the flavor of her skin and her lips, but he'd wanted to taste her.

He had all but ripped off her clothes when they'd reached the tent, then pushed her on a pile of pillows before following her down. After a frantic moment of foreplay culminating with sliding his fingers inside her to double-check if she was ready, he'd wasted no time before plunging inside her. Her legs had been tight around his waist, and her heels dug into his clenching buttocks as he'd rammed his way to release.

He knew he would take her again before she left that day, should she allow it, which he had the feeling she would. He might even take her twice more.

"Good morning," she sighed, smoothing her hand across his chest. Her cheek was pressed to his chest, one leg thrown over his thighs. Her black hair was spread out behind her, draped over his arm.

He smiled, realizing that, except for some whispered or groaned words before, they hadn't yet said anything to each other.

"Now it is," he answered, stroking her shoulder.

"Tell me more about the continent. I've now heard of the Black Sands and Stillwood. Where else have you been?"

"Hmm," he said, wondering where to begin. He could tell her of the Northern Highlands, where they had a...different way of controlling crows. Or the area known to most as the Barrier Forest, which held back... "The Creep is a lifeless wetland that lays partway between here and the Black Sands. It is largely uninhabitable, but there are a few settlements."

"How can a wetland be lifeless?" she remarked, lightly exploring the muscles of his abdomen.

"It's not really known. Something in the soil, perhaps. I know the water isn't safe to drink, but it rains almost constantly. The locals survive by selling rainwater to travelers, and dried peat to traders.

"On top of the mud traps that can suck you in you're not paying attention, the mire stretches for many leagues, and the lack of sunlight or color can make a solitary traveler feel just as lifeless as the mire."

"How can anyone live there?"

"There are spots of land that can support buildings, and some game to hunt or trap. Most locals are in self-imposed exile, and they do not like visitors, especially ones who seduce the only unattached female."

He winced remembering their escape from the young woman's room into the pitch-black night. Rosuke had been right on his heels as they'd tramped through the mud with absolutely no light to show the way. They had been lucky their horses could hear their whistles and were able to come to their aid.

"So you and Rosuke were there together?" she asked, voice tight.

"Are you all right? You sound upset," he said, looking down at her, but her face wasn't at the right angle for him to see her expression.

Shumei squeezed her eyes shut, angry at the pang of jealousy she felt from hearing about one of his past lovers. She didn't even like him. Well, that wasn't true. She had come to like him. He wasn't what he had seemed to be, and she wanted to help him. He had once been human, after all. Worse, he'd been forced to become exactly what he'd fought against.

So perhaps she was jealous of his previous lovers, but she was also envious of how much he'd seen and experienced while she'd been stuck in a tiny village for twenty years. She wanted to travel, to have adventure. She wanted to see the endless expanse of swamp, to see the city of tree houses in Stillwood. She wanted to see the heat waves rising from the Black Sands—at a safe distance, of course.

"You've been to so many places," she eventually replied. "The farthest I've been is the next village over. I wish to see what you've seen, to experience it. The world feels so much bigger when I'm with you, and I want to embrace it."

"You can have your wish, Shumei," he said, tilting her head up to look at him. "End our deal, and I will be glad to take you wherever you wish."

Her lips parted at his generous offer, but she knew she couldn't leave—at least, not yet. She had learned something extraordinary with her last visit to the witch, and if Majo had stashed a spell book in that locked case...

"You haven't asked me about the kiss I received yesterday," she said. He showed no outward reaction to her blatant dodge. She knew he had felt the kiss on his lips when it had happened, that he would know the witch had not only kissed her this time but had also touched her breasts.

"I was preoccupied with taking off your clothes," he admitted, and she wasn't quite sure if he was joking.

"I asked her about the Incubus Curse." He stiffened beneath her, verifying the name of the spell that had turned him into a demon.

"You let her kiss and touch you just to learn about my curse?"

"Yesterday, I removed what I assume was some sort of spell the witch had cast on the village leader's wife—"

"And you performed magic in front of a blondie?" he asked, incredulous. She lifted her head. "Why haven't you been banished from the village yet?"

"Because I saved her life and because it could happen again, so she promised to keep my secret, but that's not the point." She pressed close. "If I could break Majo's spell when I've had no training, then perhaps I can dissolve your curse," she said fervently. "I asked the witch about it, and she said there was a counter-ritual to unmake the curse."

"She knows about me? By the dueling gods, Shumei, you risked yourself in front of the village leader's wife, and now this—"

"I asked in the vaguest way I could think of. I would not let our secret be known to anyone I don't trust. And I don't trust her, but she has knowledge I need."

"You could have asked me, Shumei. I only have the limited kind of magic granted to a sex demon, but I still know everything I learned in the Dark Court. I do not want you to let that woman near you. She is dangerous," he said vehemently, sitting up. She sat up as well.

"What would I have to trade with you to get answers to my questions?" she asked flippantly. "You already have my body, and I have no money. The last payment you could ask is one I will not give." She spoke firmly, pulling her dress toward her to cover her nudity. She was tired of being naked during their fights.

"I would not ask for any payment," he scoffed. "I didn't think I would, but I enjoy speaking of my time in the Dark Court. I enjoy sharing my knowledge and experiences with you despite how those experiences came to be possible. But you didn't trust me enough to even ask if I would answer your questions. Did I not tell you about the history of the way things used to be before magic was maligned? Did I not tell you my sordid history, even the things I'm deeply ashamed of?"

He sounded hurt, and she realized that being the only person he'd talked to about his past was a rarity she hadn't even recognized. Likely none of his previous lovers had even known about his human past. He had trusted her with something painful, and she had too readily hinted at his possible existence to Majo.

Vallen couldn't hide his pain in that moment. By her own admission, and even knowing Majo practiced destructive magic, Shumei had gone to the witch for a way to be rid of him. Breaking his curse had been merely secondary.

He wasn't sure why he should be bothered by it, though. Why wouldn't she seek the advice of someone she knew to break her bonds with a demon? He should have been gladdened to know he may finally be free of his curse, but to know she was trying to escape him? That rankled.

"Did you not discuss your transformation with Rosuke?" Shumei answered his question with her own. Though he hadn't seemed to notice her staring yet again at his naked lap, she forced herself to focus on his face.

"Losing our magic that night... Even now, talking about it is painful," he said, shaking his head and closing his eyes. "That warm weight you feel inside was torn out of me. We were all screaming. I thought I was being gutted. How could I talk about that with Rosuke? How could I dig it up, knowing the memory would hurt him?"

Tears stung the backs of her eyelids, and she almost crawled into his lap. She had already formed an attachment to the solid lump of warmth in her belly, and the thought of it being violent ripped out made her want to wrap her arms around her stomach.

"Tell me about him?" she asked.

"Rosuke?" He turned quiet as he stared at nothing. His expression softened. "He's my best friend. I was an only child, so he's the brother I never had. I trust him with my life."

"What was he like?"

"Was?" He glanced at her before she could conceal her grimace, but she was quick to correct herself.

"Before the curse, I mean. I'm sure he changed afterward." It wouldn't do to imply Rosuke had died in the fifteen years since Vallen had last seen him. Vallen had already lost so much.

"He's always been funny. Quick to make a joke. And he's so confident."

"What does he look like?" She made sure to use present tense this time.

"He keeps his hair long. The women of the Dark Court used to say his eyes were like the ocean. Though it's been many years, I still remember his face. A pretty face, I suppose. Better-looking than mine."

She was taken aback at that. Everything about Vallen made her mouth water. She thought him the handsomest man she had ever seen. Rosuke was better-looking?

"He would still make jokes after we were cursed," Vallen continued, "but they grew in bitterness the longer a cure eluded us. Sometimes I'd see a different person when I looked at him, when he thought I wasn't watching. He seemed...destroyed," he said, pain in his voice.

"Why did no one cure you? Surely others knew of the counter-ritual?"

"The noblewoman had bound herself to a demon, but no one in the court had learned of this. In return for her soul, the demon gave her incredible knowledge, including a book that was lost soon after she was killed. The curse and the cure vanished with that book. My father, realizing he and his men had destroyed the only person who knew the counter-ritual, searched for the Devil's Hand."

"The Devil's Hand? Is that the spell book's name?" she asked.

"Well, no. I don't think it has a name, but it's my only clue for identifying it. The book's black cover is said to have a large handprint pressed into the surface."

"So your father never found any trace of it?" she guessed, shoulders sagging.

"No." He looked away, bringing up one knee to lean his arm against it.

She glanced at his well-displayed cock sitting innocently in the white hair between his thighs, and her heart skipped. Forcing her gaze elsewhere, she directed her thoughts back to their discussion. *Could it be possible?* The witch had known about the curse and the cure, saying the details were lost to her because the spells were in a language she didn't know.

"Vallen, the language we're speaking, is it different from what was spoken in the Dark Court?" she asked, trying not to get her hopes up too soon.

"Yes. At the time, Common was the language of the lower classes. Its grammar and writing system is completely different from the court's language, Mahou, which was based on the first empress, Suzu. She would speak in tongues for days at a time after communing with the Divine One. It is the language of magic."

Shumei nearly got distracted at the idea of communing with the Divine One but managed to stay focused. "If someone who speaks and reads Common saw a written form of Mahou, would they be able to study it and learn it on their own?"

"Over several decades, maybe. Otherwise, they'd have to learn it from someone who knows Mahou, and that is few people."

"Do demons know it?"

"Demons can speak many tongues, including Mahou. Bane supposedly knew dozens of languages, some of them long-forgotten, even to me."

She locked eyes with him. "What if I told you the Devil's Hand might be in Majo's possession?"

He went stiff with surprise, but his expression was unconvinced. "I would say that's impossible. My father spent the rest of his life searching for that book. Rosuke and I searched for it for dozens of years after Father passed." He shook his head and closed his eyes. "After a hundred leads turned up nothing, we lost hope and gave up. All we grew to care about was staying alive and keeping our souls out of Oblivion."

"Did your long search turn up any evidence the book had been destroyed?" she asked, leaning forward to touch his arm. It flexed under her grip.

"Like I said, the book disappeared. No one knew anything about it, not even if it was destroyed. Given that, I still wouldn't believe the book sits so close at hand," he said, dropping his head. "Please, Shumei. I don't want to hope. All the things taken from me that night—my magic, my humanity... None of it destroyed me, but losing hope? That nearly broke me. I can't do it again."

"Majo didn't merely claim there was a cure," she said, pressing on. "She actually described parts of the curse and its counter-ritual. She was vague because she said she couldn't decipher everything, but she talked of a complicated, special circle and said completing it was the most difficult part of the curse." He slowly raised his head, eyes blazing. "At the center of the circle, the man to be cursed is placed on an altar." His nostrils flared, but he didn't interrupt. "The witch didn't know how it's used in the ritual, but the main component of the spell is semen. Once that component is consumed, the focus casts the Incubus Curse with an invocation."

Vallen let out a harsh sound, releasing the breath he had been holding. The naked shock on his face confirmed Majo had known more than anyone should have.

She had it. Majo had the Devil's Hand.

It explained why the witch had trouble making her spells work and why she hadn't actually done even more damage yet—she couldn't read all of it. It also explained why she was using magic powerful enough to kill dozens of people, suck the life from another, and perform vain enhancements using potions mixed with rice wine. It explained why she always ordered such large amounts of herbs and roots. She was experimenting, perhaps selling some of her more successful results for exorbitant prices.

"Vallen, your cure is in a locked chest in the witch's hut. You can have hope again," she said, gripping his arm.

"There is no way for me to get it," he said, defeated and slouching. "The witch would not give up such a book, and though I can get inside the village's barriers, the witch has barriers I cannot pass. I could sense she was practicing strong magic inside her home, but I could not come close without tripping an alarm spell that tells her of visitors."

Which explained why Shumei never needed to knock.

"When I had my magic," he continued, "I could have easily dispelled everything she has in place and bound her magic before she could even say half a word. But now? Now I'm powerless. It's one thing to search for the book and another for me to get it." She frowned, disliking his desolate tone. He always acted so confident and pushy, but to hear him talk of giving up after locating the single object he had been seeking for centuries...

"I could trade her for the information we need. Perhaps she'll trace a copy of the right page for—"

"No, she'll definitely know of our affair then. She'll use it against you, and I don't want you to trade anything more with her," he commanded, slashing his hand through the air. She jutted her chin at his authoritarian attitude. "If you're lucky, she won't use her magic on you, but she'll ask for much more than a kiss. No one touches you but me." He snatched her wrists, forcing her to drop her dress.

Neither of them spoke. Enthralled by the heated look he was giving her, she took a deep breath of the charged air swirling between them. Arousal stirred and quickened. Her gaze flicked to his lap. He wanted her again.

"Don't you want to be human again?" she asked.

"Of course," he said, teeth clenched. "But not if it risks you." He pulled her to him, sprawling her across his lap. His show of strength stunned her, and she could only cling to him, overwhelmed, as he hungrily pressed his lips to hers.

She opened for him, letting in his expert tongue, but this kiss instantly felt different. It was desperate, almost angry, and it made her heart pound. He wasn't seducing her this time, evoking pleasure with every swipe of his tongue and every pull of his lips. He was conveying an emotion. She wished she could see his eyes. She was certain she'd find something other than cold emptiness.

They came up for air together. She swept her hands across his shoulders and down his back. He kept one arm around her and squeezed his other hand between them to grasp her breast. Her pert nipple grazed his rough palm. He captured it with his fingers and pinched.

Both moaned low as they sought each other's lips again. She ran her thumb over the shell of his ear and savored the pleasant tingle she knew he was feeling. Vallen was rougher, tugging her nipple before massaging the abused flesh with his palm.

"Gods, I want you again. Even more than before," he rasped when their mouths broke apart. He pressed his hand between her legs.

"Then have me. Take me," she begged, eagerly opening her thighs to give him more room. He slipped two fingers inside her and rubbed her clit with the heel of his hand. Moaning, she twined her arms around his shoulders.

"Bear down," he hotly whispered into her ear. She fervently did so, clamping around his thrusting fingers while he licked and sucked on the side of her neck.

A thought popped into her head, one that gave her a great thrill. She brought her hand down, found his stomach, and stroked lower, searching for the part of him she'd been sneaking glances at for the last ten minutes. She grasped his cock, and he grunted against her cheek, fingers pausing. His hair brushed her cheek, and his breath was hot on her ear. The jolt of his reflected pleasure was so strong it was almost painful.

He was so hard—as hard as stone—but also as smooth as the expensive pillows they reclined upon. Her fingertips barely met on the other side and the heat of him was surprising.

"Does this feel good?" she asked.

"You know it does," he rasped, voice dropping to a pitch that made the air shudder. He wrapped his slick fingers around hers and helped her find the right grip, the right speed. It felt so good she could hardly breathe. "Up and down like this. Y-Yes."

"Oh gods," she gasped.

"Use your thumb and press on the tip like thi—" He groaned against her neck as she followed his instructions. She cried out, pumping her hand faster.

"I want more," she pleaded.

"Then put those beautiful lips around my cock and suck the pleasure out of me." He wrapped his hand around her nape, lay back, and pulled her head between his legs.

Still holding the base of his cock, she rolled onto her stomach and took in the sight of him before her. His muscular thighs, spread to make space for her. His heavy-lidded stare, hot and eager. His chest, heaving with excitement. He was so masculine, and the part of him grasped within her greedy fingers was the most masculine part of him.

She pressed a chaste kiss to the tip and mewled at the mirrored pleasure she felt. The tip was the most sensitive part, like her clit. Slowly sliding her mouth down the length of him, she softly moaned the entire way, stopping about halfway when the back of her throat stopped her. She heard another, deeper moan and glanced up at the wild look in his eyes.

His familiar taste was strongest here. She could even smell his spicy soap. She groaned, hips curving as a particularly hard stroke of her tongue produced a pleasant result. She did it again, then again, until she and her demon lover were both gasping and crying out. Though she was having some difficulty concentrating on sucking, she didn't and couldn't stop doing it.

His hand settled on the back of her head, gripping her hair and helping her remember her rhythm as nectar seeped from the flower of her body. Following her lips with her stroking hand felt even better as she bobbed up and down. The hand in her hair tightened, and she could feel their orgasm was close.

"S-Stop. I long to come inside of you as I once did, but stop," he choked out, pulling her head up.

Thighs trembling, she licked her lips as she gazed at him with every ounce of want raging through her veins. She also wanted him to come inside her and didn't really care where anymore.

"By the dueling gods, you're beautiful," he muttered. He rose over her and pushed her onto the pillows behind her. She tried to part her thighs and make room for him, hoping desperately that he would be inside her soon, but he turned her over and packed a couple pillows beneath her hips.

"What are you doing?"

"You'll see. Spread your legs," he commanded. He braced his knees between hers, nudging her thighs wider, and she lifted her hips in understanding as she gripped the tassels of nearby pillows.

He stroked the curves of her backside, exhaling hard as if enjoying the view. One of his hands left her, and she felt the engorged tip of his cock. She bit her lip and whimpered. He worked the head against her labia until it notched in the hollow of her sex. Then, holding her hips, he sank deep.

She cried out, arching her back and twisting the tassels in her hands. He swiftly drove himself inside her over and over, slapping their bodies together and frothing their abundant mutual arousal. The pillows were soft and yielding against her belly as she rocked over them, and the rug was a thick cushion under her forearms.

He would pull out soon, but she didn't want him to. She wanted her deepest muscles clamping his cock as he pumped his warm seed into her. She wanted him grinding against her, their connection unbroken.

"You can come inside, Vallen. Please, please come inside me," she begged.

He let out a shout of exultation as he pulled her into his thrusts. The magic between them flexed like a plucked bowstring, and she knew the rule she had placed on him earlier had been altered. Bracing his knees farther apart, he spread her wide and sank deep.

She gasped into the carpet, her orgasm taking over as she drenched his cock with her pleasure. He whipped his head up, groaning her name as he exploded inside her. Her magic flared, reaching into her lover's body from where they were intimately joined. Then his sweaty chest was on top of her, and they gulped for air together.

"Oh, Shumei," he groaned before pressing a tired kiss to her shoulder. He was still pulsing inside her. "Why did you change your mind?"

"Can't—breathe," she gulped, rolling him off. He landed with a huff on a few pillows next to her, and once she'd caught her breath, she turned her head to look at him. "I liked how it felt," she admitted, pulling her legs shut.

"I thought you didn't want a demon to get you with child. Although..."

"Although what?" she asked, lying alongside him.

"Demons are sterile," he said, voice tight.

"What?"

"Well, it wouldn't do for a sex demon to impregnate every woman he siphons energy from," he tersely explained.

"Why didn't you tell me before?"

"Even if I'm a demon now, I was once a man. And for a man to admit he's sterile..."

"How do you know?" she asked, dubious.

"The Incubus Curse refers to an actual demon from Oblivion, though they're all but extinct now. I'm an artificial incubus. Early into our curse, Rosuke and I studied incubi in the court library, and we learned they, like all demons, are sterile." He glanced at her. "The Foul One cannot create that way. Thus, altering our nature altered our...virility." He rolled his shoulders in resignation and sighed. "The purpose of an incubus is not to reproduce, at any rate. The Damned One wants to kill humans, by any means."

"So incubi do kill women? Even artificial ones?"

"Yes, and incubi feel no remorse about it. Some artificial incubi kill, but some—like Rosuke and I—merely get enough energy from a woman to last a month, and then let her go. With any incubus, the woman doesn't feel any effects until they've become addicted. Depending on how often an incubus feeds, a woman may last as little as a few days or as long as a couple months, and incubi typically have many concurrent lovers in their lair."

"Effects?"

"Once a victim is addicted, they can barely move or think straight. All they want is their lover."

"But you and I—we've had sex many times. Why don't I feel the effects?" she asked, alarmed.

"You are special. Women with magic could last years, and in the days of the Dark Court, noblewomen were taught young how to recognize and kill an incubus before he could even touch them."

"I see. Well..." She pulled into herself. "I wanted you to, you know, be with me—i-in me when we both..." She hid her mouth behind her hands. "I wanted you to because you're not a demon to me, not anymore. And...I like you," she admitted, turning her face away to hide her blush.

She couldn't believe she'd admitted it. Gods, would he use it against her? She felt certain he wouldn't, but—

A rush of elation flooded her senses. Her cheeks flushed and her head grew light. Without meaning to, she nearly smiled in reaction.

Then she realized the emotion hadn't come from her. She was feeling Vallen's joy. He was ecstatic to hear she liked him.

He slid his arm around her, and she could practically hear his grin when he nuzzled her ear and said, "I like you too."

Still hiding her face, she couldn't hold back a smile. Oh Divine One, her heart was nearly choking her. How was so much happiness even possible? Surely the binding was to blame—for some of it, at least. She couldn't count on feeling this happy all the time. Could she?

Chapter Ten

Making her way home, Shumei pocketed her earnings of three kols from the Takebe family. Master Takebe had accidentally sliced his wife's leg with a hand sickle, but a clean bandage over twenty-two stitches and a poultice of comfrey mixed with a few other herbs now adorned her thigh.

The morning was quiet, and the soft thwacks of field tools could be heard from one's door. A thick cloud of mist had settled into their little valley, and her cheeks grew moist as she walked along the path that curved around to the northern end of the village.

She had realized recently that she wouldn't have ever met Vallen if the village had let her grow her medicinal plants within the barrier charms. "Tradition"—a word she'd come to loathe—demanded she not be given any arable soil within eyesight of the village, so she had to walk fifteen minutes on an unprotected path to reach her field.

Not that she'd have been able to grow her sort of plants within the charms. The village's fields tended to collect water, which made growing rice easier, but which drowned almost everything else.

A month had passed with little change. She had continued to meet Vallen one morning a week, discovering each time new ways to experience pleasure. When they weren't exploring each other, they talked of his travels and the Dark Court. She always listened with rapt attention, wishing the Dark Court would return someday. The stories he'd told of past empresses and the nobility and their achievements... It all sounded like fiction, but all of it was true.

Meanwhile, the Burning had run its course. Forty-nine people had perished. The neighboring villages deigned to resume trading with the survivors, all of whom had to be in the fields in order to grow a sufficient harvest. Young children and the elderly were spared the hardest work, but even they had to help with easier tasks.

Akiji, after staying low for weeks, had rebounded from being thrown farther than what even a strong man could have managed, and had upped his efforts in pursuing Shumei. The only time he was free to press his suit was an hour before sunset when returning home from the fields, and he usually found her after her evening bath. He even accosted her when Oka was with her, but those confrontations were short.

The days grew warmer. The village celebrated the beginning of summer with an annual festival, from which she was banned of course. Her brother was always extended a special invitation, and most years, she and her mother convinced him to go and enjoy himself. This year, though, he would not be swayed and instead spent the day fishing with her.

She grew more comfortable around Vallen, but not even his story of falling from a tree house in Kito to be left dangling from a rope, naked, had brought a full smile to her face. She was happy, though. She had developed an unexpected intimacy with him, even an easy friendship. There were, of course, times when his overbearing nature tried her patience, but she was all too eager to push back, having grown to enjoy their disagreements almost as much as their mutual pleasure.

Though she didn't want to, she continued to deliver plants to the witch. If she stopped, Majo would be suspicious, and her weekly visits were still a good opportunity to glean new information. Shumei's efforts to learn more of the Incubus Curse without any more groping were for naught, though. Majo would not divulge anything about demons without payment, and Shumei was no longer willing to let the witch touch her.

As if on cue, the witch's hut loomed ahead, emerging from the thick morning fog like a rotten tooth. Shumei had once gotten a thrill when passing by, but after learning of the terrible things Majo had done and the power of the spell book she had locked in her home, Shumei only felt a sickening anxiety.

Coming to a stop, she lifted her hand and hesitantly nudged her magic. It buzzed happily and sent out a trickle of power that filtered up to her fingers. Warmth suffused her arm and hand, and she slowly stepped forward, hoping to feel the alarm spell surrounding Majo's home.

Time slowed as she walked toward the back wall of the hut. Shumei made sure to keep her hand in front of her feet to avoid accidentally tripping the alarm with the wrong limb. She was ten feet from the house when a sizzle of power passed over her fingertips, making her gasp with surprise. She jerked her hand back and then more cautiously explored the spell's perimeter. It felt rather like the prickly surface of a cheap blanket.

Her magic fluttered happily in her stomach as she passed by the hut without tripping the alarm. She surmised the alarm spell was on the house rather than on a certain area, for the spell's edges matched the dimensions of the hut. When she was past the witch's home, she dropped her arm and continued on her way, walking down the path with her back to Majo's door. She was almost behind the next house when the witch's door creaked.

Heart racing, Shumei froze with indecision for a painful second before flattening herself against the house next to her, hiding behind the corner as she watched Majo's door swing inward. The miller's youngest child, a daughter of marriageable age, crept from the witch's home and looked around for any prying eyes. Shumei pressed herself even closer to the house she'd hidden behind, grateful for the field tools hanging on the wall that made seeing her difficult.

The witch leaned out of the doorway, lips curved in an indulgent smile, and Shumei's stomach clenched. Then Majo kissed the miller's daughter. Shumei's jaw dropped, but she refrained from making any sound. The young woman returned the kiss, and when it ended, she sighed happily.

"It was wonderful, madam," she effused in her high, young voice. "When can I come again?" The witch's whispered response was too low for Shumei to hear, but judging by Majo's face, she was saying something flirtatious. The miller's daughter giggled before giving Majo one last kiss and walking away.

Shumei almost tsked aloud but stopped herself. The miller's daughter was stupid for having such a relationship with the only woman in the village more hated and feared than Shumei was. Then again, Shumei hadn't heeded the rumors about how dangerous the witch was, either. She knew that Majo might simply have a sexual relationship with the miller's daughter, but she doubted that was all that the witch wanted with her. Majo would likely test a new spell on the naïve young lady, if she hadn't already, but Shumei could do little about it right now.

She backed around the corner of the home she'd been hiding behind, staying as quiet as possible. When she heard the witch shut her door, Shumei allowed herself to breathe. She decided to wait another a moment before continuing on her way, and made sure she escaped without showing herself to the closed door, putting several houses between her and the witch before stepping onto the path again.

Vallen watched from the safety of the trees as Shumei entered her home. Whenever he had nothing else to do, he watched over her and had been waiting for her return from what he assumed to be a house call. Her expression seemed strained as she ducked into her hut, and he faintly heard her call her brother's name. He made a mental note to ask her about what had upset her.

Lately, new emotions had stirred within him, feelings he hadn't even experienced when he was human. More than ever, he wanted to have Shumei for his own, but not to own her, if that made any sense in his head. He also felt the warm flare of hope and wondered when he might have an opportunity to filch the Devil's Hand from the witch's fortified home.

He remained hidden, thoughts swirling, as the sun rose above the shoulder of the mountain, cutting into the cloud of mist that had settled over the village.

Though she hadn't said anything, he knew that Akiji had been bothering her lately. He'd occasionally feel a spike of fear followed by a rush of anger, and only after he'd caught sight of them one early evening had he realized who the source of her distress was. They had been too far away for him to hear anything or to see much of Akiji other than his hair color and build—nor could he have intervened even if he had seen him from a closer vantage—but the uneasy dance of their interaction had been clear. Akiji trying to prevent her from leaving the conversation, Shumei trying to walk past him without being within arm's reach.

A few weeks ago, Vallen would have secretly wished for Akiji to successfully steal a kiss. His deal with Shumei would be broken, and he'd be free to have her the way he wanted her. Now, however, it wasn't enough. He didn't want her to be with him because of a clause in their bargain. He wanted her to choose him. He wanted it more and more every week, and it was slowly whittling away at his patience.

He dealt with his selfishness as best as he could by giving her subtler, easier-to-hide gifts such as a few extra logs for her family's cooking fire or clearing spiderwebs from her path to the field after learning she had an aversion to them. He also savored the small signs of her growing fondness for him. Oh, they still disagreed on occasion—whenever she brought up a new strategy for stealing the Devil's Hand, in fact—but she played with his hair whenever he carried her to the tent, and kissed him goodbye without prompting or begging. The last time they'd been together, she had even reached for his cock when she'd grown hungry enough for a second round.

And of course, he showed her how he felt whenever he gave her pleasure, always striving to keep her clutching him close and gasping and focused solely what he was doing to her. Besides kissing and rubbing where she was most sensitive, whispering softened vulgarities into her ear never failed to send back a flare of elation. She especially liked hearing, in specific detail, how much he'd wanted her over the last week.

If she was feeling bold, she'd admit her desire as well. How many times had he recalled his favorite whispered confession that she sometimes wanted him so much she wished she could touch herself? But of course, with her brother sleeping nearby, she didn't dare.

He wondered when she'd admit how often she had sexual dreams. He didn't sleep, but he recognized the difference between the slower simmer of waking desire and the sudden, intense flare of dream-induced lust. And he was curious to know whether he made regular appearances in her sleep.

I'll ask next time I see her, he promised himself. And if she were willing to share any details, he'd be sure to make her dreams come true.

TWO DAYS BEFORE her next appointment with Vallen, Shumei was scrubbing the small bit of cheap wooden flooring at the back of her home. Oka was outside hitting their sleeping mats with his wooden sword to chase the dust away. She had done well to keep up with the medicine field and had earned a day at home, though half of it had been spent cleaning. She and Oka were almost finished, though, and she would be able to have her bath and spend the rest of the afternoon playing with her brother.

With her thoughts turning to Vallen as usual, she wrung out the cloth in a fresh bowl of water, already half-finished with the floor. She had always hungered for the pleasure he brought her, but lately, she was growing increasingly restless to be in his arms again.

She found herself wishing impossible things—that he was just another villager whom she could meet publicly—and a few things she was afraid to admit even to herself, such as whether she wanted to take him up on his offer to run away with him. Yesterday morning, she had even contemplated calling out for him even though it wasn't their usual day to meet. She had become addicted to him. Not a good sign.

"Shumei," Oka called, frantic. Pulling out of her distracted thoughts, she turned to the reed door just as someone pushed it aside to walk in.

"Akiji, you're not allowed in my home without permission," she said, sighing like a mother with a troublesome child. He smirked, eyeing her as if she were his to ogle.

"What a thing to say to your future husband," he chided, staring overly long at her breasts.

"I. Am. Not. Marrying. You. How much longer must I say no? Doesn't it hurt you?" She didn't know what she was doing wrong. Nothing she said seemed to deter him.

"That you worry about my feelings shows you care, my love," he cooed. She tensed. Something in the way he held himself frightened her. His expression and his voice were mild, but he stood restlessly, limbs subtly twitching as if he were barely keeping himself under control. Her magic swelled in reaction to her fear.

Oka rushed inside, sat next to her, and wrapped his arms around her waist. "She doesn't want you here."

"Do not fret, young master," Akiji said with condescension. "I merely bring news this day. A warning." She felt a tickle at the back of her neck. "It seems last night, the miller's daughter went missing." The tickle turned into a drop of cold fear running down her spine, and she knew her face showed it.

"The rumor is a sex demon stole her away to feed off her until she perishes, the poor girl," he said, crossing his arms as he stared intently at Shumei.

She had to physically stop herself from surging to her feet in shock, but allowed herself a gasp of surprise. Having no reaction to such dire news would be damning.

Had Vallen abducted the young woman? He couldn't have. Wouldn't have. Was he being framed? That had to be it. So who had found out about their affair? And if that wasn't the source of the rumor, was another sex demon in the area? She thought of Rosuke, but then her mind pivoted yet again.

The miller's daughter. She and Majo had been together, and the witch liked to experiment. Majo had the Devil's Hand. She was the only one to whom Shumei had spoken about sex demons.

Majo had done something terrible.

"What will the elders do?" she asked with real dread in her voice. She clutched Oka close, trying to act the tremulous and naïve maiden, but she wasn't sure if she had fooled Akiji or not. His face gave away nothing.

"They and Leader Kimen are organizing a search party." He perused her hut as he spoke. "We hope to find the girl before the sun sets."

"We?"

"Yes, I am going with the search party. I'm young and fast," he said, slapping his athletic legs for emphasis. "All others will stay in the fields today."

"Then why have you come to me? Daylight is wasting." She was glad there was a reason for him to be gone the rest of the day, but she worried for the miller's daughter. The young woman was innocent. She couldn't have known whom she was dealing with when she'd decided to take Majo as a lover.

"I'm here because I love you, Shumei," he said, eyebrows crinkled with hurt, as if he were astonished to have to explain himself. "I wished to warn you of this demon's presence. If it ever touched you..." He gulped, eyes closing. He breathed in deep but was shaking. "I would go completely mad," he whispered. She wondered whether he hadn't already passed that barrier.

"I shall stay alert. Please go," she said. Oka trembled.

Just as quickly as it had come, the anger drained from Akiji like water from a pierced skin. He relaxed, hands hanging limply at his sides. When he opened his eyes again, he was calm and composed.

"Yes, I should go," he said, backing up. "That demon must have a daytime resting place. If we find it, we'll destroy it. I'll protect you." She remained silent, hoping he would leave on his own. She didn't know if what she chose to say would hurry or delay him. "Stay safe, my love," he professed, one hand raised toward her. Then he was gone. The door swayed from its two flimsy hinges, but it wasn't the only thing still reeling.

She needed to warn Vallen. Perhaps he already knew the village was aware of him—or at least, someone like him—and he could certainly take care of himself, but if warning him helped at all, she would do it.

"What's wrong?" Oka whispered, tilting his head up to look at her. "You're pale. What are you not telling me?"

Even if she had managed to fool Akiji into thinking the presence of a sex demon was news to her, she wasn't so sure about Oka. She hadn't told him what kind of demon Vallen was, but that didn't mean he couldn't suspect the truth.

"Please finish cleaning. I'll be back in an hour." She sounded calm but couldn't smooth the worry from her face as she disengaged from the tight circle of her brother's arms.

"Where are you going?" he asked, still clinging to her sleeve. "Isn't it dangerous right now?"

"Don't worry for me," she said with a shake of her head. "Worry for the miller's daughter. I'll be back soon." She bent to kiss his cheek before leaving.

The day was beautiful, clear, and breezy, but one could feel the tension in the village. Shouts occasionally disturbed the peculiar silence. No one was in the fields. The wind tossed her hair, and the sun warmed the side of her face as she stealthily crept between huts.

From behind the corner of a hut a few doors away from her own, she spied upon the raised wooden stage in the heart of the village, where festivals and occasional town meetings were centered. She first spotted Kimen, who was directing a large group of young men. Then she saw Akiji, the miller's two sullen sons, and about ten other men, all wearing grim faces. She couldn't hear a word of what Kimen was saying, but after a moment, small groups broke out of the larger, each moving in a different direction.

Each group would likely search their own slice of the surrounding wilderness, but probably not as quickly as she could run. If she started now, she could gain a large lead on the pair going in her intended direction. They would have to sweep the surrounding forest, but she could run flat out.

Deciding on her course of action, she turned and made for the path leading to the medicine field. She clambered up the first hill and skidded down the other side, not for Oka's sake this time, but Vallen's.

Not watching her feet, she accidentally slipped and landed hard on her hip, forcing a pained cry from her lips. After a few tears, she stood and kept going, furiously wiping away the moisture on her cheeks as she half limped, half ran the rest of the way to the clearing where they'd first met.

She couldn't let them find him. They'd kill him, or he'd kill them. Either way, someone would die, and she didn't want that to happen if she could stop it.

"Vallen! Vallen, I need you," she screamed, turning in all directions. Birds were startled into flight. "Vallen, where are you?" For several minutes, she ran about the clearing, going from edge to edge, calling his name.

Time was running out. The searchers would be drawing near, and she couldn't run the risk of them hearing her shouts, but she still called for him, hands cupped around her mouth to carry her cries farther.

Yet he didn't appear. She tried screaming at her loudest, calling his name over and over again despite the pain in her throat. She turned in a full circle, seeing nothing but trees and grass, and screamed his name one last time. By the time her shout faded, she was staring teary-eyed at the empty path from which she had come. He couldn't die. Not when the restoration of his humanity was so near.

"Vallen," she weakly called, voice cracking. She gulped past the scratchy lump in her throat, pressing a hand to her stomach where her magic fluttered. Her eyes stung and she shut them quickly, willing the tears to go away. She wouldn't cry, not for him. Who was he that she should cry for him? Who was he that she should feel any need at all to protect him?

By the dueling gods, he was the man she loved. That was it. That was the restless longing building up inside. She wanted to be with him because of love. She loved him, may the Divine One help her.

A twig snapped and she cried out in surprise, whirling around. From the edge of the clearing, Vallen pushed a low branch out of his way and stepped into the open grass. His sky-blue eyes, clear and bright, looked at her with obvious concern, and as she took in his unscathed appearance, a tear escaped and slid down her cheek. The gold tree embroidered on his dark green jacket was clean. No dirt or blood. The same with his pants and boots. He was perfectly fine.

"You screamed?" he called, mouth turning up in a smile as he completed his own inspection of her well-being.

"Vallen," she whispered. Her feet moved of their own volition, and she propelled herself toward him. He came farther into the clearing, brow furrowed. She quickly closed the distance between them and threw her arms around his shoulders, pressing herself flush against him. "You're safe," she sighed, nuzzling the bend of his neck. His spicy musk filled her nostrils and assured her he was really there. His arms came around her, holding her close, and his lips brushed her temple.

"What's wrong? Your screams scared the life out of me," he muttered. "And you're limping. Did someone hurt you?"

"They're coming. They know about you," she whispered, pulling back.

He knitted his eyebrows. "Who's coming? Villagers?"

She nodded. "About fifteen men. They're searching for a young woman who went missing. Everyone says a sex demon did it." His forehead tightened even more. "I know you wouldn't do that. I know." A second tear slid down her other cheek. "And what's more is I saw this girl leaving Majo's hut last week." He brushed at the tears glittering on her cheeks. "Whether she knows you're real or not, Majo is using my questions to her as inspiration for some story to cover up what she did. She's framing you."

She fisted her hands in the fine material of his shirt and pulled him tight to her. Vallen engulfed her in a comforting hug, and his heart swelled almost painfully. She was worried about him.

He'd had his suspicions when he'd found her screaming her heart out at their meeting place. Judging by the tear on her cheek and the relief on her face when she'd seen him, he had guessed the inevitable had happened. He was ready for her to ask him to take her and her brother somewhere safe, having been either banished or slated for execution. He'd expected her to beg him for protection.

And he'd have gladly given it, but instead, she was there to warn him. To protect him. On top of it all, she didn't believe the rumor. She knew he was innocent.

"Shumei," he uttered, gently urging her with a roll of his shoulder to lift her face. Tears stained her cheeks. Her eyelashes were spiky with more of them. He looked down at her pink lips, which were puffy from her worried bites. Her heart thudded against his chest.

Something inside him crumbled, and he pressed his lips to hers, willing her to shed the despair on her face. He should have been the hopeless one, not her. She was already soft for him, lips parting to accept his tongue. She stretched her arms to encircle his neck, and he leaned down to deepen the kiss, trying to comfort her with his body.

He ran his hand over every inch of her he could reach. But she was still clutching at him and shaking, so he wrapped his arms around her and concentrated on their kiss for as long as he dared before disengaging the slow wrestle of their tongues.

"I'm safe," he whispered against her mouth. "I'm safe, Shumei."

"Thank the Divine One." She sought another kiss, which he eagerly gave.

"I want you," he growled, palming her backside. "I want to wrap your legs around me and take you right here, standing up." He felt her shudder as she curved closer to him, but then he heard a sigh of disappointment.

"I want you too." An understatement. She wanted nothing more than to climb his body. "But the men will be through here any moment, and I told Oka I'd be back within the hour."

"Yes, of course," he said, disappointment knitting his brow. He relaxed his arms, and soon they stood clasping only one hand.

"Be careful," she bade.

"You as well. I'll see you here in two days," he said, a smile kicking up the corners of his mouth.

A smile pulled at her lips, but apprehension wouldn't let it come out. The best she could give him was one final squeeze before their hands pulled apart. She missed the contact immediately but forced herself to walk away. Then, after a quick wave, she turned and jogged back the way she'd come.

WHEN SHUMEI RETURNED home, she pushed aside the reed door that hung across the entrance and was engulfed in a hug. She looked down at her brother, who had pressed his face into her stomach.

"Oka?"

"Don't do that again," he sobbed, voice muffled. "Everyone is talking of demons and people dying, and then you left me here. Don't do it again, please."

"What do you mean 'people dying'? And who's 'everyone'?" she asked, combing her fingers through his hair out of habit. The reed door still tapped the wall.

"Ikuro came by and asked for something to hang from her door to drive away demons. She was scared because demons had gotten past the barrier in Taba and killed a lot of people, but no one knows how."

"Oh, Divine One. H-How did she hear this?" she asked, hoping the attack was only a rumor. Taba, the closest of the plains cities, was too far away for anyone to quickly confirm such an alarming report, but close enough for the villagers to sleep with one eye open that night.

"A couple merchants arrived this morning. They saw what was left of Taba. Said the same thing happened in Aizan a week ago." Sniffing, he hugged her tighter. "They told everyone to get out and go to a big city like Houfu."

"Divine One protect us," she whispered. Ever since she could remember, her life had been relatively untouched by the danger demons presented, at least up until now. She had been told that once, as a child, one had nearly gotten her, though she had no conscious memory of it, and perhaps twice had another villager seen one from within the safety of the village when walking around at night, but never had demons hurt anyone she knew.

Sure, there were stories, some passed down through the village elders, some from travelers staying the night in their village. But never had any of them feared the prayers protecting them would fail.

Shumei gasped with a horrible revelation.

"What is it?" Oka said, pulling back. She barely managed to slap on a neutral expression.

"I-I'm just tired," she said, squeezing his shoulders. He looked at her with disbelief. She didn't want to hide things from him like this, especially when he knew she was hiding something, but to tell him the naked truth would scare him even more. She would rather have his resentment than see him afraid.

"Why don't you talk to me anymore?" he asked.

Oh, who was she fooling? She knew shame rather than protectiveness drove her silence. She also knew she had to swallow her guilt—not only for the choices she had made over the past two months, but the mistakes she had made. She realized, looking back, that she had been and probably still was incredibly naïve, just as Vallen had said.

She had never needed to make a deal with a sex demon. Now that she knew him better, she realized his threats had been nothing but bluffs. Thinking of her feelings for him now in the face of the way he used to act toward her... She wondered if she was delusional, but something about him made her want to protect him, and at the same time be protected by him. Something about him called to her. They had met under such hostile circumstances, but what they found in each other's arms... That was magic.

Many times, she'd wondered if the binding had done this to her, but she knew it hadn't, the same way she could feel her magic lolling about in her stomach. Her love was real. Inexplicable, but real. If only he returned her feelings...

Other things were more important now, though, and she knew she should sigh about her love life at a later time. Pressing her lips together, she took in a deep breath and slowly let it out as she released her brother's shoulders. He took the hint and stood back, regarding her silently.

"Let's have a seat," she said.

Chapter Eleven

Standing at the door of the village leader's home, Shumei used the knocker this time. She wouldn't abuse her knuckles anymore.

Kimen had requested a dose of *kavua*, greatly rousing her suspicions, for it was the best choice on the second day of the Burning. Kimen opened the door as quietly as he could. His wife was notably absent. He backed up a considerable distance, gesturing for her to come inside.

"Let's not waste any time. How much is the medicine?" he asked, reaching into his shirt for his money bag.

"Just one kol, Leader Kimen," she replied. Then, holding out a bag of crushed leaves, she listed off instructions on how to take the medicine.

Kimen took the bag while carefully dropping a single kol coin into her hand as if he didn't want to touch her directly. Though grateful for his restraint, she had a feeling Akki had let slip something to Kimen that had made him wary of Shumei—likely her newfound "talent." *Good. Let him be intimidated.*

"Are the stories about demons in the plains cities true?" she ventured. She hadn't thought she would have an opportunity to ask such a question of the leader, but most news came directly to him, so he'd know the most about anything happening outside their village, or at least be the best person to ask for a guess. Whether he shared any news, though, was up to him.

He frowned at her, jaw working as he ruminated. "Yes, it's true. We are lucky every morning we wake up untouched. I've heard those fleeing the plains will be through our area soon, seeking a safe place to hide. Many have died already," he muttered the last under his breath. "No one knows how many demons. Maybe a hundred, maybe ten thousand. But they've been picking off towns one by one."

"Oh dueling gods," she breathed. "Why now? Why all of a sudden?"

"That I don't know. Now stop asking me questions, crow. Go about your business and leave me to my own," he grumbled, stepping back. The hairs on the back of her neck rose as she heard the soft moaning of his wife from the back of the house. Kimen disappeared down the hall, not even bothering to wait until she had left.

His answers to her questions had shaken her. She hadn't expected the truth, nor had she expected it to be so ugly. Her hands shook as she brought her medicine bag to her chest.

May the Divine One help them. It was only a matter of time, if everyone was to be believed. Their village would be under attack soon, and her thoughts were wild and confused as she tried to think of how she could protect her brother. She couldn't protect the entire village, but him... She could at least save him. She only hoped she could save herself as well. She didn't want to leave Oka behind with no family, no one to look out for him.

There was only one person she could think of who could protect both of them, but she needed to do something first. Turning, she reached for the handle of the door, mind working overtime as she formulated a plan. It would be risky—maybe suicidal. She had to proceed cautiously or else everything could fall apart. As she briskly walked to her next delivery, her mind buzzed with scenarios.

It was going to be a long day.

*
**

VALLEN TOOK ONE last look at the tent he'd pitched—this time just beyond shouting distance from Shumei's field—and tightened the nearest corner line. Perfect. He was a day early setting up, but his newest effort at surprising her would be a fresh-cooked meal, and he'd need time not only to catch a few fish but also prepare them.

Walking back to his horse, he was already imagining the look on her face. He'd be carrying her when she caught the scent of fried fish, fluffy rice, and whatever vegetables he could find—stewed and generously seasoned. She'd look at him with disbelief, then realization, and then he'd finally see her lovely lips curve upward with delight.

So far, she had refused to let him see what was no doubt a winsome smile, but he had heard joy in her voice the last few times they'd been together, the proof of which she had hidden every time. She'd cover her mouth or turn away or press her face against a pillow. He could guess why she felt the need to deny her emotions, and had concluded that whoever had taught her, either through word or action, to smother her happiness was a dishonorable fool. No doubt her village was full of such fools.

She'd smile for him this time, he was certain. He'd serve her a hearty meal, washed down with the best rice wine he could find within a reasonable distance of her far-flung village, and then he'd bring her such pleasure that she'd forget about the world outside the cloth walls of the tent.

He was a few steps from his horse when trepidation gripped his chest. The anxiety was not his, though, but Shumei's, and it was far stronger than he'd ever felt from her before. Perhaps Akiji had caught her alone somewhere isolated. If that were the case, her magic would help protect her, he knew that—and he had promised through the binding never to "accost" Shumei outside of their negotiated trysts—but upon mounting his horse, he found himself turning it toward her village. He'd simply check on her, as he had done many times before, and he'd find her unharmed, as always.

So then why was he nudging his horse to go faster?

SHUMEI STAYED A step outside the border of the witch's alarm spell, tightly clutching her medicine pouch against her roiling stomach.

The magical aura around the hut had radically changed. Before, she had only felt Majo's power in a vague sense, like catching the scent of lightning on the air, but now it exuded malice as tangible as a hot, putrid miasma.

The witch had gained a great deal of power practically overnight. Perhaps the other villagers could sense the change in the same way one might decide to avoid a shortcut for no other reason than just "a feeling," but Shumei had a difficult time acting as though nothing was wrong. Another villager approached, and she tried her hardest to school her face to something resembling normal. He passed without comment.

The miller's daughter had been found yesterday, hands tied behind her back and throat slit. Everyone was blaming a sex demon, but she knew it was no incubus, real or artificial. Someone like Vallen would have seduced the young woman and moved on, and a real incubus intent on sucking her dry of life energy would not have resorted to cutting her throat. Moreover, the young woman had been raped, and Shumei knew that sex demons were only nourished by the willing.

No, the miller's daughter had been killed by something else, and Shumei was about to enter the murderer's home. She had never asked Vallen to teach her defensive magic, but now she wished she had. She hadn't thought she would need it yet. But if she were to achieve her goal, and soon, all she needed was courage.

She stepped forward, tripping the alarm spell around Majo's house. The witch's magic clung to her like cobwebs. The door opened on its own, popping past the catch in the doorjamb and swinging inward with a soft, scraping sound.

"Come inside, young lady," Majo said, not seducing but commanding, voice brimming with confidence. Shumei entered, guard up.

The door closed on its own behind her, shutting them inside the witch's candlelit room. Majo wore her spiderweb dress and looked far healthier than the last time Shumei had spoken to her. She stood straight, her posture full of grace. Shumei had the distinct impression of a spider at the center of its web. She tried not to let her fear show, but her magic prickled with anxiety.

Fighting hard not to curl into herself, she asked the obvious question. "What did you do?"

"Something I've been preparing for years. I sacrificed a lot to get to this day."

Shumei's fright congealed into a cold weight on her chest that stole her breath. The witch's magic pressed down on her head, brushing close by her ears as if she were an insect flying too close to a web. It surrounded her on all sides, touching her, almost as real as drapes hanging from the ceiling, but it wasn't soft... It was wet, clinging threads that oozed sticky sap.

"Have a seat," Majo invited. "I have some tea you should try. A special blend of leaves that came all the way from Houfu." She winked knowingly as she turned to the chest in the corner. Shumei didn't move, couldn't. She didn't want to know what would happen if she ventured farther into the witch's web.

Majo knelt and produced a key from within her belt. The lock on the chest opened with a heavy snap. Inside, a dark, book-shaped object sat on top of the money pouch the witch sought to retrieve. She lifted the book, and a flicker of candlelight flared at just the right angle, just the right second, for Shumei to catch a glimpse of a huge handprint on the cover. She barely stifled a gasp.

So it was true. Majo had the Devil's Hand. Shumei's fear shrank as her desperation grew. The book secured within that chest held Vallen's cure. She had to get it.

Taking the witch's advice, she made her way toward her usual spot, grimacing at the feel of Majo's magic sticking to her. When seated, she set out the plants Majo had ordered and quickly slung her bag across her chest to keep her hands free. If the witch noticed she hadn't removed her shoes, she didn't say anything, nor did she even look at Shumei's feet as she lowered herself onto her usual cushion.

Majo didn't bother to examine her order, hand out to offer payment. Shumei lifted her arm, glad she wasn't shaking, and ten one-hundred-kol pieces tumbled into her palm. She nearly dropped the money in shock and wondered what game the witch was playing at now.

"You can have all of that if you kiss me, Shumei," Majo offered, leaning close.

She should've guessed. Shumei laid the money on the floor and moved away, maintaining the distance between them.

"I cannot do that, madam," she said, trying to stay polite, but the witch sneered.

"Why not? You allowed me two kisses before. You even let me touch you. Think of what you can do with all that money."

"I don't need it."

"Information, then." She stared at Shumei's lips with longing. "Let me kiss you, and I shall tell you anything you want to know."

"Why? You already have someone more willing than me in your bed," she revealed.

Angry surprise flashed across Majo's face. Shumei tensed. She had just baited the woman. There was no going back now. It would escalate from here...

"What did you say?"

The invisible webbing of Majo's magic slid past Shumei's shoulders, sticking in places and otherwise pooling around her in thick folds. She flinched. From the corner of her eye, she swore she saw the threads themselves, more shadow than light. Her own magic reacted in kind, and its warmth spread, filling a larger space inside her.

"The miller's daughter," she continued, despite the fear lodged in her throat. "I saw her leave your home. I saw you kiss her." The witch remained silent, probably unsure of what to say next. Shumei decided for her. "You're the one who killed her, aren't you?" she accused, matter-of-fact. "You did something to her that gave you the power you have now." Her magic swelled upward, its heat relaxing her as well as energizing her. She stiffened her spine. "The only thing I don't understand is the rape. She would have lain with you willingly."

"Little bitch," Majo hissed, curling her fingers into claws. Her webs drew tighter. "I should have bewitched you the last time I kissed you."

"Who did it, then, if it wasn't you?"

"It *was* me, you ignorant brat," Majo spat. She was no longer the calm, confident beauty from a moment ago. The spider had come out. "The one I called upon sits within me. When it came time to perform the ritual, he entered me and took the offered sacrifice as was his right as the King of Oblivion."

Majo moved toward her, and Shumei shot to her feet, feeling lighter than usual. Her magic had spread to her limbs and she felt strangely buoyant.

"I am, as you say, madam, ignorant. How is such a thing possible?"

"My king gave me so much more than I could ever give him. More power than I ever dreamed of, fluency in languages no longer spoken by anyone living, and the ability to change myself however he and I like," she boasted, pulling at the belt of her gown and ripping it in her maddened frenzy. "He now knows me better than anyone ever has or ever will."

Shumei would have watched with horror as the witch flung open her dress, but her magic had pushed out any and all fear. Its warmth was like sunshine bursting under her skin, like the roar of a bonfire raging through her veins. Its heat waves lifted her hair, swirled the skirt of her dress, and raised her onto her toes. She felt safe, calm—even invincible. She looked at Majo with pity rather than fear.

Majo tossed her dress away, and the faint clink of a heavy key hit the floor. She spread her arms and feet, and her skin stretched and rippled. A corded thigh, wide shoulders, and a broad chest... Not the witch's slim form. Whatever demon she had invited into her body was pushing himself to the surface. A hardened male organ, thicker and longer than a human woman could possibly handle, pressed against the skin of Majo's abdomen and threatened to break through at any second. But though the demon had a masculine form, not all of it was human. Bony protrusions broke through at the witch's shoulders, hips, and the crown of her head.

"You see, dear girl," the witch whispered, "I can satisfy you. I can do more than that sex demon you've been lying with. Oh, yes," she said, seeing the surprise on Shumei's face. "I knew about him. From the way you scream, he must be quite skilled."

"Why me?" she asked, too full of magic to stay surprised for long. Her toes left the floor.

"You are far more important than you know," Majo said. "I envy you and your luck. But if I can't be in your place, I'll assume the opposite, as destiny requires. Now that I've done so, my king commands me to make you ours. It's not a hard choice, Shumei." She stroked the long bulge that wanted free of her skin. "There is much more pleasure to be had within his arms than those of the Divine. Much more power to be gained."

Heat was pouring out of Shumei, pushing back the dark threads of Majo's magic.

"And what is my place, madam? What are we to each other?"

"Don't think of what we are now. Think of what we can be. Lovers, powerful on our own and unstoppable as a pair."

How dare she? Majo had killed dozens of villagers, including Shumei's mother. She had framed Vallen, had killed the miller's daughter, and now wouldn't even give Shumei a straight answer.

"Never," Shumei declared. "The things you've done are unforgivable."

Majo frowned, and the demon inside her retreated. "I knew you wouldn't yield."

"For the last time, what is my place?" she yelled. "Who am I?"

Majo smiled wickedly. "My enemy."

The witch sprung at her with a shrill scream. Her sticky threads turned into shards of obsidian, and they sliced through the wall of magical heat keeping them at bay. The world slowed again, like it had with Akiji, and the same low-pitched hum filled Shumei's ears. She twisted, preparing to strike and hoping to dodge the spear-like fingers of Majo's power. She could tell she'd be hitting hard by the strain in her waist.

The witch's hateful face came closer. Shumei knitted her brows with determination. Her right fist connected, impacting the center of Majo's chest.

Disbelief contorted the witch's face. A shard of her magic reached Shumei, slowly slicing the top of her shoulder. It left fiery pain in its wake.

The world slammed into real time. The air whirled around her in a tight spiral as Majo flew back. The witch hit the rear wall of her home with a sickening crack before crumpling onto the floor.

Shumei took in a great gulp of air. She had been holding her breath for those precious seconds that had saved her life. Wincing, she tenderly touched the wound on her shoulder, and her fingers came back covered in blood.

A wave of exhaustion hit her. She swayed and nearly fell. For a split second, she seriously considered taking a nap on the witch's sleeping mat, but shook that ridiculous thought out of her head. She had to stay upright and on guard. She wasn't out of the worst of it yet. The witch wasn't moving, but she was still breathing.

She could end it now. Though she didn't entirely understand, she knew somewhere deep inside she had to kill Majo. It wasn't just because the woman was dangerous. It was somehow her duty, her destiny to kill this woman.

Her mind rebelled. It wasn't natural to want to kill someone. The mere thought of searching out a weapon and using it made her sick. She hadn't come here to do that. She'd come for one reason only, and she had little time.

She scrambled to the case in the corner, remembered it was locked, and rummaged through the witch's discarded dress on the floor. After quickly locating the key, she returned to the chest and unlocked it. Her shoulder throbbed terribly and her head was swimming, but she pushed aside the heavy pouch of kols and pulled out the book she had been seeking.

It was heavier than she would have guessed, and the cover wasn't made of leather or any other ordinary material. It was hard, almost like glass or rock. The handprint on the front was twice as large as hers, and her fingers came away blackened by some dark substance just from touching it. The page edges were dirty and uneven, looking almost as if they had been burned down to the correct size for a book.

She hastily pulled open her pouch, shoved the book inside, and secured the flap with a leather string. The pain in her shoulder had seeped down her arm, leaving it half-numb and tingling. She was losing a great deal of blood. Though unsteady on her feet, she made it to the door and flung it open.

The limp threads of Majo's magic still clung to her as she closed the door behind her. She hobbled a few steps away, the pain in her tweaked hip returning, and paused for a breath of fresh air when she was free of the sticky web.

"Shumei," a familiar voice called. Her heart shot to her throat as adrenalin pumped anew through her veins. She turned in a circle, peering into the mist still lingering in the valley, but she didn't see Akiji anywhere. She had known he'd be seeking her out today. His father was still ordering hangover medicine every week. But she couldn't deliver medicine to him anymore. Nor to anyone.

She ducked onto the path that looped around the village and hurried in the direction of her home, needing to stop there for a precious minute to collect her brother and medicine for her wound. She hoped Vallen answered her call quickly today.

She rounded a sharp corner at a jog and passed behind Master Takebe's home. His wife, already standing after a couple days' rest, was outside collecting firewood from their personal pile and was startled to see her. "Shumei?"

Shumei shook her head. She put several more houses behind her and cut through a grouping of abandoned homes. The families who had once lived here had been the first to succumb to the Burning. It was Majo's fault these homes were dark and silent. She turned another corner—

"Found you," came a growl.

"A-Akiji!" She tried to take a few hasty steps back, but she was too rattled for one morning to move quickly enough. Akiji grabbed her arm. His face was tight with either anger or concern—she couldn't tell yet.

"What happened to your shoulder?" he asked, jerking her closer, which brought a gasp of pain. His eyes widened. "Was it the sex demon? Where is he?"

"Let go of me," she said, strength gone after fighting off Majo.

"No, I'll never let go! You've evaded me for the last time, you d-damned whore."

"What? I-I'm not—"

"I found a note on my door," he said, voice shaking with anger. He brought his hand up so fast she flinched, but then she saw the edges of a crumpled bit of paper poking out of his fist. "Someone was good enough to tell me that the one woman I desired as my wife, the only one in the village I loved above all others, who I swore to care and provide for, was fucking a demon of her own will."

She didn't know what to say. She didn't even know how to look at him. His grip on her arm turned painful.

"Why?" he asked, eyes shimmering.

"Y-You're hurting me."

He shook her. "Tell me why. Why don't you love me?" She felt a pang of pity and knew there was no way to answer him without telling the truth.

"When I look at you," she whispered, "all I feel is fear and disgust. You cannot make me happy."

"And t-this demon doesn't frighten you? Disgust you?" he asked, grimacing at her insult. "He brings you happiness?"

"Yes."

The slap across her face was abrupt, too fast for her to dodge, and it whipped her head to the side. There was an immediate sting in her mouth, and she knew she had cut her lip on her teeth. She took in a fast breath, a tear slipping from her eye.

"I loved you," he screamed in her ear. Blood dripped down her chin from her cut lip, and she turned her head toward him.

"Not love," she insisted. "You only want power over me."

"How dare you dictate my feelings to me." He grabbed her neck and pulled her closer, squeezing too hard for her to breathe. She thought of using her magic, but she was already so exhausted. She didn't know what would happen to her if she tried it for a second time. She might fall unconscious, and who knew what would happen to her while she was at her most vulnerable.

"I was willing to forget what happened the other day," he seethed. "I was willing to help you with your work, give you children, everything I could to make you love me. Why wasn't I enough?" He dragged her close and fisted his hand in her hair. She yelped at the painful tug on her scalp.

He leaned forward to kiss her, and this time, she let him. His lips, hard and rough, bruised as they attacked her unresponsive mouth. The second they touched her, the string of magic tied around her soul snapped. In her head, she heard a gasp followed by thunder.

Akiji pulled back and glanced at the sky. His chin was smeared with blood from her bleeding lip. Evidently, he had heard the thunder too. He looked back at her, and his gaze dropped to her mouth.

"It's not love you want, Akiji—not from me," she said, lip stinging. "You want control. You want the control your father has taken from you."

"You know nothing about what I want." He slammed their mouths together for another kiss, this one more brutal. She was forced to open her mouth and let in his tongue. She could have bitten it, but that would only make things worse. She tried to wriggle away from him, but her strength was gone.

She heard a soft thump. Akiji's sloppy lips mashed against hers. His hand in her hair went slack, and he stumbled a step away before collapsing like a puppet cut from its strings. She dragged her sleeve across her mouth, heart soaring the second she saw who had come up behind him.

"Vallen," she sighed, tears of relief running freely down her cheeks. His expression was a mix of anger and concern, and a long, serrated sword was tightly gripped in his hand. He must have used the hilt to knock out Akiji. She wanted to leap into his arms, but she was barely standing as it was.

Vallen winced at the sight of her. There was blood on the torn shoulder of her dress and on her chin. Her cheek was red where someone had hit her. He could guess who, sparing a brief glance at the waste of breath lying on the ground.

He wanted to pull her into his embrace and tell her everything would be all right, but in that moment, there was only one thing more important than comforting her.

"I never meant for a kiss like that to break our deal," he said as he sheathed his sword. "It wouldn't be fair for me to—"

"It's all right. I wanted to break it."

Heart leaping, he took a step closer. "Why?"

"Because I'm happy when we're together. Happier than I ever thought possible. You're all I think about. All I want," she said, voice breaking. He held his breath. "I love you."

A euphoric smile broke across his face. He wanted to roar his exultation to the sky, but he was too short of breath to gather any air. He hadn't felt so alive in... No, he had never felt so alive. Ever.

Careful of her injuries, he drew her against him and covered her in kisses. "*I love you*," he whispered in Mahou. "I love you so much.

155

The centuries were worth it for you." Clutching at his back, she shuddered against him and sniffed as though crying. He pulled back to check on her and was rendered speechless. Though tears swam in her eyes, what had seized his tongue and his heart was the bright, beautiful smile on her face. Just when he thought she couldn't be more stunning...

A pained moan drew their attention, and they both looked down at Akiji weakly testing his limbs. Vallen held his beloved closer, elation and rage warring within him.

"Leave him. We need to go. I can explain once we've left the village far behind."

Shumei tried not to think about the people who would still need her and her medicines. Ikuro and her unborn baby. Master Takebe's wife, who would soon run out of the poultice for her injured leg. And many people would have summer colds soon.

"We shall collect your brother, then," Vallen announced, picking her up.

"I can walk," she protested.

"You were limping two days ago, your shoulder is bleeding profusely, and you're nigh ready to pass out. Let me carry you, my love," he said in that luxurious voice of his. She smiled again, unable to help herself, and grabbed hold of the front of his jacket. He lit into a run, his steps even and long to avoid jostling her. In only a moment, they arrived at her hut.

"Oka! Grab your things, quickly," she called, trying to speak in a loud whisper as she ducked inside. Oka was stirring what would've been their breakfast, two logs lit underneath the pot, and he turned in surprise when she limped through the door.

"S-Shumei," he squeaked.

"I'm okay, but we have to go. Vallen is taking us away." She threw the last of the water in their washing bowl onto the flames of the small fire. "Gather your things while I get some medicine for this wound. Be quick." He squeaked again, and she turned to see that Vallen had followed them inside.

"A-Are you him?" Oka asked, pointing at him. Vallen let out a puff of air that was probably a laugh, and nodded.

"Oka, now." She reached up with her good arm and pulled a basket of prepared medicines off the shelf. Then she opened her bag, and her eyes bulged. She had actually forgotten about the spell book she'd stolen.

With precious little time to flee, she put off any discussion of it and instead packed up some medicine, a roll of clean cloth to use as a bandage, and the comb Vallen had given her. By the time she turned around, Oka was holding a small bag of his things and standing next to Vallen, ready to go.

"I'm all set," she said.

Vallen ushered them outside and produced a loud, high whistle. Not a moment later, his horse galloped into view from the path behind her house. Shumei had worried they wouldn't all fit onto the animal's back, but she could tell just from looking at the monstrously large horse that she was wrong. Vallen lifted her up first and then set Oka in front of her.

"Hold tightly to the pommel, young man," he ordered.

"Hey, what's going on here?" a man yelled. With a gasp, Shumei looked over her shoulder. Her nearest neighbor, the one Vallen had said was having an affair, had come out of his house. Behind him were several more people, their mouths open with shock as they took in the strange scene before them.

"I'm leaving, Master Akito, and I may never come back," she announced. Vallen pulled himself into the saddle, fitting snugly behind her. "And by the way, shame on you for cheating on your wife." Akito stood there spluttering. Even more people appeared.

"Let's go, Vallen. We've little time," she said, feeling a strange urgency as dread twisted her stomach. Or maybe her magic was warning her.

"As you wish, my love," he purred in her ear. He seemed to relish the new pet name. He nudged his horse's flanks, galvanizing it into a gallop. They took the path behind her hut and were soon out of sight.

Chapter Twelve

Vallen could tell Shumei was anxious to put some distance between them and the village. Every couple of minutes, she glanced back. When they came to the stream—the same one where he had first spotted her—he steered the horse to follow it. His mount had to move slowly to keep its footing, but anyone attempting to track them would have a tougher time of it.

They followed the stream south for quite a distance, stopping only for a few precious minutes to tend to Shumei's wound, but no one said much. His curiosity burned intensely as to where she had gotten her injury—he hadn't seen any sort of weapon on Akiji—but even when Oka asked, she begged they get somewhere safe first. Eventually, the stream crossed an old wagon path overgrown with patches of grass and fallen tree limbs. He turned them again, and the horse agilely picked its way along the trail.

He felt Shumei sag in his arms, and though he worried for a split second that she had lost too much blood, he remembered the fatigue on her face when he had first found her that morning. She hadn't yet explained, but he suspected she had used her magic. She had little experience and no training, so she must have worn herself out. The same had happened often to young amateurs in the Dark Court.

"This is the farthest I've ever been from home," Oka said. Even a voice as quiet as his was startling in the still forest, but Shumei didn't stir from her slumber.

"This is where the adventure begins," Vallen said as the horse swerved around a fallen tree.

"She's asleep?" Oka asked, looking over his shoulder.

"Seems like it."

"Where are you taking us?"

"To my estate, a few hours farther."

"Why did we have to leave?"

"You'd have to ask your sister. I'm as clueless as you." He adjusted his hold on Shumei, making sure she didn't get a cramp in her neck.

"What's going to happen when we get there?"

"Some of that depends on what your sister has to say, but we'll be safe for a while, and we can plan what to do next." Oka fell silent for a moment, but Vallen could tell by the way he fidgeted that another question burned in the boy's brain.

"What's on your mind?" Vallen prompted. "Whatever it is you wish to ask, feel free."

"What are your intentions toward my sister?" Oka blurted.

Vallen was taken aback, not because of the question itself, but because of how the boy had worded it. Oka seemed rather eager to be grown up.

"Well?" Oka prodded, half turning.

"I love her. I intend to make her happy." He sincerely wished he could give Oka something more definitive to go on, but all of their lives were uncertain at the moment.

"Good." Oka then fell silent, seemingly content with Vallen's answer.

Shumei shifted in her sleep, snuggling deeper into his embrace with a satisfied sigh. He pressed a gentle, silent kiss to her forehead, and savored the sweet ache in his heart.

WHEN SHUMEI WOKE, a branch was slowly coming at her face. Then an arm pushed it up and out of the way. Taking in a deep breath, she straightened.

"Where are we? How long have I been asleep?"

"A few hours," Vallen said. "We're not far from our destination."

"Which is?"

"My estate. I had prepped for guests when we first met, so there are a few clean rooms for us, but most of the main building is in disrepair. Be careful where you walk."

"What's that up ahead?" she asked, inclining her head. She could see a break in the road, a thin path only wide enough for a narrow cart. A post driven into the ground served as a marker. Some sort of faded image was carved into it, but she couldn't tell what it was yet.

Oka swiveled his head in all directions. "What's what?"

"You can see that?" Vallen asked, pointing at the fork.

"Of course. It's as obvious as day," she said, puzzled. "It's right there, Oka. To the left?"

"*What's* right there?" he asked despite looking where she pointed.

"A path and a road marker. Can't you see them?"

"I only see trees." Oka's shoulders slumped in confusion.

"Don't worry, young Oka. You weren't meant to see it. The path is hidden by old magic, and though I'm surprised Shumei can see through the spell, I shouldn't be." He turned the horse at the fork, following the hidden road. The image carved into the post was that of a tree once painted green, but the color had nearly washed away.

"You can use magic to do that?" she asked.

"Whoa! I didn't see this?" Oka exclaimed, glancing around.

"One of the old empresses once said there was no limit to what magic could do, only how much we knew. The Divine One grants such knowledge when it's time."

"Empress?" Oka asked, turning back to look at them.

"I'll explain later," she assured him. Oka pouted before facing forward.

Their journey continued without incident, though Oka was reluctant to cross a bridge that only he couldn't see. Once the horse set foot on the first plank of wood, the bridge became visible to him and he quieted.

At last, the path turned to follow an imposing stone wall that was more than twice her height and, as far as she could see, hundreds of feet long in either direction. It stopped just below the canopy and wound around or sometimes through the trees. Vines and other foliage concealed it entirely in some places, but not one stone had fallen out of place. Studying it was difficult, though. She felt compelled to turn away and forget it existed.

"Why don't I want to look at it?" she asked. Meanwhile, Oka was searching for the wall he couldn't yet see.

"It's a spell similar to what hid the path and the bridge, but stronger," Vallen explained. "It makes the object seem unimportant and trivial, like how one would ignore an ant on the ground. Even for a powerful magic-user, this version of the spell is potent."

"I see," she said.

"The longer you stare at it, the weaker the feeling becomes. We'll find the gate soon." He nudged the horse into a canter.

"I assume the wall surrounds the estate?" she asked.

"What wall?" Oka huffed, throwing his arms up. She patted her brother's shoulder in sympathy. Surely he was tired after taking in so much at once.

"You'll see it soon," Vallen said. "Just keep looking to our right, and it'll slowly appear." Shumei watched with amusement as Oka glared at the wall slowly passing them by, making small noises as he resisted the urge to shift his eyes away. "And yes, we're at my estate. Besides the hidden-in-plain-sight spell, there are other nasty traps spaced along the wall and even on some of the trees that appear climbable."

"Magical traps?" she asked.

"Of course," he said near her ear, and she shivered from head to toe. Her shoulder felt stiff and achy, but the rest of her wanted to melt into his arms.

"So how do we get in?" Oka asked, excited. His gaze was pointed at the top of the wall, so it seemed to have become visible to him. She hadn't heard him sound so eager in a long time.

"We'll come upon the gate any moment now. Young Oka won't be able to see it, but I'm curious to know if Shumei can."

Pressured by his comment, she tried to concentrate, but as the seconds ticked by with no gate in sight, she wondered if he had passed it on purpose.

Then she spotted it: an entrance consisting of two large doors taller than the wall and situated beneath an elaborate arch. She could tell some of the forest growth had been pruned, and peered closer at the magical markings carved into the wood. She didn't recognize any of them, but she could feel something powerful on the gate. Her eyes watered as she tried to maintain eye contact with it.

"Very good," he said, close to her ear again.

He dismounted. Oka was rapt as Vallen approached the gate, and Shumei had to admit she was also excited. She expected something grand, like the wave of his hand and a flash of light.

However, he merely leaned into the gate, pushing with what seemed like a minimal amount of effort, and it swung open with hardly a sound.

Oka's shoulders drooped. "That's it?"

"For a normal human, the weight of the door would be much more difficult to push open, but yes, that's it," he said with a smile. "My father cast all the spells protecting this estate. If anyone but me and a few others had tried to even touch it, there would have been a great clanging noise right before you were punched away from the entrance."

"I'm certainly glad, then, that you were the one to open it," she replied with raised eyebrows. "Ah!" A jolt of pain in her wound made her hiss and wince. She touched the bandage Vallen had wrapped around her shoulder. Apparently, the numbness of some hastily applied medicine was wearing off.

"Are you all right?" Oka asked, trying to twist in his seat to look at her. Vallen quickly returned.

"I think I need a new bandage and probably some rest. I still feel exhausted for some reason," she said with a sigh.

"Then let us not delay." Vallen took the horse by the reins and it obediently followed him into the compound.

Like the wall surrounding it, the estate had been built to minimize impact on the forest. Though a few trees had been removed, the largest ones were still in place, and their canopy threw a deep shadow over everything, blocking the midday sun and its heat. The shade also cast a gloom about the place, which had clearly seen better years—better centuries, in fact.

The architectural style was not one she recognized, though what she knew of construction was limited to her village. The main building stood several feet above ground level on an array of stilts and braces. A covered porch appeared to wrap the structure. Most of the outer walls were lattice-type, wooden doors that slid open on tracks, and the paper-thin material stretched over them had ripped in several places. She would expect to see storm doors but supposed either the closeness of the forest or magic—or both—prevented most weather damage.

"I'll take you around to the side with the bedrooms and drop you off at the sitting room. The horse must be taken care of before I forget things in our haste, but I won't be long," Vallen said, guiding them around the nearest corner of the main building.

Though she could see inside a couple of rooms through large holes in the paper doors, the rest of the expansive building was a mystery. The porch, it seemed, had not been cleaned in a while, though it had been swept recently.

"It's pretty dirty," Oka commented.

"The estate hasn't had any staff to clean it in centuries. Maybe that'll be your job soon." She stiffened as the movement of the horse jostled her wound. "I just hope there are no spiders."

"I'll do another sweep as soon as I can," Vallen called over his shoulder.

They arrived at the back of the building, and Vallen hopped up to the porch to slide open one of the doors. The paper looked white and fresh, as though it had been replaced recently. She smiled at a mental picture of Vallen cleaning.

The room beyond the sliding door was immaculate—and dark. Shumei spotted several sets of floor-level tables and cushioned seats with wooden backs. Vallen quickly lit a couple of lanterns, which cast a warm, soft glow. When he reemerged onto the porch, he made a clicking sound with his mouth, and she made a noise of surprise as the horse obediently sidestepped toward the porch, bringing them flush to the edge.

He helped Oka off first, who quickly made his way inside to inspect the room after shucking his shoes.

"This must be an expensive table," Oka marveled. She looked to Vallen with an apology on her face, but he was smiling with amusement.

"Your turn," he said, sliding his arms around her. He plucked her off the horse as easily as taking a jug off a shelf. She found her footing quickly, but he held her in a hug long enough for her to feel the erection confined within his pants and hidden behind the fall of his jacket. Of course, thanks to the binding, she had already known it was there before she had even gotten off the horse.

"If you weren't injured and if we had privacy..." he whispered.

"Me too."

"Whoa, this shelf thing is huge," Oka exclaimed.

"That's a cabinet, young Oka," Vallen said as he guided Shumei into the room.

In addition to the furniture, a sunken hearth sat to the left, ready to be lit. Suspended from a metal rod above it was a large kettle. The rod went all the way to the bamboo ceiling, which was shaped to let out smoke through vents. The cabinet Oka had noted held other cooking implements, and a neat stack of firewood sat against the wall. The floor was made up of a mosaic of straw mats, some of which had been recently replaced. Sitting in one of the legless chairs, Oka wiggled his bottom against the cushion and stroked the smooth, dark wood of its arms.

"What kind of wood is that? It looks as black as night," she said, gingerly sitting in the chair next to Oka's. She gratefully leaned on her right elbow in favor of relaxing her left shoulder.

"The coal tree is found only in the Dead Swamps," Vallen said. "One of the previous empresses liked black, so the entire court copied her when she requested all her palace furnishings be made with coal wood." He moved toward his horse. "I'll be back within the hour with food, water, and some medical supplies. Try to sit still while you wait," he instructed. "You'll look after her, won't you?" he directed at Oka. After he had Oka's agreement, he curtly nodded and left.

"Dead Swamps?" Oka asked, turning to his sister. Shumei smiled.

She spent the next hour talking about their continent and of the old empire once ruled by magic-users, preordained by the Divine One to battle the minions of the Damned One. She had never seen Oka so absorbed.

"How were empresses chosen?" he asked.

She blinked. "I don't know. I never thought to ask." But it was a good question. Oka had opened his mouth to say something else when they heard Vallen's footsteps.

"He's back!" Oka said with glee. He ran to the doors and slid one open. Vallen appeared in the doorway, arms full.

"Do you need any help?" she asked.

"Yes, actually. Young Oka, if you could take the two jugs on top I can manage the rest." Vallen bent his knees so Oka could grab the jug handles, and Oka brought them to the table.

"What's in these?" she asked, leaning forward. The two jugs were made of what looked to be a glassy, white material.

"One is water and the other is rice wine. Forgive me for forgetting which one is which, but it will be obvious when a cup is poured. I'm sorry, Oka, but you cannot have any wine," he joked.

"I know," Oka said petulantly.

Vallen laid the rest of the supplies on the table, including a pile of cloth strips—too many, really—on top of which sat a plate of sliced apple and a bag that clinked when he set it down.

"There's an apple grove on the other side of the main house, but it's early in the season, so only a couple were ripe enough to eat. For now, we have no other food supplies."

"I haven't eaten an apple since before Papa died," she said. Oka's eyes lit up as he grabbed a slice. "What's in the other bag?"

Vallen sat in a chair on the other side of the table. "A mortar and some empty bottles from the supply room. I thought we could use the herbs you brought with you to make a salve. I told you I specialized in defensive magic, and that included medicines, though most of the old recipes have a touch of magic in them. The ones you make are 'all natural,' so to speak." He opened the bag and pulled out small, serviceable bottles that looked more expensive than her shoes.

She was thinking of her own bag of herbs and powders, which probably weren't nearly as effective as what Vallen could make, when she remembered the powerful magical item sitting against her hip.

Her loud gasp drew everyone's stares. Vallen leaned over the table, full of concern. "What's wrong? Are you in pain?"

"N-No, I just remembered! Oh dueling gods, how could I have forgotten?" Using her good arm, she hauled her medicine bag onto her lap and pulled at the knot holding the flap shut. Then she grasped the chalky, black book and drew it out.

"I got it! I got Majo's spell book," she announced with triumph. The shock on Vallen's face was almost comical. Then his expression hardened.

"That's how you got hurt, isn't it?" he asked, too accusatory for her liking. Her defenses slammed into place.

"She attacked me, yes, after I got a confession out of her. She sacrificed the miller's daughter to a demon in exchange for power."

"So you went there to interrogate her. Was that your only reason?" he asked, looking at the book. She could feel how fast and hard his heart was racing.

"There's troubling rumors of demon raids in the plains' cities—massacres—and I felt this urgency to—"

"You're not answering my question. Was interrogation your only reason for going into that woman's house?" Vallen pressed.

"Well, no. I wanted the Devil's Hand. I knew where it was and where Majo kept the key, and I knew I couldn't leave until—"

"If she had traded her soul for power from practically any demon that can answer a summoning—which means it's powerful—then she could have easily killed you," he said, voice raised. "You must have felt the aura of her new powers. You knew she was stronger, and yet you picked a fight anyway. You almost got yourself killed over a book!"

"It's not just a book. It's your cure! I wanted to do this for you. I wanted to give you something you couldn't get yourself." The weight of book was starting to tire her wrist, so she set it in her lap.

"If you had died in that house, trying to give me something I've lived without for countless years, your death would have been in vain. Did you think of what would have happened to your brother?" he railed.

"I took a risk, yes, but it paid off, didn't it?" she yelled back.

"Um, sorry to interrupt," a small voice interjected. Vallen and Shumei glared at Oka, but he didn't flinch, to his credit. "Vallen got something important to him, Shumei's alive, I'm alive, and we're all together. Why argue about something already over and done?"

Vallen clenched his jaw, and Shumei slumped with humility. Her brother had a point.

"It was still a foolhardy decision," Vallen grumbled, sitting back. "She should avoid that in the future."

"I know that, but I couldn't leave without trying."

Silence pervaded while Oka ate enough apple slices to give himself a bellyache, she was sure.

"We need to change that bandage," Vallen said eventually.

"I'll need the mortar and some water," she said.

"I can make the medicine. You'll have a hard time crushing the leaves with that injured shoulder," he pointed out. She nodded silently and handed her bag to him. The all-important, powerful spell book sat on the floor next to her chair, momentarily forgotten.

"What about a needle and thread? Do you have anything like that left?" she asked.

"Don't worry about the dress. There are more where that one came from," he said, pulling out a mass of jumbled herbs.

"No, I... I think I need stitches," she said.

Vallen stilled. "That'll hurt."

"It won't heal properly otherwise. No amount of comfrey will adequately close the wound on its own, even with a tight dressing."

Vallen frowned as he sorted the plants on the table. "Oka, the cabinet behind you, middle shelf."

"Shumei," Oka said softly.

"Please, Oka," she said. "Then take the rest of the apples and explore the forest out back. Don't stray too far, though." He nodded somberly as he stood.

Vallen pulled out the pestle and mortar and began to grind up a couple of carefully chosen leaves. Shumei wasn't sure why, but she was pleased he'd chosen the right plant. Oka placed the sewing set on the cluttered table, grabbed some apple slices, and disappeared into the trees.

Ten minutes later, Shumei sat naked from the waist up and wiped her tears as Vallen tied off the last stitch in her shoulder—sixteen in all. He washed the area with a clean cloth, then smeared it with the salve before wrapping it tightly with a fresh bandage.

"Stay right there and relax. I'll be right back," he said.

She drew the remnants of her dress up to her exposed chest and watched him disappear into the complex's interior, wondering how he could see where he was going when there was no light in the hallway as far as she could tell. She reached to the plate sitting close at hand, plucked the last apple slice, and bit into it, comforted by its sweetness after her ordeal.

When Vallen returned, she gasped at the beautiful dress in his arms—forest green and embroidered with shimmering gold leaves. The artistry reminded her of the jacket he'd worn two days ago.

"Oh, Vallen," she effused. Eager to touch it, she held her blood-stained dress in place and stood.

"The stone oak was my family's symbol," he revealed. "We revered trees in general, so this estate was partially built with the few trees my father cleared, and it was designed to blend in with the forest." She nodded in understanding and stroked the soft dress in his arms.

"Let me dress you," he roughly uttered, stepping close. The emptiness in his eyes was gone. In its place, devotion. He saw her. Really saw her. His lips looked in need of a kiss. They always did, it seemed.

"Please," she said simply. She released her dress and it fell away, leaving her in only her socks.

"Gods, if only I could have you now," he rasped, curling his arm around her waist. "I want to make you forget the pain you went through this morning, but I don't want to tax your stamina right now, not when you need to heal."

"I know. Perhaps in a few days. Can you last that long?" she asked, referring to his demonic need. Vallen chose to take it the other way, grin full of mischief.

"Even if you promised me your body in an hour, I wouldn't last that long. You're too tempting," he said huskily, caressing her backside. His light touch almost tickled and it made her gasp. "I suppose this could be an opportunity, though. I will teach you enough magic to reverse the Incubus Curse, and while you're studying, I shall teach Oka sword fighting. Your injury might have saved you several days on your back, my love."

"Or it may have cruelly denied me the same," she said. He chuckled against her cheek.

"Your brother may return soon. We had better get you dressed." He stepped back, tossed a bright gold belt over his shoulder, and held the dress open for her. She slid her arms into the sleeves.

"It's even softer than the other dress," she said as he wrapped her up in silk. The gentle caress of the liquid-smooth cloth made her nipples pucker.

"This one is of a quality that befits a woman of the Dark Court. I meant the more serviceable black dress to be less conspicuous in your village, little good that it did you. It was a maid's dress," he explained, knotting her belt behind her back.

"That was a maid's dress?" she exclaimed, amazed at the wealth of the nobles of old.

"I meant no insult," he said, touching her arm.

"N-No, I mean— Was your family really so wealthy they could give such an expensive dress to a maid?"

"No noble of the Dark Court would have a poorly dressed servant. Fine clothing was a well-accepted part of their compensation. I suppose you could say my family was rich, but only moderately compared to other families."

"You once said the Dark Court was made up of several houses. How did that work?"

"There were thirteen major houses, each aligning itself with one of the four seasons. Spring had five, summer had four, and autumn and winter had two each," he said as he finished tying her belt. She turned around. "My house, signified by the tree, belonged to summer, and our members were proficient with fire magic, plant magic, and a few others. Rosuke's house was the dragonfly and also belonged to summer."

"And the previous empress? Which house did she come from?" she asked with fascination, wondering what all of the houses' symbols were, and what their most prominent families were like.

Vallen tucked and straightened her dress while he spoke. "The empress didn't belong to a house. When she gave birth, her daughter would become the next empress."

"What if she didn't have a daughter?"

"The empress was our most direct link to the Divine One. Her line was holy, and her firstborn was preordained to be a daughter. Any subsequent children chose a house on their twentieth birthday based on their seasonal affinity."

"Their what?"

"Magic-users have a time of year when their power waxes, and the season tends to color their spellcasting. Green for spring, yellow or sometimes orange for summer, red or occasionally brown for autumn, and blue for winter. If, for example, one of the empress's younger children aligned with autumn, they had two houses to choose from."

"That's kind of sad, joining a house by yourself," she said with a frown.

"And troublesome," he agreed with a nod. Still listening, she walked to the doors. "An empress with siblings or multiple children had to solve house squabbles without showing favoritism. Siblings sometimes came to resent an empress and would work to undermine her."

"Couldn't she change the rules?" She opened the door as a signal for Oka to return.

"I suppose, but the court staunchly defended its traditions."

"How was the first empress chosen?" she asked, sitting at the table. Vallen sat next to her and tidied up the mess they'd made.

"That far back, it gets vague and poetic, but as the story goes, all magic-users felt the pull of their intended leader and came upon Empress Suzu in her home, where she sat waiting for them. They could feel the aura of her magic and knew it to be the mother of their own. Thus, she came to lead them in battle against the Damned One, whose minions were driven to the shadow of night and the Damned One's dimension of Oblivion. She established the language of magic, local defenses for all cities and towns to protect them from demons, and formed armies to fight demon uprisings."

"Wow. She did all of that?" she asked.

"She had help, but yes, she made the world that existed before this one. All of her successive descendants had the same aura, called the Pull of the Empress. Whenever an empress became pregnant with her heir, the whole court knew."

"Could demons feel it? Wouldn't they use it to find her?" she asked, absentmindedly stroking the fine material of her dress.

"No, a demon's magic is not born from the empress but from the Foul One. They can't tell which noble the empress is, though it was often obvious if you just looked for who had the most guards," he said with lopsided smile.

"What happened to the last empress?"

"Killed. She was still a young woman and hadn't yet taken a consort, so she died childless, unfortunately. When Rosuke and I found out... We had known her when she was barely tall enough to kick our shins. It was a dismal day when news reached us of the people's uprising."

"So there are no more empresses?"

"A new empress hasn't been born yet, anywhere. One might never be born," he said.

"Shumei," Oka groaned.

She jumped in surprise and looked at her brother, who stood at the doorway. The light beyond indicated the sun was close to setting. Oka had wrapped his arms around his stomach.

"Apples not agreeing with you?" she guessed.

Oka slid the outer door shut. "Do you have any *yagikusa*?"

"You'd have to chew the flowers raw," she said and reached for one of the piles of herbs Vallen had neatly arranged while they were talking.

"I don't care. Just as long as the pain stops," he said as he came forward. He took the small, yellow petals from her hand and tossed them into his mouth.

"I'll have something better ready for dinner," Vallen promised, stowing the remaining plants in Shumei's bag.

"Are you going to be okay?" Oka asked, staring at the blood-stained bandages.

"I'll be fine," she assured him. "I trust my own plants, don't I?"

"You'd better. I'm chewing on them," he joked. "Nice dress, by the way." He settled into his original seat.

"It is," she said, stroking her skirt.

While Vallen cooked a simple dinner consisting of rice and a medley of vegetables, she filled them in on what had happened in Majo's hut that morning, which had her dodging a barrage of questions from both Vallen and Oka. By the time she and her brother had eaten, they reached the subject that concerned her most.

170

"A couple of merchants passed through the village with tales of demon attacks on Taba and Aizan," she said. "Both saw the aftermath in Taba firsthand. Those who survived fled and are heading toward us." Everyone's expression was grim.

"I've heard...similar reports," Vallen concurred.

"You? How?" Oka asked.

"It's easy to stop someone on the road and ask a question. Either fear of me or enough kols will get me the information I want."

"Not to put too fine a point on it, but as a demon, don't you get news from 'the other side'?" Shumei asked.

"I'm artificially made, so I answer to no one, except in death. Real demons wouldn't dare share information with me."

"Have you ever met one?" Oka asked with wide eyes.

"Of course. I killed quite a few when I was a member of the Dark Court. After my curse, I met a few then, too, and was just as motivated to kill them. Real demons that meet artificial demons have an annoying habit of attacking."

"But why now?" she asked. "After all these years, why would so many demons rise up? We rarely saw any from behind the charms, and half the time, I suspect the witness was drunk."

"That I do not know. Perhaps Majo would. She has a direct link." Vallen idly tapped the arm of his chair, lips twisted in contemplation.

Oka loudly yawned. She looked to the closed doors leading outside and saw night had fallen.

"I'm sure you're both tired," Vallen said, coming to a stand. "I'll show you to your rooms so you can get some rest."

"I have my own room?" Oka said with excitement, his sleepiness momentarily alleviated. She smiled, preparing to stand, and gasped when a pair of strong hands pulled her up to her feet by her waist.

"This way," Vallen said, gesturing at the inner doors.

The hallway, leading off in both directions, was only dimly lit by a couple of small lanterns, but the floor was clean and uncluttered. They turned right, and Vallen pushed Oka ahead of him with one hand on the boy's shoulder until they came to a room at the end of the hall. The door was already open. Oka ran inside.

In the center was a thick, luxurious sleeping mat made up with a thick blanket. The walls were adorned with simple artwork, and a cabinet sat against the wall to the left. There was also some sort of table with drawers and a floor chair.

"I get to sleep here?" Oka whispered.

"You do indeed. And you can answer nature's call next door. It's not difficult to use," Vallen said. Oka ran to the water closet to look inside.

"I just...pull this handle?" he asked. Vallen hummed in the affirmative. Shumei drew her eyebrows together in curiosity and leaned over Oka to see what this "handle" was.

"Let's go see your room," Vallen whispered in her ear, making her shiver despite the lingering warmth of the expired afternoon.

"Good night, Oka," she called. She waited for her brother to come get his good-night kiss before following Vallen down the hall. As she walked away, she heard the thump of Oka flopping onto his bed.

Her room, which she assumed she'd share with Vallen, was at the opposite end of the hallway, separating their room from Oka's by at least a dozen others.

"I can only assume why this room is so far from my brother's," she teased, watching her lover slide open the bedroom door. He smiled at her over his shoulder.

She leaned in for a look, gasped, and went inside. The room had two cabinets, one of which was open and held a dozen dresses. The bed was laid upon a raised area, two steps leading up to it on all sides. It was large enough for four people, but rather than a set of simple white pillows like what Oka was probably snuggling at the moment, the head of their bed was strewn with black-and-green pillows much like the ones that had decorated the floor of the tent where they had made love so many times.

The artwork on the walls was more ornate, though not gaudy, and its obvious central theme was forest scenes. Even the straw mat flooring was dyed to match the décor better.

"It's...far too grand for me," she whispered, overwhelmed. She started when he slid his arms around her from behind, resting his chin lightly on top of her head.

"This was my room," he said, voice rumbling against her back.

"O-Oh" was all she could say, flushing.

"You deserve at least this, and much more," he went on. "I would have you live like an empress, if I could. The next few days, weeks, or months may be difficult and full of uncertainty, but I'd like to give you a place of comfort and rest that makes you feel how you're feeling now."

She melted a little. "Thank you."

Twenty minutes later, they closed their door, confident Oka had fallen asleep in his room after checking on him. Shumei settled onto the mattress, shoulder still numb thanks to the well-made salve. She looked up at Vallen, who had stripped down to his pants.

"I know you don't need to eat food, but do you sleep?" she asked, eyelids heavy.

"I haven't had a wink of sleep since the night I was cursed."

That woke her up a bit. "Then, do you not get tired?"

"If I haven't taken energy from a woman for two weeks, I start to feel fatigue. It's not until the last few days that I feel really drained, but even then, the prospect of getting energy is more than enough motivation to spend my strength on wooing her."

"I see," she said, petulant. She didn't like being reminded of his many other lovers. She laid her head back, and only when she opened her eyes did she realize they had shut on their own.

"You must be exhausted," he said in a low voice as he lay next to her.

"What will you do while I'm asleep?"

"I'll hold you for as long as possible. I must attend to some things before you wake, but I shall be here when the sun rises."

She turned her head to him. "Living without sleep and without your friend, constantly alone with your thoughts... I'm amazed at your courage and strength of will."

"I'd endure it all again if it meant being with you." He sidled close, and she was too overcome by his words to think of a response. "Just promise me you'll keep yourself alive."

"I-I can't really control that," she said, laughing softly, "but I promise to try not to ascend to the garden prematurely." They looked at each other for a moment, and she had to fight the weight of her eyelids.

"Kiss me," she begged, curling toward him.

"With pleasure." He carefully moved over her to avoid putting pressure on her shoulder. His lips gently settled upon hers. She moaned into his mouth, bringing up her free hand to cup his cheek.

But it didn't go further than that. After a moment, they reined in their passion, slowing the kiss until they pulled away from each other. And though he could not resist a few fleeting kisses to her chin and cheek, he eventually settled against her side, one arm thrown across her chest.

She was out in seconds. His body and the blankets kept her warm as the day's heat seeped away from the house, and though she woke once when he moved away from her, a small kiss and a reassuring whisper sent her back to sleep.

Chapter Thirteen

She dreamed...running through fields, darting between trees, and skipping lightly over the surface of rivers and lakes, the rising sun always to her back. She ran as fast as the wind, body as light as a cloud. She passed hundreds and hundreds of people as she sprinted through a dozen vistas. All of them had black hair. Some of them, she was sure, were figments of her imagination, and some of them, undoubtedly, were born from Vallen's stories.

The people looked on as she sped past, their faces full of wonder as though witnessing a vision from the Divine One. She was more a part of the earth than a member of the human race. She was the quickening in the soil, the heat of the sun, the wind in the trees, the water in the lakes and clouds. She was the embodiment of the Divine One's grace and love.

Her journey ended at Vallen's secret estate, where dozens and dozens of crows greeted her. Only one head was blond. Oka was running to greet her, followed closely by two people she had never seen before.

The one face she had hoped to see was not there.

THE CHIRPING OF birds and the sigh of a breeze slowly brought Shumei out of sleep. Her injured shoulder was warm and stiff, and her stomach growled for the mouthwatering scent of cooked eggs wafting to her nose, but she otherwise felt fine.

For a blissful moment, she watched the play of shadows on the wall, cast by the swaying branches of trees under a full sun. She was both loath and eager to get out of bed. There were many things to be done, starting with Vallen's cure. She also had to worry about Majo, the village leaders, Akiji, and, oh yes, the demon raids on human villages and cities after centuries of peace.

Oka's laugh echoed faintly and she turned her head on the pillow, taking in a deep breath. Then her bladder made its need known, so she sat up. A few small throbs of pain started up in her shoulder, but they were minor and not a sign of anything wrong. She was lucky her wound hadn't become infected, what with their hasty retreat from the village and their half-day journey to this place.

As she stood, she found herself face-to-face with the mirror above the dressing table next to the bed. Her bed-tousled hair was rather silly, but her skin was clear and fine that morning, most likely due to the long night of sleep she'd enjoyed despite her injury—twelve hours' worth, if the light of day was any indication.

She would have to get her bandage changed again before breakfast, but first came a quick visit to the room with the mysterious handle. As she passed by the sitting room, she looked in to see Vallen entertaining Oka with his story of falling from a house in Kito to be left dangling naked in the breeze.

Vallen had dressed in all black again, though he also wore a leather vest cinched snugly to the contours of his upper body. His pants were leather rather than cloth, and they clung to his narrow hips like a second skin. Oka also wore new clothes obviously meant for a nobleman's child. They were Vallen's house colors, and finely stitched saplings adorned the shirt's hem.

"How did you get down?" Oka asked.

"Thankfully, only a shocked old man was awake to see my predicament," Vallen said. "In the dark of night under trees, he probably thought I was a blondie with my light-colored hair, so he kindly unknotted the end of the rope holding me to the balcony of the house, and I fell the last few feet to the ground."

"This must be a favorite memory of yours for you to share something so embarrassing," she said.

"Good morning," Oka said, grinning.

Vallen turned to her. She had taken time to comb some sense into her hair with her fingers but was certain she still looked bedraggled.

Even so, judging by the spread of warmth low in her belly, she knew his delicious-looking leather pants were getting tighter.

"The old man's reaction stuck with me. He was far more flustered than I was," Vallen replied, smiling. "I was simply grateful for the assistance." He and Oka had finished eating, but a plate of eggs, a few slices of meat, and some freshly made rice waited for her under a glass lid. "How do you feel?" he asked as he stood, medicine bag in his hand. "I checked on you a few times, but you never seemed to be in pain."

"My shoulder aches a bit, but I don't feel feverish. I think I'd prefer to change my bandage before eating," she decided, touching her shoulder and feeling minimal pain from the pressure. It was like touching a bruise several days old.

"Let us change your bandage in the bedroom," Vallen said, reaching for her elbow.

"Yes, I need only a moment," she said, pointing shyly at the water closet nearby.

"I'll wait for you there, then."

The water closet was clean and well designed—a much more civilized solution than leaves and a private spot in the woods. After completing her business, she eagerly pulled the handle and watched with fascination as the system of pipes flushed everything away. She wondered if magic made it work.

Oka was gone by the time she walked past the sitting room, probably off to explore the woods again. She felt a strange need to walk to the porch and call his name to tell him not to wander too far, but she resisted the urge, knowing they were relatively safe within the estate's walls.

Coming upon her bedroom again, she looked in to see Vallen sitting on the edge of the bed with his bare feet on the steps, a bandage draped over his thigh and a nearly completed mesh of medicines in the mortar he held in his hands. He raised his head.

"Were you as amazed at the handle as Oka was? He couldn't stop talking about it when we first started breakfast," he said, chuckling. She smiled and walked to the bed.

"You're dressed rather handsomely today," she said, sitting next to him.

"I could tell you liked it," he murmured with a lopsided smile, setting the mortar on the first step. He leaned toward her. His fingers swept up her thighs, curved around her hips, and slid sensually to her lower back. He deftly loosened her belt, and her heart skipped in reaction.

"Now, now," he said with a small shudder. "I can't control myself if you get worked up too."

"I can't help myself," she whispered. Her sex was already warm and heavy as her dress slipped down her arms, revealing the bandage wrapped tightly around her shoulder. She kept enough fabric over her breasts to avoid teasing Vallen too much, but hiding herself seemed to inflame his lusts even more.

"I don't want to tear out any of your stitches," he said hoarsely, adjusting his position to lessen the pressure on the erection ridging his pants. "I'd never forgive myself." He unwound her old bandage and tenderly peeled the last layer from her shoulder. She looked down at her wound and felt a great wash of relief. It was healing remarkably well.

"Your shoulder feels warm, right?" he asked, dipping a cloth into a basin of water.

"Yes, why?" she asked, enjoying the cool touch of his hands on her shoulder.

"That's your magic helping." He wiped away dried bits of salve. "In the days of the Dark Court, when nobles and their house soldiers battled the minions of the Damned One, even those with nearly fatal wounds could make a full recovery after only a few weeks' rest. Those with more minor wounds, like yours, could heal in a matter of days."

"Really? I'll be well in only a couple days?"

"It's my guess," he said with a nod.

"So my magic is healing me?"

"I should say it's speeding up the natural healing process, but don't worry. You can handle it. Drowsiness and a little stiffness are the only side effects."

She nodded, watching as he spread a new layer of salve over the wound. The stitched flesh looked red and raw, but it had already fused. The *yagikusa* blossoms mashed into the salve began to work within only a moment, and the mild throbs of pain faded a degree. Vallen wrapped a new bandage around her shoulder and then helped put her dress back to rights.

"And now I have something important to tell you, which cannot wait any longer," he said gravely.

"What is it?"

"I returned to your village last night," he revealed. She started in surprise to think he'd gone all the way back. He answered her question without even hearing it. "When we came here, it took us half a day, but I was forced to keep my horse at a trot to avoid exhausting it."

Ah, it had been carrying two adults and a child, after all.

"There was a town meeting happening when I arrived, even though it was hours past sunset," he continued. "The leader, whose name I forget—"

"Kimen," she supplied. He nodded.

"Right. He told many lies and few truths, but I can tell you with a fair amount of certainty that Majo left the village and took most of her belongings with her."

She swallowed. Dread sat heavy in her stomach.

"She had screamed that demons would kill them all, and...that she would find you and kill you," he said, mouth stiff.

"She was at the meeting?"

"Kimen recounted the events to those who hadn't seen it, though I'm sure those who hadn't seen it had heard it from their gossiping neighbors. Kimen also lamented that Akiji had gone with her."

"By the dueling gods," she whispered. "Akiji is a bully, but he's not evil. He doesn't know what she is."

"I imagine he knows now," he said haltingly.

"What else did you learn?"

"That's..." He slid his warm fingers around hers, and her chest grew tight with worry. "They were deciding what to do next when absolute chaos broke out. A hundred demons swarmed the village—"

"No!" she gasped.

"I killed a handful, but there were simply too many. I could only get a few villagers out. I told them to get to your medicine field and stay there until dawn, for it has the correct prayers on its barrier charms. But I don't think they believed me."

Of course. His hair was white and they wouldn't recognize him. They'd think he was tricking them. Shumei couldn't stop her tears, and he held her in his arms while showering the top of her head with kisses.

He continued after she'd composed herself. "Human-born demons had sabotaged the village's barrier. They were the ones I went after first. I didn't know any of them, and I don't know how they were recruited. I tried to ask one, but he thought attacking me was a better idea."

"You're worried Rosuke was recruited," she said, hesitant.

"Yes," he admitted.

"What are we going to do?"

So many people she'd grown up with had just died. It was the epidemic all over again, but far more frightening. Yes, many had not been kind to her, or at least most of them hadn't, but she had helped birth several children, had healed dozens of wounds, and reversed many fevers. And in their own way, people had expressed thanks, whether it had been a soft word or a sigh of relief with a glance at her face.

Now all except for a few had died. She wondered if the leader and his wife had survived, if Ikuro and her many children had escaped, and if Master Takebe and his wife had been able to run away with her leg still so tender.

Vallen pulled her into his arms again, letting her cry against his neck, and promised everything would turn out all right. But she couldn't help thinking of her dream from last night and how he hadn't been there at the end.

Chapter Fourteen

The next couple of days went by fast. That first morning, Vallen taught her some of the basics of Mahou over breakfast while scanning the Devil's Hand for the counter-ritual to unmake his curse. The centuries he'd spent as a demon had eroded his fluency, but he was certain they wouldn't run into the same problem Majo had.

His eyebrows jumped in surprise with almost every turn of the page. Translating as he went, he found spell effects in every flavor of destructive, cruel, and sadistic.

One ritual was powerful enough to summon a tsunami of any height, anywhere. It required vanishingly rare and expensive components, such as bone shavings from an ocean animal Vallen claimed was extinct. Another ritual made its victim rot as though dead, not allowing an escape from the pain until their brain had completely decomposed. Shumei shuddered to think of it.

Vallen also found the ritual Majo had used to siphon youth from Akki. Although the spell had been broken, thus allowing Akki to return to her normal appearance, the life stolen from her was gone forever. Vallen estimated Majo had stolen a year of Akki's life, assuming she wasn't dead already.

He also found instructions for vain enhancements, such as longer hair, larger breasts and penises, and different eye colors. Majo had likely been missing an ingredient when she'd tricked Shumei into drinking the potion for larger breasts—the flower of a plant that only blossomed once every few years, and only in the far north. According to Vallen, it would have prevented Shumei's nausea.

The most well-worn page was at the back. Vallen gripped the book tightly as his gaze darted across the heavily annotated ritual. He grimaced and cursed. He shook his head in disbelief. When Shumei couldn't stand it any longer, she begged him to tell her what the ritual did. And in a hoarse voice, Vallen explained...

Majo hadn't summoned a demon general, but the Damned One himself. Shumei asked him what that meant exactly, but Vallen wouldn't tell her.

"If you don't feel the pull," he'd said, "then I'm not sure."

"What pull?" she'd asked.

"Don't worry about it right now."

Since then, she had spent almost all her time practicing the steps for the counter-ritual, acting them out without the spell components. Her magic would sit up and watch every time, like a dog spotting a rabbit.

She had blushed fiercely to learn she would have to bring Vallen to climax with her mouth for one of the steps. Every time she acted out the spell for him to check her memorization, she knelt in front of one of the tables in the sitting room to symbolize that all-important step, and her cheeks were never anything paler than bright red, amusing her lover to no end.

The difficult part of the ritual was the circle she had to draw around the altar upon which Vallen had to sit. It had to be drawn within an hour, with absolutely no mistakes, and it was as artistic as it was complex. She spent all her waking hours trying to memorize the circle's pattern and fell asleep two nights straight at their favorite table in the sitting room, leaving Vallen to carry her to bed.

During the daytime hours when Vallen wasn't instructing Shumei in the basics of magic, he and Oka cleaned the estate. The boy protested, insisting he'd rather learn sword techniques, but Vallen coerced him into helping by saying he had to build up his strength first.

They scrubbed the porch and its columns and replaced all the paper on the doors. Oka praised his "strength training" at dinner, admitting he certainly felt sore all over. After Oka had fallen into an exhausted sleep on the third night, Vallen checked Shumei's wound, hopeful he could finally have her naked and moaning beneath him without hurting her shoulder. However, seeing it still needed one more day, he held her until she fell asleep.

His ache for her was one he could live with for a bit longer, but he sorely wished to rip off her dress, shove her thighs apart, and plunder her dew-drenched flower all night long while savoring her sweet, shuddering cries. His only distraction was spending the nighttime hours spying on the events outside their walls and bringing back reports in the morning.

After several days without word on Majo, a midnight conversation with a demon had produced results. Of course, he had to pierce the demon six times with his serrated sword and hold it by its hairy neck against the ground to get answers, but the demon spilled a bit of information as well as blood as it died there in the dirt.

The witch was relentless in her pursuit of the young woman who had stolen her prized spell book. She terrorized the villages as yet untouched by the demon raids, searching for available information on Shumei's whereabouts. But no one had seen a young crow, her blondie brother, and the demon they traveled with. One merchant gave him a horrifying account of Majo abducting a woman from a village that had yielded no information and sacrificing her in a ritual. The merchant had once sold bolts of cloth to the young woman, whose ravaged corpse was later found in the woods.

Vallen decided to keep this last piece of information to himself. To know her act of thievery had inadvertently brought about such an intense search would only make Shumei feel guiltier.

On their fourth morning at the estate, Oka managed to coax Vallen into some actual sword practice before they dusted the interior rooms, and they were parrying in the small bit of open space in front of the sitting room. Shumei sat inside with the spell book on the table, trying to draw the circle from memory on a piece of paper. It was slow work and the urge to peek at the book for a hint was strong, but she resisted and finished the circle, having taken nearly an hour and a half to draw it.

She looked up to see Oka trying his hardest to land a hit on Vallen and failing miserably, but her brother seemed to be enjoying the effort. She smiled at his red-cheeked excitement and then checked her circle to see how well it matched the one in the book.

After a quick count, she found she had made around twenty mistakes. Sighing in disappointment, she began to study the mistakes to make sure she didn't repeat them, but a shout outside made her look up.

"Rosuke," Vallen hollered before taking off out of sight. Oka stood transfixed, his wooden sword hanging loosely from his hand. She banged her knee on the table in her rush to stand.

Vallen shouted his friend's name again. Too flustered to think, she limped toward the door, knee throbbing. When she got to the porch, she couldn't see Vallen and figured he had vanished around the corner. She glanced at Oka, who looked at her fearfully.

"Come inside, Oka. Sit quietly," she instructed. He left his shoes on a stone step below the porch and disappeared behind her.

She ran as fast as she could when wearing soft socks on a smooth, wood porch. At the corner, she stopped dead in her tracks. A horse stomped irritably beyond the two men on the ground, where Vallen held a fatigued but handsome man in his arms.

She had assumed Rosuke's hair would be white like Vallen's, but it was a bright, flaming red. She had never seen red hair, and she stared as if he were a two-headed ox. His clothes were torn and filthy, his skin drawn and pale. He looked at Vallen with such relief that she knew he had missed Vallen as much as Vallen had missed him.

"What happened?" Vallen asked. She could hardly hear him, but she hesitated to get any closer.

"I was in Houfu. I hadn't eaten for over three weeks." He shook his head. "I barely survived the night. I'd hardly begun my search when demons swarmed the streets, at least a hundred. Not an army but more than enough. The city guard was overwhelmed. Many died." He closed his eyes and grimaced as though revisiting the memory.

"You—you've not had a woman for nearly a month?"

Rosuke nodded lethargically, looking as though he'd fall asleep right there. "I will fade by morning. I could not find a woman between Houfu and here. All the villages are deserted, full of corpses, or too dangerous to approach. I knew I would die this time and I wanted to die here," he said, voice raspy with fear. "Where you might find me."

Shumei snuck a few steps closer, and oh dueling gods, the pain on Vallen's face. How badly she wanted to hold him.

Vallen brushed a lock of hair from Rosuke's cheek. "Don't give up yet."

She took another step, and the soft sweep of her foot alerted the two demons to her presence. Rosuke's deep blue eyes flared with surprise. And Vallen's expression was a wordless plea.

He didn't... Did he? Did he seriously want her to...?

"Who's this?" Rosuke asked.

183

"This is Shumei," Vallen said, still beseeching her with his gaze.

Vallen knew what he silently begged for was a horrible thing to request from someone who had confessed her love only days before. She instantly figured out what his expression meant and flinched with pain. Without saying a word, she turned and walked away.

"You love her, don't you?" Rosuke asked, face unreadable. Vallen nodded. "Then I shall not ask it of you. Just be with me when the time comes." Rosuke looked as though he would take a nap right there.

"Don't you fall asleep yet," he said, shaking Rosuke until he opened his eyes again. "I'll take you inside the house. We'll see from there."

"I'd rather walk in, though I may need you to steady me. Just pretend I'm drunk. You know, like old times?"

Vallen tried to smile and laugh at the joke, but the heavy press of sadness made it difficult even to breathe. After all this time, Rosuke had returned, but only to die at his feet.

When he and an exhausted Rosuke entered the sitting room a moment later, he saw only a shocked Oka sitting quietly at the table where Shumei had been studying. She was nowhere to be seen.

"Did your sister come through here?" Vallen asked.

Staring at Rosuke, who stared back, Oka nodded and pointed at the doors leading in. Vallen walked Rosuke through the room.

"Her brother is a blondie?" Rosuke asked as they turned right. Vallen headed toward Oka's room with the intent to let Rosuke rest there while he spoke with Shumei. It was only midday. He still had time to convince her.

If only the guilt he felt would let him take a full breath...

"Yes," he answered. "It amazed their village to no end that a crow woman had birthed a blonde child." He helped Rosuke lie down.

"I haven't slept somewhere so comfortable for months," his friend moaned. His bright red hair spread across the white pillow like fresh blood.

"Try to stay awake. I'll talk to her." Vallen made a mental note to give Rosuke a new set of clothes. That is, should he survive the next twenty-four hours...

He left Oka's room behind and started down what felt like the longest stretch of hallway in the world. Oka had remained in the sitting room, no doubt according to Shumei's request. The door to the bedroom he'd shared with her the last few nights was open.

When he arrived, Shumei was staring at her reflection above the dressing table. He wondered what she was thinking. She looked at him in the mirror, then turned to face him.

"I know you love him," she said unsteadily. "Even before the Incubus Curse, he was like a brother to you, and his companionship made the long years of your curse more bearable. You've known him longer than I've been alive—many times over—and I cannot begin to imagine the strength of your attachment. I only know it must be far more profound than what you and I mean to each other."

"That's not true," he vowed, taking a step closer. "I love you so much I sometimes wonder how my heart hasn't burst. You've saved my life more than once with the gift of your body. You risked yourself for that damned book and love me despite what I am. If you cannot do this, you need only say so. The decision is up to you."

"How can you say that?" she asked, tearing up. Gods, he wanted to hold her. His feet carried him closer. "It would kill you to lose him, and you'd place that decision in my hands?"

"It is not I who can save him! It's not my decision in the first place and so it is yours."

"S-Sex demons cannot share energy among themselves, then?" she asked, hand pressed against her heaving chest.

He shook his head and searched for the right words. "I do not sense him as a source of energy the way I sense you," he explained haltingly.

"Does he...have to be inside me?" She hugged herself protectively.

He nodded. She grimaced and stared at her feet, thinking. He dared not speak a word, knowing she might relent after she'd discounted every alternative—as he already had—but only if she came to the conclusion herself.

She looked up at him. "The spell I'm studying to cure you, would it also work on Rosuke? Could I do the ritual for both of you at the same time?"

"Could you perform it correctly tonight?" he asked, gently reminding her of their time limit.

She made a sigh of frustration. "No, not tonight. I tried to make the circle earlier on paper and made too many mistakes on top of taking too long."

Again, he held his tongue, thinking that sex was the only option—and soon.

"Gods," she said with a tremor in her voice. "I keep thinking 'I don't know him' and how I'd be s-spreading my legs for a stranger, but..." She winced and turned her face away. "Then I'm ashamed to remember how I acted when I met you."

He decided to ignore the facts of their less-than-ideal first encounter, as lifesaving as it had been for him. After all, he had used every trick he possessed, short of mind-altering magic, to seduce her.

"You do know him," he said. "How many times have I told you stories about Rosuke? His sense of humor, his penchant for taking risks, the younger brother he lost to the same curse he and I both suffer. You know him."

"But I don't love him," she whispered with teary eyes.

"I do."

Shumei looked at her lover, at the defeat slouching his shoulders and the despair furrowing his brow. He didn't want to share her, either, she was sure. But he also didn't want to watch his friend waste away. He likely felt as trapped as she did.

"Would you...be here with me?" she asked.

Hope lifted his head. "I'd prefer it. We're still bound, and I can help you relax. Rosuke is kind. He'll be gentle with you, I promise," he swore, stepping close to set his hands on her shoulders.

"What would my mother think?" she said, dropping her gaze to the floor.

"You'll be saving the life of someone cursed," he reassured her. "Believe me when I say Rosuke knows the sacrifice you'd be making."

A part of her had known the second Vallen had silently beseeched her that she'd be the one to feed Rosuke. She had searched for any other way but had known there was none. And now that she had come to grips with it... She raised her head and squared her shoulders.

"All right. I'll do it," she said, heart racing. Oh, what she had just gotten herself into? Or rather, who she had just gotten into herself? By the dueling gods, her crude thoughts made her wince.

Vallen breathed deep with relief and smiled ruefully. He pulled her to his chest and wrapped his arms around her, a flurry of thanks falling from his lips.

"To have one person I love save another person I love is a gift I can never repay."

"You can spend the rest of your life trying." Her petulant comment earned her a surprised laugh.

She made to follow him when he pulled away and turned to the door, but he stopped her with his hands on her arms. "Wait here. I'll bring him," he said, guiding her to the bed.

"O-Oka," she said, blushing.

"I'll take care of it," he said before briskly leaving the room.

She was definitely going to Oblivion for this, Shumei thought.

Vallen stopped by the sitting room, poked his head in, and met Oka's nervous gaze.

"What's going on? Who's that man?" Oka said, standing.

"I hadn't had a chance to tell you about Rosuke. He was also cursed the night I was turned into a demon, and I've known him for a long time. He's injured, though, and I need Shumei's help fixing him. But there might be...screaming, so—"

"Screaming?" Oka said with wide eyes.

"Your sister would rather you not hear it, so I'd like you to play in the orchard for a while and practice that move you had trouble with." He picked up Oka's wooden sword from where it sat on the table and put it in his hand. Squinting as though sensing the lie, Oka nodded but said nothing.

Vallen saw him off, shut the door to the outside, and then made his way to Oka's room where Rosuke rested. Rosuke had sat up, and he gazed at a painting of a maple sapling growing in a small patch of sunlight. He raised his head when Vallen called his name.

"She said no, didn't she?" he surmised, his question more of a statement.

"Actually, she agreed," Vallen corrected. Rosuke turned in surprise. "I don't think I'll ever love her more than I love her now."

Rosuke somberly nodded and took a deep breath as he made to stand on his own. Vallen almost rushed forward to help him, but as it was with sex demons nearly at their limit and presented with an energy source, Rosuke seemed to have gotten his second wind.

"The little one?" Rosuke asked, walking slowly but steadily to the door.

"He has been sent off to practice his sword swings in the orchard."

As they made their way down the hall, the only sound was their heavy footsteps. The closer they came to Shumei, the faster her heart beat—he could feel it through the binding. His face felt warm, and he could tell her cheeks were almost as red as Rosuke's hair.

"She's nervous," he warned. "Very nervous." He took slow, deliberate breaths as his own heart raced in response. The anxiety he was causing her... There was nothing for it now, though. He and Rosuke would simply have to do everything possible to reassure her.

"Nervous about a pair of sex demons about to ravish her? I wonder why," Rosuke replied, making him smile.

Sitting primly on the corner of the bed, right where Vallen had left her, Shumei couldn't help second-guessing herself as two sets of feet approached her door. She sensed a sympathetic response from Vallen—a steady stream of calming energy—but it did little. Her palms were sweaty and she couldn't stop fidgeting with the end of her sleeve.

Vallen entered first, and everything about the hesitant wince on his face spoke to how well he understood her state of mind. He stood aside, and the tall, lean frame of a red-haired sex demon entered her bedroom. The second his eyes found her, they glazed over with hunger. Soon, she would be spread beneath him. She tried to picture it and to start getting used to the idea—for she had little time. The thought of Vallen watching when she cried out with pleasure, feeling it himself when her orgasm transported her...

Red-faced and overwhelmed by how much she liked the idea, she clamped her thighs together and tucked her bent legs tightly to her chest. Her nervous fingers would start doing damage to the edge of her sleeve if she didn't calm down.

"Rosuke, relax," Vallen whispered even as he struggled to breathe normally. His erection was painfully thick. Shumei was clearly anxious, but the binding told him she was hot and wet between her thighs.

"I'm trying," Rosuke whispered back. "But the look on her sweet face..."

"Perhaps we should sit and talk first," Vallen suggested to everyone. "Things seem to be getting intense."

"Isn't that the point?" Rosuke asked, walking forward.

Vallen followed. "I believe Shumei is more anxious than excited."

Shumei wiggled with uncertainty as two devastatingly handsome sex demons stalked toward her. Vallen's erection was obvious beneath his tight-fitting pants, and she couldn't deny what the bulge tenting the front of Rosuke's traditional trousers was.

"It's all right, love." Vallen sat next to her on the edge of the bed, pressing himself against her body. Rosuke sat on her other side without touching her at all.

"What are we supposed to talk about?" she asked, soft but clear.

"Anything you wish," Rosuke said.

She stared at the death grip she had on her dress and racked her brain for something to discuss while the two men on either side waited to flip open her dress and have their way with her. Nothing seemed to come to mind except raunchy images of her between their bodies. Then a lock of Rosuke's red hair caught her eye.

"Why isn't your hair white like Vallen's?" she asked, overjoyed to have found a topic that didn't involve sex.

"That's kind of a long story," Rosuke said, antsy. He kept shifting next to her.

"Not that long," Vallen countered. "The woman who cursed us made a mistake in the ritual."

"She did?" she asked, forcing her hands to relax.

"We had been drinking heavily that night, and I was nearly passed out while the woman was with Rosuke, having already been with Yasuke and me."

Shumei went red to the tips of her ears. So much for avoiding the topic of sex.

"None of us had noticed the cup she was supposedly drinking from. And after...servicing each of us, she would pretend to take a drink, but she was actually collecting the curse's required component. She had already taken mine and Yasuke's, but she spilled some of Rosuke's by accident. Thus, his magic was only partially ripped out. It still died, but his hair turned red and remained so from that night on."

"I, I see." She cleared her throat, face burning with discomfort. Rosuke shifted again, and she realized he was adjusting his erection. She coyly eyed his lap, the direction of her gaze hidden by her hair, and wondered how he would feel inside her.

"H-Have you two shared a woman before?" She needed to know even though the question embarrassed her to no end.

"We have," Rosuke admitted. "Some women sold sex, but some were merely curious." He sidled closer and offered his palm to her. She took it hesitantly. He gently closed his fingers around her hand and lightly brushed her knuckles with his thumb.

"So how does that...? How does that position work, exactly?" she stammered, though she had started to relax. Rosuke wasn't crowding her, and the stroke of his thumb was soothing.

"There are...several variations," Vallen said, voice dropping.

His mind produced an image of Shumei on all fours, her body jerking back and forth as two men thrust into her. Her hair swaying, her back arched with pleasure, her mouth open and crying out. The man beneath her would massage her breasts, and the man behind her would control how fast they plunged into her. She'd hardly be able to draw breath as she writhed with ecstasy.

Half a dozen more possibilities flooded his mind. Shumei on her side, her legs tangled with theirs. Shumei on her back, one cock between her thighs and another between her lips. Shumei suspended between them. Shumei's moans turning rough from screaming too long and too loud as they spent the whole evening touching her, tasting her, covering her with their—

The sudden rush of blood to his cock had him groping her thigh with need.

"G-Gods," Shumei breathed, shivering. "Vallen, y-you're..."

Shumei had spread her knees without even realizing it. Whatever Vallen had imagined had aroused him greatly. Her sex practically dripped with lust. He pressed close and rubbed her thigh. Wondering where her shyness had gone, she turned to Rosuke.

She hadn't seen him up close yet—hadn't been able to bring herself to look at anything but her fidgeting hands. His face was almost feminine. A soft complexion, deep-set eyes with long lashes, high cheekbones, and full, upturned lips. But the hard line of his jaw and brow ridge sharpened his features. Looking at him felt almost the same as when she'd seen Vallen for the first time. Beauty so perfect and unearthly that she couldn't turn away.

"Did you...?" Rosuke asked, staring at Vallen.

"Yes, I invoked a binding upon her," Vallen acknowledged, slipping his hand beneath the fold of her dress. The greed with which he dug his fingers into her thigh nearly outmatched the greed that hardened Rosuke's delicate features.

"So I'll be making love to both of you?" Rosuke asked, softly panting. He then nailed her with his gaze, groaning so low it was more like a growl. She pressed her back into Vallen's chest almost by instinct, and Vallen wrapped his other arm around her waist. Rosuke moved toward her.

Shumei put her hands out, flattening them against his shoulders. "R-Rosuke?"

"I had many lovers at court. Women and men. Only once at the same time." Inhaling deeply, he palmed her knee and eased her thighs wider.

"Ah!" She grasped his wrist. "Y-You and Vallen...?"

"No, he prefers only women, and we are friends first." He dragged her skirt open, exposing her leg, and they both moaned when he touched her bare skin. "But the thought of making love to him through you—"

He ducked his head and took her mouth in a kiss. His lips were warm and passionate. He thumbed her chin down, opening her mouth, and then his tongue was parrying hers.

Groaning, Vallen slid his hand on her thigh up to her breast and tugged at her belt. Rosuke pulled back for a second, and she turned her head to suck in a breath of air, already hot and heavy. They were going too fast. She still had concerns that needed addressing before any clothes were removed, and they hadn't even touched her earlier question. So she wrenched herself away, stumbling out of reach as their hands trailed after her.

"Shumei," Vallen called with an ache in his voice. Rosuke remained silent.

"You didn't answer me. How does that position work?" she repeated, only marginally calmer now that she wasn't within arm's reach. Vallen and Rosuke glanced at each other briefly, as if speaking telepathically, and Rosuke nodded.

"For Rosuke and I, the most pleasurable position has both of us inside you at the same time," Vallen said, speaking carefully as he considered his words. "We would need time to prepare and something to ease—"

"I don't understand. I couldn't p-possibly take both of, of your...d-down..." she said, losing the nerve to finish her sentence.

"Usually, the second one uses your other orifice," Rosuke explained.

"Other o-orifice?" she asked. "But that's... That cannot be comfortable. It's—"

"It can be...coaxed wider," he averred, digging his fingertips into his thighs. "It's quite pleasurable, when done well. Women enjoyed it as much as anything else we did to them."

"Wouldn't it be crowded? I mean, legs a-and all that," she stuttered, mind whirling with mental images of what that might look like. Blushing like mad, she felt like the most naïve fool.

"I shall be glad to explain it to you later," Vallen said roughly. "For now, I think we should decide on something less time-consuming."

"Is there another position, then?" she asked.

"Yes. Rosuke between your legs, and me between your lips. But with the binding, the sensations might be too much for you to concentrate."

Shumei recalled the first time she had taken Vallen into her mouth and the pleasure she'd felt through the binding. The memory had her pressing her knees together.

"Oh, that—that sounds nice," she sighed, taking an unconscious step forward. Vallen blinked in surprise. "But you're probably right."

"In that case, you'll just be with Rosuke," Vallen said, glancing at his friend. "But I'll be here with you." He touched the bed for emphasis.

She steeled her shoulders and nodded. "All right, then."

Rosuke tugged at the ties of his pants. Vallen removed his leather vest and tossed it aside. Her belt was already loose from Vallen's attempt to take it off earlier, so she simply pulled, and it fell away without fuss. Her dress sagged open, revealing a line of flesh down the center of her body. Vallen licked his lips, and Rosuke held his hand out, inviting her closer.

She walked toward the two demons on her bed. Their hot stares slid down her body as each step widened the gap in her dress. A wave of desire from Vallen rolled up her body, and she whimpered with need.

When she was within reach, they drew her onto the bed and followed her down as she reclined upon the plush pillows. The sides of her dress fell open, baring her chest.

Vallen lay along her left side, palmed her breast, and brushed their mouths together as he sought a kiss. She eagerly turned her head to him, eyes sliding shut. His lips and tongue were gentle, even adoring. Meanwhile, his hand on her breast rolled and squeezed.

Rosuke watched for a moment, an interloper in their intimacy even though he wanted to join them and pleasure the tender young woman lying between him and his best friend. He hadn't seen Vallen in years, and yet within an hour of reuniting, Vallen and his lover, who didn't know him at all, were saving his life. No, more than that. They were saving his soul.

He could scarcely believe not only his luck but the depth of Vallen's friendship. Though it wasn't any sort of argument that drove them to part ways fifteen years ago, he could hardly call their last conversation friendly. Rather, they had both grown so tired of the tedious, never-ending struggle of their existences that neither could stand to have the same conversation for the ten-thousandth time. Vallen had simply suggested they split up, permanently, and Rosuke had agreed. The next morning, Rosuke had left Vallen's estate with hardly a word of farewell.

Blinking, he pulled out of the deep, murky depths of his memories in time to see the tip of Shumei's breast puckering in sympathy with her other well-pleasured nipple. He licked his lips, heart hammering. His gaze continued down and stopped at her lower half, still partially hidden beneath one side of her dress. He slowly pulled the silky cloth aside, exposing her completely, and her thighs compressed as she moaned into her lover's mouth.

Vallen lifted his head and glanced at Rosuke, who hadn't yet taken any initiative. His friend seemed distracted, his eyes glazed in a way Vallen easily recognized. Rosuke was lost in his past, something that had happened to both of them more and more the longer they'd lived. When he seemed to return to the present, Vallen nuzzled his lover's cheek, pushing her face aside, and whispered into her ear.

"Tell him what you want." He felt her shiver on his own skin as he shifted lower. She wrapped her arm around his shoulders. He mouthed the peak of her breast, making her gasp, and slid his hand to her other breast.

Shumei sighed with pleasure as she shyly turned to Rosuke, who still held himself up on one hand and hungrily stared at her. She lifted her other arm to him.

"Will you undress? I want to see you," she said, breath hitching every time Vallen flicked her nipple with his tongue.

With a nod, Rosuke hurriedly peeled off his clothes. Unlike Vallen, whose physique was that of a warrior, Rosuke's toned form was on the leaner side. His clear skin was marred only by a few thin scars that swept around his left side. They looked rather like the wound in her shoulder, which was still covered by a thin bandage. Old injuries from a magical attack?

Rosuke's blood-red hair spilled over his shoulders and down his chest, reaching the dimple of his navel and coyly hiding the nipples on his wide, tight pecs. He pushed his pants down, and his cock stood straight up, long and thick. Vallen's rock-hard erection dug into her thigh, barely held back by his leather pants, and the thought of both shafts rubbing against her made her shiver.

Rosuke tossed his clothing to the floor and sidled up to her. She hesitantly laid her arm across his back, unsure of where to hold him. The opposite of shy, he hooked his leg around hers, pulled her knees apart, and thrust his thigh between hers. She hardly got a gasp out before he covered her mouth in a kiss.

He touched her stomach with calloused fingers that were at odds with his delicate features. As his hand traveled down her body, she sighed into his mouth and shivered beneath his rough touch. He gently cupped her mons and pressed his finger between her labia.

She and Vallen groaned as he teased her clit. Vallen urgently rolled his hips against her leg, and Rosuke deepened his kiss, clearly pleased his touch aroused them both.

Shumei felt overwhelmed already. She kissed one demon, who had his hand between her thighs, while another mouthed and rubbed her breasts as he bucked his erection against her leg.

Rosuke lifted his mouth and took his fingers from her, trailing moisture over her stomach as he took in her dazed expression. Her lips were so soft and full, and he couldn't decide whether he wanted them wrapped around his cock or parting beneath his kiss.

"She's wet, Vallen. Feel for yourself," he invited. He grasped his erection and rubbed it against her thigh. Vallen lifted his head and swept his hand down her body. While Rosuke hollowed his cheeks around her other nipple, Vallen worked his hand between her legs.

"I want to see you too, Vallen," she moaned. With a rough sigh, he pulled his fingers from her and rose to his knees. His shirt joined his vest on the floor, leaving him wearing only his leather pants, which tied shut with black lacing over each hip. Fascinated, Shumei explored the lacing over one of Vallen's hips while he loosened the other side.

Rosuke brought his head up, still idly massaging her breasts while they slowed down for a moment.

"Where did you get these?" she asked, tugging at a knot to loosen it.

"I wondered as well," Rosuke added, pinching one of her nipples. She slid her fingers through his long hair to rest her hand on his shoulder, arching her chest into his massaging hand.

"A young merchant in Kaizoku was offering custom-made leather clothes. These had already been made and fit rather well, so I bought them," he explained, having loosened his pants enough to remove them.

Shumei didn't hesitate to wrap her fingers around his erection, making him groan and forget what he was doing. The head was wet with arousal, and her breaths were shallow as she pumped it within her fist, watching his face and gasping along with him.

"By the dueling gods, how I want you," Rosuke gruffly whispered, turning her face toward him as he took her mouth in another kiss. Then he plunged his hand between her legs once more.

Shumei cried out even as his tongue swept inside to taste her, and Vallen groaned in reaction, clambering off the bed to kick his pants to the side. When he climbed back on, he sought out any spare inch of his lover he could find, and Shumei nearly swooned as two naked, aroused demons pressed full-length against her, their hands and mouths doing their best to drive her crazy.

Unable to catch her breath, she pulled her mouth away from Rosuke, who tried to follow her lips and capture them again. She turned her head, only to be caught in a kiss with Vallen, who also had one leg hooked around hers. The two of them had pulled her thighs wide, and she groaned into Vallen's mouth as Rosuke thrust his fingers into her while thumbing her clit. Vallen plucked the tip of her breast with his free hand while Rosuke mouthed her other nipple, the flat of his tongue rubbing the tight, sensitive peak.

Gasping, she pulled away from Vallen. "Please, I need someone inside me. Now." Rosuke took his fingers from her and licked them, and she sighed as the tension temporarily released her.

"Let's finish this," Vallen declared. He climbed up the bed and arranged a few pillows before lying back, his upper body propped up. She wondered if he would watch from there, but he slid his hands under her arms and pulled her up, settling her between his spread legs. They worked together to strip her dress from her shoulders, and she lay back on his chest. His cock was warm and hard against her lower back.

Rosuke crawled to follow them. His raging erection swung heavily from his pelvis, framed by his red hair flowing over each shoulder. He was going to fit himself between her thighs, trap her between his body and Vallen's, and—

Ambushed by renewed shyness, she tried to close her legs, but Vallen hooked his hands behind her knees and pulled them wide.

"Vallen," she yelped, grabbing his wrists. Her heart raced.

"You're so beautiful," Rosuke groaned, staring unabashedly at her sex. He caressed her wriggling leg as he moved between her thighs.

"Beautiful and bewitching," Vallen said, low. He kissed the shell of her ear. She ceased her struggles, cheeks radiating heat.

"I'm rather jealous," Rosuke confessed. He braced one hand on the bed and grasped the base of his cock. "Vallen's found someone so sweet and passionate." He rubbed himself over her wet lips.

Her head spun. "Divine One be merciful."

"He will be," Vallen said in a rough whisper.

"I shall enjoy watching you come—both of you." Rosuke pressed his hips forward.

"G-Gods," she sobbed out, grasping his shoulder in one hand and the bedding in her other. Vallen breathed hard against her neck.

Rosuke went slow, sinking in only halfway. Then he slid his palms beneath Vallen's, replacing them and freeing Vallen's hands. She made a small, embarrassed sound as he widened her legs, then a choked gasp as he pushed deep, fully sheathing himself inside her. Vallen slid his arm around her waist and dipped his other hand between her legs to tease her clit. She moaned, long and loud, and then again when Rosuke began moving.

"You feel so good." Rosuke squeezed her thighs as he smoothly pumped his hips. "Warm, wet..." He pressed deep and swirled against her insides. Vallen groaned into her neck, and his heart thudded against her back.

"I c-can't believe this is h-happening." She laid her head on Vallen's shoulder. He rocked his hips as if he couldn't help it—off-rhythm and erratic. His slick erection slid along her spine.

She was certain she'd pass out at any moment. Having both Vallen's hand and Rosuke's cock between her thighs had pushed her to a new level of pleasure. She had never thought she could feel so aroused in a situation such as this, a situation she wouldn't have even dreamed of before today. Rosuke said everything she needed to hear to feel desired and confident, and Vallen's embrace made her feel safe. His presence was a solid, comforting weight behind her.

"How are you doing?" Rosuke asked when she covered her eyes. His voice had dropped in pitch, like Vallen's did when he made love to her. The sound of it reminded her of a dozen other orgasms, and her body clamped down on the demon driving into her. Rosuke grunted in reaction.

"Overwhelmed," she breathlessly answered, sighing as another wave of that wonderful, dizzying sensation radiated from where she and Rosuke were joined. "Don't stop. I'm so close already." Rosuke thrust harder, slapping against her body with each stroke.

"By the gods," Vallen growled while he nuzzled her ear. His finger on her clit didn't stop. He felt everything she felt, and knew how to touch her, pulling back when she was close, pushing her hard when Rosuke's angle was perfect. She wanted to wrap her legs tight around Rosuke, tense her abs, and fall apart in Vallen's arms, but she also wanted the delicious friction to last as long as possible, even if only a few seconds more.

Vallen knew he was exhausting Shumei, but now was the only time he'd feel only her side of their lovemaking. He wanted to learn how her body responded, what she liked, and how high he could build her anticipation. Only he would know the best way to touch her, taste her, tease and release her.

"Please, Vallen," she mewled. "Let me come. Please, please."

"Rosuke," he grunted, earning his friend's frenzied attention. "Deep, short, and slow." Rosuke nodded and did as directed. Vallen swirled her clit.

She stiffened with a gasp. Vallen growled and bucked against her. Through the binding, he felt her pleasure rise. It was like a warm wave, a flood of heat. Nothing like the sharp, sudden satisfaction of his own climaxes. No, this was intoxication.

"Thank you, Shumei," Rosuke moaned. His deep voice clashed with another, and Vallen realized he was groaning as if in agony.

"A-ah!" Shumei cried out, high and airy. She clamped on to Rosuke's shoulder, threw her head back, and spread her thighs wide. Pleasure filled her, hot and dizzying. She moaned over and over, toes curling and nails digging into the shoulder of the man between her legs. Rosuke writhed against her, forehead furrowed with ecstasy.

Her magic, awake and watchful, shot out from her wet, pulsating core and shocked Rosuke with one of its feelers, feeding him energy in one big dose. Rosuke gasped as though he had been splashed with ice-cold water. Vallen gave a deep, sharp groan and covered her back with his seed.

Rosuke released her legs in favor of grabbing on to her knees, and her thighs came to rest around his hips. He hissed, emptying inside her as he slowly thrust. Vallen squeezed his hand between her body and his, and pumped himself as he humped against her, still covering them both with endless streams of his pleasure. Shumei sighed, content to lie there in all of that mess while her orgasm—and Vallen's—still warmed her sex.

They stayed that way for a moment, catching their breath as Rosuke rubbed inside her to stretch out her climax. Eventually, his erection abated and he pulled out.

"That had to be immoral," she croaked. She drew her shaking legs together. Vallen wrapped his arms around her and kissed her cheek.

Rosuke sat back on his heels, head spinning. He had an insane urge to giggle.

"No, it felt too divine," Vallen countered, nuzzling her ear. Rosuke lightly laughed in agreement. "If we could, I'd gladly spend the rest of the day putting you in every possible position I could think of, just to see if the noises from your throat sounded different each time."

"Perhaps after the little one has fallen asleep tonight, we can use one of the separate buildings where the old servants used to stay," Rosuke suggested, leaning back on his hands. His cock felt well used, but the idea appealed enough to make it twitch with interest.

"I don't think my throat would last," she whispered, putting her head back on Vallen's shoulder.

"You'd be amazed how long a woman can scream with the right men making love to her," Rosuke rejoined, rolling his neck. The dizzy feeling was starting to fade, and he realized with a grin that she had completely replenished him.

"I believe she's passed out," Vallen observed, craning his head to see her slumbering face.

Rosuke tilted his head to the side and with a smile said, "Sleep well, Shumei. And thank you again for saving my life."

Chapter Fifteen

Deep whispers drew Shumei from sleep. She felt clean...and far too warm. Not only was she dressed again, she was also covered in blankets and bracketed on both sides by two sex demons. Their soft conversation had woken her, but the room was still dark. How long had she been asleep?

"When do you think she'll have learned the circle?" Rosuke murmured.

"Perhaps another week," Vallen said.

"Vallen?" she croaked. Both demons jerked in surprise.

"Sorry, did we wake you?" he responded.

"I need water," she said, then swallowed around the scratchiness in her throat. Rosuke pulled away from her and she heard the bedroom door slide open.

Vallen kissed her forehead. "How are you feeling, love?"

"I think I'll be fine once I drink some water. What time of day is it?"

"The sun rises in about an hour."

"What? Why have I been asleep so long?"

"Well, you've been feeding me weekly, and then you gave Rosuke a whole month's worth of energy. And I know you've been depriving yourself of sleep while trying to memorize that damned circle for the ritual. You were exhausted."

She turned toward the scent of his spiced soap. "How's Oka? Is he worried?"

"I told him casting magic takes a toll on beginners. He assumed you waved your hand over Rosuke to heal him and then passed out from the effort. He doesn't know what happened in this room."

"That's good. He's not yet ten as it is." She breathed a sigh of relief, snuggling close.

Rosuke returned a moment later bearing a cup of water, and though she didn't need any help, both demons pulled her to a sitting position. She gratefully downed the water without stopping for breath, and the cup was taken away from her before she could even ask. She felt like a pampered princess, and she wasn't sure whether she liked it.

"Are you still tired?" Vallen asked. She blinked the sleep from her eyes and saw that both of them were half-naked. The light of a single lantern in the hallway outlined their bare upper bodies, and for a second, she remembered being pressed between them, hot and sweating and mewling for more.

Blushing, she looked down at herself. Someone had dressed her in a silken under-robe that was nearly see-through. The shadow of her aureoles was easy to see, even in the dim light. She quickly covered herself.

"Did you bathe and dress me?" she asked Vallen.

"Rosuke wanted to, but I didn't let him," he said with a cocky smile. "He took care of the bedding instead—on the condition that I dress you in that."

"I'm not a doll," she said sternly. The two demons exchanged a glance that said neither of them were at all contrite.

"Would you have preferred we put you to bed naked? Many nobles slept as such, including me," Vallen said. Shumei huffed, wondering where all his appreciation from earlier had gone.

"Well, we should all be awake—and dressed appropriately—when Oka comes to breakfast. After that, I'll continue studying the ritual to cure you. What you do with your morning is up to you, obviously," she said, tossing her mane of hair over her shoulder.

"It seems we've been dismissed," Rosuke joked, sliding off the bed again and making a show of it as he flashed a sultry look at Shumei. Vallen rolled his eyes at his friend, knowing he was joking when he flirted. It was Rosuke's way of coping.

After they'd put Shumei to bed, they'd had quite a long conversation with Oka concerning what had happened to his older sister. The boy had been much more suspicious than they'd led her to believe, but they had successfully quelled his concerns.

Only after that intense inquisition was Vallen finally able to tell Rosuke of the news about their cure. Rosuke had cracked a joke, certain Vallen was kidding about finding the Devil's Hand, and only when Vallen had pointed out the open spell book on the table did Rosuke believe him.

Rosuke had lost the ability to speak, then the ability to sit straight, slumping in shock and putting his face in his hands. He'd muttered to himself for a moment, sending up prayers of thanks to the Divine One.

"I know you love her, Vallen," he'd eventually said, "but for what she's done for me—for us—and for what she's about to do, I swear on my life to spend what remains of it doing everything in my power to show my full and undying loyalty."

They had spent the rest of the day preparing a separate bedroom for Rosuke and cleaning the inner ring of hallways, but one of the three of them felt the need to check on Shumei more than a dozen times. As they worked, Rosuke had him and Oka laughing several times, his spirits higher than Vallen had seen in centuries.

Of course, Rosuke had not yet used his bedroom. As demons, neither of them needed to sleep, and with an end to their curse in sight, they wouldn't have been able to even if they'd tried.

Looking at Shumei, who regarded Rosuke with feigned anger, Vallen realized just how much she had given both of them, and how much more she was going to give them. He wondered how he could ever repay her.

"There are some dresses to choose from in the cabinet over here," he explained, getting off the bed as well. She turned to him. "You may join us for breakfast in the sitting room in about an hour, I would estimate." He headed toward the bedroom door, through which Rosuke had already left.

Shumei hadn't told him about her dream yet. She had dreamed it again last night, and it had been longer this time. More details about the land had become clear to her, and they hadn't faded into the vague memories of dreams one usually had after waking.

She still remembered the many vistas, the faces of leaders who had witnessed her passing, and even the dress she'd worn as she'd traveled through all these realms—white with a golden sun pattern. At the end, when she had arrived at Vallen's estate, she had recognized one of the black-haired people who'd come to greet her. Rosuke's smiling face was right behind Oka as both ran up to her, including a third person—a woman with confident eyes.

"V-Vallen," she started, rising to her knees. He turned back to her, eyebrows raised. She stared at him for a moment, and the words she wanted to say were on the tip of her tongue. "It's nothing, never mind."

"Take your time getting dressed," he said, smiling. He slid the door shut behind him, and his footsteps faded as he walked down the hall.

"I dream about you," she whispered, staring sadly at the closed door. "And in my dreams, you're dead."

**⁎
⁎⁎**

EVERYONE HAD FINISHED the midday meal, and Shumei sat on the edge of the porch, swinging her legs. The dress she'd chosen was deep blue and covered with a koi fish pattern from collar to hem. The turquoise belt had given her difficulty, being of a style she'd not worn before. The two ends of the bow in back were meant to drape low, and it had taken her forever to keep them short enough not to touch the floor when walking around. She rather liked the effect, though, for it looked like a bright blue tail.

Vallen and Rosuke had liked it as well, but Oka had wondered why anyone would wear something so hard to fight in.

"Why would I need to fight if you three are protecting me?" she had asked, and in response, Oka had straightened with pride. She knew being equated to two skilled warriors would please him.

Thus, the three of them had been engaged in sword practice all morning. At present, Oka was taking a break to watch Vallen and Rosuke show off their rather impressive techniques using real swords. The wide-eyed look on her brother's face made her smile every time she glanced at him.

She, however, was busy memorizing the ritual circle. She returned her gaze to the spell book, which lay on a cloth draped over her lap to protect her skirt from the cover's chalky black residue. Frowning with concentration, she scrutinized the complicated pattern.

Several basic shapes overlapped, each containing symbols Vallen had explained were the written form of Mahou. One read *sunder*, another read *lust*... This complex array was then surrounded by several concentric circles of different thicknesses, which apparently determined how much magic was fed into different stages of the invocation and how quickly. Within these rings were longer phrases in Mahou, each describing desired magical effects.

She was only grateful there was no specific order in which to draw the circle, and the dimensions didn't have to be perfect. Vallen had told her of spells where the time limit was even smaller, and the circle could only be successfully drawn if the caster never lifted the writing instrument they were using. She wished she could have the spell book next to her and open for reference when drawing it for real, but allowing another representation of the circle within the ritual space disrupted the casting.

Both hands on the pages in front of her, she leaned down and stared at the circle she had come to loathe, wishing with all her might that she knew it by heart. She wanted to be able to draw it in fifteen minutes, eyes closed. But so far, the fastest she'd managed was twenty minutes too long.

Her vision blurred. She lifted her head and blinked but couldn't get her focus back. She shut her eyes, waited a moment, and then opened them again. The pages had turned black and looked as deep as a canyon, as vast and powerful as the ocean Vallen had once described to her.

Then she lost her balance.

Her hands sank into the book, through her legs, through the porch, and then she tipped forward, falling into the pages. Her feet flew over her head. Her whole body was being sucked into the book.

Panicking, she tried to look around, but saw only darkness. She couldn't even see her hands in front of her face. Then a faint figure appeared before her. It looked like a person, but it had no clean shape, as though it wasn't solid.

The circle appeared in front of her, giant and shining. It glowed so bright the air hummed at a resonance that hurt. She slapped her hands over her ears, eyes watering because she couldn't close them. Then the humming cut off and the circle burst into a thousand pieces, all jagged shapes like broken glass. She screamed in fright as they flew at her, but she couldn't move. She could only float there as they came zooming at her.

The first one pierced her body, warm and liquid. She fell silent with a gasp when there was no pain. The pieces all fell into her, then into place inside her, reassembling themselves. Her mind's eye traced the circle over and over again, starting from a new spot every time. She watched it being traced hundreds, thousands of times and knew she would never forget its shape.

Then a new circle appeared in front of her, and she somehow knew it was the circle drawn to invoke the Incubus Curse. It burst as well, flying into her body and imprinting itself on her brain.

Another circle appeared, and then another. One for curing a particular magical illness, one for growing whole forests, one for casting a defensive shield over a city thousands of miles away, one for a ritual to pay homage to the Divine One.

A hundred circles, a thousand circles—they all appeared in front of her. So bright was their glow that her eyes ached, and they continually fell into her. She convulsed as she took them all in, and the knowledge of their shapes was a boiling heat that made her think she was melting. Days seemed to pass, and the only way to tell how many circles were left was the slowly fading glow all around her.

The last circle appeared, and she knew it as she had known all the others. It was a circle no one but she could draw, meant only for her. She memorized it as well, a tear falling from her eye as she realized its significance. It was the last circle, yet somehow she knew it was just a taste of the knowledge she was meant to learn.

It was dark again, and she floated there alone, exhausted. Her eyes slowly adjusted to the darkness, and she saw the figure of a man in front of her once more. He had been there all along, watching her absorb the magical patterns. He moved forward, his dimensions barely discernable, like smoke hovering in the dark of night. His hands, foggy and unclear, reached out to her, and she felt his cool touch on her face.

His outline grew more distinct, glowing as though the sun had risen behind him. He leaned forward. "Soon, my chosen one," he whispered. "I am already proud."

He kissed her forehead, and she fell immediately to sleep, head rolling back. All was quiet for a long while.

"Shumei! Please wake up," a familiar voice begged. "Divine One be merciful."

Then came a young voice. "What happened? What happened to her?"

"We don't know, little one. Fetch some water, quickly," a third voice said.

She groaned, feeling as if she had been lying there for a week. The back of her head throbbed with pain, and her throat hurt.

"Shumei. Thank the Divine One," Vallen said, touching his lips to her forehead. He held her in his arms, and when she opened her eyes, she found herself still on the porch.

"What happened?" Rosuke asked, kneeling by her other side. She tried to speak, but her throat was so dry.

"*Mizu...mizu hoshii*," she croaked. Both demons gasped.

"What did you just say?" Vallen asked.

"Want...water," she whispered, wondering why they hadn't heard her the first time.

"Is she awake?" Oka panted, running up to them with a jug and a cup. Rosuke jumped off the porch to make way for him.

"G... Give her some water first," Vallen said, face frozen.

"She just spoke Mahou," Rosuke whispered vehemently. He and Vallen shared a look she could not understand. They watched as she gratefully gulped down the water.

"Shumei, what happened?" Vallen asked again once she had caught her breath.

"I was...studying the circle and watching you." She paused, wondering how to describe her experience. It had been as vivid and upsetting as her recurring dream, and she was certain both events were more than what they'd seemed. She felt as though she was going crazy.

"I remember wishing to have the circle memorized, but then I fell." She looked from one concerned face to another. "I fell *into* the book. I must have just fainted, but...the dream I had felt so real." She snuggled closer to Vallen.

"What was the dream?" Rosuke asked.

"I saw the circle, and it broke apart and fell into me. And then more and more circles appeared, and they did the same. It felt like days had passed, and I was ready to faint from the heat."

Vallen and Rosuke exchanged another enigmatic look. With Vallen's help, she sat up and discovered the book still sitting in her lap. She had merely slumped backward. Vallen sat on one side of her while Oka sat on the other. Rosuke stood upon the ground in front of them, arms crossed.

"What did you see happen?" she asked.

"I was watching them fight," Oka began, "and I heard a thump. You were lying on your back. I called your name but you didn't answer."

"Rosuke and I realized something was wrong when Oka called your name a second time," Vallen said.

"That's when you screamed," Rosuke said.

"I've never been so scared in my life," Vallen said, banding his arm around her shoulders. Oka wrapped his smaller arm around her waist.

"We all ran over to see what was happening, and by the time Vallen picked you up, you were convulsing and your face was red," Rosuke explained.

"Whatever it was, it made it possible for me to draw that damned circle. And I could do it with plenty of time to spare. I could do it with my eyes closed," she boasted.

"Really?" Rosuke asked, leaning forward to grasp her knees. Vallen and Oka pressed in close, and Vallen echoed Rosuke's excitement.

"Can I watch you do the spell?" Oka asked. She gasped and looked down at him, realizing she had no way to explain it was a ritual he really wouldn't want to see.

At once, both demons said no.

"What? Why?" he asked. "You always tell me to leave the room or go somewhere else. What's going on?"

Rosuke shrugged. "Vallen and I have to be naked for the ritual, and I'm too embarrassed to be naked in front of a child." Shumei's jaw dropped at how quickly Rosuke had revealed such a damning fact.

"Why do you have to be naked?" Oka asked.

"Rosuke," she said in a warning tone.

"There's plenty of time when you're older to see naked people," Rosuke said, no doubt to distract Oka from his original point.

"I-I don't," Oka exclaimed. "I just want to see some magic."

"I'll show you something else, then," she offered, latching on to his true wish.

"Really?"

"Sure," she said, thinking quickly. She had never tried to perform magic on command and was hoping one of the many circles she had memorized would surface in her mind. On cue, the perfect one appeared.

She made to move, and all three of them stopped crowding her. After setting the spell book on the porch behind her, she slipped on her shoes and hopped to the ground. While searching for the right spot, she picked up a stick lying beneath a tree a few feet away.

Whereas other circles had to be drawn with some sort of implement and an "ink," whether chalk, coal, blood, water, or something similar, this circle merely needed to be traced over the ground—no lasting marks necessary.

When she had found an area about fifteen feet across and free of large tree roots, she stood in the center and closed her eyes. A tree had once grown here, long ago, and it was now part of the house. Its roots had rotted away, becoming a part of the earth again. There was room for a new tree to grow.

Vallen watched in stunned silence as she whipped the small branch through the air, and even he could not recognize the circle she was creating. All he could tell was its similarity to patterns used by his family's house. A pattern for plants.

He felt the pulse when her circle was complete, a tightening in the air. She backed away, tossed aside the branch, and spoke one simple evocation.

"*Ki.*"

There was a great rumbling, and the trees around them groaned as a large vine shot out of the ground, twisting and sprouting branches and leaves as it grew taller. The ground churned and broke as the vine widened, rising higher and higher. Its branches spread, filling in the space where sunlight had once hit the ground, growing bigger and fuller until the new tree hardened and came to a stop with one last shudder.

"Wow," Oka cried out, clapping. He scrambled off the porch and ran to her. No doubt having taxed her magic, she struggled to smile while yawning. "Do it again, again!" He grabbed her skirt and danced around.

"It takes a lot of energy to do that. Maybe later, when I feel stronger?"

Rosuke and Vallen stood by the porch, speechless.

"I've only seen your grandmother do that," Rosuke said.

"Maybe she's meant for House Tree," Vallen wondered, chest swelling with pride.

"She may," Rosuke agreed. "We're going to be cured, Vallen. I don't know about you, but I'm shaking."

"I can hardly believe it, nor how ill I'd treated her at first." By the dueling gods, he'd taken her within minutes of meeting her—and in a field, no less. If he had been human, he'd have wooed her as none ever had even at the height of the Dark Court. He'd have given her flowers, poetry, and adventure. And when she was ready, he'd have made love to her so gently he wouldn't have needed the virginal spell.

"Time will move forward for us, starting tonight, and you'll have the rest of your life to make up for it," Rosuke said.

"I'll need all of it to express the full depth of my love and gratitude."

Chapter Sixteen

V allen ordered Shumei to take a nap and refresh herself before the ritual. Everyone else spent the afternoon cleaning and preparing one of the three rooms on the estate meant for magical rites. Rather than straw mats, the floor was a smooth, hard wood that was easy to draw upon. The only furniture was an altar large enough to hold a *rakuda* and a table meant for preparing ritual components.

Vallen and Oka scrubbed the floor of old chalk markings. Rosuke cleaned the altar and table, draping both with heavy black ceremonial cloths that hadn't been used for nearly two hundred years, but that remained as serviceable as the day they'd been made.

The remaining chores included replacing the paper in the sliding doors and the candles throughout the room. After new chalk was placed on the table, all that was left was to wake the witch to perform the ritual.

"Shumei?" Oka whispered, kneeling on the edge of her bed to shake her shoulder.

"Is it already time?" she asked sleepily, turning languidly toward his voice. "Are they in the bath now?"

"Yeah. Rosuke said they wanted to 'look pretty' for you," Oka said with a laugh. "Are you really going to see them naked? Is it because they'll transform?"

She groaned in embarrassment, cheeks lighting up. Now was one of those moments when she wished her brother were entirely the mature adult he sometimes seemed to be.

"All you need to know is that Vallen and Rosuke were once human and will be again soon," she said, soft but firm. She ruffled his feathery blond hair.

Oka pouted but nodded. "I'll be back before dark, but I'll go straight to my room until someone comes for me." He stood and went to the door.

"Be careful," she called, sitting up.

After rubbing the sleep from her eyes, she gingerly moved off the bed. She was still wearing her goldfish dress but carefully removed it and put it back in the cabinet. Wondering what she should choose to wear for the ceremony, she pawed through the dozen or so choices hanging in the cabinet. The spell did not specify any particular outfit, but considering the ritual component she had to obtain, she took one look at the nearly see-through robe she'd been wearing that morning and smiled.

Rosuke and Vallen waited in ritual room, twiddling their thumbs impatiently.

"I'm nervous," Rosuke admitted, flashing a smile at Vallen. "Sitting naked on an altar like this reminds me of that night."

"It should. We're going to reverse what happened back then."

"Do you think we'll get our magic back?"

"I want to hope we will, but the reversal spell didn't say for certain," Vallen answered, gut aching. As a fully charged sex demon, he had far more strength and stamina at his disposal for protecting Shumei than a mundane human did. If his magic were restored, the situation would be completely different, but no one could predict whether the Divine One would grant such a gift again.

"Good evening," a soft voice called.

Both demons twisted their heads toward the door, where a young, black-haired witch stood wearing a robe so thin and sheer that she seemed clothed only in a thin veil of mist. It was the robe they had dressed her in earlier, and which had left Vallen's cock straining against his pants as they'd tucked her into bed.

Shumei smiled coyly as both demons quickly grew erect. Rosuke lightly stroked himself and stared at her openmouthed.

"No need to get ahead of ourselves, Rosuke," she chided, closing the door behind her. He swallowed hard and took his hand away.

"You remember all the steps?" Vallen asked, mouth dry. Shumei's breasts bounced lightly as she walked to the preparation table, her raspberry nipples teasing him behind their veil of cream-tinted cloth. She looked like a forbidden dessert.

"Of course. The first step—placing the subjects on the altar—is already complete." She smiled at them over her shoulder. "The next step is the circle. It must be completed within an hour once started, with the same writing instrument, and must be used within three hours."

The night Vallen and Rosuke had been cursed, the noblewoman had completed the circle and had covered it with a large rug before luring them away from a party. The altar had simply been a table laden with food and drink, where they had finished off several bottles of rice wine. She had flirted with all of them, and none of them had balked when she had pulled at the ties of their pants.

She had begun with Vallen, who had been too drunk to care who was pleasuring him, and only when he felt something wet swiped across his stomach did he begin to suspect. He had lifted his head and had seen blood on his skin—her blood. But before he could do anything, she had already completed the short invocation, and the excruciating pain had started. The noblewoman's cackle had haunted him for decades.

Shumei gingerly picked up the chalk on the preparation table and approached the altar. Rosuke and Vallen watched anxiously, but she didn't let it affect her concentration. She was determined to make this work.

Legs bent and eyes closed, she touched the chalk to the wooden floor and began to draw, moving her arm in wide sweeps and zipping around the corners of the inner array of shapes. She stepped carefully as she formed the circle, wary of smudging any lines, and was halfway around the room in only five minutes. She heard whispers from the altar, but ignored them, continuing until she reached the spot where she'd started. With one final flourish of her hand, she finished.

When she opened her eyes, she discovered only a small piece of her chalk was left. She breathed a sigh of relief that she hadn't run out. Other circles required even more detail than this one.

"Wow," Rosuke breathed as he stared unabashedly at her breasts.

"Looks perfect to me," Vallen said gruffly, also staring.

"So is the circle," she said with a chuckle as she stood. "Or is that what you were referring to?"

"Of course not," Rosuke said, writhing with impatience. Smiling, she walked the short distance to the side of the altar where her two subjects sat.

"The third step is the main spell component—man's essence," she said, slowly unknotting the belt of her diaphanous robe. Both demons watched intently, mouths open. "Who's first?"

"Me," Vallen growled. Air sawed in and out of his lungs. Her heart raced as she held his gaze and nudged her robe open. It slipped past her shoulders and clung to the bends of her elbows. A long, hot slide of arousal filled her, undoubtedly Vallen's reaction. His cock thickened and subtly twitched in time with his rapid pulse.

"A-Are you ready?" she whispered, propping her hands her hands on her hips in an attempt to seem calm, but she didn't pull it off very well.

"I'll always be ready for you." He leaned back and braced his palms on the altar as he widened his knees to make room for her.

The picture he made had her practically drooling. His smooth, wide chest, the tension in his abdomen that spoke to his desire, his powerful thighs, and the look he was giving her. Aching to be touched, she thumbed her nipples to make them pucker, then lightly pinched them until the jolt of pleasure she felt reflected on Vallen's face. His back stiffened. Then he closed his eyes and bit his lip. A glance at Rosuke confirmed he was looking at her as if awaiting an enormous feast.

Vallen opened his eyes again, lids low with need. She slid one of her hands down her body and between her thighs. She had never touched herself in front of him before but knew he'd enjoy it as much as she'd enjoy being watched.

"Shumei," he grunted, panting. She found and massaged her clit, rolling it gently while her other hand was occupied with her breast. Vallen winced and tensed again as a drop of arousal seeped from the tip of his cock. She pressed a second finger between her labia, using both to press and swirl her clit.

"By the dueling gods," Rosuke whispered.

"Come to me," Vallen pleaded, reaching for his erection, but he hesitated and sank his fingers into his thigh instead.

The temptation to use her power over him was too much to resist, and she slid her longest finger into her vagina, pushing it deep.

"S-Shumei, I beg you!"

Exultant, she pulled her hand away and stepped between his knees. Vallen grasped her wrist and brought her hand to his mouth.

"Vallen," she choked out as he sucked on her fingers. Then he pulled them from his mouth with a pop. After leaving one last kiss on the back of her hand, he pushed her to her knees.

She knelt on one of the pillows lining the altar's base and hummed with excitement as he pulled her head forward. She opened her mouth and watched him guide his glistening cock between her lips.

"Take it," he said, pushing her head down his shaft. He hissed when his erection touched the back of her throat, then groaned as she bobbed her head. Settling into a rhythm that pleasured him, she curled her arms around his waist.

Vallen wished he could see the gentle sway of her breasts, but the sight of her soft, pink lips wrapped around his cock was also fascinating. Her small, warm hands gripped his sides. Her long hair and silky robe brushed his legs. The wet sucking sounds her mouth made filled his ears. He forced his hands off her head and braced them behind his hips, which he couldn't stop from rocking upward.

He croaked her name and threw his head back. "I'm c-coming. Got so much for you."

A roar exploded from his throat. She writhed between his legs, struggling with her own climax while swallowing his.

"Y-Yes," he groaned, white-knuckling fistfuls of the black cloth beneath him. "Suck me dry."

"Gods," Rosuke rasped. "She really might."

Shumei licked her lips as she lifted her head. Nothing had spilled, but she had nearly lost herself to pleasure. She brought her hands back to wipe at the tears of effort clinging to her eyelashes. Then Vallen collapsed onto the altar.

"Vallen," she cried out. She pulled herself to a stand, barely able to keep her trembling legs beneath her, and leaned over him.

"Did she kill you?" Rosuke joked, flicking one of Vallen's cheeks.

"I'll be fine...in a few weeks," he answered with a slow, languid smile.

"You scared me." She lightly punched his shoulder, then laughed with relief.

She hadn't known whether she could...properly consume the ritual component. She had never gotten that far whenever they'd been together. If any had spilled from her mouth and touched the floor, the spell would have become useless. She wouldn't have forgiven herself if she'd made the same mistake as the noblewoman. She had to make sure both of them became human again.

"My turn?" Rosuke asked, deep and sultry.

She blinked, having been lost in thought, and noted the desperate set of his brow. He stroked himself, and the movement made her look at his lap. His cock was flushed and hard, its deep red head glistening with arousal. Her heart kicked.

"Will you suck me dry too?" he whispered, brushing his thumb over the sensitive slit on the tip. "Will you make me scream at the ceiling while I come at the back of your throat?"

"Rosuke," she stammered, blushing fiercely. And she'd thought Vallen was generous with sexual banter.

"It saddens me you'll be all his again after the ritual. I'll have no excuse to touch you." He tilted his head and leaned toward her, red hair spilling over his shoulder. "There are so many things I still want to do to you."

"Oh my," she whispered, bashful despite all she'd done right in front of him. "Rosuke, how do you do that?"

"Centuries of practice," Vallen said, eyes closed.

Rosuke gave a lopsided smile and beckoned her. She took his outstretched hand, feeling again the calluses on his delicate fingers from his sword use, and stepped between his knees.

"I'll remember this moment forever," he vowed. "And not just the pleasure. You... You're saving my life and my soul, Shumei."

She swallowed, feeling pressured, and shrugged off her robe. Vallen still lay on his back catching his breath, and she set her scant clothing beside him.

Then she touched Rosuke's chest, brushing aside long locks of his red hair. She pressed the pads of her thumbs against his nipples and rubbed in slow circles, watching his eyes darken. He made a sound so soft she hardly heard it, and his small nipples stiffened. With a gentle push on his shoulders, she urged him to put his hands back, and it put his chest at the perfect angle. Pressing close, she braced her hands by his and kissed his right nipple.

Rosuke sharply inhaled, whispered her name, then groaned as she tongued his nipple while staring at him. How could she look so innocent and so sexual at the same time? The silky skin of her stomach brushed against his cock, and the sensation made the room turn blurry. Then she molded her lips around his other nipple and sucked gently.

Jealousy churned in his gut even as he closed his eyes with delight, and he wasn't even sure whom he was jealous of. Vallen, Shumei, or both? How he wanted every night to be like last night. The three of them intertwined on a wide bed. They could introduce Shumei to so many things, so many ways to feel. He and Vallen would bring her to multiple climaxes and then sleep with her tucked between them. He wished it could be the three of them, but Shumei and Vallen were deeply in love and it was too late even to think about intruding. They would have each other and he would be alone.

Such melancholy thoughts flew right out of his head, though, when Shumei touched his cock. Her warm hand, gentle but firm, squeezed with just the right pressure as she slowly rubbed up and down. He opened his eyes and bemoaned his blurry vision as she knelt on the floor. She pulled her mass of long hair over one shoulder, as if knowing he wanted to watch, then leaned into him, mouth open.

He couldn't get any air into his lungs. His breaths came in shuddering gulps. When her lips and tongue touched him, he moaned louder and louder the farther she went down his shaft. He settled one hand on the back of her head as she pulled her lips back, sucking hard and nearly leaving him before gobbling him up again. Then she followed her mouth with her hand. He rolled his hips and hissed as every muscle in his body clenched so hard he shook.

"Oh dueling gods, this feels good," he groaned.

He had wanted to hold out, to make this last as long as possible and remember it well, but now he wondered whether he could. She sucked faster, harder, and his face heated. He gritted his teeth and fisted his hand in her hair.

"My cock's g-gonna melt." He tried to slow her down with his hand in her hair. She coughed and wrapped her free hand around his wrist.

"Don't choke her," Vallen said.

Rosuke gasped at the soft, deep voice in his ear. He hadn't even realized Vallen had sat up. Close enough for Rosuke to feel his body heat, Vallen watched everything Shumei was doing to him. By the dueling gods, his heart would rip itself in half.

"Put your hands back and let it come," Vallen said in a serious tone.

Rosuke realized he had almost ruined everything. If Shumei wasn't prepared to swallow, the spell would be wasted. So he nodded in understanding, leaned back on his hands, and let her dictate the pace. She licked her lips, smiled briefly, and then resumed.

"How does it feel?" Vallen whispered. Rosuke grunted, jerking his hips involuntarily. He couldn't tell whether he liked her mouth or pussy better. He had loved giving her pleasure but damn did he also love receiving it. And how long had it been since he'd loved either? Years? Decades?

"How does it feel, Rosuke?" Vallen uttered. "Tell her."

"Like she's sucking out my soul," he sobbed. He was going to explode. Burning heat coalesced and rose up his shaft. She paused, lips still wrapped around the head, and rapidly pumped his cock in her fist. "I'm c-com—"

He gave a choked roar as pleasure seized his voice. He wanted to press deep into her mouth but forced his ass to stay where it was, and twitched as each throb rolled through him. He came and came and came, hardly able to breathe. When the stranglehold on his throat ceased, he gave an agonized cry and slumped back with exhaustion.

Vallen watched as Shumei swallowed the ritual component with the most beautiful, determined look on her face, hand at the ready to make sure absolutely nothing spilled. She was gorgeous in the midst of all this sex and magic, so different from the first night he'd met her. Then she had been naïve and uncertain, if no less adventurous. Now she was provocative, confident.

Though he loved Rosuke like a brother, and though he knew yesterday and today had been necessary to save his life, jealously raged inside him. He wanted to rip Shumei away and prevent Rosuke from ever touching her again, or even looking at her. So he consoled himself with knowing that from tomorrow on, he alone would be responsible for her pleasure, and that her lust-glazed eyes would only ever be directed at him, her moans only ever because of him. From that night on, she would be his and he would be hers—and no one else's.

Never again would he take another woman. Never again would he even want another. She owned him, mind, body, and even soul should the spell work. With the completion of the ritual, she would wash away his demonic taint, making her something close to a god. He would love her until the day he died.

Vallen held Rosuke's hand as the redhead caught his breath. Shumei had risen to her feet, and the expression on her face...

Something inside her had changed. She was growing more powerful with each passing second, as if her magic would unfurl endlessly.

They were nearing the end of the ritual. Having obtained the ritual component from both of them, the next step was two final kisses and an invocation in Mahou. Beyond that, no one knew what would happen precisely.

Shumei leaned toward him. She kissed him, tongue shyly touching his, and he eagerly responded. He expected to taste the musk of sex, but heat poured into his mouth. It slid down his throat like a breath of air in the Black Sands and settled as a pool of warmth in his stomach. It spread from there, and the farther it went, the sleepier he became.

"S-Shumei," he whispered as she pulled her mouth away. He fell back on the altar, too weak to move. His eyelids felt heavy, and the last thing he saw was Rosuke reaching for his kiss.

Shumei rested her hand on Rosuke's chest as she kissed him in the same manner as she had Vallen. It was happening, she could feel it. The magic was sparking. Its heat traveled from her mouth to his, and like Vallen, Rosuke fell away when she lifted her lips. They both looked so delicious lying there, naked and satisfied.

She had to stand on a certain spot within the circle, so she carefully picked her way to it as power sizzled over her skin, washing up, down, and around in all directions.

Both demons, now drunk on power, lay helpless on the altar, as they had been when the noblewoman had spilled the cup of their essence on the circle. It had symbolized the rejection of their lust, but Shumei had accepted it when swallowing. The blood spread on their stomachs had been symbolic of the death of their magic. But with the Kiss of Power, Shumei had passed some of her magic into their bodies to germinate. Divine One willing, those seeds would quicken with her invocation. She clenched her hands in silent appeal.

"*Saa, noroi ga tokareru toki ga yattekita.*" The words flowed easily from her lips, and the translation she hadn't natively understood before seemed perfectly clear now.

The time has come to undo this curse.

"*Kono kotoba wo motte, kanzen ni moto no ningen ni modoshiteyaru.*"

With these words, thou shall return fully human.

She drew her fists tight and hoped with everything she had.

"*Kai!*"

The sizzling sensation surging over her skin grew exponentially, flowing into the circle in great waves. Her magic buzzed in her core. Its hum filled her ears, blocking out everything else as it had done before. An immense buildup was forming, slowly filling in the lines of the circle like blood pumping through veins.

She kept her eyes open, wanting to watch the result, no matter if it was the desired one or not. But the room was so bright, as if the sun itself sat in the corner. The circle pulsed with energy, riding the beat of her heart. The two demons on the altar still lay motionless, and she had to resist the urge to check on them. She mustn't move. Mustn't even lift her foot off the floor lest it somehow disrupt the flow of power. The humming grew louder, roaring inside her head like the deafening din of a massive waterfall. *Please...*

He was lying in a river, completely submerged. The warm current gently washed the sticky remains of blood from his abdomen. Through the shimmering surface of the river, he saw the sun, bright and warm, in a clear blue sky.

He smiled as hope and love and joy filled him with every passing second, as though he were a sapling and the sunshine were feeding him. Then the sun grew larger, spreading outward. It was coming to him, sinking closer and closer, so huge he could see nothing but bright, divine light. He shut his eyes as searing heat pushed against him. The water of the river burned away, evaporating into nothingness, and all that was left was him and the heat of the sun.

A weight on his abdomen grew heavy, particularly upon his navel. He gasped as the heat pierced him, then again as it flowed into his stomach, filling his body. His sex became erect. His limbs spread as he floated in that warm space, near to bursting with heat. Every inch of his skin tingled, from the crown of his head to the soles of his feet. He arched his back in breathless discomfort as the scorching heat pumped into him, never-ending.

"Welcome home," a voice said close to his ear. He could only croak in response, too overwhelmed in more ways than one.

The last of the heat filled him, having settled into every pocket of his flesh, and he felt the splash of his release against his stomach. He became aware of a hard surface beneath his back as the world fell into place around him, reminding him he was still in the ritual room.

Shumei watched with awe as both demons writhed on the altar, tossing their heads and giving sharp cries. Their rigid cocks swayed heavily. The circle's glow pushed into the middle, and the lines faded as the center filled with yellow light.

They grunted and shot their seed across their stomachs as if consecrating the ritual and bringing it to a close. Then their hair began to change color, starting at the roots. It was turning black.

"Vallen," she whispered.

The divine flame was abruptly extinguished, plunging the room into relative darkness. She stayed still until her eyes had adjusted to the lantern light and she could discern her two subjects moving sluggishly.

Vallen sat up first. His hair was as dark as midnight, and he had never looked more handsome. Then Rosuke sat up, and his longer, wavier hair was just as dark as Vallen's. They stared at her as if in a trance, mouths open, and she wondered if they were as moved as she was.

"Shumei, you..." Vallen said, voice thin.

"You're our empress," Rosuke finished for him.

She blinked. "What?" She had thought they'd say something about being human again, being magic-users again—being happy...

"I can feel it," Rosuke said. "We, we couldn't before because we had lost our magic, but now..." A tear slipped down his cheek.

"It's the Pull of the Empress. I didn't know it could feel so strong," Vallen whispered. "Didn't think I'd ever feel it again."

"That—that can't be true," she said, hands trembling.

"It's true. Gods, it's true," Rosuke declared.

"But I'm nobody," she insisted, shaking her head.

"You were chosen by the Divine One to be his champion," Vallen said. "To lead others like us in battle against the Damned One and rule over the land, for everything under the sun is your empire."

"I don't know how to lead. I-I don't know nearly as much magic as I should. This can't be," she cried out. Her cheeks were wet with tears. Worse, exhaustion was setting in after expending so much power.

"You will learn, Empress," Rosuke assuaged, face full of joy. "We'll teach you."

"We'll help you take back your empire," Vallen said.

"Don't talk to me like that," she sobbed. "You sound more like a soldier than the man I love."

"As a magic-user standing before his empress, I am one of your soldiers first and foremost. We both are," he said, gesturing to Rosuke with the tilt of his head.

"I, I thought I was solving all our problems," she bemoaned, turning away. "And now this?"

"You won't have to do this alone. I'm rather surprised no other crows had found you before we left your village. Your pull is powerful, and any magic-user would be hard-pressed to ignore it. More are sure to find us soon, and you have me and Rosuke until then."

She whirled around. "Listen to yourself! You're talking about overthrowing our rulers, about taking on the armies of the Damned One."

"*You* are the ruler," Rosuke affirmed. "You have the power of the Divine One inside you and an immense potential of which you've only had a mere taste. As empress, you could lay low a field of demons with but one word from your lips."

"It's...too much," she whispered, legs trembling. "I... I can't—" The edges of her vision went gray, and the room tilted...

"Vallen," Rosuke warned.

Vallen was off the altar in a flash. There was no way he'd let Shumei—his empress—hit the floor. Smearing the chalk lines of the used-up circle, he skidded to her side and caught her as she fainted. Though her magical stamina was still low, he surmised that learning she was the first empress in 300 years was the real reason she'd lost consciousness.

"She needs to rest," he said, brushing her hair off her cheek.

Rosuke went to the door and opened it. "You take care of bathing her. I'll ready her bed and clothes."

Vallen gave him a curt nod and Rosuke walked off in the direction of her bedroom, although he assumed Rosuke would stop by his own room first to clean up and get dressed. He then gazed at the sleeping face of his lover. She had been the new empress all along. A jumble of emotions too numerous to feel all at once swirled in his chest.

He was proud she was already shaping up to be an excellent wielder of magic. She had already proven her talent with her show of power to Oka and with her completion of the ritual to make him human again. Her stamina was her biggest weakness, but it would improve quickly.

He was also afraid. Majo had to be the Damned One's champion. The King of Oblivion excelled at corrupting human magic-users, especially talented ones, so selecting Majo could not have been arbitrary. And even though Majo and Shumei had both been newly awakened, Majo had seriously injured Shumei. Defeating her would be a difficult, dangerous task.

Newly awakened... By the dueling gods, he'd felt such guilt over the last few days for the way in which he'd introduced Shumei to sex, not to mention his callous attitude toward her at the river the next morning. Worse, he kept thinking of how he'd have treated her differently had he known she would be empress, a sign he had not grown at all since his time at the Dark Court. She deserved sincere passion no matter if she were empress or not.

But she was empress. That was undeniable. Even now, he felt her pull, and he wondered how he should act toward her. He was her lover but also her subordinate. He had vowed to advise her but could not make demands of her. If she decided to risk herself, he could not stop her, only argue his case.

Oh, but what relief he felt. Relief an empress had finally returned, that the ritual had worked, that his and Rosuke's magic had been restored, and that everyone was safe behind the estate's powerful enchantments—at least for now. He only hoped they had time to train Shumei and build up her stamina before she had to face Majo. Already, time could be running out...

Chapter Seventeen

A night's rest and a smiling, black-haired Vallen to kiss her awake did much to restore Shumei's good mood. They spent most of the morning eating breakfast, rejoicing in a successful spell, and planning their next move. Oka seemed thrilled to be a part of it all, though he had been rather dubious of Rosuke and Vallen's claims that his older sister was preordained to rule an empire. They spent half an hour convincing him they weren't joking.

Rosuke and Vallen determined Majo had been behind the demon attacks on human cities. She had figured out the flaw in the barrier charms and knew human-born demons could exploit it. No one could guess how long they had until Majo found them, but they assumed they had less time than desired. In the meantime, all they could do was wait for more crows to follow Shumei's pull, and train for their next confrontation. Vallen altered the spells on the path, bridge, and walls to allow safe passage for those seeking the empress.

After they'd eaten the midday meal, Rosuke began training Oka in a few effective sword stances, leaving Vallen to teach Shumei defensive spells. They were already proving difficult for her.

"One more time," he said, watching her carefully. He raised his hand and aimed it at Shumei, who stood ready to deflect his spell. His magic filtered up his arm, and he gathered a small amount of yellow energy in the curve of his hand—only enough to nudge her.

"*Kaihou*," he said, loud enough for her to hear and be prepared. The mass of energy blasted from his hand, shooting at her like a rock flung with a slingshot.

"*Tate!*" She willed her magic to form a shell around her body but got only a small sputter of energy in return. The yellow mass hit her, and she stumbled back. Releasing a disappointed sigh of frustration, she dropped her arms to her sides. Her magic bristled as if distressed, and she wondered why it didn't know what do. She'd said the correct word, right? Something like *tah-tay*?

Vallen walked toward her. "Are you all right?"

She nodded, grateful she hadn't fallen down yet. Not only would it hurt, but she was also wearing what was most certainly the finest dress on the estate. Red as blood, made of the purest silk, and covered with gold, falling leaves. Vallen wouldn't let her wear anything else, saying that as empress, she should wear only the best. She'd been too hungry to tell him off and had put it on to hasten the start of breakfast.

She smacked her thigh with her fist, cursing softly. "I don't understand," she bemoaned. "Why won't my magic do what I say? I can feel that it simply doesn't know what to do, but I said the word, didn't I?"

"What are you thinking when you try to create the shell?" he asked, stopping a couple steps away.

"I'm thinking about saying the command word right. I understood what I was saying yesterday, but now I'm back to barely knowing any Mahou." Would an empress be so inconsistent and useless? She doubted she could actually call herself empress when only two people in the world really believed it—unless you counted Majo. That made three. She didn't believe for a second that Oka was convinced. She wasn't even sure she was convinced.

"Empress Suzu would speak perfect Mahou only after communing with the Divine One and without even knowing she was doing it. You'll come to know it as well as Rosuke and I do. I promise," he said, squeezing her arm comfortingly.

"But did I say it incorrectly? Did I mess it up?" she asked, looking at him with pleading eyes. She needed to know how to do these kinds of things. Majo would clean the floor with her if she didn't.

"You said it beautifully. It's the feeling behind it that's stunting the spell. You have to really want protection from a blow. Some people use fear to build up their mastery until they're confident. Others use anger."

"Isn't it a bad thing to be afraid?" she asked, wondering how anyone could survive a battle against a horde of demons and be scared.

"Only if you let it take over you. Otherwise, it's an incredible motivator. My father used to say, 'Courage is being able to act even when you're afraid.'"

"So you're saying I should try using my fear to make the spell work?"

"It's worth a shot," he said, flashing his brilliant grin at her. Her stomach flipped.

He was so dashing in his all-black traditional clothing. She had once walked past a small group of mercenaries hired to protect the road to the next village, where she'd gone with her mother once for seeds, and compared to them, Vallen was a warrior king. His black hair suited him so well, complimenting his icy-blue eyes and bright smile and making him look more like a sex demon than ever before. He was human again, though—that was certain.

She was going to miss a couple things about his former status. The binding, for one. The magic of their sexual connection had been dissolved after last night's ritual, having "lost its authority" when he became human again—at least, that was how Vallen had explained it. He wouldn't be able to arouse her through the binding anymore, but he'd also have more control without her arousal compounding his. She was looking forward to nightfall.

"All right, then," she said and took a big breath. "Let's try again."

He returned to his earlier position. "This one's going to hit harder. Should give you more incentive to block. Ready?"

Nodding, she braced her feet apart. Vallen formed the ball of energy again, and it spun tightly in his palm. If she didn't block it, it would knock her over.

"*Kaihou.*"

The ball flew at her almost faster than her eyes could follow. She tensed, remembering a horrible summer afternoon when a girl had thrown a rock at her for daring to spy upon the solstice festival. She still had a small knot on her head from where it had hit her.

"*Tate!*"

The shell formed in chunks, appearing before her as a shimmering white wall, but it came together too slowly and only deflected the ball of energy by a small degree. It punched her shoulder and she stumbled back, barely keeping her feet under her.

"What in Oblivion is this?"

Shumei gasped, heart in her throat, and for a split second, she thought Majo had walked in and caught them off guard. She wheeled around and spotted the newcomer only a stone's throw away.

The woman stood next to a large tree, hand braced on its trunk. Her black hair, woven into two thick braids, reached all the way to her waist. Rather than a dress, she wore plain, dark blue traveling clothes similar in cut to what Vallen wore. A sheathed sword hung from her belt, and a black satchel was slung over her shoulder. Her skin was darker than was typical for the people in the mountains, but Shumei had seen many merchants with the same complexion. Her eyes were the most arresting thing about her. They were the most brilliant green Shumei had ever seen. And they glared at her.

Though she had never met the newcomer before, Shumei knew her. Had dreamed of her. She had been one of the faces behind Oka, but in Shumei's dream, she had been smiling.

"Who are you?" Vallen demanded, having appeared at Shumei's side.

"That's the empress?" the woman asked, voice husky and dripping with sarcasm. If Shumei's mouth hadn't already been open, it would have dropped open then. The woman had just called her the empress, and no matter her tone, her question made the shocking truth hit home.

"Who are you?" Vallen repeated. That he didn't step in front of her as though she were a child made her feel authoritative, but Rosuke had no such considerations and completely blocked her view of their new arrival. She looked around for Oka and spotted him near the porch. He watched their exchange with wide eyes.

"I've come to answer my empress's call and this is what I find?" the newcomer scoffed. "She can't even block? And she's—what, barely twenty?"

"Give me your name, woman, before I lose my patience," Vallen thundered.

"I'll only answer her questions," she retorted.

"Move aside, Rosuke," Shumei calmly ordered. She squared her shoulders as Rosuke reluctantly stepped away. The newcomer looked her up and down. Her dissatisfaction made a crinkle between her eyebrows, but Shumei took no offense. "What is your name?"

"Mai," she said, forehead smoothing. Her answer was as simple as her clothing, as straightforward as her manners.

Having been told her whole life to speak with utmost politeness to her "betters," Shumei wondered how this Mai could have developed such a blunt way of speaking.

"My name is Shumei."

"Why are you so inexperienced, Shumei?"

"You will address her as Empress," Vallen interrupted.

"I'll do no such thing," she promptly slung back.

"What did you just—"

Shumei touched his side to calm him. "How well would you handle magic if you had discovered it only a few weeks ago? If you found out you were supposedly an empress, how well would you be able to lead others the next day?"

"Y-You mean..."

"How old are you, Mai?"

"I'm but twenty-five," she said. "I'm not much older than—"

"And when did your magic awaken?"

"Fourteen." A chilling shadow passed behind her eyes.

"You've had eleven years with it, then," she surmised, resisting the urge to rub her arms for warmth. "That's a great deal more than a few weeks."

"But this is unacceptable. You are the empress! You should be more powerful than this," Mai insisted.

"You have no right to question her power," Rosuke said in a raised voice. "She has incredible potential. I've seen with my own eyes more than once."

Mai's eyebrows shot up. "Potential?" she parroted. "Demons are running amok, and she has potential?" She walked toward them, and both men tensed in readiness. "Prove it to me."

Shumei wanted to hunch her shoulders but forced herself to stand straight and look this overbearing person in the eye. Not only was this newcomer taller, older, and more confident than she was, but also more experienced, and she wanted proof?

"Why should your empress have to prove herself to you? You insult her by even asking it," Vallen said.

"I'll not accept an empress who is so weak," Mai insisted, fisting her hands at her sides. "The path, the bridge, the wall, and the gate were all enchanted against demons, but not with her magic, am I right?" She pointed at Shumei, her expression as disappointed as her voice. "And what do I find after all these powerful enchantments? A contingent of witches like me, training for battle? A grand estate brimming with activity? A fearless empress with the presence of our deity and the mind of a leader? No. I find an empty, run-down building, two men, one blondie, and a weak, child empress who looks as though a breeze could knock her down. Unless she proves herself, I'm leaving."

Vallen and Rosuke both gathered a breath to argue with her, but Shumei's voice stopped their words in their throats. "Fine," she agreed.

"But Empress—" Rosuke said.

"She's right," Shumei argued. "How would I react if I was in her position? If the world was falling apart and the one person I hoped could fix it seemed incapable? Wouldn't you be angry, Rosuke? Disappointed?"

"Nothing about you disappoints me, Empress," he said, gentle.

"Because I proved myself, didn't I?" she prodded.

"I'll be here if you need me," Vallen said, pointing at the ground. She gave him a small smile, grateful for his instant support. Rosuke's face hardened, his reluctance obvious, but he backed up in concession to her wishes.

"Oka?" she called, startling her brother, whose gaze was fixed on Mai.

She beckoned him and he obediently came, bringing along his wooden sword. In his finery from the day before, he was Vallen's opposite. Whereas Vallen was a deadly warrior king, Oka was a naïve little prince. She smiled down at him, cupping her hand around his cheek.

"Working hard?" she asked.

"Rosuke's a good teacher," he said.

She nodded in relief. "That's good. I need you to stay with Vallen and Rosuke over here. Mai and I want to test each other out," she explained, trying to soften the harsh exchange he'd overheard.

"A-All right." He gripped his sword tight, and she steered him to stand between Vallen and Rosuke.

"Don't interfere," she said sweetly to Oka's two handsome buffers. "I want to know just how much potential I supposedly have." Vallen nodded, but Rosuke jutted his chin. "Well then, Mai. Let us find some space."

Having watched the scene in silence, Mai nodded and set her sword and satchel down.

They kept their distance from one another but walked toward a more open area. The canopy didn't allow more than a few small patches of sunlight, but the breeze was strong enough to pierce the denseness of the forest and flutter the ends of her hair. They were soon out of earshot but stayed well within eyesight of the men.

"That blondie is your brother?" Mai asked, speaking through her teeth as though the question had been burning in her throat.

"Yes. His name is Oka, not Blondie," she warned.

"A blondie is a blondie—"

"A blondie is a snake-eyed tyrant who feeds on hurting others. Oka is a sweet, pure boy, and I'll not have you call him such," she corrected her.

Mai stiffly nodded. "I'll make my own judgment before calling anyone names, I suppose, and that includes you," she said with a hard edge to her voice. "I'll not call you Empress unless you're fit for the title."

"If you must."

Mai seemed annoyed by her answer, based on the sneer that briefly wrinkled her nose. "Prepare yourself."

The woman's magic burst out of her with an audible crack that made Shumei jump. Green-tinted magic swirled around Mai, pulsing with heat and energy. It was like watching a bonfire through green glass, and at the center, Mai burned without burning. She was meant for a spring house, it seemed.

A gust of wind from Mai's direction sent leaves and twigs flying, and Shumei brought her arms up to protect her face. Her heart raced, and the cold hand of fear gripped her heart. She watched Mai the best she could despite the bright glow of power, and when Mai put her foot back, she realized Mai was going to rush her. What would happen when Mai reached her, she couldn't guess. Nor did she know how to defend herself from a magically enhanced physical attack. She was in trouble.

"Empress," Rosuke shouted with a twinge of panic.

She spared two seconds to glance his way. Vallen held him back even though Vallen's face was filled with concern. Oka was tense with fright, his wooden sword forgotten on the ground.

Shumei gasped as Mai sprinted toward her holding two bright orbs of energy in each palm. Bracing herself, she breathed in to speak the shield invocation, but the command she'd been practicing all morning would not come. Was it *toh-tay* or *tah-tay*? Casting that option aside, she pulled at her magic, trying to will it into her legs to help her dodge, or her arms to help her block, as it had with Akiji and Majo, but her concentration was scattered, and Mai was only a heartbeat away.

Divine One help her, she was useless. Why had he chosen her? Why hadn't he chosen Mai, whose experience and strength of will were readily apparent? Was Shumei really meant to be empress? Or had it all been a mistake?

A high-pitched whine filled her ears. Mai rapidly slowed, then froze. Swirls of her green-tinted magic hung like smoke in a windowless room. Indeed, the wind blowing off her had also stopped, and Shumei's hair now hung straight. Forest debris floated in midair, and all sound had ceased except for the buzzing in her ears. The entire world had stopped.

"There's no denying it, Champion."

She turned and swung into a new world. Mai was gone, the estate and the trees had disappeared, and even the screaming whine had faded. She once again stood in a familiar darkness, barely able to discern the semi-solid, smoky figure in front of her. Her gasp of recognition was loud in the stillness.

"Are you...?" But she couldn't bring herself to finish the question.

"You shall reign as empress. Your court shall bring peace to the world, and your power shall destroy him, once and for all."

Him? Have mercy, did he mean the Damned One?

"A-Are you the...?" she tried again.

"I shall teach you as your need grows, and your next lesson is now." He floated closer.

"Are you the Divine One?" she blurted. As faint as it was, she detected a smile on the figure's indistinct face.

"I am. Come to me," he commanded, spreading his arms.

Tears stung her eyes, and she pressed her fingertips to her lips to stop their trembling. Her belief in the Divine One had been one of the few comforts in her life, even on the worst days when the villagers had been especially cruel—even when her father, and then her mother, had passed. Belief that he loved her as much as the rest of his people. Hope that he would accept her soul, her love, her faith. Now here he was, arms open to her, accepting her as she had prayed he would.

She took the three steps separating them and threw her arms around him, hugging him tight. His smoky presence seemed to be an illusion, for his body was solid and warm.

He wrapped his arms around her, and she felt as at home as when her father had been alive. Love radiated off him like perfume from a bed of flowers. Every safe feeling one could have filled her—the kiss of a mother, the hug of a father, the laugh of a friend, and the passionate touch of a lover. Her tears flowed freely, and she happily accepted his kiss.

Heat poured down her throat as power filled her from head to toe, bone to skin, and with it came incredible knowledge that passed by her mind's eye in disorienting flashes. She tried to focus on the thoughts and experiences flowing into her—a demon's bones cracking, the splash of magic reflected away, the feel of raw power surging through her arms—but concentrating only made her head pound.

She became light-headed and her knees shook. He held her more firmly, keeping her upright, and she listened to her heartbeat as she clung to him. He embraced her for what felt like an hour, but was probably only a moment, and when he pulled back from their chaste kiss, he laid his hand on her back.

She inhaled sharply, loudly. She felt as if she were running all-out, flying through the void at a speed her legs and her lungs could not handle. Panting, she felt faint. Fatigue turned into nausea.

"What's...h-happening?" she gasped, strength evaporating.

"You are learning stamina. The drained feeling will not last long."

Even from this close, she couldn't see his face clearly. Not the shape of his nose, the line of his jaw, or the tilt of his eyes. She supposed it didn't really matter because, as a god, he didn't have a physical form.

"W-Why...can't I...see you clearly?" she asked. Her legs lost their strength, and her grip on his shoulders slipped, but he gently and easily kept her in place against his chest.

"You haven't decided what I look like yet," he answered, wearing that hazy smile again. "That's enough." He took his hand off her back and lifted her higher in his embrace. "I'll now share my strength with you. I know you shall use it well."

She could no longer even hold her head up, she was so exhausted and sore, but the Divine One gently cupped the back of her head and supported her as he curled close. He exhaled into her mouth, the perfume of his breath like the sweetness of honey, warm like the sun. It softened and soothed her tired muscles. Her aches faded, leaving behind only a heavy drowsiness like what she felt when waking too early.

He exhaled a second time, and the scent was of mint and fresh rain. Her limbs tingled as her lungs absorbed his divine breath, and she was able to lift her arms again, which she wrapped around his shoulders. The soles of her feet found purchase and she stood straighter in his arms.

He exhaled a third time, filling her with cinnamon, ginger, and laughter. Her heart sped, but her body felt loose and ready. She thought of Vallen and the scent of a rare spice on his skin.

The Divine One kissed her once more, light and gentle, this one simply meant to comfort. A tear slipped down her cheek. He caught the tear with his lips and lifted his head. She felt energized and limber, prepared for anything, and opened her eyes.

"Time for you to prove yourself to the head of House Sakura. Her childhood was rather painful, Champion. She readily mistrusts others. Help her find a way to heal."

He gently released her from his embrace and she looked at him pensively, turning his words over in her mind. The Divine One placed his hands on her shoulders.

"Don't hit her too hard," he said with a smile in his voice. Then he turned her away from him, and she swung back into her world. Mai was still there in front of her, her long braids suspended behind her.

"Now," he whispered in her ear.

The world slammed back into place. Dodging left, Shumei swiftly leaned back to avoid Mai's fists. The balls of energy, what Shumei now knew as Flying Fists, shot out of the other woman's hands as she shouted the keyword, and both spun away harmlessly to hit the ground, sending leaves into the air.

"*Tsuyosa*," Shumei whispered. Her magic eagerly complied with her wishes, and every muscle in her body tightened, burning with strength.

Mai stumbled to a halt, whipping her head around in surprise, but she quickly recovered, much to her own credit. She brought up her hands, and a giant ball of energy rapidly formed in her palms.

"No," Rosuke hollered. Shumei ignored him this time. Mai was simply creating a large version of the Flying Fist called the Flying Kick. It would be easy to deflect.

"*Kaihou*," Mai called out, and the monstrously large green ball flew at her like lightning.

Shumei crossed her forearms in front of her. "*Kagami*," she shouted, and a large shimmering circle appeared.

Mai gasped as her Flying Kick bounced off Shumei's summoned mirror and was sent shooting back at her at twice its original speed. Mai tried to use a blocking spell, but she didn't even finish the keyword before the ball slammed into her, knocking her back. Luckily, she didn't hit a tree before she landed.

"Go, sis, go," her brother exclaimed.

Having hardly broken a sweat, she stared at Mai's prone form for a moment. She expected Mai to get up and try something new, but Mai didn't even twitch.

"Don't hit her too hard."

"Shimatta," she whispered.

She quickly ran to Mai, worried she had seriously hurt her. A stride away, Mai flipped over.

Shumei threw her arm in front of her. *"Tate!"* Mai's Flying Fist ricocheted off her magical shield, smacking into a tree and scattering shards of bark. She then kicked at her, but Shumei dodged aside and landed a hit on Mai's leg that made her opponent cry out.

Mai shot to her feet, wincing as she put weight on her injured ankle. She darted forward and dropped her shoulder. Shumei saw Mai's fist coming a mile away. She had already called upon her strength spell and blocked with one arm as she brought her other hand up to catch Mai's second fist. She jerked Mai forward and onto her raised knee, softening the blow as much as she could. She didn't want to rupture anything.

Mai grunted, the wind knocked out of her, and jerked out of Shumei's grasp. Her furrowed brow and gnashed teeth spoke to her frustration as she stood there, rubbing her stomach and wincing. Clearly, she was about to do something rash.

With a shout, Mai ran at her at full speed, intending to tackle her to the ground, but Shumei dropped low with perfect timing, shouldering the woman as she hit her and tossing her away like a rag doll. Mai shrieked, then landed with a huff as the air was knocked out of her—again.

Now also frustrated, Shumei marched to where Mai lay panting. She grabbed the front of Mai's jacket and lifted her high enough to leave her feet dangling. Mai's eyes were wide with surprise, and she gripped Shumei's wrists as she wiggled like a hooked fish.

"Do you yield?" Shumei asked, frowning.

"How can this be? You, you couldn't even do a blocking spell a moment ago."

Amazed she could hold up someone about as heavy she was without breaking a sweat, Shumei shook Mai. "Do you yield?" she repeated, louder this time.

Mai hastily nodded, kicking her feet. Even though Shumei wanted to drop her, Mai's ankle was already hurt, so she gently set her down.

Mai went to her knees and pressed her forehead to the ground. "I beg your forgiveness, Empress. I should not have judged you so harshly before, o-or at all! I didn't have the right," she said with sincerity.

Shumei glanced at the men and almost giggled at their expressions. Oka was grinning, dancing where he stood, but Vallen and Rosuke seemed ready to collapse. Their arms were limp, their postures slack and their mouths ajar. They almost looked sleepy, except their eyes were wide with shock.

She smiled at them and then looked down at Mai again, gentling her expression as Mai gazed at her with the same awe Vallen and Rosuke now often turned her way.

"No apologies necessary, Mai. Please stand and join us," she said, holding a hand out to help her up. She easily pulled the woman to her feet and realized her strength spell was still powered. She willed her magic to relax.

"Very impressive," Vallen said, walking up to them, Rosuke and Oka keeping pace.

"I'm sorry for distracting you, Empress. I should've had more faith in you," Rosuke muttered, contrite.

"*Daijoubu*," she said with a smile. Wait, that hadn't been Common. Vallen and Rosuke grinned. Oka pinched his eyebrows in confusion, and Mai cocked her head to the side. Apparently, Mai wasn't well versed in Mahou either. "Uh—I mean, that's all right." She scratched her cheek in embarrassment. All this attention was unnerving.

"I think that's enough training for today," Vallen announced, full of obvious pride. Rosuke nodded in agreement.

"Refreshments are in order, then. We should get to know our new arrival," he said, winking at Mai. She turned a frosty look upon him, quickly cooling his flirtatious smile.

"I brought a couple of rabbits with me, if you would like those for dinner, Empress," she offered.

"Rabbit meat?" Oka asked, practically drooling. "Sounds yummy." Shumei smiled at him and stroked his hair.

"Thank you, Mai. I'll gladly help you prepare and cook them."

"I w-wouldn't dream of asking that of you, not after what I did," Mai said, flustered.

"I'll help you, then," Vallen offered. Mai coldly glared at him.

"Oka will help you," Shumei said, trying to placate everyone. "He needs to learn more cooking skills than what I've taught him."

"Hey, my soup is good," Oka said, hurt.

"When have you ever cooked meat?" she asked gently. He twisted his lips in petulant silence, and she winked at him before looking to Mai, who seemed pacified by her solution. "First, let's make sure your ankle is all right." She reached for Mai's arm. Mai let her grasp her elbow but would accept help from no one else. Everyone followed them into the building.

Chapter Eighteen

The rest of the day was an interesting affair. The rabbit ended up a little burned—Oka's fault—but it still tasted delicious. *Hunger is the best sauce*, as the saying went. Shumei was starving by the time it was ready, having been through a lot in only one afternoon.

They learned Mai was from a smaller city in northern Stillwood, but her parents were originally from Kaisui on the southern edge of the Black Sands, where the residents were generally darker-skinned. Oka had begged to know if she'd seen the ocean, but because her parents had migrated to Stillwood before she was born, all she'd ever seen was forest. Her father had died in a logging accident when she was eight, and her mother had died of an infection when she was fourteen. Losing her had awakened Mai's magic, of that Shumei was certain. Having been through the same loss, Shumei offered what commiseration she could.

Mai had taken care of herself after her mother's death, cleaning homes and cooking meals for a living, and bargaining such services for sword lessons from anyone who would teach her. The magic and history she knew had been gleaned from her mother's old journals.

As soon as she'd felt the Pull of the Empress, Mai had packed only enough food for a week and a few basic possessions, abandoning her home and village to seek out her empress. She'd stumbled upon the forest path leading to the estate by pure luck—and not a day too soon, for Vallen had only recently made it visible to people like her.

They spent the rest of the day talking of the Dark Court and establishing a new one. Rosuke would drop the occasional flirtatious comment, earning a smile from his empress and a glare from the newcomer. Vallen offered as much history as he could remember, and Mai repeatedly questioned the reasons behind certain court traditions, often putting him on the defensive. Only when Oka spoke did Mai soften her words.

As their discussion wore on, Mai learned how Shumei had met Vallen and Rosuke. Of course, Shumei evaded any specific details, especially those of an intimate nature, but Vallen's knowing smile had nearly tripped her tongue and given her away. Mai also learned of Shumei's village, the witch, and the demon attack that had taken place only a few days ago.

Vallen had been unable to find the survivors he had sent to the medicine field, nor could he find anyone else who had survived the night. He couldn't even find any bodies except for a small fraction still lying about in the village. No merchants or neighbors had come calling, what with all the problems lately, so the bodies had remained where they fell, which made for a gory scene in the light of day.

Burying them would have required more time than he'd had to spare, so Vallen had reluctantly left the bodies where they lay and had searched the empty homes for supplies they could use, such as foodstuffs. He had also harvested some plants from Shumei's field, which was growing well despite her absence.

They used some scavenged flour that night with dinner, and Shumei ate bread for the first time in many months. They spent the rest of their daylight preparing a room for Mai, who ended up choosing the one next to Oka's. Her choice relieved Shumei no small amount. However remote the possibility, she secretly feared something would sneak in to hurt Oka in the middle of the night, but with another ally sleeping so close, he had even more protection now.

As night fell, Rosuke retired first, saying something about a chill in the room, and Shumei couldn't help but make eye contact with Vallen. The heat in his eyes was more than enough to make her tremble right on the heels of Rosuke's comment, which led Mai to inquire after her health. Clearly, Mai hadn't caught the undercurrent in Rosuke's remark.

"I'm fine, Mai, really," she said without breaking eye contact with Vallen. She preferred to bathe in the warmth of his hungry gaze. Only when her brother yawned was she was able to break free from her trance. Blinking, she glanced at Oka's sleepy face, stood, and straightened her clothing.

"What is it? Are you retiring for the night?" Mai asked, standing.

"I believe it's Oka's bedtime. He's had far too much excitement for one day," she said, walking to her brother and helping him to his feet.

"But the sun's only been down an hour," he complained, trying to stifle a second yawn.

"No buts. Time for bed," she said, steering him toward his room.

Vallen watched Shumei with appreciative eyes. She would make a good mother. She was gentle with Oka and commanded his obedience without much fuss. He couldn't wait to start working on their first child.

That he even could father children now filled him with immense joy. He was the last of his line, the only son to a high-ranking officer of the Dark Court. If he had never regained his humanity, his line would have died out along with the dozens of other noble families who had perished in the uprising.

"Your room is that way, so you may wish to follow her," he suggested to Mai, not glancing at her as he walked toward the door through which Shumei had already disappeared. He could feel the woman's icy glare on his back and smiled.

Mai watched as the other male left the room. The empress had clearly chosen him as her consort, and they were likely on intimate terms. She couldn't suppress a shudder.

The other one, though, appeared unattached, and his lewd jokes troubled her. It wasn't so much their content as it was their intended audience. She wanted nothing to do with him. Men like Rosuke, with looks like his, were dangerous. As she moved to follow the empress into the hall, she vowed to bar her door that night.

Shumei sat by her brother's bed, hand on his chest as he quickly succumbed to sleep. She checked one last time that he was tucked in and kissed his forehead, silently thanking the Divine One for sparing her brother from all the dangers that had been constantly hovering over him.

"You love him greatly, Empress?" Mai called softly.

"Yes, greatly. He's a precocious boy and the only family I have left." After one last stroke to his cheek, she stood and padded quietly to the door.

"I...was speaking of another," Mai admitted.

"Vallen," she supplied, stepping into the hallway. She slid Oka's door. "I love him greatly as well." With her hand on the wooden frame of the paper door, she cast a spell of protection with one whispered word.

"The other male—Rosuke, I believe... Is he to be trusted?"

Shumei smiled, recalling the Divine One's command to her.

"Truthfully, Mai, the most untrustworthy person here is you. Rosuke is certainly crude at times, but he's fiercely loyal."

"Me? I..." she stuttered, looking ill at ease.

"You did challenge me today, and you've refused to acknowledge Vallen and Rosuke, who are your comrades-in-arms," she pointed out. Mai seemed to appreciate bluntness. "Have no fear for your safety, or mine. At least not when it comes to any 'male' in this building. Try to sleep, and do not think of enemies."

"Y-Yes, Empress. I understand," Mai whispered. She bowed stiffly, belongings in hand, and shut herself in the room next door.

Shumei stared down the hallway, pulse audible in her head as she walked toward the open door at the far end. It seemed so far away. The candle in the sitting room, halfway down the long length of hall, had been blown out, and it appeared Vallen had not lit a candle in their room, so all was dark and quiet in the slight chill of night. Midsummer would be upon them soon enough to make the nights hot and sticky, but not tonight.

Tonight, she would be hot and sticky for an entirely different reason. Tonight, she and Vallen would make love as humans. There would be no magic between them except what they made together.

She stopped at the door and took a bracing breath. Stepping inside, she looked at the bed, but it was empty. She scanned the back of the room but saw no movement.

Then a spicy scent wafted to her from behind and the paper door slowly slid shut, scraping softly along the frame. She didn't turn, only glanced behind her, and saw the faint outline of his shoulder. He stepped close. She faced forward, heart racing as she waited anxiously for his touch.

He slipped his arms around her and pressed his wide chest against her back. His heat seeped into her, melting the tension in her spine. She lifted her hand to the back of his neck and gripped his forearm in her other. The lean muscles under her fingers flexed as he hugged her tight.

"I dreamed of this," he rumbled in her ear. "Of holding you, not as a demon but as a man."

She turned in his embrace, needing his lips against hers, and wrapped her arms around his shoulders as she stood on tiptoes. Vallen obliged her with a slow, sweet kiss, one that promised to escalate and continue all night. She moaned into his mouth as he clamped her to his chest with one arm. His other hand yanked at the knot of her belt.

"I need you," she murmured against his mouth. Her belt fell to the floor, and her dress sagged open.

"I know. Even without the binding, I know."

"Vallen—"

A loud boom shocked a cry of fright from her, shattering their intimacy. Vallen grasped her close as a heart-stopping, shrieking noise followed.

"The alarm," Vallen said, releasing her. He ran for his sword in the corner of the room.

"W-What's that mean?" she asked, breathless and pulling her dress shut.

"They're here," Vallen said. "Majo and her demons are here!"

Chapter Nineteen

N-now?" Shumei asked, stunned.

"Quickly, love, you must dress," he pleaded. "They are at the gate!"

She heard a deep shout down the hall that could only be Rosuke, then his heavy steps as he ran toward their bedroom. Mai called out to ask what was wrong. Vallen tossed her belt to her before attaching his sword to his waist, hands working fast.

It couldn't be now. She wasn't ready. There was still so much she had to do. So much she had to learn.

"Vallen," Rosuke called. "They'll come to the front. I'll scout their numbers. Follow as quickly as you can!"

"Be careful," Vallen said. Rosuke ran off, footfalls fading fast.

"What is this noise?" Mai called. "Is the enemy here?"

"Follow me. Bring any weapon you have," Rosuke ordered.

Vallen turned to look at her, hand on the hilt of his sword. He was ready? How could he be ready? They were about to be slaughtered.

"I-I'm not a fighter," she said, voice brittle. Vallen retrieved her belt from where it had fallen to the floor and pulled her dress shut, then wrapped the belt around her.

"You are. You can do anything, Shumei. You restored my humanity, my magic, my hope. You performed spells I've never been able to do myself. You defeated a veteran magic-user in only a minute." Not caring about aesthetics, he finished tying her belt into a sloppy knot. "You are the light of the Divine One, his champion, and our empress.

240

He has elevated you above all others." He grabbed her shoulders, looking her dead in the eye. "You can do this."

Warmth flooded her chest, but it wasn't magic. It wasn't excitement, nor was it fear. It was determination.

She wondered for the space of a heartbeat if the Divine One himself hadn't taken Vallen's place for just that moment, for she felt uplifted. Nodding once, she followed him to the door.

"Find Rosuke," she said. "I'll join you shortly." Vallen whipped open the bedroom door, sword in hand, and ran out.

She entered the hallway and extended her right hand. Finding the inner wall, she rapidly drew a circle with the tip of her finger. A light followed where she traced, a bit of magic she'd added to reveal the lines and ensure accuracy. The ball of warmth inside eagerly awaited the circle's completion. As she finished, a crackling sound, not unlike the sizzle of summer fireworks, filled the hallway. A whoosh of warm air burst out from the completed circle, throwing her hair back over her shoulders, and the blare of the alarm faded.

The circle she had just activated overrode the one she'd placed on her brother's room earlier, and worked much like the barrier charms, only stricter and more powerful. It wouldn't keep the Foul One's evil creations out forever, but quite a while. She ran down the hall and whipped open her brother's door. Oka was awake and sitting up, eyes wide with fear.

"W-What's going on? Did I have a nightmare?"

She rushed to plant her hands on his shoulders. "Listen carefully. The enemy is here, but the house is safe, so promise me you'll stay right here. We'll be fine, but you must not come outside. Obey me in this, please." She quickly kissed his cheek and pulled him into her arms for a fast, tight hug before running out his door.

"What? Shumei," he screamed. She ran to the front of the house, mind working overtime as she went through a dozen scenarios in the space of ten seconds.

What if the fighting had already begun? Would she need to help Mai? Should she go after Majo first? Should she think of ways to coordinate the four of them? Or could she let them worry about themselves?

The walls zipped by as she ran, and she wished both that she had more time and that she was already there. Her heartbeat was loud in her head, her breathing harsh.

The main entrance, centered on the opposite side of the building as the sitting room, was a grand piece of architecture. The doors were made from coal wood and opened into a large entryway lined with elaborate shelves meant for the shoes and belongings of guests. Every piece of wood in the entryway, from practical to ornamental, was also made of coal wood, and the shelves were lined with delicate white molding that depicted tree leaves and ivy. An ornate desk on one side was meant for the estate secretary.

The main doors were shut when she ran into the foyer, surprising her no small bit. She had thought they'd be wide open. As she placed her hand on the door, ready to push it open, she grabbed at her belt to make sure it was secure.

She could hear nothing on the other side of the door. No talking or fighting, as if no one had come through here. However, there was no mistaking the sickening, sticky feel of Majo's magic. It wasn't inside the house yet, but it was trying, feeling along the wall of protection she had set up and looking for a flaw.

Her magic, still and watchful inside her, was no longer the playful entity she sometimes felt it was. Even it, with the small bit of personality she imagined it to have, was now serious, ready to do anything she asked.

She slid the door open. Rosuke and Mai stood to the right, a step away from the base of the stairs that led to the ground. Both had their backs to her, standing guard. Vallen still had one foot on the bottom step and stared gravely at her.

All three held swords—their blades bare, sharp, and ready. Vallen's looked as wicked as it had before with its serrated edges. The blade of Rosuke's wide sword curved sharply. Mai's was the plainest, but also the longest. Shumei was only able to see her three allies because of dim moonlight reflected off them, but a few feet beyond Rosuke, who stood the farthest away, was a dark mystery.

"She wanted to wait for you," Vallen said, subtly gesturing with his head to something among the trees—someone who lay in wait for the four of them. Scanning the darkness ahead, she descended the steps, raised her arm, and aimed her palm at the sky.

"*Hikari.*" With a low pop, like pulling a stopper from a jug, a ball of light shot into the air.

It was all she could do to gasp rather than let instinct and fear draw out a scream. There had to be nearly a hundred demons, all standing still and attentive. A few of them flinched at the light, but the majority didn't react. After all, her simple spell was not true sunlight.

She had never seen so clearly a demon born from Oblivion. She instantly felt sullied. Each face was twisted and malformed—teeth protruding from noses and necks, eyes askew, multiple mouths, arms and legs in the wrong place and backward... Some had fur, but some were hairless. Some had tails, horns, or claws.

Shumei broke out in a cold sweat. She wanted to run but felt frozen in place. Only when Vallen touched her arm did she snap out of her horrified trance.

"Empress, your enemy wishes to speak with you," Vallen said.

Her spell, still hovering in the sky, cast enough light to see the large group of demons waiting for the inevitable fight, and it was bright enough to see the only one among them who looked human. Although "human" was an overstatement.

"It's been a while, Shumei," Majo purred. She stood at the front of the legion, decked out in red silk and black leather that left hardly any of her assets to the imagination. Her sleeves were embroidered with white symbols that Shumei recognized as granting magical armor. They were automatic shields, powered at all times. Exhausting, she imagined, but like Shumei, Majo had undoubtedly been imbued with superhuman magical stamina.

Majo's face, though... Her eyes were completely black. Shumei wasn't even quite sure if they were still there. The skin around her sockets was ashen, as if the pits of her eyes were black holes that would suck the soul out of anyone who looked at her. On the right side of her face, the veins under her skin seemed to flow with indigo ink. The left side of her face wasn't much better. A deep scar ran from the corner of her mouth down to her jaw, making her smile lopsided, and another scar broken the clean line of her high cheekbone.

"Not long enough, Majo," she answered, grateful her voice was loud and strong.

"It seems having your lover around suits you. You look positively delicious."

"And you look like a doll that a dog chewed on," Shumei said. Majo's smile only widened, becoming even more lopsided.

"Just trying to fit in," she said with a chuckle, gesturing to the horrors standing around her.

"How did you find us?"

"That's what I love about you, Shumei. You're so direct. To answer your question, the only downside to joining the other side was I lost any ability to track you using the Empress's Pull, but finding and following another crow trying to find you? Well, that was simple."

243

"You followed Mai," Shumei deducted, not realizing such a thing could happen and yet now, it seemed obvious. She couldn't help but glance over at her newest ally, whose face was horrorstruck.

"I-I'm so sorry, Empress. I didn't know," Mai said in an aside. Shumei turned back to the witch. There were more important things to do right now than comfort Mai.

"And where is Akiji? Is he still alive?"

"Do you actually care?" Majo asked, looking down at her nails as though bored. Her fingertips were black.

"He's a bully, but...yes, I do."

Majo huffed, clearly annoyed. "All I can tell you is that my king has decided to keep him for as long as he is...entertaining. He'll not join us this eve."

"Why is the Damned One doing all of this? Why did he not wipe out all of humanity while it was unprotected by an empress?"

"So many questions. You have been thinking a lot about this moment," Majo said with a smirk, her good mood returning.

A mutable temper like hers had been one of Vallen's worst qualities when Shumei had first met him. Was it a demonic trait?

Majo took a deep breath. "Very well. After all, even I didn't know until he told me. Listen well. The last empress, slain in her bed by a blondie, was not killed quite as quickly as many believed. She had enough time to utter one of the few powerful invocations reserved only for a champion—the Ceasefire."

Vallen make a small noise of surprise. Did he know of the invocation? Or was he reacting to something else?

"It only works if the champion is not killed by her enemy, and if she has no heir. And it guaranteed a temporary truce between both sides until a new empress was born. The last empress was a quick thinker. She knew a blondie uprising would dismantle her court and demolish her army. The new empress would be vulnerable. One such as I would easily slay her and charge into the Divine One's territory with no army to hold me back.

"So the Divine One waited, patiently watching, until the population of dark-haired humans had built up again. Then he chose one female from among them and gave her the Light of the Empress. Until her magic awakened, she would be just another crow girl, living out her simple life. It wasn't until I found the Devil's Hand that I was able to prophesy the empress's identity.

"What a terrible surprise to find out it was you and not me," Majo said a frown. "But it was easy to gain my king's support. I told him of the barrier flaw and your identity, and even promised the return of his high general's long-lost spell book. Losing it again earned me my due punishment." She traced the scars on the left side of her face, and for brief instant she seemed frightened.

"Of course," she continued, "my king cannot control all of his servants, just as the Divine One could not prevent the blondie uprising. Some demons still preyed upon humanity during the three hundred years of peace, but they were punished for violating the ceasefire."

"And now that the ceasefire is over?"

"My dear, this war has been raging for millennia. The ancient rules of battle set by both sides, long-forgotten by most, are still valid."

"And those are?"

"One champion must kill the other. Only then can the winner take her army into the enemy's domain and attempt to assassinate the other god. She has one year to do so, or else she must defeat a new champion. If she perishes in her attempt to kill the other god, then both sides must choose a new champion and start again."

"So in all those millennia, not one champion succeeded?"

"Oh, a few managed to lead their armies into Oblivion. But defeating a god, Shumei? Only a champion of champions can accomplish such a thing, which is why I pity you for being chosen." Majo giggled, and Shumei's back stiffened as if a drop of cold water were running down her spine. "You won't survive this battle," Majo growled, voice dropping to an earth-shaking rumble, "let alone a fight with my king." The building behind them shook. The leaves in the trees rustled.

"What makes you so confident?" Shumei asked, folding her arms. Majo's threats would not cow her. She had heard too many from the other villagers over her short life for Majo to dent her will.

"I know what scares you, Shumei," the witch replied in a normal voice. "I know what makes your stomach clench. What thoughts wake you in the middle of the night. As the Damned One's champion, I know everyone's strongest fears. For example, that girl there, holding her sword so tightly. She is deeply afraid of a man's touch—of sex."

"E-Empress," Mai whimpered. Shumei hastily looked over at Mai, whose sword was violently jerking as she tried to keep it up and in front of her. Rosuke glanced at her as well, though Shumei couldn't see his expression. She hoped Rosuke would keep an eye on Mai.

"It's not going to end here, Mai," Shumei said. "I'm on your side." Her assurances seemed to bolster Mai, whose blade steadied.

"You see what I mean?" Majo tittered. "With just a threat—"

"Fear can be overcome. I wonder if the Damned One is as stupid as you. If so, killing him will be easy," she bragged, hoping to incite Majo. If it was going to happen, it had to happen soon. Otherwise, Majo's taunts would weaken their resolve.

"You are the fool. You think a few words can so easily defeat one's fears?" she asked. "We'll see about that."

Vallen and Rosuke tensed. Then she felt it too. Her magic was rapidly expanding, as if it knew something she didn't. Within seconds, her skin emanated heat as though a bonfire raged inside her.

The witch raised her hand, which made one of her long sleeves slip down to her elbow, revealing a series of intricate tattoos on her forearm.

"*Kurayami*," she invoked, snuffing out the light that had been hovering so innocently above their imposing scene. Shumei heard Mai's gasp, and then the screaming began. Every demon howled, bayed, and roared their war cry.

She had only a couple of seconds to think. The demons closest to them would undoubtedly leap forward to dig their claws and teeth into the nearest bit of human flesh. Her side needed to see in order to avoid it. She needed to see in order to kill Majo.

"Rosuke, come to me!" she called over the demons' deafening barks. She took a step toward Vallen, placing her hand on his arm. Rosuke's fingers touched her elbow, and she quickly grasped for his sword hand. She did the same with Vallen and gripped the base of their blades. Neither of them questioned what she was doing. There was no time.

"*Sokobikari*," she whispered. She carefully ran her hands up the length of the blades, and a bright glow followed her fingers, giving the blades their own inner light. It was bright enough to see a several yards in all directions, something Majo could not dispel from afar.

"Rosuke, touch blades with Mai and stay close to her," she hurriedly told him. "Vallen, keep them away from me as long as you can." Both men nodded and Rosuke ran toward Mai. She heard a clang and the glow of her spell spread to Mai's blade as well.

This was the best she could do for them now.

"*Tsuyosa*." She invoked her strength spell, watching as the first few demons entered their ring of light. Rosuke hollered as his fight began.

"*Tajuu*," Vallen called. His sword multiplied into five more, the blades of which hovered in front of him as if ghosts wielded them. He lunged forward, and all six swords thrust in unison, directly striking four demons. It was time.

She darted forward, jumping over felled demons and swiping her arms to both sides. She knocked demons aside as though she were flinging branches out of her way, smashing them into trees or each other in her race to reach Majo, who had been standing only fifty feet away before the light spell had been extinguished.

She didn't look back to see if Vallen was following. If he simply fought to keep himself alive, that was good enough at this point.

She had what felt like a million ideas as to how to hit Majo first, and then second, and then third... The problem was which one would penetrate Majo's shield, deal a lot of damage, and be unpredictable, giving the witch no way to counter it before it could hurt her.

She punched one last demon aside, sending it into a tree trunk and audibly breaking its back. Then Majo appeared before her, barely visible in the light thrown from Vallen's sword.

"*Tate!*" Shumei quickly gasped out, blocking the two Flying Fists that had rocketed at her almost faster than she could think. Majo blinked in surprise, probably not expecting that she could have blocked them. Shumei had to do it now.

"*Moui*," she muttered under her breath. Her arms seized up, burning with power, and she planted one foot in front of her. Time slowed down, and her magic's high-pitched whine filled her ears. The witch was bringing up her hands, but she was too slow. Twisting quickly, Shumei put as much weight into her punch as possible, putting every bit of the spell's energy into her clenched hand, and made bone-crushing impact into the witch's abdomen.

It was a direct hit. The armor manifested by Majo's embroidered spell only blocked magical attacks, just as she had hoped. Her enemy was flung back. Several other demons were mowed down as Majo flew out of the light's range.

A heavy body slammed into her, bearing her to the ground beneath it. The breath was knocked out of her, and for a couple seconds, she could only see stars. The light of Vallen's sword was closer now, but a dozen demon bodies separated them. He was probably too occupied with fighting them back to see she was down.

"Little human," a hollow voice rasped.

Every muscle in her body froze. Her heart seized. She looked up at the hairy face of a large demon standing over her, and then took stock of the terrible predicament she was in. The multi-legged spider demon had pinned each of her limbs to the ground, and still had a few left over to feel around on her body.

Memories flooded her mind. Running through the woods, being chased by a mysterious, evil voice that wanted to play, being picked up and nearly eaten... She had been saved, but by whom? Her father?

The demon had a pair of fangs above its mouth, which was filled with sharp, jaggedly spaced teeth. Its head had clearly once belonged to a human, one with a thick beard that the demon had chopped close to his face, as if he cut it himself with the edge of a dagger. His eyes were askew, one pointed in the wrong direction, and any skin not covered with fur or bone was covered with strange bumps.

The other demons stayed back as though yielding to the much larger one standing over her. They prowled around the two of them in a circle, clearly ready to eat her, bones and all, if they had the chance.

"How I shall be rewarded," it tittered. "Excellent, excellent!" She couldn't speak, couldn't move or look away from its horrifying face. She couldn't even think. The memories of what had happened to her so many years ago had taken control. The hot, disgusting breath. Hanging in the air by its grip on her four limbs.

A spicy cologne. Yes, a stranger had saved her, and his scent was now undeniably familiar.

"But first, I'll get some pleasure out of this," it rasped, roughly palming her breasts. "Ooh, soft, very soft indeed."

"S-Stop. Stop it," she whimpered. She both hated and feared spiders at the same time. Ever since that night, the eight-legged creatures had always destroyed her composure. Seeing one from afar was enough to make her stiffen with terror.

"Shumei," Vallen screamed. "Where are you?"

Vallen. His estate was half a day from her village. He had to have been there fifteen years ago when he'd previously parted ways with Rosuke. He had no qualms about traveling at night. He must have heard a young child scream for her mother. And his spicy scent hadn't been like anything Shumei had smelled before. Kaisuian soap.

It was Vallen to whom she'd clung, crying into his shoulder while he'd shushed her. He had slain the spider demon—had saved her, all those years ago. He had saved her and didn't even know it.

A bright light swung past. Hot blood splashed onto her dress. The spider demon screamed in agony, releasing her and scampering away. It had lost two of its arms—the ones that had been groping her.

"I'll chop off every limb that's touched her!" Vallen shouted, standing over her. The light off his sword revealed the many demons stalking around them. She sat up, trying to get a hold of herself. Even with her strength spell still active, she hadn't been able to escape that spider demon. Perhaps Majo had been right about the power of fear.

Vallen leapt past her, slashing again at the spider demon still roiling about in pain. It screamed, and more blood sprayed from the stumps of its severed limbs, spilling onto the ground in buckets.

She stood to get her bearings. The demons seemed to be staying away instead of attacking. Why? Where was Majo?

"Behind you, dear," a guttural voice said, the words sounding wet as though spoken through a mouth full of blood.

Shumei dropped and rolled to the side, barely dodging the white lightning that sizzled by her and hit another demon instead. It died instantly, unable to even make a sound before it fell to the ground.

"Perfect," the witch said, but it wasn't her speaking. It was the evil inside her.

Why was missing her with that spell "perfect"? Too late, Shumei realized Majo wasn't looking at her, but at the back of her lover, who stood over the dead spider demon.

No.

Majo raised her hand, blackened fingertips pointed at Vallen's back. Shumei made to stand, to come between them with her mirror spell, but she hadn't reacted fast enough.

"*Shokushi.*" Lightning erupted from her hand, and Shumei screamed Vallen's name. *Please, please let it miss him.* If it didn't, the Touch of Death would—

Vallen turned around just as the bolt from Majo's fingers hit him square in the chest, and Shumei watched, horrified, as the light left his eyes. His mouth was open, hand still gripped tightly around his bloody sword. He fell to his knees.

"Vallen! No, no," she screamed. His body slumped to the side, and he breathed his last. His eyes were still open, looking at her.

Only moments ago in their bedroom, he had been holding her, kissing her, loving her. And now he was... He had been human only a day. Three hundred years of wandering the land as the exact thing he'd once fought, and he was... He would never hold her again, never tease her again, never make her heart flip with only a slow smile, never turn a heated look her way.

She would soon be as lifeless as he was, if the agony in her heart continued any longer. She never thought pain alone could kill. It stole her breath and made her want to throw up. She shut her eyes, dug her fingers into the ground, and shrieked. When she ran out of breath, she took in another and screamed again through the harsh sobs that threatened to choke her.

A deep, loud laugh tumbled down to her. She fell silent, shaking, cheeks wet with tears.

"How truly pathetic. You loved him, did you? Even better," the witch said.

"Champion," a familiar voice called. Shumei opened her eyes.

"Your friends still seem to be doing well, but we'll overcome them," Majo said. The toe of her boot came within a step of Shumei's dirty hands.

"Remember what I taught you." She took in a deep breath, aware of fluttering in her belly. Her magic wanted something. *"Time is running out."*

"We won't kill you just yet. We'll make you suffer first, all of you." Majo was gleeful, and Shumei could taste her laughter. "I think we'll start with your lover's body. You'll watch, of course."

"She's so close, Champion. She's in your grasp."

"Then, after we've thoroughly enjoyed you," she continued, "we'll find a way inside that house and bring out the one you're protecting. Your brother is my guess. Playing with him shall be fun."

"No more despair, for nothing is lost. You are my beloved chosen. Everything I have, I give to you."

"There are still many hours until sunup, and I shall make them feel like an eternity, I promise you," Majo snarled.

"You will not touch him," Shumei said, voice hard.

"What did you say?"

"You will touch not Vallen, Rosuke, or Mai. You'll not even see my brother." She lifted her head and gave Majo's marred, angry face her own glare of contempt. "But I must thank you for one thing."

Majo sneered. "Such brava—"

"Thank you for coming to me."

She grabbed Majo's ankle and squeezed as hard as she could, crushing bones. The witch gave a wide-mouthed scream and tried to kick at her with her other foot, but Shumei rolled away and shot to her feet. Majo took a step back, crying out with agony and almost falling as she tried and failed to put weight on her broken ankle.

Shumei sprang at her, and though the demons around them obviously wanted to help, it seemed they dared not interfere. Not that they'd be able to.

"*Jouzaikousen,*" Shumei barked. The Ray of Cleansing.

Her magic began spinning. Majo whimpered and struggled, but Shumei grasped the witch's throat to silence her. Heat poured off Shumei, and a hot wind swirled around her. Her magic spun faster and faster. It scraped her insides, curled her hair, and made her shake. Then lightning flashed, and a ray of light powerful enough to turn night to day burst from her body, reaching into every shadow and every tainted soul.

The air was filled with the screams of demons, who burned so hot and bright they turned to ash in a matter of seconds. Majo also cried out in pain, but her human origin kept the light from incinerating her.

"*Nikuken,*" Shumei invoked, still gripping Majo's throat as she brought her other hand back. Her magic fed its power into her arm, and her fingers melded together, hardening until her entire forearm had become a Blade of Flesh, sharp enough to slice through a tree trunk.

"No! I can't fail. D-Don't send me to him," Majo pleaded, sounding innocent and human for the first time that night.

Shumei punched her transformed hand into the witch's chest. Bone crunched and flesh tore. Majo croaked. Her grip on Shumei's wrist went slack.

Shumei drew her hand from Majo's chest. Blood ran like water over her magicked flesh, which was already softening into her normal hand. Then, remembering her dead mother, she threw the witch to the ground like so much garbage.

The light of her cleansing spell was fading, but it was still easy to see in all directions, especially after every demon had been incinerated. Blood and ash dirtied Vallen's fallen form. Weak with despair and exhaustion, she lurched toward him and fell to her knees at his side. She pulled him into her lap with the last of her powered strength spell, but no spell could stop the tears that flowed anew.

"Empress, that was amazing!" Rosuke called, coming closer. Mai's relieved laughter followed him. "By the dueling gods, you're glowing! What spell was that?"

Shumei loosened the ties of Vallen's shirt and parted the cloth to reveal his chest. The small scar on his ribs that marked where the Touch of Death had hit him was shaped like a broad, red flower that had wilted. She grimaced as a sob swelled in her throat.

"Empress, we..." Rosuke said, slowing as he approached. "Are you all right?" Mai stopped beside him, and Shumei spared them only a brief glance. They were both splashed with demon blood but appeared uninjured. "Is that...? No." Rosuke shook his head. "No. No, he's not dead." He backed up and bumped into Mai, who covered her mouth with her free hand. "S-Shumei, he's—" Rosuke's voice broke, and he turned away.

Tightening her jaw, she gazed at the slack face of the man she loved. She had to do this in the next ten minutes. She had plenty of time, but she wouldn't waste even ten seconds on an explanation, nor could she spare any energy. The Ray of Cleansing had nearly put her under. By will alone was she still conscious. Vallen's sword was still clutched in his death grip, and she used the sleeve of her dress to wipe the blade. The ink for this spell had to be clean.

When she was satisfied, she sliced the tip of her finger along the blade's edge. Hissing at the pain, she tried to ignore it as being the smallest of sacrifices for such a powerful spell.

"Empress?" Mai called in a small voice, afraid she'd shatter the sudden quiet of the forest. The light from the empress's spell had faded to that of a sunset, and the empress didn't look up from what she was doing. Mai turned to Rosuke, who had dropped to his knees. He stared at nothing, his expression slack and unblinking. Tears shined on his cheeks.

"Rosuke," Mai whispered. She felt an unwelcome impulse to put her arms around him and instantly denied the urge.

"I'm going to save him," Shumei said, voice rough and breathy with fatigue. "I'm going to save him because the alternative is too cruel. Because he's one of us. Because he loves me." Her voice softened. "And because I love him."

Shumei began to draw on his skin, her blood acting as the ink for the most powerful of the known set of magic circles—a spell only she could cast, for it would kill anyone else. She drew one circle on the spell's scar and another over his heart. Then she carefully traced a complicated pattern to connect the two. Several times, she had to pinch her finger to make more blood well up.

When she finished, she double-checked and triple-checked the patterns, but she knew they were perfect. Careful of any extraneous blood drops, she then painted both her lips and his, making sure plenty of life's essence covered them.

"Come back to me," she whispered, leaning down to give him the Kiss of Power. She pressed her lips to his and stiffened as an immense amount of power poured out of her, though the sensation was more like it was being sucked out. Her magic vibrated and trembled so violently it shook her body. But the seal of their mouths was solid, and even if she'd wanted to pull away, she couldn't have.

"You have done well, Champion. I gladly give of myself to restore your precious treasure." The Divine One's voice muffled the headache pounding in her brain. *"But remember, your greatest challenge is yet to come."* Vallen took in a breath, and his lips twitched as he tried to react to her kiss. *"You have one year, Shumei. Use it well."*

"The Divine One has blessed us," Mai cried out. "Look, Rosuke. He's moving!"

"V-Vallen?" Rosuke called.

Shumei's tears dripped onto her lover, whose lips moved with slow passion as he kissed her back. He combed his shaky fingers through her hair, and she sobbed with both joy and grief as she hugged him closer.

"I can hardly believe my eyes," Mai said, awed. Leaves crunched as she stood. "Where did…?"

Something was happening around them, but Shumei couldn't pull away from Vallen just yet. He slowly sat up and wrapped his arms around her, still pulling magic from her.

"There's so many," Rosuke said.

The flow of magic abruptly slowed to a trickle, and Shumei went slack in Vallen's arms, utterly spent. Vallen held her close, and she tucked her nose into the crook of his neck to inhale the spicy scent of his soap. How she hadn't slipped into a coma yet…

"You saved me—again," he said.

"Only as…many times as…you've saved me," she panted. "Besides…I couldn't live…without you."

"Shumei!" Oka's voice was unexpected, and it startled her into paying attention to their surroundings. She opened her eyes, intending to reassure her brother—and then scold him for leaving the building—but the sight before her rendered her speechless.

"She's… S-She's fine," Rosuke said, distracted. "Everyone is…just fine."

At least two hundred people were spread among the trees. Vallen stood, then helped Shumei to her feet. She leaned heavily on him, and they both stared with mouths agape. Oka attached himself to her left side while Vallen stood on her right and scanned the sea of faces that had appeared before them.

"Who are they?" Shumei asked softly, hoping Vallen could explain.

Mai answered instead. "Your followers, Empress. Only the first wave. The light from your spell told them where to go."

"This, this is correct," a young man said, his peers prodding him to come forward. He held a bag over his shoulder, gripping the strap tightly.

"You've been searching for me?" Shumei asked.

"Yes, for weeks. We thought we were close when the attacks began, but we felt you move away from us. It was difficult to follow, but...the light showed us the way," he said, breathless and looking elated simply to be speaking to her.

In the sea of crows, those with lighter hair easily stood out, and she gasped when her eyes landed on Master Takebe and his wife. Next to them was Ikuro, who held one of her children asleep in her arms. Her oldest boy stood behind her. She didn't see the woman's husband. All three adults stared at her with shock but also fascination.

"V-Vallen, what do we do now?" she whispered, watching as Rosuke and the young man conversed, bringing them up to speed on where they'd been before now and where they'd come from. Mai spoke to an older woman standing at the front of the group.

"We train to do battle with the Damned One. It is your destiny," Vallen said. Her stomach cramped with anxiety. "But you have me, Shumei. You have Rosuke and Mai. You have all of these people behind you, and more are coming."

She felt the weight of the world settle on her shoulders, and the words of the Divine One came back to her.

"You have one year, Shumei. Use it well.
Your greatest challenge is yet to come."

Chapter Twenty

Ikuro's husband and two of her children had been slain when demons had attacked the village. Only the oldest and the youngest children still lived, not including the baby yet to be born. Master Takebe had lifted his wife into his arms and had carried her all the way to the medicine fields. His missus still praised his strength.

The only other survivor was Ryoushi, the village huntsman, whom Shumei later found in the crowd. He had led the handful of survivors from the attack on Shumei's village to safety when the sun rose, and when the pilgrimage of crows had come upon them, his tale of Shumei and Majo's abrupt departures had been her followers' best lead.

Everyone spent the night preparing the estate for all who had come, which used up all the bedrooms and sitting rooms in the main building and the secondary buildings meant for servants. Shumei knew they would need to either build more shelter or find another place to call home, for there was no doubt more would arrive soon and all would need a place to sleep.

She had been eager, however exhausted she felt, to talk with all who had come, and to start organizing a new court, but her subjects had insisted she rest, an opinion wholeheartedly supported by Vallen, who had taken her gently to her room. Somehow, everyone had known where she was sleeping, and by the number of gifts sitting about the room, she wondered if anyone hadn't brought her a present.

The eastern sky was folding back into day when she lay on her bed. She snuggled into Vallen's arms, having bathed in the manmade pools that pumped in water from the hot springs farther up the closest foothill. The bath had been made even better with a pair of masculine hands and a bar of Kaisuian soap. Her skin still tingled from its spicy suds.

"I can't believe you didn't pass out in the bath," Vallen murmured against her damp head.

She squeezed him close. "Why's that?"

"You vaporized a hundred demons with one spell, defeated the Damned One's champion, resurrected the man holding you—who is more grateful than you could ever know—and you greeted, housed, and fed the first two hundred of your subjects, all in one night."

"All the excitement kept me going, but it's fading fast." She smiled lazily, rubbing her cheek against his chest.

"Then sleep, my love. I shall hold you until we both wake," he said, sounding as though he needed the sleep as well. Relaxing into his embrace, she inhaled deeply. Then, a thought occurring to her, she opened her eyes.

"Vallen?"

"Mm?"

"This is a strange question," she said slowly, fidgeting with the edge of the blanket. "Fifteen years ago, when you were here with Rosuke for the last time, did you...come upon anything strange or noteworthy? In this area, I mean."

Vallen was silent a long while as he dug through his memories. Many things had been lost to time, but his last few days with Rosuke before they'd decided to part ways had stuck with him.

"I did, actually. A little girl had become lost in the forest at night and was being terrorized by a demon. I took her back to her family after I slew the creature. Thinking back on it, he must have been breaking the— My love, what's wrong?" He tried to look at her face. She was shaking, and he heard the telltale sounds of weeping.

"Vallen... Oh, Vallen, I love you so much," she sobbed, pulling herself up to press her face against his shoulder. He held her close, uncertain what had changed.

"I love you as well. You know this. Did I say something wrong?" He stroked her naked back, enjoying her soft skin but wishing she wasn't quaking with sadness. "Or are you impressed by my valor?" he then asked, laughing. She choked up even more, and he realized she was trying to say something clearly enough for him to understand her through her tears.

"That l-little girl," she said, hiccupping twice, "was m-me."

His hands on her back paused. Heart pounding, he swiftly banded his arms around her, crushing her to his chest as if he would pull her into himself.

"Shumei," he whispered into her ear. "Oh, my love." He kissed her shoulder, her neck, her cheek, and her lips, as if needing to know she was still here with him. She sobbed again, but he comforted her with gentle kisses and loving hands.

They didn't speak again after that, at least not with their mouths. They searched out the places they knew, the places that reduced them to gasps and choked sighs. Exhaustion made the room swirl, but love and passion made their hearts race as Vallen covered her with his body and fit his hips between her thighs. Neither closed their eyes as he moved over her. Then, shuddering and writhing, they softly groaned as pleasure overtook them.

They fell asleep flushed from sex and tangled together, their cheeks damp with tears of happiness and relief. The morning sun slowly spilled into their room, lighting upon the dark highlights in their raven hair and bringing a glow to their skin.

And when Shumei dreamed, it was only of Vallen.

Thank you for reading
Caught in the Devil's Hand!

If you enjoyed Shumei and Vallen's story, please help readers like you find this book by leaving a review on your preferred retailer or book review site. (It would also mean the world to me!)

Don't want to miss out on future books, contests, or price promotions? Head to my website to join my mailing list.
www.rubyduvall.com

Eager to know what happens after CAUGHT IN THE DEVIL'S HAND? Keep reading for a preview of the next book in the Dark Court series, DRAWN INTO OBLIVION. Out now!

Excerpt: Drawn into Oblivion

The Dark Court #2
Copyright © 2008, 2019, 2021 by Ruby Duvall

Chapter One

T he day was hot and sticky, a testament to the fact that full summer was upon them. As the days grew long and lingering, everyone in the palace used every hour of sunlight efficiently. The halls and courtyards buzzed with activity—lectures on magic, combat drills, or a combination of the two, festival preparations, and wedding preparations. The complex practically overflowed with people, all walking somewhere, carrying something, or talking to someone else.

Mai stepped down from the covered walkway ringing the main courtyard of the inner palace, needing a break from the ruckus. The midday meal had left her feeling lethargic, and a walk through the palace grounds had helped. She had also taken the opportunity to speak with two women belonging to another of the thirteen major houses of the court regarding the upcoming festival. They were overseeing the building of a stage for performances and had reported excellent progress.

She was glad she hadn't dawdled, though. A special combat demonstration she didn't want to miss would soon be underway in the courtyard. Dozens of men had all gathered at the far end. Their deep voices resonated, some sober and others cheerful. Judging by their easy familiarity with each other, everyone liked everyone else and was glad of it. The empress and her young brother were also in attendance, albeit seated in a place of importance.

Rather than join them, Mai availed herself of the concealment offered by a pair of cherry trees at the opposite end of the courtyard and tried to stay as inconspicuous as possible while waiting for the sparring match to begin.

Even though she recoiled from the idea of standing with the men, despite the open space in full view of the empress, Mai marveled at seeing so many black-haired people together, and at how far they'd all come. Just three months ago, everything had been so different.

Demons had attacked human cities with a brutality not seen in anyone's lifetime, ending the centuries-long reign of a class of humanity once praised for their utter lack of magical ability. In the blondies' place, black-haired magic-users ruled once more. Leading them all was the empress and ordained champion of the Divine One. Shumei was the most powerful magic-user and the one who would end their war with the Damned One and his demons once and for all.

But the empress had once been like many of the black-haired people who now followed her: vilified for the color of her hair and thus her connection to magic. Up until recently, she had languished in a small, isolated village, supporting her family and herself on a meager living as an apothecary.

Then, on the cusp of major changes in her life, she had met Vallen, and her latent magic had emerged. With it came an end to the temporary truce between humanity and demons, one put in place when the blondies had seized power centuries before. Thankfully her magic had also sent out a powerful call known as the Pull of the Empress to all magic-users.

Mai had followed the Pull without hesitation or regret, leaving behind her village in Stillwood. She'd spent weeks looking for her empress and had been one of the first to find her living at a magically hidden estate, one from the days of the Dark Court. Her hopes had been high—too high, she now realized. What had she expected after centuries had passed between one empress and the next? Certainly not just four people rather than the dozens or even hundreds of energized followers she'd hoped to find. Shumei had looked as uncertain and inexperienced as a child, and much to Mai's shock, her young brother was a blondie. The two black-haired men, Vallen and Rosuke, had piqued her suspicions from the moment she'd laid eyes on them.

Betrayed by her expectations, Mai had lashed out and had demanded a duel with the empress. That she had been so impertinent still made Mai blush with shame, for not only had Shumei dodged or deflected every single attack, she'd also given Mai bruises that had lasted two weeks. Mai counted herself lucky that she'd narrowly escaped with no broken bones.

The evening of her first night at the hidden estate, Mai had shared dinner with the four of them while rebuffing the attention of the one named Rosuke and wondering with disbelief why her empress had become intimate with the one named Vallen. That the empress shared her bed with him had been obvious despite how little Vallen had spoken. The heated looks they'd shared had been more than enough of a hint.

She'd also learned Vallen and Rosuke had been original members of the Dark Court, and that a curse placed on them before the court's destruction had granted them immortality, which had carried them through three hundred years of blondie reign—something few people knew, even now. And only Shumei, Vallen, and Rosuke knew the exact details of the curse, for Shumei had cured it not long before Mai's arrival.

Mai's blush of shame deepened as she recalled the battle that night. Unbeknownst to her, she had led the enemy right to the empress, and they attacked when night fell. Shumei's brother, Oka, had been confined to the house, but the four adults had stood against a hundred so-called "dog soldiers"—demons that looked nothing like dogs but sounded like them when howling their battle cry.

Leading them had been Empress Shumei's equivalent under the Damned One. Majo, once human, had lived in the same village as Shumei. She had been like an intimidating older sister to Shumei, and the villagers had called her "the witch" behind her back. Majo's thirst for power, her jealousy of Shumei's destiny, and her hatred of the villagers had sent her spiraling into evil. As a powerful crow woman, she had been the ideal choice for the Damned One's champion.

Majo and Shumei, compelled by their appointed roles as much as their own hearts, had to defeat one another. Whoever survived would be able to breach the boundary between the material plane and that of her enemy god—but only for a year. Within that amount of time, the victorious champion had to lead her army against her enemy god and destroy him.

The empress defeated Majo that night, earning the right to enter the Damned One's plane and attempt to kill him, which would end the war between humans and demons. But gathering, training, and leading an army was far easier said than done. Moreover, no one knew much about the Foul's One domain. Whatever the Dark Court had known about Oblivion had largely been lost in the burning of its library.

All anyone living could say of Oblivion boiled down to folktales and rumor. Stories of unlucky persons wandering through mysterious gates, falling through planar rips, or being abducted by magic abounded, and all agreed that traveling to Oblivion changed a person forever. They supposedly lost a piece of themselves and gained something else, something they'd carry for the rest of their lives—assuming they came back at all.

Most challenging of all was formulating a strategy for assassinating the Damned One. The night Shumei had killed Majo, she had asked why no previous empress had ever succeeded. Majo had scoffed, "Defeating a God, Shumei? Only a champion of champions can accomplish such a thing."

Before her death, Majo and the Damned One's army of demons had wreaked utter havoc upon human cities. During blondie rule, priests had used barrier charms to keep the occasional demon out of cities and villages, which had only worked because of the priests' mild magical abilities. But Majo had discovered a loophole in the wording of the prayers etched onto the charms, and had sent human-born demons to sabotage the barriers. Then, with nothing to hold them back, her demon army had razed every city and town they'd targeted.

Houfu, the largest city in the plains and considered the jewel of the nation, had been devastated. The brightly colored roofs of the homes that ringed the center of the city had been dulled with layers of ash. The large and imposing wall that surrounded the capital had collapsed in many places. The smell of burned wood and flesh and the fetid stench of decay had hung in the air, and the city had been disturbingly silent.

Most of the population had been slaughtered, including the blond king and his family. A substantial portion of the surrounding city had burned to the ground. Those sections untouched by fire were gruesome scenes of death.

With a hard swallow, Mai remembered the walk from the city gates to the palace at the center. The bodies of men, women, and children had lain rotting in the streets alongside one or two dead demons, with no one to cremate or bury them. The few survivors had been too frightened to come out of hiding.

Several women had been abused before their deaths, their dresses twisted up their bodies or completely torn away. The few children who hadn't been eaten whole had instead been torn to pieces. Men had been brutally butchered, and the streets had been black with dried blood.

Despite the carnage, Houfu was where Empress Shumei had chosen to reestablish a new court. The enormous palace complex, consisting of fourteen halls, seven squares, five gates, and several hundred outbuildings, had been largely untouched by the invasion.

Large sections of the palace's outer walls had collapsed when demon forces had believed the royals were still within, but they had ceased their advance after the king had been killed fleeing the city. Mai assumed the demons had intended to leave the complex intact for the Damned One and his champion. Workers were now restoring and improving the damage to the outer walls, but they needed at least five more weeks to complete the repairs.

The palace grounds alone were three times larger than Mai's hometown of Toubou, and the sheer size of them still amazed her. The surrounding city was even larger, and though many parts of it were charred and broken, the beauty and wealth of the capital shone through. Even the humblest homes had glass windows, colorful tile roofs, and bolts for their doors.

The complex's largest building was the residential palace: several stories of slate-colored stacked roofs, matching dormers, and white stone-and-plaster walls. It housed the empress and her retinue, including the empress's bodyguards, high-ranking military officers, and house elders. Mai lived in the east wing, her room adjacent to her fellow Spring elders'.

As for the nearly eight thousand black-haired followers who had answered the Pull of the Empress, some crows lived outside the complex, but much of the city's housing was still in disrepair in the wake of the demon attack, so most had found temporary shelter in the numerous outbuildings of the palace complex while more of Houfu was restored, an enormous task.

The day their enormous caravan had arrived in devastated Houfu, the empress's first priority had been performing a powerful spell reserved only for the Divine One's champion. The spell had drained her, and she had slept in a near coma for several days, but the result had placed magical shells of protection over every major and minor city in the empire. Such a powerful spell would ensure that any populated areas demons hadn't attacked would continue unmolested, at least until the new court could train and establish local protection.

Still awaiting the sparring match, Mai looked past the groupings of soldiers at Empress Shumei, who sat upon a thick cushion beneath the courtyard's covered walkway. A headdress consisting of stiffened loops of silver-and-white silk braids adorned her long hair, which was artfully twisted away from her face. Her dress was a study in shades of blue, patterned with a flock of white birds flying about her in an upward spiral. She watched the soldiers with alert brown eyes, hands folded in her lap.

Next to her sat her young brother on a cushion of his own, but he sat on the edge of it, eyes alight with anticipation for the sparring match that would soon begin. His garb matched his sister's, though it lacked the birds, and the vibrant blues were a perfect combination with his golden hair.

Mai was still stunned at how much the empress had changed since the day she'd met her...and challenged her—Mai couldn't forget that shameful moment. Shumei had been practicing defensive spells with Vallen, and though she had been dressed well, she had seemed uncomfortable in her finery. Exertion had tangled her hair and flushed her face. The empress of today, however, was the epitome of poised beauty, all soft skin and luscious black hair. Mai found herself wishing she could look half as regal as her empress.

Looking down at her own clothes, Mai smoothed her fingers over the unadorned silk. Her dress that day was a muted gray, and her under-robe was a lighter shade of the same color. She preferred not to draw attention to herself with flattering patterns or colors. Any men giving her even the briefest of glances put her on edge.

At first, she had been harsh to almost everyone around her, distrustful of the men and unapproachable to any women seeking her advice as one of the few crows with experience wielding magic. After all, she had been self-taught. Why couldn't others do the same? she'd figured. Then the empress had pointed out that sharing her knowledge was not only her duty as a house elder, but would help her improve her own skills.

And of course, the empress had been right. Moreover, Mai's rapport with her fellow female crows vastly improved. The men, however?

She knew what they muttered about her. Ice-cold. Stiff, distant, reticent. And she hoped to keep it that way. No amount of wheedling from the empress would convince her to be anything but arm's length from them—or even farther, if she could help it.

The sparring match the empress had come to witness was part of the training for the advanced soldiers, a talented subset of her force of eighteen hundred men and women—mostly men, a most irksome imbalance. Vallen and Rosuke, high general and commander respectively, were off to one side, joking with each other as they stretched their bodies and tested the balance of their swords.

Though the empress was the most magically talented—her knowledge of circles and incantations was unmatched—Vallen and

Rosuke were the deadliest fighters, not just with swords but various weapons. The two of them sparring was something to behold.

Mai's heartbeat picked up as Vallen and Rosuke readied themselves in the center of the demonstration space at the other end of the courtyard. Their observers hung back by the walkway.

These advanced soldiers had several paths of assignment ahead of them. Some would become part of the empress's personal guard, some the house elders' personal guard, and some would command the empress's army when she took them into Oblivion. Mai knew the names of only a few of the high-ranking officers in attendance, such as Captain Yuushi and Commander Jun. She had seen the former talking with Elder Kagumi of House Berry a few times—and suspected the two were secretly attached—and the latter was a quiet, gloomy middle-aged man. He was also broad-chested, and significantly taller than even Vallen or Rosuke, so Mai kept her distance.

Despite how serious their future responsibilities, the majority of the advanced soldiers cheered and teased their superiors while waiting for the match to begin. Mai could barely hear Vallen and Rosuke over the soldiers' shouts.

"You hear that? They cheer loudest for me," Vallen boasted as he faced Rosuke. "They see the real talent." Though he was quite tall, he wasn't bulky. Rather, his physique was battle-ready—lean, quick, and flexible. He had clean, sharp features, and a set of sky-blue eyes Mai's fellow crow ladies swooned over, even though he was very much taken. In fact, the empress was set to tie him to her as her official consort in just ten days.

As if on cue, the men shifted their loyalties to the commander, earning a good-natured grin from Vallen. Rosuke shook his head. "No one likes cockiness, my friend." He pointed at Vallen while holding his sword suggestively in front of his pants. "Unless it's *my* cockiness, of course."

Vallen and the rest of the advanced soldiers barked with laughter. Mai quirked her lips and glanced at Empress Shumei, who wore a similar expression of mild admonishment.

As Rosuke twirled his blade and chuckled, Mai cast her eyes over his athletic form. He was leaner than Vallen, but just as quick. His humble sparring clothes could not hide the clean lines of his wide shoulders and slim hips. The more formal military garb he sometimes wore only enhanced them.

Today wasn't the first day she'd found herself studying him—a disturbing preoccupation she strove to smother—but even as she stood there, her fingers twitched with her desire to feel his wide shoulders and stroke his sword-calloused hands. But only out of jealousy, she told herself. His skill with a sword had honed his body into that of a warrior.

When it came to his face, something about his good looks struck her as almost feminine—not that she personally found him attractive, of course—and it wasn't his long hair, full lips, or high cheekbones. Perhaps it was his eyes, she realized—deep-set with thick lashes and irises "like the sea," according to some. She had never been to the ocean, so she couldn't say for sure, but if his eyes were the color of the sea, it was a place she wouldn't mind visiting.

Vallen turned away from Rosuke to the semicircle of soldiers. He held up his hands, and the men immediately obeyed his command for silence. Mai couldn't see his face, but the way the soldiers straightened and focused on him spoke to his sober expression. Rosuke sheathed his sword.

"Today, Commander Rosuke and I shall demonstrate a dangerous kind of close combat. Most of the Damned One's creations have excellent dark-vision, and thus prefer to fight in darkness. That is exactly what happened when we engaged the Damned One's champion in battle just over three months ago."

Mai frowned as she recalled that terrifying night and the moment the empress's light spell was snuffed, plunging them into darkness. She looked to Empress Shumei, whose expression was inscrutable from across the courtyard.

"That night, the empress's quick thinking saved us. She casted an impressive light spell on our blades that the enemy could not magically douse from afar, but casting such magic in battle, even for soldiers as talented as you, is rather difficult. It's a touchy spell that requires concentration and finesse." Some of the men glanced at their watchful empress with pride and adoration. "Her light spell evened the playing field for the four of us, but you may not have such an opportunity. You may not even have moonlight or starlight to see by."

Vallen paused to take a length of cloth from inside his shirt, and one of the soldiers raised his hand.

"Yes, Minoru?" Vallen prompted. Rosuke also pulled out a length of cloth.

"You said 'the four of us.' I had always thought the battle was fought by you, the commander, and the empress. Who was the fourth person?"

Several others nodded as though they had wondered the same thing. Mai squeezed herself tighter to the cherry tree, wishing she could become part of the trunk rather than endure the wave of embarrassment swamping her. No one knew she had been at that battle?

"The elder of House Sakura was the fourth," Rosuke answered. "Elder Mai and I fought back-to-back while the high general and the empress pushed through the demons to reach the Damned One's champion."

The men buzzed with conversation. Mai curled her fingers against the tree trunk and bit her lip. She couldn't explain what hearing her name on his lips did to her heart rate or why it made her cheeks red. But she did know she wished this Minoru hadn't opened his mouth.

"Elder Mai?" Minoru obnoxiously exclaimed, making her wince. "I had no idea she could fight. She never practices with any of the advanced troops. Doesn't even speak to us."

Even from the other side of the courtyard, Mai saw Rosuke stiffen. Her first impression of him had been that of an unreliable flirt, someone who feigned confidence but ran at the first sign of trouble. However, when the dog soldiers had bounded toward them, baying and snarling, Rosuke's focus had saved her from injury countless times. Though she had slain several demons, not too bad with a sword herself, Rosuke had killed a couple dozen, some of them aiming for her. His attentive eyes and fast reflexes had kept her covered without getting in her way or doing all the fighting.

"Elder Mai fought bravely, which is all I could ever ask of any of the empress's soldiers," Rosuke said, voice stony. His defense of her made her heart pound even harder.

"Very true, my friend," Vallen agreed. "Let us return to the demonstration. As I said, circumstances may turn against you, forcing you to fight in near or total darkness. Perhaps you've had no time to prepare your weapons for such a fight, or you've been disarmed. Perhaps you've been blinded in battle."

The soldiers shifted uncomfortably as their instructors blindfolded themselves, and Mai couldn't blame them. Fighting without the benefit of sight was a serious disadvantage.

"The *darksight* spell isn't without its limitations, but mastery of it will be essential for achieving victory in Oblivion. Observe." Vallen drew his sword, a wicked-looking blade with serrated edges, and confidently turned toward Rosuke, who casually held his wide, curved sword in one hand.

Mai glanced at the empress, wondering if Shumei looked as concerned as Mai felt, but the empress wasn't even watching them. Instead, Shumei had found Mai hiding behind the tree, and Mai's heart raced as the empress commanded eye contact without moving a muscle.

She had dined with the empress many times, and normally felt rather comfortable around her, but as the empress bent her regal gaze upon her, Mai felt as if she were being squeezed. She shrank even more against the cherry tree, pulling herself as far behind it as she could, and breathed a sigh of relief when the empress looked away. Only then was she able to return her attention to the sparring match.

With a sudden lunge, Vallen was in front of Rosuke and swinging his sword. Mai nearly called a warning before Rosuke brought up his blade, deflecting Vallen's blow as certainly as though he was fighting with his vision unhindered. He twisted and pushed Vallen's sword aside, and a bit of footwork gave him an opening. Vallen deflected Rosuke's jab and then raised his sword to block another swing. The men who watched cheered them on, and the only thing louder than their voices was the clang of steel.

Mai looked to the empress again, wondering if Shumei was as worried as she was, but the empress seemed relatively calm. Next to her, Oka had pressed his hand to his head while grimacing. Confused, Mai wondered if he was anxious, but his eyes were shut rather than on the sparring match. He was in pain. The boy had recently shown quite an interest in sweets, though, so perhaps he'd eaten too much sugar.

Several soldiers in front of Oka scattered, pulling Mai's attention back to the two men on the verge of killing each other. Their fight was taking them all over the other end of the courtyard and forcing those on the ground to fling themselves out of the way.

After several nail-biting minutes, Vallen tripped Rosuke and became the first to gain the upper hand. Mai gasped at how hard Rosuke landed on his back, and Vallen swiftly brought down his sword, looking as though he intended to drive it right through Rosuke's throat. Without thinking, she jumped out of her cover and screamed. But Vallen's blade sank into the dirt several inches from Rosuke's neck.

The soldiers cheered uproariously. Vallen pulled off his blindfold and turned toward Shumei as though seeking her praise. Indeed, her expression toward him was warm. Rosuke stood, his blindfold already off, but his back was to Mai. He brushed the dirt from his clothes as the soldiers swarmed him, showering him with compliments.

Vallen approached the walkway, took the empress's hand, and kissed it. Oka leaned forward in his seat, eyes bright as he clapped Vallen's shoulder and no doubt gave his own compliments. His headache must have subsided.

Mai glanced at Rosuke again and gasped, pressing her hand to her heart. He was looking at her with a degree of focus not unlike what she'd seen the night of the dog-soldier fight. Mai couldn't help wincing with embarrassment. Had he heard her scream? He must have, it had been so loud. She was such a fool for coming here.

Then his expression became something else, something more predatory. He lowered his arms to his sides and faced her more directly, almost daring her to respond somehow. A blush burst across her cheeks, and a quick sweep of those nearest to him confirmed the other men had noticed her standing there. She was quick to retreat, hopping up the stone steps that led to the covered walkway and shucking her shoes. She picked them up before disappearing inside the building, but she swore his gaze lingered on her as she cowardly fled the courtyard.

Also By Ruby Duvall

(time-travel romance)
<u>Love Across Time series</u>:
Stay with Me
Escape with Me

Eidolon (*BDSM romance*)
The Fisherman's Widow (*erotic horror*)

(fantasy paranormal romance)
<u>The Dark Court series, in order</u>:
Caught in the Devil's Hand
Drawn into Oblivion
At the Maze's Center